THE DAY BEFORE SUNRISE

have happened?

"I happen to have interviewed Dulles about his Swiss espionage exploits and readily concede that Wiseman has created a highly convincing facsimile of the man who served as go-between the German peace emissaries and the United States. Wiseman . . . melding fact with fiction so seamlessly (builds) an authentic picture of Hitler's Third Reich writhing in its death throes."   —John Barkham Reviews

"THE DAY BEFORE SUNRISE
is a psychologically believable and always fascinating interior look at a dying Nazism."
                          —**Publishers Weekly**

"Serious and credible . . . intriguing reading."
                          —**Houston Chronicle**

Could

THE DAY BEFORE SUNRISE

have happened?

"Wiseman mixes historical figures with imaginary ones masterfully," says **The Pittsburgh Press.** "It will have the reader on edge," agrees **The Oregon Journal,** evoking "all the horrors of war plus a pathetic and doomed love story." Whether or not you decide THE DAY BEFORE SUNRISE was probable or even possible, you'll agree with the **West Coast Review** that "the book works just fine."

ABOUT THE AUTHOR

Thomas Wiseman was born in Vienna in 1931 and went to England at the age of seven. Before the publication of his first book, *Czar*, in 1965, he had worked as a full-time journalist for sixteen years. His third novel, *The Quick and the Dead*, published in 1969, was hailed by *Time* magazine as "a brilliant tour de force of rare psychological depth and complexity." Mr. Wiseman is also the author of *The Romantic Englishwoman* and two works of nonfiction, *Cinema* and *The Money Motive*.

THE DAY BEFORE SUNRISE

A NOVEL BY

Thomas Wiseman

WARNER BOOKS

A Warner Communications Company

WARNER BOOKS EDITION

Copyright © 1976 by Thomas Wiseman
All rights reserved, including the right to reproduce this book or
portions thereof in any form.

Library of Congress Catalog Card Number: 75-21482

ISBN 0-446-89213-0

This Warner Books Edition is published by
arrangement with Holt, Rinehart and Winston

Cover art by Larry Noble

Warner Books, Inc., 75 Rockefeller Plaza, New York, N.Y. 10019

 A Warner Communications Company

Printed in the United States of America

Not associated with Warner Press, Inc. of Anderson, Indiana

First Printing: April, 1977

10 9 8 7 6 5 4 3 2 1

THE DAY BEFORE SUNRISE

The
ESCAPE ROUTE
taken by
SCHÖLLER and ELLIOTT
out of BERLIN
April 21-23, 1945

0   Miles   50

N

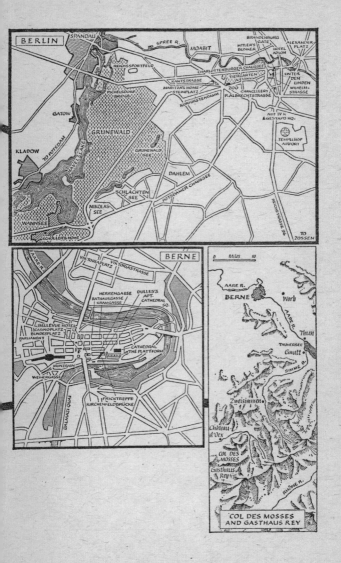

BERLIN

SPANDAU

SPREE R.

BRANDENBURG GATE

MOABIT

HITLER'S BUNKER

ALEXANDER-PLATZ

REICHSSPORTFELD

CHARLOTTENBURGER CHAUSSEE

HOTEL ADLON

UNTER DEN LINDEN

KANTSTRASSE

TIERGARTEN

WILHELM-STRASSE

MARITZA'S HOME

PICHELSDORF BRIDGE

STEINPLATZ

ZOO

CHANCELLERY

P. ALBRECHTSTRASSE

KURFURSTENDAMM

GATOW

Amt IV K.

GESTAPO HQ.

TO POTSDAM

HAVELLAND

GRUNEWALD

TEMPELHOF AIRPORT

KLADOW

GRUNEWALD SEE

DAHLEM

RINGSTRASSE 36

SCHLACHTEN SEE

POTSDAMER CHAUSSEE

NIKOLAS-SEE

TO ZOSSEN

WANNSEE

SCHULLER'S HOME

BERNE

AARE R.

VIKTORIASTRASSE

VIKTORIAPLATZ

HERRENGASSE

DULLES'S APT.

RATHAUSGASSE

CATHEDRAL SQ.

KRAMGASSE

BELLEVUE HOTEL

CASINOPLATZ

BUNDESPLATZ

PARLIAMENT

CATHEDRAL THE PLATTFORM

MUNZRAIN

WEIHERGASSE

DALMAZI QUAI

FRICKTREPPE

KIRCHENFELDBRÜCKE

0 Miles 10

AARE R.

BERNE

Worb

AARE R.

Thun

THUNERSEE

Gwatt

SIMME R.

Zweisimmen

Château d'Oex

COL DES MOSSES

Gasthaus Rey

RHÔNE R.

COL DES MOSSES AND GASTHAUS REY

◆ | ◆

In the second week of February 1945 the weather in Upper Silesia suddenly turned warmer, and along parts of the frozen River Oder cracks began to appear in the ice.

Seeing that their line of retreat was about to melt away, a unit of German tank destroyers, who were dug in on the eastern bank of the river, south of Breslau, started to fall back. This was contrary to orders, which forbade any German soldier to retreat or surrender.

The tank destroyers made their way to the river, on foot, on horseback, in armored trucks, on the platforms of gun carriages. The heavy vehicles caused the cracks in the ice to widen. To spread the weight of the vehicles the soldiers threw long wooden planks over the thawing river surface and drove very slowly along these heaving tracks. They crossed in single file, one vehicle at a time. It was slow going.

By early evening only a few were across. And now the melting ice came pouring down from upstream, producing a minor avalanche. Loose, swirling ice blocks struck the horses. As their hooves pounded upon the precarious surface, it began to open up beneath them in places.

Animals, gun trailers, and men were swallowed up in a black jaw that a moment later had closed again with the shifting of the ice. These sights and the screams of drowning men and the bellowings of terror-stricken horses added to the confusion and the fear of the others trying to get across. Wheels slipped off the wooden planks and spun uselessly as engines whined and roared without producing movement. A two-ton truck began to spin like a top and then was gone on a wild zigzag course downriver.

As more cracks appeared in the ice, the solid surface very slowly began to move. Finding themselves carried away from their chosen crossing point toward a broadening section of the Oder, soldiers within shouting distance of the western bank abandoned their vehicles and called to those of their comrades already across to throw them ropes. They got no answer: only the fusillade of cracking ice. Then for the first time they saw the white forms in the shrubs along the bank, stiffly still. And as the tank destroyers drew level with these waiting men, who were wearing white snow camouflage over their uniforms, somebody spotted the SS runes on their sleeves. Moments later the SS men opened fire on their fellow countrymen, turning the ice floes into floating biers.

Next day, February 11, when Marshal Konev reached the eastern bank of the Oder, the tank destroyers' bodies were moving slowly downriver, in solemn procession.

Using the same technique of throwing wooden planks across the breaking ice, but doing it more skillfully and selecting the crossing points more carefully, Konev's army succeeded in getting a large force of tanks across.

A few days later, Zhukov established a firm bridgehead on the west bank of the Oder, north of Küstrin, bringing the most advanced Russian forces to within two hours' drive of the center of Berlin.

As this news spread through the capital, there was mass panic. There were word-of-mouth stories of Soviet soldiers raping and killing indiscriminately as they advanced. The word went out: *Sauve qui peut.* Now it was every man for himself.

· 2 ·

"Listen to this, sir," Howard Elliott said. He was sitting at the reconstructed German cipher machine in the code room of the American legation in Berne. As he tapped the keyboard of what looked like a combined typewriter and miniature telephone exchange, the deciphered text was emerging in a series of jumps on the fast printout. "This beats everything. Even for them. Listen to this, Mr. Quantregg."

Quantregg, a tall Californian with a crew cut, whose every movement was imbued with a sense of urgency that he was continually trying to get others to share, had just burst in, his normal way of entering a room, and was standing in the doorway, head nodding fast like someone beating time to a jive beat.

Reading off the printout, Elliott translated:

"Certain unreliable elements seem to believe that the war will be over for them as soon as they surrender to the enemy. Against this belief it must be pointed out that every deserter will be prosecuted and will find his just punishment. Furthermore, his ignominious behavior will entail the most severe consequences for his family. Upon examination of the circumstances they will be summarily shot.

"It is an act of racial duty according to Teutonic tradition to exterminate even the kinsmen of those who surrender themselves into captivity. . . ." Elliott stopped, and added: "Signed guess who?"

For some time now Elliott had been monitoring the internal communications of the Reich Main Security Office. So he was familiar with Himmler's mystical

11

bloodthirstiness and bizarre forms of self-justification.

Quantregg slowed the up-and-down head movements to a savage nod.

"It's kinda brilliant in a way," he conceded. "What else'll stop the funky bastards running? Except that it's not gonna work, even shooting their old mothers is not gonna work." His tone of voice changed, became judicious. "Hope you boys keep a record of all this sort of stuff, not just for the intelligence quotient but also bearing in mind the war crimes angle."

"I imagine War Crimes is pretty organized on that."

"Let's make double sure. I wouldn't want any of these babies to slip their head out of the noose just on account of somebody forgot to take notes."

"I've kept some notes," Elliott said.

"Glad to hear that."

He came farther into the room, looking steamed up as he always did when he got on the subject of Germans.

Quantregg sometimes had to have meetings with Nazi emissaries who came to see his chief, Allen Dulles.

"I tell you one thing," Quantregg said. "I won't ever shake one of 'em by the hand. It's a principle with me."

"That must bother them, sir," Elliott said. He couldn't resist it.

"That's right," Quantregg said.

"Mind you, sir," Elliott said, "I heard Mr. Dulles is pretty free with the liquor when they come and see him."

"That's something else," Quantregg said. "You offer them a shot of something, gets 'em talking. Not the same as shaking hands."

"You don't have to drink from the same glass," Elliott agreed.

"That's right," Quantregg said. "That's right." And then, catching on, said sharply, "You being smart with me, sonny boy?"

"I wouldn't dream of being smart with you, Mr. Quantregg."

"You better not be, I tell you."

"Right, sir."

"Right."

Elliott was a smart young fellow. Maybe too damn smart for his own good. Quantregg, an ex-FBI man, the mere cop on the team, always felt he was being put down by the Ivy Leaguers with whom Mr. Dulles had largely staffed the Berne mission, and he thought of Elliott as one of them. He had that same clean-cut superior look. Very light brown hair which in places was actually fair, neatly parted and brushed back, cut sharp around the ears and at the back. Pale blue eyes. Button-down collar. Gray knitted tie. Gray suit. Plain gray socks. Triangle of handkerchief in top pocket. Neat. Soft-spoken. But a wise guy.

These smart young fellows who'd been to the best Eastern colleges and knew all about the history of Fascism and Nazism and all the other isms. They stood around theorizing about this eventuality or that and constructing scenarios of action. Quantregg felt out of his depth with them. His qualifications were of a more practical sort.

Herb Entweiler, the code room chief, had come over with a pink flimsy in his hand. "This just came in," he said, giving it to Elliott. "It's a triple S, so you better take it. It's for Mr. Dulles."

Quantregg said, "When you're done, get it over to him toot de sweet. He wants everything brought to his apartment. He can't move. Got the goddamn gout again. That's what I came to tell you. Got it?"

"Got it. *Sir*."

"Right."

Quantregg left looking in a huff and in a hurry, as always.

Elliott glanced at the triple S. The designation meant it could not be machine-decoded. Very special messages were sent for extra security in a code that could only be deciphered by reference to a one-time pad.

Entweiler had gone over to the code safe and unlocked it; he stood by while Elliott flicked through a printed schedule and looked up the keyword for April 5. Then he got the reference number for that day and selected the appropriate code pad, which he took over to his green metal-top desk. The keyword was

13

made up of a series of random letters which were added to the ciphertext to render it structureless and therefore unbreakable by cryptanalysis.

Elliott dug out a cigarette from a new pack of Chesterfields, and using the code pad in conjunction with the keyword, began to write with a soft pencil on a single sheet of cross-lined paper, with nothing underneath. When he had the whole of the plaintext written out, he read it through to make sure it made sense. His lips puckered slightly as he took in the import of what he had just decoded. He folded the message and put it in a manila envelope.

"I was told to take this round to Mr. Dulles at his apartment. Toot de sweet."

"I'll arrange transport," Entweiler said, picking up the internal phone.

"I can make my own way."

"Not with a triple S in your pocket, you can't. You'll go in a legation car, with a security officer."

It was a black Cadillac, flying the stars and stripes on each mudguard, with bulletproof glass windows. All doors locked from inside as well as outside. The security officer sat in front next to the driver.

They moved off smoothly through the quiet residential district around the Dalmaziquai where the Aare was on the same level as the street, affording residents the possibility of a pleasant riverside stroll under the trees.

Nobody was strolling today. It was a dull cold gray day. The weather had been very changeable at the beginning of April, some days bright and clear with sunshine, while on other days you thought it might snow again anytime, with those sudden squalls of stinging cold rain, and the sharp air currents coming down from the Bernese Alps.

The car passed a deserted tennis court. Signs pointed to the Tierpark, a swimming pool, a convalescent home. Most of the houses around here were private two or three story residences, built in a variety of styles in the first and second decades of the century. The solid dwellings of solid Swiss citizens. Some of these houses were now occupied by embassies, with little more than their country's heraldic shield over the entrance door to distinguish them from houses still in private occupation.

Dulles's apartment was only a few minutes' drive away in a street of fine old sandstone houses on a ridge above the river. He lived at the point where the Herrengasse widened into the great cathedral square. Just a little farther on was the Plattform, a high tree-lined terrace from which there was a magnificent view of the whole city laid out below and of the Bernese Alps rising in a sudden massive upsurge just on the other side of the river.

Outside Dulles's front door the Cadillac stopped with a gentle bounce of its luxurious suspension. Elliott got out and rang the bell. It was the cook who answered. "Ah yah," she said, seeing the legation car, and let him in. There was an OSS man sitting just inside the door, by the main stairs. He relaxed when he recognized Elliott.

"I take your coat, please," the cook offered, and Elliott handed it to her.

Quantregg appeared at the top of the stairs, "OK, OK," he said, fingers snapping impatiently. "Bring it up." His whole body was vibrating with impatience as he waited for Elliott to come up the stairs. The slowness of these guys. Quantregg invariably took stairs three at a time, as if raiding the joint.

Walking a short way along the corridor, Quantregg knocked lightly on a door, and after a moment went in. Elliott waited at the top of the stairs, holding the envelope. He shifted his weight from one foot to the other, started to get out a cigarette, and then thought better of it.

After something like ten or fifteen minutes the door opened. Quantregg came out and stood in the narrow passage, virtually taking up the whole width of it with his big frame, his back to Elliott. He was showing some people out. Three men. Elliott couldn't see their faces. Quantregg took them down the corridor to the back stairs. As they were taking their leave, Elliott heard heel-clicking and saw a hand extended.

It was drawn back again immediately as Quantregg conspicuously refused the offered handshake.

The visitors disappeared down the stairs and Quantregg came back down the passage toward Elliott.

"OK. Go in," he said. "He'll want to dictate a reply."

Dulles was sitting in a low armchair, his left leg stiffly extended, supported under the knee by a pillow on a velvet footstool. He was in his socks, shoeless. He had a cane by him, and a pipe in his mouth. The room was full of tobacco smoke. There were papers and files and newspapers in several languages on tables, sideboards, the floor.

Dulles didn't look too good. He was evidently in pain, and feverish. A film of perspiration covered his yellowish skin. Below his brow his eyes were distant lights. He wore rimless spectacles. The eye pouches were deeper, and his mustache was almost white. He looked older than fifty-two.

Officially, Allen Welsh Dulles was Special Assistant to the Minister at the American legation in Berne, but when shortly after his arrival in November 1942 a Swiss newspaper printed a story describing him as the chief of the American Secret Service in Switzerland, the OSS, and President Roosevelt's personal representative, Dulles issued no denial. He took the view that a man in his position must let people know he is in business. It brought some oddballs to his door, and some pretty unsavory characters, but Dulles was fond of saying that someone in his profession must be ready to deal with the devil himself, if it was in the interests of the United States and the free world. Therefore when emissaries of Himmler's SS sought to contact him, he had not rebuffed their approaches. He had been willing to meet them, secretly, or to send one of his aides to hear what they had to say.

Some of his men were bothered by these contacts. But Dulles took a longer view of history and of his mission to protect the American way of life, and since he was never in any doubt that he and God were on the same side, he could look into the eye of the devil, even offer him a drink or a cigar, without feeling uneasy. He would sit there, drawing on his pipe, look-

16

ing politely at his visitor, whoever he was, and consider each proposal pragmatically, on its merits.

Of course, there was some risk in seeing such men, and sometimes Dulles was troubled by visions of newspaper headlines that said: PRESIDENT ROOSEVELT'S ENVOY RECEIVES HIGH SS OFFICERS. For this reason he usually conducted such meetings at one of his many secret apartments in and around Berne and Zurich. But this damn gout had immobilized him.

As Elliott came into the room, clutching the manila envelope, Dulles frowned, suspecting that he was not going to like what he was about to hear. He held out his hand for the envelope, and then remembering he had a reputation for courteousness of a somewhat Old World variety, said, "Thank you, Elliott. Appreciate you coming here. Got this damn gout again. Knee. Can't move it, dammit . . ."

Elliott mumbled something sympathetic.

"Excess uric acid in the blood. 'Fraid I'll have to make you run around the next few days, till I get mobile again. You won't mind some legwork, you've got strong young legs. Hear you play a mean game of tennis . . ."

"I sometimes beat Mr. Quantregg," Elliott admitted.

"That *is* mean."

Dulles seemed to be postponing the moment when he'd have to read the cable.

"Now how about fixing me a scotch and soda," he said. "Medics say beer is bad for the gout, but whisky's OK. That's something to be thankful for—hmm?" He gave his resonant chuckle. Elliott went to a sidetable and poured out a scotch. First time he'd heard about whisky being OK for gout, but you didn't argue with Mr. Dulles. Everybody in Berne knew how important Mr. Dulles was. How close to the President. A man with the highest family connections. There'd been a Secretary of State in his family, hadn't there?

Elliott carried the drink across to him, and Dulles took a long gulp and held out his hand for the envelope. Then at the last moment he changed his mind, and said, "You read it out." He pushed his spectacles up onto his damp forehead and massaged his eyeballs

17

as he waited to hear the triple priority signal from Washington.

Elliott tore open the envelope and in an expressionless voice read out the message.

WASHINGTON
DATED: APRIL 5 1945

URGENT—TOP SECRET
ADMIRAL LEAHY TO ALLEN W DULLES
JOINT CHIEFS OF STAFF INSTRUCT DULLES TO TAKE NOTE AS FOLLOWS:—
1. A CRITICAL SITUATION HAS DEVELOPED WITH THE RUSSIANS. STALIN HAS SENT A LONG ACRIMONIOUS MESSAGE TO ROOSEVELT ACCUSING HIM OF DOING A SECRET DEAL IN BERNE WHEREBY THE GERMANS WILL "OPEN THE WESTERN FRONT AND PERMIT THE ANGLO-AMERICAN TROOPS TO ADVANCE TO THE EAST."
2. ROOSEVELT HAS SENT A PERSONAL MESSAGE TO STALIN SAYING: "I AM CERTAIN THERE WERE NO NEGOTIATIONS IN BERNE AT ANY TIME, AND I FEEL THAT YOUR INFORMATION TO THAT EFFECT MUST HAVE COME FROM GERMAN SOURCES, WHICH HAVE MADE PERSISTENT EFFORT TO CREATE DISSENSION BETWEEN US IN ORDER TO ESCAPE IN SOME MEASURE FOR RESPONSIBILITY FOR THEIR WAR CRIMES. IF THAT WAS SS-GENERAL WOLFF'S PURPOSE IN BERNE YOUR MESSAGE PROVES HE HAS HAD SOME SUCCESS. IT WOULD BE ONE OF THE GREAT TRAGEDIES OF HISTORY IF AT THE VERY MOMENT OF VICTORY NOW WITHIN OUR GRASP SUCH DISTRUST, SUCH LACK OF FAITH, SHOULD PREJUDICE THE ENTIRE UNDERTAKING . . .
"FRANKLY I CANNOT AVOID A FEELING OF BITTER RESENTMENT TOWARDS YOUR INFORMERS, WHOEVER THEY ARE, FOR SUCH A VILE MISREPRESENTATION OF MY ACTIONS AND THOSE OF MY TRUSTED SUBORDINATES IN BERNE."
3. ACCORDINGLY DULLES IS ONCE MORE INSTRUCTED NOT TO UNDERTAKE ANY ACTIONS OR NEGOTIATIONS THAT ARE OR COULD BE SUSPECTED OF BEING IN VIOLATION OF THE PRINCIPLES AGREED BETWEEN OURSELVES AND THE RUSSIANS.

When he had heard it all, Dulles said "Damn" very softly. He turned to address Quantregg. "I had it . . ." He extended the palm of his hand and slowly closed his fist on some invisible object. "I had it . . . and they've blown it. Damn."

"I guess they don't trust Wolff," Quantregg said. "I guess they think he's leading us on a wild goose chase."

"They don't know Wolff, and I do," Dulles said.

"I guess in a way you can't blame them, not trusting him," Quantregg said, "considering who he is."

Suddenly remembering Elliott was still in the room and waiting to be told what to do, Dulles turned to him and said, "All right, Elliott. Sit down a minute. Just give me a moment to collect my thoughts."

Closing his eyes and drawing steadily on his pipe, he concentrated. After a minute, he said, "All right. Take this down." He began to dictate.

ALLEN W DULLES TO ADMIRAL LEAHY:
YOUR MESSAGE RECEIVED AND CONTENTS NOTED.
VENTURE TO SAY THAT THE PRESIDENT IS ENTIRELY JUSTIFIED IN REJECTING STALIN'S POLITICALLY MOTIVATED ACCUSATIONS WHICH ARE UNFOUNDED AND MOREOVER INSULTING TO THE HONOR OF THE UNITED STATES AS WELL AS REFLECTING UPON THE PERSONAL INTEGRITY OF THE PRESIDENT.
STALIN'S INFORMATION IS UNDOUBTEDLY A GERMAN PLANT DESIGNED TO DISRUPT RELATIONS BETWEEN US AND SOVIETS. I CAN CONFIRM THAT OSS ACTIONS CONFINED TO NORMAL INTELLIGENCE OPERATIONS AND CONTACTS WITH SS-GENERAL WOLFF COME WITHIN THIS CATEGORY. I CAN ASSURE THE PRESIDENT THAT NO SECRET DEALS HAVE BEEN MADE IN HIS NAME OR THE NAME OF THE UNITED STATES IN VIOLATION OF AGREED PRINCIPLES, I.E., UNCONDITIONAL SURRENDER OF THE ENEMY.

While he was taking down this message, Elliott must have revealed something of what he was thinking. Having read the young man's mind, Dulles now leaned forward, and placing a hand on his knee, said with a flattering air of taking him into his confidence: "Elliott, let me tell you something. An intelligence officer is supposed to keep his home office informed of what he is doing, that is true. Sure, sure. But he can overdo it. If, for example, he tells too much, or asks too often for instructions, he is likely to get some that he doesn't relish. You understand?" He paused and took several puffs at his pipe. "You see, Elliott, only the officer in the field is in a position to exercise judgment on the fine details."

"Yes, sir," Elliott said. "I'm sure you're right, sir."

• 3 •

Elliott returned to the legation in the office Cadillac, encoded Dulles's reply to Washington, and took it into the radio room for immediate transmission. That done, he left.

As he was leaving the building, Quantregg came out of his office and they walked down the street together.

Elliott said lightly, "Who was the heel-clicker with the dirty handshake?"

Quantregg looked much more annoyed than the bantering tone of the question warranted, Elliott thought.

"Once you have gotten more experience in this line of work, Elliott, you will learn there are certain questions you do not ask."

"Seems sort of silly to me, sir," Elliott said unabashed. "Considering the messages I am required to transmit—not *only* to Washington—on Mr. Dulles's behalf. Seems sort of pointless, keeping other things so secret."

"There's no reason why a code clerk has to know who Mr. Dulles's visitors are," Quantregg said. They wanted to know everything, those smart-aleck college kids.

"What's Mr. Dulles up to?" Elliott asked.

"Up to?"

"It wasn't a downright lie I just sent off to the President, but it wasn't exactly the plain unvarnished truth either, was it?"

They had reached the high Kirchenfeldbrücke. Quantregg stopped and looked hard at Elliott, who was huddled inside his coat and turning away to avoid a sudden gust of stinging cold air on his face. He found himself looking far down to the serpentine coil of the Aare, shimmering with the lights of the bridges that spanned it at different heights.

Quantregg said, "Mr. Dulles is a very clever man . . . if you want my opinion he's going to be one of the key decision-makers after all this is over . . . he's a man who's always thinking ten moves ahead."

"Is that a fact?"

"You being sarcastic?"

"No, sir. Absolutely not, sir. I also have the highest respect for Mr. Dulles. I was just wondering what he was up to . . ."

"Mr. Dulles is running a complicated operation. All sorts of angles to it. I think you're a little too inexperienced in this line of country to understand all . . . all the ramifications. . . ."

"I just asked a question," Elliott said.

"Well, don't," Quantregg told him. "OK?"

"OK. OK. Sure. Whatever you say, I guess."

Quantregg left him, and Elliott continued alone across the bridge.

From this high point the city was compressed into a single view: the sandstone houses with their mansard roofs and long rows of dormers, on the other side of the river; the cathedral spire, a serrated silhouette against the white of the mountains; the sky line continuing in a broad sweep of domes and cupolas and

21

pinnacles. There were some flat-roofed modern apartment buildings too.

He had crossed this bridge dozens of times. Why did it feel special tonight? As if he had got wind of something. He shivered. It was damn cold for this time of year. Something was going on, of which he had caught glimpses, seen a few bits of a jigsaw puzzle. But he wasn't supposed to see the whole picture. And yet from the few pieces that he had seen, he couldn't help starting to build up a conjectural whole . . .

Oh hell, he thought as he walked, trying to figure it out—oh hell, it's like Quantregg says, I'm just a code clerk, it's none of my business what Mr. Dulles is up to.

But he decided he'd drop in at the American Bar of the Bellevue, see who was there. It was the place where you could always pick up the latest rumors.

• 4 •

Without the glistening pince-nez, the naked eyes—so rarely exposed in this state—were like the vulnerable parts of some stricken beast, soft and gray and jellyish. The face was of a doughy whiteness, the jowls puffy, sparsely bearded. The neck was shaven to the back of the skull, up to the tops of the ears, in the Prussian manner. The mouth was slightly open, and the breathing of the man lying flat on his back in the narrow iron hospital bed was heavy, as if he had been running for a long time and could not get his breath back. From time to time he sighed heavily. His mouth was dry and his gut full of gas. His head felt like a ball of fire.

The Venetian blinds were closed, and only very faint lines of light penetrated between the wooden slats. In the white-walled room there were bowls of wild flowers on various white pieces of furniture. At the sick man's side, on the bedside table, stood a glass samovar containing an infusion of gentian and dandelion tea. Next to it was a copy of the Koran.

The sick man lay with his eyes open, staring up at the ceiling. He appeared to be in a long, long daydream.

He was dancing the Boston . . . yes, *he*! With his bristly little mustache and puffed-out cheeks. Finally, he had learned it. Maja! How pretty she was. Frivolous, of course. A Rhinelander. Those easygoing, hot-blooded creatures. Like the Austrians. Not stern-minded, at all. Always putting off the serious business of life until tomorrow. Ah . . . but how he had danced the Boston! *Who would have thought, then, in 1922, what my destiny was.*

He held on to the fading image: the solemn awkwardly shaped young man (hips too long, legs too short) dancing, *dancing*. . . . A delicate tapping sound on his door broke the memory thread. He frowned, reached into the drawer of his bedside table for the pince-nez, and placed them carefully on his nose before pressing the button which illumined a light outside his door, giving permission to enter.

The visitor came in cautiously, head first, feet following tentatively behind, ready to go into reverse in a moment.

"May I express the hope that the SS-Reichsführer's headache is somewhat better?" the shuffling man inquired.

"It is no better," Himmler said. "What do you want, Brandt?"

"I thought the Reichsführer would wish to be informed . . . that SS-Major General Schellenberg has been waiting for five hours."

"Schellenberg. Why wasn't I told?"

"The SS-Reichsführer expressly forbade . . ."

"Send him in."

The Foreign Intelligence Chief came in briskly, his

sharp many-faceted face pale with excitement. With military formality, he approached the bed, nervously avoiding the flashing glass lenses of the prostrated man. To look directly into those demanding eyes was, he knew from experience, too exhausting.

"In view of his dramatic recovery, on which I congratulate him, I venture to burden the SS-Reichsführer with a matter of the gravest urgency . . ."

"Well?" said Himmler in a voice so low it was almost inaudible. The agony in his bowels had begun again, emptying his brain of blood. Had he been standing, he would have fainted. A black veil hovered above his eyes, threatening to descend at any moment.

"I have evidence that SS-General Wolff has been in Switzerland, discussing surrender terms with Dulles . . ."

"I saw Wolff only a few days ago. I questioned him closely myself, as did Kaltenbrunner and Schöller. We were satisfied with his explanations . . ." Schellenberg opened his mouth to interrupt, but a warning finger silenced him: the Reichsführer was merely pausing to catch his breath, he had not finished yet. "I will not hear these accusations against Wolff," Himmler said. "He would never be disloyal to me. I have created for him the rank of *Highest* SS-Leader, to set him above all other High SS-Leaders. We have been together since the beginning, in everything." This time, whether for lack of enough breath to go on, or because he had finished what he had to say, he fell back onto his pillows.

"For that reason," Schellenberg said, encouraged by Himmler's labored breathing to believe he might have a chance to finish what he had come to say, "for that reason, Reichsführer, it is all the more shocking that SS-General Wolff has been making deals with the Americans to save his own skin—at the expense of the Reich. I have evidence that . . ."

But Himmler was shaking his head to indicate that he did not wish to hear more. Schellenberg stood for a while silently waiting, rebuked but patient. After a while, he said softly, deferentially: "May I inquire, what is the Reichsführer's own *alternative* plan for ending the war?"

At this, Himmler seemed to revive a little, reinvigorated by the treasonable suggestion that lay in the air.

"Have you gone mad?" he said.

"It is my opinion," said Schellenberg boldly, "that only the SS-Reichsführer himself possesses the cards to bargain for the best terms with the Allies, and if I may venture to say so he will come to recognize this eventually. . . ."

"The cards?"

"The Jews," Schellenberg said, shrugging.

"You are mad to dare to talk to me of surrender," Himmler said. "I take it you are ill. I will excuse it for reasons of health," he added quickly.

"If I may allow my madness to speak, in that case. SS-General Wolff must be arrested. Should his negotiations with Dulles succeed, it must preempt my own endeavors, on the Reichsführer's behalf, through Count Bernadotte . . . which are, I may say, close to bearing fruit."

The basilisk eyes of Himmler were still but glittering secretly behind the thick glass lenses.

"The allegations against Wolff are being investigated by Schöller," he said with the last of his strength. "It is a matter for the police."

"In that case, I am confident that the Reichsführer will shortly have incontrovertible evidence in support of what I say, and will, I trust, then take the appropriate actions."

Himmler nodded feebly, and with a small finger movement dismissed his Foreign Intelligence Chief from his sight.

· 5 ·

As far as the eye could see, the traffic had come to a sudden halt. In his large, gray, armor-plated Mercedes, SS-Colonel Ritter von Thedieck lit an oval Turkish cigarette and beat against the steering wheel with a tightly gloved hand. No telling what was causing this holdup. Could be the road was blocked by shot-up vehicles. Or else there was yet another control point ahead, or perhaps . . . But it was no use speculating. There was nothing to be done except wait . . . wait for something to happen. . . . The next disaster.

In this exposed position they were sitting targets for the strafing British Mosquitoes. The open beet fields on either side of the autobahn afforded no cover and it was a long way to where the pine forests began.

People had got out of their vehicles and were looking to see what was causing the holdup.

Von Thedieck did not move. The SS-Colonel sat in a daze of having no choice, no alternative but to wait—for whatever was going to happen next.

Behind him lay the burning city of Berlin, which he had left during the night by the Reichstrasse 96; two hours ago he had been in Zossen, the underground High Command headquarters. They were preparing for evacuation. Inside the great telephone complex, Exchange 500, which linked up with all German-held positions, he had seen several of the flashing lights on the consoles go out even while he stood there.

The road he was on ran along the narrowing corridor between the eastern and western fronts. Anytime now the Russians and the Americans would meet and link up, and then the only remaining escape route south to Switzerland, Austria, and the Alps would be closed.

There were a few private vehicles on the road. Most of the others were large staff cars, bearing the gilded swastika medallions of high Nazi officialdom. The flapping tarpaulins of army trucks revealed cargoes of antique furniture, paintings, crated chinaware, bronze statuary. Only the highest party functionaries, or the richest, had been able to obtain gas and travel passes.

Nothing was moving. The tightly gloved hand beat faster on the wheel. A sudden slight forward lurch of the long line. Another halt. Then another move forward. Then another long halt. In this way they progressed for the next twenty minutes. After the last forward movement, von Thedieck was able to see the cause of the holdup: another control barrier. It was situated at a point where the road ran between high banks under an iron road bridge. Guards were moving along the line of cars, and one of them, seeing the SS runes on the mudguards of the Mercedes, signaled for von Thedieck to pull out and drive on. A traffic lane had been kept clear for such priority treatment.

At the control window, von Thedieck pulled up and handed out his papers. The plainclothesman sitting in the temporary wooden booth was wearing an overcoat, a hat, and a muffler around his neck. He fixed the expressionless eyes of officialdom on the SS-Colonel, scrutinizing his features and comparing them with the photographs on his military orders, his travel pass, his passport, his top priority designation. Then his eyes went rapidly down a long list in front of him, and stopped after the first half-dozen names. He must have pressed a button, because a foghorn alarm call was sounding out, and men were running about, black-helmeted guards with sub-machine guns.

Two guards had got into the big car and were ordering the SS-Colonel to reverse along the free traffic lane. He did not ask where they were taking him. Such questions were neither permitted nor relevant.

Farther back, there was a gap in the line of cars and he was told to drive through it and down a short tunnel that passed beneath the main road. Prods and

27

gestures. One-word commands. He must take the over-pass which curved back across the autobahn and connected with a minor country road on the other side. This was flat for a short distance and then descended steeply toward the village of Rudolphstein, dominated by the steeply pitched roof and towers of the Schloss.

Von Thedieck drove down the hill and through high gates into a courtyard, where he was told to get out, which he did.

The area between the barns and outhouses was full of cars being searched. Some had been virtually pulled to pieces, leather door linings ripped away, seats slashed open, parts of engines removed. Von Thedieck glimpsed what was going on as he was pushed up some steps and through a heavy iron door into a hall full of silent waiting men. He was conscious of great-coats with fur collars, of bright red lapels, of silver braiding on caps and shoulder tabs, of collar patches with silver stars, with oakleaves. . . . These were men not accustomed to the indignity of being kept waiting. They stood upright and unmoving, as if each one were alone here. They did not attempt to communicaté with each other. Von Thedieck's escort pushed a way through their midst.

He was taken up broad carved oak stairs, and then along twisting corridors, through several doors, along more corridors, and up narrow winding stone steps that rose in spirals inside the curved walls of one of the castle towers. At the top his gun belt was removed, his pockets were turned out, and he was searched for concealed weapons. One guard felt inside his mouth for cyanide capsules. After that, he was taken to a bare unheated room. The door closed. He heard a key turn.

There was very little space. The ceiling sloped down at one side to only a couple of feet from the floor. Light came through a narrow slit window. With precise controlled movements, von Thedieck took out his crocodile cigarette case which he had been allowed to keep, and from behind the silk band withdrew an oval Turkish cigarette and lit it in the long flame of a gold lighter. There was nowhere to sit. He decided against sitting on the floor. It was not dignified to do so, and he knew the importance of maintaining as much dignity as possible in the situation he was in. He made himself as comfortable as he could against the wall. He knew he would be made to wait: that was part of their method. He tried to empty his mind of those forebodings that the method was meant to induce.

The room was silent except for the regular creaking of soft leather in rhythm with his breathing.

About an hour went by. He was beginning to feel very cold and stiff. He exercised his fingers the way a pianist does before he begins to play, and rotated his neck. He tidied his fine head of hair; he puckered his lips into an elegant little moue. His left eyebrow lifted. He was conscious of the possibility that he was being watched through spyholes.

When the door opened and an official voice from across the corridor called, "Enter," von Thedieck went in unhurriedly, as befitted an officer of his rank. This room was much larger and was heated by a big tile stove. The walls were covered with mounted antlers and deer's heads; stuffed owls and eagles occupied branchlike perches. The usual expressionless official sat at a table with stacks of files, an array of rubber stamps, and lists. He had von Thedieck's papers in front of him.

"Your destination, SS-Colonel von Thedieck?" he demanded routinely.

"Fasano, as you can see," said von Thedieck petulantly, pointing to his military orders.

The official held the papers very close to his eyes, examining them carefully, taking his time. In the end, he seemed satisfied and addressed a man in civilian clothes who was standing with his back to von Thedieck, looking out of the window: a powerfully built individual, with broad shoulders, a thick neck, and large ears. The back of his jacket and the seat of his trousers were shiny from wear. His pockets sagged.

"This appears to be SS-General Wolff's signature," the first official said.

"Yes, yes, yes, but what about the Château Mouton Rothschild?" said the big-eared man. He turned. "Four

29

dozen bottles. Are you giving parties on the Italian front, Thedieck?"

"Do you begrudge a little wine to men going to their death?" the arrested man said in a superior manner.

The large individual in the shiny worn suit appeared amused by this answer. He gave a sour grin. He was examining the immaculate SS-Colonel; starting at the patent leather boots, his eyes ascended the elegant upward slope of the long flared black leather great-coat, soft doe skin of the finest quality, waisted; silver plaiting on the shoulder tabs; fastidious nose; pomaded hair, lying smoothly on the well-proportioned head.

"It came from my own cellar—the wine," von Thedieck added irrelevantly.

"No doubt, no doubt," the big shabby man said. There was a kind of permanent disbelief in his eyes. It was the expression of someone who has long ago stopped expecting to be told the truth. Von Thedieck noted the big strong hands, the rough common face. What a peasant! He assumed a superior attitude to-ward him, deciding he was someone exploiting his moment of authority.

"I must warn you," he said, "that SS-General Wolff will take a very poor view . . ."

"And the French soap?" said the large coarse fellow. "Do men about to die also have to smell nice?"

"A matter of taste," von Thedieck said, looking pointedly at this unkempt individual. "If one prefers to meet one's maker unwashed . . ."

"So it's for Him you got yourself all smartened up, is it?" He laughed crudely and turned again to look out. This room afforded a panoramic view of the sur-rounding countryside. The noise of the cars on the autobahn starting up after being cleared through the control point came at this distance in a succession of soft explosions. "Listen to them," he said, cocking his big ears, "the bigwigs starting off, with their art treasures and their women and their official authoriza-tions. *You* weren't heading for Switzerland, by any chance, Thedieck?"

"Fasano, as I have already told you. If there is any

doubt, I suggest that you telephone SS-General Wolff immediately at his headquarters."

"You were at Zossen a few hours ago. For what purpose?"

"I saw Major General Gehlen."

"For what purpose?"

"There were certain matters that General Wolff had instructed me to raise with General Gehlen."

"What matters?"

"As you are aware, I am not at liberty to disclose such things."

"You can to me," the large man said intimately.

"I am not aware that I can."

"You can."

"I would require instructions from General Wolff to that effect . . ."

"What I tell you is good enough . . ."

Von Thedieck looked at this shabby individual in puzzlement.

"You don't know who I am?" He seemed amused at being unknown to this dandified SS officer.

"I presume you are a policeman of some kind," said von Thedieck.

"A policeman, yes. Yes. That's right. I'm the Reich Special Investigator. Schöller."

Seeing that von Thedieck had gone rather pale, the Investigator kicked a chair toward him.

"You understand that you must answer my questions."

"If I might be permitted to phone General Wolff."

"Refused," Schöller stated curtly, and turning to his official told him, "Leave us, Grafeneck."

"Perhaps in that case," von Thedieck said, maintaining his composure, "I might be allowed to phone SS-Reichsführer Himmler. He knows me. I was his translator in Italy."

"I know, I know. That you speak languages is not in question."

"May I ask what is in question?"

"Certain trips that you and General Wolff made to Switzerland to see Dulles."

31

"Dulles," von Thedieck repeated, as if the name was unfamiliar to him.

"Dulles. Allen Welsh Dulles. A very important man. President Roosevelt's *personal* representative in Switzerland."

"You are misinformed, Reichskriminaldirektor."

"About his importance, oh I don't think I am. It is my job not to be misinformed."

"I meant about the alleged trips."

"I am not misinformed about those either." He laughed.

"I would respectfully beg to differ."

"You would, would you?"

He gave a snort and bending down took a bulging folder out of his briefcase. Making space on his desk by pushing stacks of files to both ends, he opened the folder and took out a photograph. He studied it briefly and then placed it rightside up before von Thedieck, who was standing on the other side of the desk.

"Not a very good photo, is it? A bit blurred. But then the circumstances in which it was taken were not ideal for photography. Who would you say that man was?"

From his side of the desk he pointed with a sharpened pencil to one of a group of men on a railway station platform. Only the backs of their heads could be seen. They all wore hats and coats and scarves—they were perhaps excessively muffled up against the cold.

Von Thedieck glanced at the picture and said, "It could be anyone."

"You don't recognize the build, the clothes? Let me jog your memory, Thedieck. Think back. Chiasso. March eighth."

"The date is of no significance to me."

"Really? Have a look at another picture."

The one placed before him this time was not quite so badly focused, and one of the men in the group had turned a little more toward the camera and was revealing a narrow profile. Von Thedieck continued to shake his head negatively.

"You don't recognize the posture?" Schöller said. "The elegant bearing. Yourself. Who else?"

"The person is totally unidentifiable."

"And this one?"

Very quickly Schöller placed another photograph in front of von Thedieck. This one was an enlargement of the head seen in narrow profile in the previous picture. Von Thedieck's features were just about recognizable.

"That could be me," he conceded, "but the picture might have been taken anywhere at any time. There is no background to be seen."

"But it wasn't taken anywhere. It was taken at Chiasso railway station on March eighth. Who were the men with you?"

"I must repeat, respectfully, that I am bound by the officer's code of conduct in the matter of divulging information about a military mission."

"A military mission? To Lake Maggiore, at Ascona?"

Schöller produced another photograph. It showed a house on a lake and a group of men standing on a veranda talking. The photograph had evidently been taken from a considerable distance, with a telephoto lens, and the definition was not good.

"Isn't that General Wolff?" Schöller demanded, pointing to one of the blurs. "And the man with him, Gaevernitz? Owner of the villa at Ascona, and Dulles's close associate. And that one, with the sharp nose, and the glasses, smoking a cigar. Major Waibel of Swiss Intelligence. And in the background—have a look with the magnifying glass." He passed the glass to von Thedieck. "Wouldn't you say that was Captain Wirth talking to you?"

"I would not say so, with all due respect."

"All right, leave you out of it. Look at Wolff," Schöller said gruffly. "Look at the head—that hook nose. Unmistakable. Look at it in profile, there, and the light-colored hair, thinning on the dome of the forehead. That *is* General Wolff. No question."

"Such features are commonplace," von Thedieck said.

"Compare the features," Schöller said, producing another file from his briefcase. This contained very clear photographs of General Wolff. They showed him in black SS uniform at Himmler's side on various ceremonial occasions, invariably occupying a position immediately to the right of the SS-Reichsführer, as befitted the Deputy and Chief of Staff. There were also a number of photographs of Wolff in the company of Hitler. In these he was more in the background, granting pride of place to the protocol-conscious Göring.

"Look! Look! Look!" Schöller said roughly, jabbing his pencil point at the hook nose and high forehead in all these photographs and then pointing again to the somewhat similarly shaped blur.

"I agree that it could be General Wolff," von Thedieck said, "but it could also be a hundred other people."

"All right, Thedieck. All right. . . . I tell you what I'm going to do. I'm going to have you taken to the rigorous interrogation room, and I am going to leave these photographs with you, so you can study them. And then I will talk to you again, and perhaps by then you will be able to recognize the people in the pictures. I would advise it."

"I am indebted to the Special Investigator for his advice."

• 6 •

Coming through the revolving door of the Bellevue, Elliott felt himself being scrutinized.

In the spacious lounge, under the high stained-glass

dome, several men sat singly or in pairs, reading newspapers, or smoking, or just waiting and watching.

Elliott made his way along a central aisle. He strolled on through a succession of sumptuously appointed rooms that opened into each other and led to the dining room and terrace. He nodded to one or two people that he knew, turned around, and walked back again, pausing for a few moments at the long oak table on which newspapers in wooden-frame holders were laid out. He glanced at the headlines and then walked back to the entrance and turned by the stairs toward the American Bar. He went in and seated himself on a high stool at the curved end of the dark oak counter.

He ordered a Jack Daniel's on the rocks and looking around saw the handsome Captain Wirth, sitting in a green leather alcove, raise his glass to a girl at the bar, inviting her to a drink. The girl was smiling noncommittally. Not accepting exactly, but not refusing either. Nobody refused anything too firmly in this ambience. Everything was a matter of delicate negotiations, and Captain Wirth of Swiss Intelligence was, like so many of his compatriots, a master of the ambiguous approach. He had a reputation as a womanizer, but some people said this was just a convenient cover for gathering information from a variety of women agents. Others maintained that he used the pretext of gathering information as a cover (for his wife's benefit) for his sexual exploits.

He was not being too insistent in his offer of the drink, just smilingly waiting. Seeing Elliott, he asked him to sit down.

"A drink?"

"You looked as though you might be occupied," Elliott said.

"Perhaps, perhaps," Captain Wirth conceded, "but meanwhile you can keep me company. She is very attractive, no? The trouble is, nowadays you can never tell if they are professional, and if so *what* profession."

Elliott sat down and looked at the girl, who was still smiling faintly, waiting for a firmer invitation.

"You like her?" Captain Wirth asked.

"She's fantastic," Elliott said enthusiastically.

"Maybe she likes you," Captain Wirth hinted.

"No. It's you she's interested in."

The waiter had come with his Jack Daniel's. Captain Wirth clinked glasses with him and said, "It won't be long now. A few weeks at the most. What will you do when the war is over, Mr. Elliott? You will stay with the legation?"

"I just happened to get into that when the borders closed, and nobody could leave."

"Your father is a distinguished correspondent of the press. Perhaps you will choose his occupation?"

"It keeps you on the move, there's that to be said for it."

"You like to keep on the move?"

"On the other hand—newspaper work, I dunno. You're always around the people who make things happen, but *you* don't make things happen. Sort of like being the eunuch in the seraglio."

"What sort of things do you wish to make happen, Mr. Elliott?"

"I don't really know, but *something*."

Captain Wirth smiled understandingly. "Then you have not chosen your character yet," he remarked.

"*Chosen* my character."

"Yes. André Gide once wrote to a friend asking him at what age he had chosen his character, and it occurred to me how true. We do, at a certain time, choose our own character—though we may only come to realize it long afterward."

"Who says you've got a choice?"

At the bar the girl of indeterminate calling had finished her drink; she was looking around.

"The question of choice," Captain Wirth said. "Ah, yes. For myself I must believe that one has choice, though I agree it is sometimes so narrowed-down as to appear virtually nonexistent. A neutral country, entirely surrounded by belligerents—ah!" He spread his hands expressively. "You quickly learn how little choice you have. But still *some*, I venture to say."

"Your people—Major Waibel especially—have always been very helpful to us," Elliott said.

"One endeavors to reconcile neutrality with one's conscience," Captain Wirth declared.

"I've often wondered how you swing that," Elliott said. "With General Guisan. When the Swiss General Staff meet . . ."

"Major Waibel does not report everything he does to the General. The General does not press him to do so."

"That's very easygoing of the General."

"He naturally has complete trust in his senior intelligence officers."

"Colonel Masson enjoys the same complete trust in his liaison with the Germans?"

"Absolutely."

"I wouldn't go so far as to call it two-faced," Elliott said, smiling, "but it's a pretty damn good illustration of not letting your left hand know what the right is doing. . . ."

"Ah—" Captain Wirth said, "Switzerland is neutral but she also must live. We must protect our vital interests. Both sides accept that. The Germans allow our merchant ships to leave from Genoa. The British let them pass through the Strait of Gibraltar. You Americans do not bomb the Swiss quay at Genoa, nor our rail links."

"That why you people set up the Wolff deal?" Elliott said.

"The Wolff deal?"

"Come on, I know about it. I code and decode the messages. . . ."

"Let me put it this way," Captain Wirth said cautiously. "We are aware of the consequences for my country should the Germans in northern Italy fall back fighting every inch of the way, blowing up everything in their retreat, as they have been ordered to do by Hitler. It would be disaster for us."

"I guess it would be."

"The Germans have many divisions in northern Italy. We would not want them deployed on Swiss soil. Therefore we are as interested as Mr. Dulles in achieving an immediate German surrender. . . ."

"I see your point, Captain." He laughed. "It's not

37

only conscience you have to reconcile with neutrality, it's also eating."

"That comes into it too," Captain Wirth admitted.

The bar waiter came over to say that the Captain was wanted on the phone. He went to take the call at the bar, standing close to the charming girl. Throughout the call, which was brief, they exchanged smiling, flirtatious glances.

"I shall attend to it," Captain Wirth said, putting down the phone while still smiling at the girl, a little sorrowfully now. He returned to the alcove where Elliott was sitting.

"I am sorry, I must leave. A matter of work, you understand." He looked regretfully toward the girl and then said, "But perhaps you, Mr. Elliott, if you have time on your hands. Please, please allow me. . . ." He was already making the preliminary motions of inviting the girl over, and it didn't look as though she was going to refuse.

"No, no, thanks a lot, but I've got things to do." He got up too, and they went out of the bar together.

Automatically Captain Wirth made a mental note about the young American. Unsure of himself with women. Probably because he couldn't bear to lose. . . . Yes, he knew that type.

• 7 •

Von Thedieck's watch had been taken away. There were no windows in the rigorous interrogation room. It was a dank cellar. In one corner there was an old cast-iron bathtub, supplied by a single tap. The stone floor sloped slightly to a drain, and there were coiled rubber hoses on the ground.

To counter the sense of desolation that he felt, von Thedieck reminded himself who he was. The personal envoy of the Highest SS-Leader and Reich Pleni-potentiary for Italy. By now General Wolff would have instigated inquiries about him at top level. He, von Thedieck, had translated for Himmler. Had sat next to the SS-Reichsführer at breakfast, lunch, and dinner, turning his theories of race and blood and destiny and nature cures into faultless Italian. He had been at General Wolff's side, translating for him, in audience with the Pope.

Impossible that he—von Thedieck—linguist, aristo-crat, authority on Puccini, a man with the highest connections, a welcome and witty guest in the palazzos of counts and princes, should be sitting in this filthy cellar waiting to be questioned by some oafish police-man.

For him, there had always been special dispensa-tions. Nobody had required *him* to go through the rigorous training—with live ammunition!—that SS recruits were normally subjected to. His special talents, and connections, had straightaway elevated him to the rank of SS-Colonel, and he had never had to fire a pistol, or be fired at.

The iron door was opening noisily on its large rusty hinges, and the Special Investigator came in carrying a batch of dog-eared files under his arm. He sat down straightaway and indicated to von Thedieck to sit on the only other chair.

"What time is it?" von Thedieck asked.

The Investigator acted as if he had not heard the question. He was busy with the files, slipping off the rubber bands that held the papers together, checking dates and subject matter inside, and arranging the folders in a different order. Occasionally he rubbed his stubbly face as if he would have liked to have a shave.

"How long have I been here?" When he received no answer he asked, "Might I be permitted a cigarette, Reichskriminaldirektor?"

"When we are finished."

"But—I must protest. I am a chain-smoker. I have been here for hours. . . . My cigarettes have been taken away . . ." His fingers went trembling over his lips. "It is a great deprivation for me."

"You are not meant to be too comfortable," Schöller pointed out.

"Might I . . . at least . . . have a glass of water?"

"Later."

"My watch. When will it be returned to me?"

"In due course."

"What is the time? What day is it?"

"That doesn't matter to you. Not till you've answered the questions."

"As I have already explained . . ."

"Your explanations don't wash with me, Thedieck. *Now*. Are you ready to cooperate?"

The SS-Colonel was silent. Abruptly Schöller rose to his feet, turned, and went out, locking the heavy iron door after him.

"Well?"

"What is the time, Reichskriminaldirektor? Is it daytime?"

"That's no concern of yours."

"I beg to differ. I must know if it's day or night."

"What for? It's all the same here."

"I am very hungry—I've been given nothing to eat. For days."

"Days?"

"Since yesterday."

"Yesterday?"

"You confuse me, Reichskriminaldirektor."

"If you answer the questions, it'll straighten everything out."

"I cannot disobey my orders . . ."

Schöller was rapidly flicking through von Thedieck's file. He had found something.

"Well, well. What have we here? School report. 'Ritter is a sensitive child, much given to brooding introspection, which cannot be regarded as entirely healthy. But his scholastic work has been well above

40

average and his piano playing is brilliant.' Well, well, well. A farting child prodigy." He continued to flick through the file, sometimes wetting his finger to turn the pages. "Now here is something—'at Gymnasium said to have had unnatural sexual tastes.' Who'd ever have believed it! Unnatural tastes, hmm?"

"I don't know where you obtained such slanderous lies . . ."

"I wouldn't bother myself about that. Now. Here is something else. This is interesting. Psychiatric report, by Professor Berners, Charité Hospital, Berlin. Dated . . . 1925. You were twenty-nine then."

"Such documents are confidential," von Thedieck began, becoming flustered.

"Oh, yes. Yes. They are not always easy to get hold of," Schöller admitted. "This is *very* interesting," he said, and began to read out. " 'The patient von Thedieck's severe nervous breakdown appears to have been occasioned in the first place by a failed love affair with a young girl of good family, the apparent cause being his sexual impotence. Character makeup of a neurasthenic type. Patient's expression typically hangdog and tense. Troubled by blushing, blanching, and compulsive nail-peeling.

" 'The patient has a long history of nervous disturbances, claustrophobic attacks, and depressions, as well as attacks of acute and irrational anxiety bordering on panic, sometimes brought on by, for example, sitting in the middle of a row of seats in the theater, or by a long-delayed revolver shot offstage. In interviews the patient gives the impression of desperation. He has spoken of suicide frequently, and he accuses himself of being a foul and vile person, of being worthless, beneath contempt, not fit to live, etcetera. Frequently breaks down into tears in the course of interviews in a womanly way. Sense of shame seems to be largely connected with his homosexual practices. His musical interests and intellectual pursuits constitute an entirely separate part of his life.'

"Well, that puts everything in a different light," Schöller said, getting up. "We know what we're dealing with now."

As soon as he heard the key being turned in the lock, von Thedieck got up and, remembering the peephole in the door, went and stood with his back covering it and then began to shake.

His face, concealed from any watchers there might be outside, had become that of a cowering child. He bit his lip, trying to control the panic that was rising in him. He had not felt like this for many years. How thin was the line between what he was and what he had been once—the Reichskriminaldirektor had brought that home to him. You couldn't get away from what you were. *If I am tortured.* There was no point in pretending—he knew very well that he could not bear pain. Never had been able to.

He had heard of electric shocks to anus and penis, of the crushing of the testicles in small iron presses specially made for that purpose, of the sequence of drowning and resuscitation and drowning again in baths of cold water, of people being hung by the arms until their shoulders became dislocated. . . . Seeking to keep calm, he told himself that Schöller would not have recourse to such methods. He was not Gestapo. Just a policeman. The Kriminalpolizei. Of course, they all came under Himmler—but that didn't mean they all used the same methods. Did it?

Being left alone was the worst. He found himself waiting anxiously—eagerly even—for Schöller's return.

When Schöller came in, von Thedieck's first question was "What is the time?" but the Investigator ignored it. He took his seat and resumed where he had left off. This time he covered von Thedieck's early years in the Nazi party, his joining the SS, his progress in that organization. It was all there. His entire life appeared in grotesque paraphrase. How did they know all these things? Events of ten, twelve years ago, of a private nature, that he barely remembered himself. Incidents, conversations, encounters—illnesses, statements made in moments of depression or despair or futility. Who had been listening all these years and noting everything down? He tried to maintain a sense of detachment about all this material being thrown at him. It was, of course, part of the interrogation technique. A good deal of it was rumor and hearsay—but how close to the true events, or at any rate, to one aspect of them. Given a particular makeup, did a man's life really follow such an inevitable course? As discreditable incident followed discreditable incident—examples of weakness, of cowardice, of self-indulgence—he saw the source of this malaise, which had been his life, in the conceited features of a hateful child, with its inordinate demands. If that child could be extinguished. The relief of it.

Of course, this calculated assault upon his sense of self-respect was meant to make him feel low and contemptible. To make him despair. He was a man of culture and education, he kept reminding himself, weak like all men, but not—surely—the useless wretch he was made out by the Investigator's careful selection of discreditable items from the dossier. Working-class youths he had picked up and used had given statements to the police, describing his sexual demands on them.

Every man had a lower nature. It was not all of him. But as vile incident after vile incident was read out in the Investigator's mocking voice, von Thedieck began to see these dishonorable events of his life following upon each other like the progressive stages of a long and irreversible illness.

"I found a meaning to my life in the SS."

"Yes?" Schöller inquired.

"In the sacrifice of self demanded of us."

"You?"

Von Thedieck said, "Are you going to torture me?" He looked around. "I have heard you have instruments. . . ."

The policeman's big ears pulled back against the side of the skull and the rumpled skin became tautly smoothed out over the large bone structure.

"Instruments," Schöller spat on the ground. He gave a contemptuous laugh. "I don't need instruments, Thedieck. I'm an old policeman. I have fists and knees and elbows. I leave instruments to my esteemed *Kollegen*." He spat again.

"Are you going to beat me up?" His eyes rolled

upward until the pupils had entirely disappeared beneath his lids, and his face was presented docilely for the expected blows.

Schöller looked at him in disgust. "Pull yourself together," he said, and went out.

Food had been brought in, and von Thedieck fell on it ravenously.

He was starving. How many hours—days?—had he been here, without food?

Hunger obliterated from his mind the realization that he was eating with his hands. Knife and fork had not been provided. He was gnawing at a bone, like a dog. Still it was decent of the Reichskriminaldirektor to have fed him. A decent type, a decent type. Doing a hard job.

Squatting over the drain, his trousers about his ankles, shivering in the cold dampness, von Thedieck felt the sudden semiliquid stream pouring out of him, and smelled the foul smell of his insides. There was nothing with which to clean himself. He pulled up his trousers again, compelled to suffer his own unclean condition.

Schöller had opened one of the later, newer-looking folders. "Last year," he said, reading, "your mother died. You did not visit her while she was dying. Why?"

"That is a lie. I did visit her."

"At the end?"

"At the end . . . at the end I could not face it. She was dying of cancer. She had changed completely. I could not stand to see her . . ."

"She asked to see you and you did not come."

"How could you know that, how could you know such a thing?"

"It's recorded."

Von Thedieck was breathing strangely, in sudden gulps. He was cold and sweating at the same time, and the sweat was rolling down his jowls and over the silver thread emblems of his collar patches. His fast-blinking eyes went around the bare walls, seeking some outlet, a break in the monotonous expanse of moldering brickwork. He tried to rise out of his chair, driven by a ludicrous impulse to run, to run.

The formerly dapper SS officer was now completely bedraggled; there were food stains on his tunic, his buttons were undone, his hair stuck out stiffly from the side of his head, his uniform hung awkwardly from his slumped body. His posture on the hard wooden chair was tensely lopsided.

"You must believe me," he begged.

There was a childlike imploring look on von Thedieck's face. Schöller recognized its meaning. Usually in the course of a successfully conducted rigorous interrogation, there came a moment when the person questioned, having lost the last shred of his self-respect, was compelled to turn and seek human comfort from the only other person present, even when that other person was his torturer. This need cut through considerations of ultimate self-interest because time had been eliminated and only the immediate relief of some form of human approval counted.

"My mother," he said, "had been so beautiful. I could not stand to see her dying. In any case, she was unconscious. There would have been no point in my being there."

Schöller studied the file. "She recovered consciousness on February third, 1944, at seven A.M. and again at three P.M. She was intermittently conscious throughout February third, fourth, fifth, and sixth, before dying on the seventh. You did not see her on any of those days. She died in great pain, screaming."

Von Thedieck's eyes screwed tightly shut as if to keep out an agonizing light.

He felt the need to confide in this man, to expose himself in all his shamefulness; he struggled against this need. It was, of course, a state of mind that the secret police methodically induced for their own purposes. But if it was only under these circumstances that the full truth could be seen . . . His sense of unworthiness stilled his fear. He was calmed by the knowledge of the inevitable justness of whatever punishment the Reichskriminaldirektor chose to inflict upon him.

"When my mother died, I was with someone—a youth—I had accosted in the lavatory at the Wannsee U-Bahnhof. While my mother was dying, I was using him; but I could not obtain satisfaction for a very long time, and then at last I thought, 'Good, she is gone now, I am rid of her at last, the old bitch,' and I—I remember thinking—supposing babies were made there, what black rascals they would be."

"You betrayed everybody in the course of your life," Schöller said quietly.

"Yes."

"Even your mother."

"Yes."

Von Thedieck began to weep uncontrollably. Schöller gave him a cigarette and lit it for him. Shaking, von Thedieck drew in the smoke. The cigarette had the effect of calming him somewhat.

"No man can go against his own nature," Schöller said, without harshness. "None of us can help what we are. Still, we must do our duty, hmm?"

The waves of tears slowly were brought under control as Schöller spoke.

"I understand," von Thedieck said.

"Good . . . good."

"What does the Reichskriminaldirektor wish to know?"

"The full details of the Berne conspiracy to betray the Reich . . ."

"We were seeking honorable terms . . ."

"*Honorable?*" Schöller said mockingly.

Von Thedieck laughed at himself for still clinging to the pretense of honor.

"We were also going to save our own skins, of course," he said with a slightly hysterical giggle.

"What arrangement did Wolff reach with Dulles?"

"It involved the immediate surrender of all German forces in Italy. An approach was to be made to Kesselring to persuade him to also surrender the forces of the Commander-in-Chief-West. But resistance to the Russians was to continue."

So it was done: the relief of having given way to the basest of impulses was a kind of ecstasy.

"What were you and Wolff and the others getting in return?"

"Immunity. We would not be prosecuted for war crimes."

"The Allies are committed not to deal with anyone except on the basis of unconditional surrender."

"Dulles and General Wolff arrived at a private— at a gentlemen's understanding . . ."

"What else is Wolff getting? Money?"

"No payments were mentioned. But it was intimated that our financial affairs would not be—probed."

"That explains your transfer of money to Switzerland."

"Yes."

"The contact with Dulles, how was that made?"

"It was effected through Major Waibel, of Swiss Intelligence."

"And the contact with him?"

"Through an intermediary, Baron Parilli, with extensive contacts in Switzerland."

"What level have the negotiations reached?"

"There was a secret meeting between General Wolff and two Allied generals."

"Where was this meeting? And when?"

"On March nineteenth. At the villa in Ascona on Lake Maggiore."

"Who were these generals?"

"They were not introduced to us by name. But later it was established that the American was Major General Lemnitzer, Field Marshal Alexander's Deputy Chief of Staff, and the Englishman was General Airey, Alexander's senior intelligence officer . . ."

"How did these Allied generals get into Switzerland?"

"It was facilitated by Major Waibel. They were in disguise and had false names and papers."

"What is Major Waibel's role in all this?"

"He initiated the entire operation by bringing us together with Dulles."

"In direct contravention of Switzerland's position of neutrality," Schöller said with a hard laugh.

"He does it on his own responsibility."

"Really," Schöller said mockingly. "You mean Guisan turns a blind eye to it."

"That may be."

"Technically, how is it done? How do you enter and leave the country for these secret meetings?"

"Major Waibel, or someone from his office, passes us through border control."

"Are papers examined, questions asked?"

"No. As we are known to Major Waibel, all formalities are waived."

"And if you have to cross the frontier unexpectedly. Without Major Waibel being told in advance. What happens then?"

"There is a password."

"What happens when the password is given?"

"The person who gives the password is conducted to a private room, where he waits until Major Waibel's arrival, or until Major Waibel has verbally indicated that he can be allowed through."

"This password. What is it?"

"Sunrise."

"Sunrise."

"Yes."

Schöller stood up. He arranged the papers, squaring them off, and then slipped the elastic bands over the files he had been using. He said, "What you have just told me will be typed out, and you will be able to make such minor corrections of detail as you wish, and then you will sign it."

"Yes." Von Thedieck closed his eyes. He had become calm and composed again.

"What will happen to me?"

"You will be taken back to Berlin, to the Plötzensee prison."

"Plötzensee."

"Yes. You will be kept in solitary confinement until this matter has been cleared up. You must talk to no one. You will sign a second confession, relating to the illegal transfer of money to Switzerland. Until my investigations are complete, General Wolff will be informed that this is the charge on which you are being held."

"And if I were to request the right and privilege of an SS officer . . .?"

"It will be granted."

"I do make that request."

"Very well. As soon as you have signed the statements."

His watch and cigarettes were returned to him, and half an hour later Schöller came in with the typed statements, in triplicate. Von Thedieck read them through carefully. He noticed one or two typing errors and spelling mistakes. He was vaguely surprised because the police typists were usually very accurate. He corrected the mistakes with his fountain pen, and signed the statements and the carbon copies.

When they had been examined by Schöller and folded in his pocket, he produced a revolver, loaded it with one round, cocked it, and slipped off the safety catch. He placed it on the chair on which he had previously been sitting.

"I am deeply grateful to the Reichskriminaldirektor."

"I shall require a statement."

"Of course." Von Thedieck picked up the pen and wrote on a sheet of paper provided by Schöller:

"In accordance with the SS code of honor, the signatory requested the right of an officer to expiate his crime so that he may be regarded as having fallen in action, and this request was generously granted by the Reich Special Investigator, Reichskriminaldirektor Schöller. In validation of the above, I append my signature, Ritter von Thedieck, SS-Colonel."

Schöller picked up the statement, read it, and folded that away too. He was about to leave, but seeing the SS-Colonel's disheveled appearance, something occurred to him.

"You'll want to tidy up," he said, "have a wash, so that you look clean and neat. I'll bring you some things." He went out and returned within a few minutes with a comb and hairbrush, soap, a small towel, and a clothes brush. He placed these next to the revolver on the chair.

"One other thing," Schöller said. He sounded awkward and was rubbing his face. "Your mother. She was not in any pain at the end. I—I regret having had to use such a story, I was in a hurry. She never recovered consciousness."

"I thank the Reichskriminaldirektor for telling me this." Tears of gratitude poured down the man's face.

"I thought you should know that."

He had no idea whether the pansy SS-Colonel's mother had been in pain at the end or not. But he did not like to let a man die with a sin against his mother on his conscience.

"You can use the bath tap," he said. "I have switched on the water."

"I thank the Reichskriminaldirektor."

Schöller went out and lit a cigarette. He felt the stubble of his beard. He could hear the racket that the water made running through the ancient plumbing system. He finished his cigarette, threw down the stub, trod it out. He walked up and down. Five minutes, ten minutes. How long was von Thedieck going to take? Of course, the SS-Colonel was very particular about his appearance. He'd want to look nice and neat.

Schöller lit another cigarette, and then another. He was on the point of opening the door to hurry up matters when he heard the shot. He trod out his cigarette and pushed open the heavy iron door.

Von Thedieck lay on the ground, hair combed flat, tunic buttoned and brushed, hands clean and white. The whole left side of his face was shattered, and the eye, on that side, had been blown out by the bullet. Schöller snorted through his nostrils, coughed up phlegm, and spat. Then he turned and went out.

• 8 •

Schöller himself typed the report of the interrogation and its ultimate outcome, hitting wrong letters at times and spelling some words incorrectly. When he was finished, he put the signed carbon copies of the confessions in his pocket. The originals he placed together with the suicide note in his document safe.

It was now five A.M. and beginning to get light. From his room at the top of the Schloss, he could see a long way across the open countryside, whitish with hoar frost. The first light fell on a peacefully curving country road, and on the moving water of a stream.

The Investigator had slept as little as his prisoner during the forty-five hours of almost continuous interrogation—no more than nine hours in three nights. His eyes were bloodshot, his tongue furred, and his throat was raw from too much smoking. He felt his cheeks and got up. There was a washroom next to his office, and there he took off his jacket and rolled back the collar of his shirt from his thick red neck. He took a shaving stick used down to the silver paper and, wetting his brush under the cold water, attempted to work up some lather from the poor-quality soap. He succeeded in working it into a somewhat thicker foam on his beard and proceeded to shave with long fast strokes, using a safety razor with a blade that was no longer sharp enough and tore at the coarse hairs. He washed the soap off in the cold water and rubbed his face and neck vigorously with the towel. His trousers were crumpled; he had been lying down in them for brief spells of sleep in the intervals between the questioning, and he decided to change. He had some fresh underwear, a clean shirt, and another suit in the closet.

When he was dressed he returned to his office. The orderly had brought breakfast and was laying it out on the desk. Bread. A large plate of various kinds of sausage meat. Cheeses. Hard-boiled eggs. Jam. Coffee. Schöller ate with appetite, at the same time looking through a sheaf of the latest reports. Some of these spoke of air strikes during the night against the southbound traffic. Army trucks had been destroyed, as well as many private vehicles. The dead numbered more than seventy.

As soon as he had finished eating, he called in Kriminal-assistent Grafeneck and gave him a message to transmit at once.

"To SS-Reichsführer Himmler. From Reich Special Investigator Schöller. Rudolphstein, April 8, 1945.

"In the matter of the so-called Wolff conspiracy, I have further inquiries to make. I anticipate that my investigations will be completed within forty-eight hours. Meanwhile, I recommend the immediate recall of General Wolff for questioning. In anticipation of the SS-Reichsführer's agreeing to this step, I have taken the liberty of placing the General's family under the SS-Reichsführer's protection, pending the return of the General himself. There was not time to consult the SS-Reichsführer in this regard, as it had come to my notice that the General's family was departing for Italy. In fact, I was obliged to have them escorted from the train at the Brenner Pass, where they are now being held in protective custody."

Having dictated the text of the message, and ordered that it be sent straightaway over the teletype line, he told Grafeneck that if he had not heard from him by noon of the 12th the document safe was to be opened and action taken in relation to material found inside.

Then he packed an overnight bag and left. In the stables where the staff cars were garaged he selected a Horch with no official markings. By now it was almost seven A.M.

On April 8 the corridor between the eastern and

western fronts was still wide enough for him to be able to take a fairly direct route to the south. The Allied armies were some distance from the Elbe, and Bayreuth and Nuremberg were not yet threatened.

But the constant danger from strafing fighter planes made it advisable to keep off the autobahn as far as possible, and the route he chose was one that followed minor country roads.

When he had to pass through open fields, he chose the narrowest, bumpiest country lanes, scarcely wider than the width of his car, and drove slowly, knowing that from the air a single slow-moving speck was impossible to distinguish from a farm vehicle, on which the British Mosquito pilots were unlikely to waste their cannon fire or incendiary bombs.

By dusk he had got as far as Regensburg and decided to spend the night there.

Next morning he set off before dawn, passing between Augsburg and Munich. Karlsruhe had fallen to the French; in Pforzheim the battle was in its final stages; but with the fighting still some hundred miles to his right, Schöller was able to take the road to Kempten, which afforded the most direct approach to the Swiss frontier.

Even so, the constant halts to have his papers examined, and the necessity of avoiding military areas that were liable to come under air attack, made the journey long.

It was night by the time he reached Bregenz, the Austrian border town on the Bodensee. He drove through the town and then for about twenty-five kilometers along a road that for a time ran parallel with the lake and the railway tracks. Half an hour's drive and he was at the border. Across a narrow segment of water lay Switzerland.

At the German control point he produced the papers of a Dr. Schultz, chief foreign buyer of the Reich Technology Ministry. It was an official incognito issued to him by Gruppe IV E of the Reichssicherheitshauptamt and known to the Gestapo frontier police as such, and it ensured rapid and preferential treatment. To cross over into Switzerland was a matter of driving over a short bridge that spanned a ribbon-like water-way. The Swiss border post was just on the other side.

When he was asked for his papers, Schöller said, "My compliments to Major Waibel. Please tell him I look forward to watching the sunrise with him."

This occasioned no surprise. He was directed to pull up at the side. One guard remained watching him while the other went into a green-tiled house that looked like a private villa. Within a minute or so a more senior official of the border police emerged and said, "Major Waibel will be told that you are here. Your name?"

"That is not important."

"I understand."

The border official politely opened the door of the Horch and indicated for Schöller to step out and come with him. He led him into the green-tiled house and showed him to a small private room in which there was a table and a hard wooden bench. It was now after midnight, and presently the border official returned to say that Major Waibel could not be reached until next morning. Schöller accepted this without demur, and making himself as comfortable as he could on the wooden bench, went to sleep.

He was awakened at seven A.M. A handsome man in his thirties was standing over him.

"I do not know you—do I?" he asked brusquely.

"But I know you, Captain Wirth."

"Who are you?"

"I am the Reich Special Investigator. Schöller."

"What do you want?"

"I want to see Dulles."

"Mr. Dulles. Of the American legation."

"The same."

"In what connection?"

"The sunrise," Schöller said with an airy wave of the hand. "Of which he and I are both devoted watchers."

"I will inquire," Captain Wirth said.

He returned ten minutes later and said, "Come with me." Schöller smiled.

An army car drove them to a military airstrip close

to the border. The small plane that had brought Captain Wirth was waiting, and in a matter of minutes they were airborne, the Swiss countryside spread out beneath them.

Schöller, looking out through the porthole, could see the whole of the Bodensee, and just the other side of it—Germany, the smoke of burning towns rising in a dozen places. Half an hour later they landed in Berne.

◆ 9 ◆

The large, round man, bent low over the hospital bed, at first sight appeared to be molding and modeling something out of the slack belly of his patient.

From childhood Felix Kersten had possessed extraordinary powers in his fingertips, an ability to penetrate the body's surface and tell the entire internal geography at a touch.

Within minutes of commencing the treatment, he had found the dilated liver, the engorged spleen, the knotted intestines, the feeble lungs. The vasomotor function of the vessels was extremely poor. The nerves were starved of oxygen. The vital centers lacked nourishment. Himmler's body was a stagnant pool, with life force reduced to faint pulses.

His eyes opened and he saw Kersten. His magic masseur!

The powerful fingers were continuing their deep mysterious exploration, pressing and rubbing, pressing and rubbing, dispersing the unwanted blood and moving the good blood toward the heart. Almost at once the heartbeat improved, and the internal secretions too.

The intestines were released from their knot. Like a logjammed river that has been freed, the Beast's body began to flow again.

A long deep sigh issued from Himmler.

He saw a white ceiling, white walls. . . . Not all his mind and perceptions were restored to him at the same time. The later man did not yet exist.

The masseur was watching his patient craftily. As the treatment took effect, things that had been dammed up in the body began to loosen. Kersten was obliged to listen to the outpour . . . long menus of food that Himmler had eaten at some time; lists of every sort; the names of people of high birth who had received him, always with joy, in their houses; his longing for arms and war and tests of courage . . . his belief in nature, light meals, dandelion tea. In work. *History will not inquire how well Heinrich Himmler slept, but how much he achieved*. It was a phrase he often repeated, though now he was usually exhausted and incapable of anything at all by the late afternoon. *Be more than you appear*, the slowly recovering man admonished. Another of his favorite sayings. The needs of the State. The requirements of history. Nordic-Westphalian blood. The *Untermenschen* who dragged everything down to their level. An official had insulted his father. It still rankled, after all these years. Evidently the rude fellow did not know that the father of Heinrich Himmler had been tutor to Prince Henry of Bavaria. A great-grandfather had been a high police official at Lindau on the Bodensee. He loved nature, Himmler. Hated the chemical production that befouled the air. Modern man was choking in his own filth. Something about the drug manufacturers, one of his favorite hates. And the so-called doctors. Quacks and charlatans, like the priests. The Jew-Popes. As a young man he had been welcomed in many fine houses, he confided, making one of his abrupt changes of subject.

He talked about someone called Maja. She often figured in his rambling thoughts, after a treatment. Maja. A dear soul. The daughter of a woman called Frau Loritz whose lodger he had once been and who served him splendid meals: dumpling soup, filet of veal, potato salad, noodles, beer, cocoa, apple pie, and *Gutterle*. For Maja he proposed learning to ice-skate so that he could ask her to come skating with him. He could master anything upon which he set his mind. Mariele Rauschmeier had made a disagreeable remark: that he talked too much. This was untrue. Sometimes it was necessary for him to explain his meaning since people often misunderstood what he said, or at any rate *meant*. These young foolish girls, all innuendos and giggling and secret meanings . . . he felt sorry for them. He hated innuendo. And crudity. Bad language in front of women, he would never tolerate. Sometimes a man succumbed to his lower nature. . . . But such things had to be struggled against, such habits conquered . . . in such ways a nation was weakened, its vital energy drained away. "Basically I am a soldier at heart," he declared, suddenly sitting up, "but first I must take my exams." His face lit up—he was twenty, peering into the future with all of his great foreknowledge. He would take part in fighting and war. To face danger was a relief to him, to risk his life. *Yes, yes*.

Somebody called Lu was referred to often. He was evidently a friend from his youth, a good fellow but petty bourgeois by nature. A bank clerk with the soul of a bank clerk. He knew nothing of the terrible sacrifices that one was called upon to make. He'd had many good friends, he told Kersten, but they lacked sternness of spirit and wasted his time.

Himmler was getting better. Talk about his time being wasted invariably signaled recovery. Kersten continued his massaging, heeding all the signs, calculating the right moment to speak. It must not be too soon, not before the relief was unquestionable, the miracle once more indubitably performed. Nor must it be too late—when the restored well-being was already taken for granted. It was a matter of the most delicate judgment to tell the exact moment of the Beast's gratitude. And so Kersten waited until Himmler's eyes indicated a return to the present, the hospital bed at Hohenly-chen, the war. The moment to speak.

"May I ask the SS-Reichsführer if he has given the

matter of my recent request further consideration?"

"Ah, Kersten," Himmler grumbled, "you get a life out of me with every rub."

"It is my privilege to do so on behalf of humanity."

"Criminals, Jews, traitors . . . "

"May I leave the Reichsführer my list?"

"You always have a list. . . . Nobody can say I do not pay handsomely for the relief you bring me."

"The Reichsführer has always been most generous in rewarding me in the past. May I venture to hope that the people on this list will be given their liberty . . . ?"

"How many this time, Kersten?"

"Five thousand, Herr Reichsführer."

"It used to be six Norwegians, four Dutchmen, seven Finns. You have been putting up the price of your treatments lately, my good Kersten. *Five thousand! Jews,* I suppose? Ah well, I am rich in Jews." He laughed at his little joke.

Suddenly Himmler had an idea.

"Consider, Kersten. If I offered Eisenhower the Jews. . . . If I gave him the lives of all those that remain . . . "

"It would be an act of humanity, Herr Reichsführer!"

"One that he would reciprocate?"

"I cannot speak for Eisenhower, but I venture . . . "

"You have no contact with him? You who have contacts with everyone."

"Not personally. But through the Swedish government, no doubt. Count Bernadotte would be the best man to make such an . . . offer."

"Yes, yes, quite so."

As abruptly as it had occurred, the idea lost all interest for Himmler.

"Perhaps if the SS-Reichsführer would free the Jews unconditionally . . . such a gesture . . . ". But the ever-perceptive Kersten had seen Himmler's face darken, and knew that the moment for making requests was now past. Himmler pressed the bell by his bedside, and almost immediately the door opened and his batman appeared.

"I wish to dress. Immediately," he commanded. "My uniform!"

"The field uniform, SS-Reichsführer?"

"No, the black."

He waited, sitting up stiffly, an expression of solemn concentration on his face, palms and fingers lightly pressed together in what might have been the posture of someone praying. In a minute the communion, with whatever, had ended: the batman came in, ready to hand out the clothes, one article at a time, in the order laid down.

Removing the nightshirt, Himmler stood momentarily naked, a man in his mid-forties, broad-hipped, with a paunch, narrow shoulders, and the spinal curvature of someone who has spent too many years stooped over paperwork. An ill-shaped figure bulging out where Nordic-Westphalian man should be flat, and receding where manliness required protuberance. His sex organ was like the partially retracted body of a snail.

Miraculously cured by his magic masseur and imbued once more with a sense of destiny, he pulled on the long underpants and the black breeches. Still naked from the waist up, he sat forward on the edge of the bed and, raising first the left and then the right leg, let the kneeling batman push on the jackboots. Next came shirt and tie, the batman tying the knot. Himmler put on the black tunic with the three silver thread oakleaves enclosed in an oakleaf wreath on each lapel. He did up the buttons. He buckled on his sword belt, hooked on ceremonial dagger, attached the crossbelt in the front, passing it under the silver braiding on his right shoulder, and gave the end to his batman to hook into the belt at the back. He slipped the swastika armband on his sleeve and finally accepted the cap with the silver braid and the Death's Head, and placed it firmly and squarely on his head, so that the peak reached to the tops of his pince-nez. Sternly, he turned to his physician:

"Your requests will be implemented, as always, Herr Kersten."

"Thank you, SS-Reichsführer."

"Although the outlook seems dark at the moment, Kersten, everything may yet turn out well. I have an intuition that fate is about to spring one of its great reversals. But, if this should not be, then my Waffen-SS will fight to the last man, as the Ostrogoths fought at Vesuvius . . . "

"And the SS-Reichsführer?"

"He will fall at the head of his men, as did Teias, the last king of the Ostrogoths."

With that, the terror of the earth, ceremonial dagger jogging on his groin, turned and strode briskly into the anteroom where a dozen men, wearied by long waiting, jumped to their feet in astonishment at the sight of their restored leader. A dozen arms shot out in the Hitler salute; a dozen voices cried "Heil Hitler," not exactly in unison. His aide Grothman and his secretary Brandt shuffled forward, offering their congratulations on his predestined recovery. There was a smirk on Himmler's face as he turned to his chief astrologer, Glass, a long, very thin man, like a piece of bent wire, with a shiny bald skull and bony fingers that were perpetually in movement.

"Well, Glass," Himmler said, "what do you see before us?"

"A death, SS-Reichsführer," the soothsayer confided in a low ingratiating voice.

"Hitler?"

The astrologer spread out his hands equivocally, by way of indicating that even his prophecies could not rise to such specifics. But his master seemed well satisfied. "The Führer is very ill," he said. "I may have to carry the burden alone."

Turning on his heels, he strode out, followed by Brandt and Grothman, his driver Lukas, his doctor Gebhardt, the Chief of the Inland SD Otto Ohlendorf, two Waffen-SS generals, a general of police, several Gestapo functionaries, Reichsleiters and Gauleiters, and their adjutants.

In phalanx they marched down the hospital corridors, and at their approach male nurses rushed to move stretcher cases, which would otherwise have been trodden underfoot in the general enthusiasm. The sound of metal-heeled boots rang out on marble floors.

In the grounds an open car was waiting. Himmler got in and stood for a moment in the back, arm lifted in the Hitler salute, face stern as when he had stood next to the Führer on the high podium at Nuremberg, backed by the great pillars duplicating the Pergamon Altar. Around him, now, a score or more of his personal staff stood in fervent attendance.

Glancing upward, Himmler saw that there were faces at every window at the SS hospital, and it seemed to him, in the moment before he again lowered his eyes to a more acceptable sight, that many of these men, badly wounded, of course, possibly even dying, did not have expressions of proper respect, indeed some of them were almost derisive in their demeanor. He made a note to talk to SS-Professor General Gebhardt about improving the mental hygiene of these men.

Then, still standing upright with raised arms, he gave Lukas the signal to drive off. As soon as they were out of sight of the hospital windows, he sat down, feeling rather weak in the legs, suddenly. He was driven straight to his private train, drawn up for maximum safety in a tunnel. As he entered his Mobile Operations Room, an aide handed him a teletype from Reichskriminaldirektor Schöller.

Himmler frowned as he read it. "Place an immediate call to General Wolff in Fasano," he said and proceeded to busy himself with accumulated paperwork. There was a great deal of it. Death penalties to be confirmed on senior officers guilty of complicity in defeatism, or of sabotaging the war effort by their pessimism, or of other even more heinous crimes, such as leaving their units without permission, faking illness to escape front-line duty, or failing to carry out one of the SS-Reichsführer's commands to the letter.

Himmler cast his eyes rapidly down the list, initialing death penalties in rapid succession. His eyes stopped about halfway down.

"But this man is on my personal staff," he said to his secretary Brandt.

"Yes, SS-Reichsführer."

"He is guilty?"

"Yes, Reichsführer. Of the most serious complicity in defeatism. He has been saying that the war is lost,

61

that those of us who still have a chance of saving ourselves, should take it. He was having a very bad effect."

Matter-of-factly Himmler initialed this name too and said, "I hereby authorize every commander to seize any man who turns back—I don't care who he is, or how high up—and put him up against the wall. See that is issued, Brandt, and have the Justice Ministry legalize it, retroactively if necessary."

He now turned to the first batch of reports. Report from SS-General Gutenberger, HSSPF West: "Colonel Kaehler (Neuss)—politically colorless, no power of decision, dismissal necessary." Report from SS-General Hofmann, HSSPF South-West: "Lieut-Col. Graf (Schlettstadt)—politically unreliable, dismissal urgently requested. Lieut-Col. von Hornstein (Rastatt)—should be dismissed, said to have a Jewish grandmother."

There were stacks of these reports, speaking of lack of planning in the higher military echelons, of disastrous irresponsibility in high places, of valuable troops and resources lying idle, of senior officers in key posts with suspected Jewish blood . . .

Hunched over these papers, Himmler worked for two hours without stop. It was night when Grothman came into the carriage to say he had finally been able to get through to Wolff in Fasano and he was on the line now. Would the SS-Reichsführer talk to him?

Himmler picked up the phone, his lips set in the expression of a headmaster obliged to cane a favorite pupil.

He spoke quietly, lecturingly: "It was impudent of you, Wolffchen, to attempt to move your family out of my immediate jurisdiction. I have rectified that situation, and your wife and children have been returned to my protection. You will return immediately to Berlin. I wish to speak to you." With that he hung up.

To Schöller, arriving in Berne on April 10, 1945, was like coming to another world. Everything here was bright, clean, whole. People strolled in the streets without fear or stood about in the arcades talking. They were well dressed and well fed and their eyes were clear. The shops were full of goods of the rarest luxury. Meat—real meat! Whole legs of ham. Pyramids of glacé fruits. Bonbons. Fresh fish. Fresh fruit. Soap: smooth, beautifully rounded and wrapped. Leather shoes, with good, hard, durable soles. Boxes of cigars. Rows of liquor of every kind and color. The aroma of freshly roasted coffee and of washed and soaped bodies.

As Captain Wirth's car carried them through the city, Schöller saw what stylish clothes the women wore, and how attractive they were. They were dressed not just for warmth, but to make themselves more desirable.

It was the lunch hour—friends, acquaintances, lovers meeting each other, exchanging greetings, going into restaurants. How freely people went about. Schöller could hardly recall such a way of living, though of course it must have been like that once in Germany too. A long time ago. He felt curiously uncomfortable, exposed to so much brightness and light. He was not used to it.

Major Waibel had telephoned Dulles to tell him about the arrival of the Reich Special Investigator.

It was a bad blow to the American group that the Germans knew the code word Sunrise. How much else did they know? Dulles had immediately sent for Howard Elliott to give him a series of urgent cables to get off. When Elliott arrived at the Herrengasse, he brought a message that had just come in. It was from one of Wolff's aides, Captain Zimmer. It said that Wolff had been ordered by Himmler to return immediately to Berlin. Wolff's family was being held in Germany, and so he would have to comply with the order.

Dulles looked around at the others in the room. They had all become grim-faced.

"Anybody know anything about Schöller?" Dulles asked.

"Chief of Amt IV K of the Reichssicherheitshauptamt," said Quantregg.

"The Gestapo."

"Part of it," Quantregg said.

Elliott made a dissenting noise, and Dulles looked toward him.

"You have a comment to make, Elliott?"

"Well, only that Amt IV K isn't the Gestapo. Exactly."

"You telling me what is or isn't the Gestapo, sonny?" Quantregg snapped back.

Elliott coughed uncomfortably. He was naturally polite and didn't like to correct a superior in front of others.

"Oh, I realize, sir," Elliott said, "that you know that setup backwards. It just so happens I know about this. Amt IV *K*," he placed emphasis on the K, "is a separate office—that whole outfit is a maze, and sometimes they attach an office to a department on paper when in practice it's separate. Amt IV *K* is part of the Kriminalpolizei if it's part of anything, it's a small office. The Special Investigator doesn't come under Müller or the criminal police chief. The office is autonomous, responsible directly to Himmler in his capacity as Chief of Police."

"Right," Quantregg said.

"It's not the Gestapo, that's all I was saying."

"I reckon this is something that might be important," Dulles said. He would sometimes feign a degree of ignorance in order to elicit the maximum information from others. At such times he had the face of a most attentive listener and willing learner. Turning to Elliott, he asid, "What else do you know about Schöller?"

"Not a helluva lot, sir."

"Tell us what you know."

"He's a cop, a former Kriminalinspektor from Munich."

"His job is what, exactly?"

"Insofar as they admit anything, they *say* it's to check into things like misuse of office, embezzlement in high places, abuses of power, misappropriation of Jewish property, you know . . . "

"That's the fairy story," Dulles said.

"Right. Right, sir."

"And his true function?"

"Well, basically it was a way for Heydrich, in the first place, to keep a check on his own top brass, Müller and his cohorts of the Gestapo in the Prinz Albrechtstrasse, Nebe and his Kriminalpolizei people at the Alexanderplatz. See they didn't get too big for their boots, and become a threat to him—Heydrich. Schöller in the role of Special Investigator, empowered to look into anything and everything, was somebody to hold over their heads. He could be used to keep them in line. And check up on them."

"That figures," Dulles said. "They have a passion for investigating each other."

"Paranoid," Elliott said. "They all are."

"They have good reason to be," Dulles said.

"Yes—I guess that's true."

"How do you come to know their setup?" Dulles asked.

"Well, you know my father, sir . . . "

"A fine reporter," Dulles said. "Self-educated man, I believe. But what a wordsmith! Hmm?"

"Yes . . . "

"You got all this from him?"

"He used to talk a lot about Schöller. He was intrigued by him. Partly, I guess, because he never got anywhere with that story. Could never get anything hard enough to print. Officially they wouldn't admit there was such a person as the Reich Special Investigator. Not to the foreign press anyhow. He was supposed to be part of the general police. His special powers were kept pretty secret. First time I heard about him, I was just a kid. It was like the sort of scary story kids love, and then it gives them nightmares. I think what got me from the start, made him stick in my mind, was my father saying there wasn't anybody the Special Investigator didn't know about, didn't have something on. Real bogeyman stuff. All the top-echelon people, he was supposed to have the dirt on all of them. So he could lean on them when required."

"That's the way the Nazis operate," Dulles said. "You ever see him, your bogeyman?"

"Once. It was just a man coming out of a building. My father pointed him out. I've also seen photographs of him. Not a lot, because he wasn't the type that posed for them exactly. But my father managed to dig up one or two and filed them away for the day when the whole story was finally going to jell."

"What sort of a man?"

"Ordinary. Very ordinary. Sort of a roughish face. Big. Big ears. Looks like a cop. Nothing special. Nothing sinister. Wouldn't stand out in a crowd. A face that could disappear anywhere."

"What made it scary?"

"Knowing all the things he knew, I guess. I dunno really. It was an atmosphere that was pretty damn scary, Berlin in the mid and late thirties. People disappearing. Somebody knocked at their door and you never knew what had happened. You just never saw them again."

"You think you could identify him, on the basis of that one time and the photographs you saw?"

"I wouldn't like to swear that I could, but I'm pretty sure, yes. Of course he could have changed a lot, but there was something about him I think I would recognize again."

Dulles raised a hand indicating he wished to get up. Quantregg helped him to his feet and handed him his cane. Dulles tried one or two steps, and let out a yelp of pain as he bent his knee.

"Pour me a scotch," he instructed Quantregg, "and make it a damn large one." He drank it down and repositioned himself, still wincing and uttering little gasps. Sweat was running down his face.

"I'm going to have to see this bastard," Dulles said. "And I can't see him here."

"You've got a fever, sir," Quantregg reminded him.

"We'll meet him at the Viktoriaplatz apartment," Dulles said. "Set it up with Waibel, or Wirth."

"How in hell's name you going to get to the apartment, Mr. Dulles?" Quantregg said.

"You're going to carry me, Dick. You and Elliott here."

"Elliott? You want Elliott along?"

"You can't carry me by yourself, Dick, and I don't want to bring any more people into this than I have to. Elliott here is the only one of us has any idea what Schöller looks like. I want him to take a look at this guy. Make sure he is who he says he is."

◆ II ◆

The small modern apartment building in the pleasant Viktoriaplatz district of Berne was equipped, as are many Swiss houses, with roller shutters that can be wound down to different levels, or extended outward on stays to make sun shades. If anyone wondered why the shutters of this particular building were hardly ever open and asked questions, he would probably have learned that two of the apartments were occupied by prostitutes, and that the third was unlet.

Given this explanation, nobody thought anything of the fact that strange men arrived at the building at all hours, that they were usually in a hurry, and sometimes at pains not to be recognized. Such behavior was quite consistent with men visiting prostitutes, or alternatively, coming to inspect an apartment for rent.

The two men who got out of a dark blue saloon car in the Viktoriastrasse on April 10 and walked rapidly to the entrance of the apartment building in the Platz could have fitted either category.

Inside, they took the self-operated elevator to the top floor and walked along a corridor to apartment C. As they approached, they were being examined through a spyhole in the front door by Quantregg.

"Well, here he is," he said. "Wanna take a look see?"

Putting his eye to the small lens, Elliott saw the knowing face and felt a shiver of old fear; it went back to God knows when, a long long time ago, he felt. The night knock breaking into sleep, catching you off guard: and encircled in the spyhole—a face that was like a metal badge, impassive authority with which there was no arguing. He knew that face from countless bad dreams: it kept turning up, sometimes in a familiar setting, other times in the unlikeliest places—there it suddenly was, opposite you in a train, or next to you in an elevator, or sitting by you in a cinema, or in church, or it was the face of one of the guests at your sister's wedding. A blank unknown face (identifiable by its extraordinary blankness) that seemed to know you, and seemed to be saying it knew all about you.

"Yes, that's him all right, I'd say," Elliott said as the bell rang with a harsh resonance inside the carpet-less and curtainless apartment.

Quantregg undid the top button of his double-breasted jacket to give him easier access to the Colt .45 automatic in his armpit holster. Then he opened the door, gave Captain Wirth an energetic shoulder squeeze, but in accordance with his principles ignored Schöller's formally extended hand. With a sharp arm movement he showed the visitors down an uncarpeted corridor, and into a medium-sized unfurnished room. It was fairly dark in there. Only a little daylight penetrated between the slats of the lowered roller blinds. There was no heating, and all the people in the room wore their hats and coats. They were standing. There were no chairs.

Schöller sized up the situation in a series of quick hard glances. The man who stood in the darkest part of the room, resting part of his weight on a cane, his face obscured in shadow, he assumed must be Dulles.

"Do I have the honor to address Mr. Dulles?" Schöller inquired of the dark form.

"You say whatever you have to say to me," Quantregg told him.

Elliott saw how Schöller quickly took in everybody's position in the room and placed himself with the wall behind him, next to the door.

When he began to speak, in accented but fluent English, he addressed himself to the farthest, darkest part of the room.

"Gentlemen, honored Mr. Dulles. . . . I trust I may speak here as a fellow professional," he began, formally, obviously having carefully prepared what he was going to say. He paused, waiting for some token response to this opening gambit. But getting none, he went on: "I see that I can, I see that we are all practical men here." He overrode their silence. "Therefore I will not go around the bush, as the saying goes. Gentlemen, your scheme—your so-called Sunrise—is blown. Blown." He beamed.

Still getting no glimmer of response, he continued in a voice that fell readily into monotonous officialese. "The traitor Thedieck confessed everything. General Wolff's meetings with Mr. Dulles. The plan to effect an immediate German surrender in Italy. The approach to Commander-in-Chief-West Kesselring to bring him into the plot. The meetings at Gaevernitz's villa in Ascona with the Allied generals Lemnitzer and Airey. And so forth and so on. I bring to your notice herewith substantiation of these matters, carbon copies of von Thedieck's confession. The original is in my safe."

He handed out the copies, one to Quantregg, the other to Dulles. The tall thin flame of a cigarette lighter came on in the dimness and showed a shadowy form studying the document. Still Dulles said nothing.

After a pause Schöller continued: "As Reich Special Investigator it was my duty to advise the SS-Reichsführer to recall General Wolff, and instruct him to present himself for questioning. This I have done."

"Why are you going to the trouble of informing us of your moves?" Dulles asked him quietly.

"Gentlemen, honored Mr. Dulles. . . . General Wolff . . . his goose is cooked. No? In short, he is . . . a dead duck—unless . . . "

"Unless what?" Quantregg demanded.

". . . Unless I let the bird fly," said Schöller in a changed voice that Elliott noted had lost its official inflection and become ingratiating, and soft.

"Why would you do that?" asked Dulles as softly.

"I am a practical man," said Schöller. He paused. "The role of a policeman," he remarked, "is to serve the regime that employs him. But he does not have to like it."

"The number of anti-Nazis we turn up these days, you'd be amazed," Quantregg said.

"I was never political, Mr. Dulles, I am just a policeman, doing his job."

"Yes, so you said. So you said."

"You can check."

"We will, Schöller. We will. You can bet your damn life we will," Quantregg told him.

"I was concerned with our own people. . . . Bigwigs lining their pockets at the expense of the State. The SS-Reichsführer holds very strong views on the subject of financial integrity. And sexual matters. Homosexuality. The SS-Reichsführer is determined to stamp it out. Plots within the leadership, motivated by personal ambition. Unnecessary brutality. I was called upon to investigate many such cases. Illegal dealings in appropriated Jewish property. And so on and so forth. The Gestapo. I was required to keep a check on its activities . . . "

"You weren't too damn brilliant at that," Quantregg said.

"My powers are limited. I can investigate and recommend. But I can *act* only upon the instructions of SS-Reichsführer Himmler."

"Tell that to War Crimes when the time comes," Quantregg told him. "Maybe they'll believe you."

"To be completely honest with you," Schöller said, lowering his voice to a confidential level, "some of the things I heard about . . . terrible, *terrible*. Such things, such things. *Schweinerei!* It disgusted me, I tell you."

"If you felt like that," Elliott said, speaking for the first time, in a quiet voice, "why didn't you do something—in your position?"

Schöller examined the young man who had just spoken. Probably some kind of technical expert or adviser, he concluded. A college graduate. Not an operative. No experience in the field. Knew it all from books.

"My position? My position?" Schöller repeated dismissively. "You know what happened to Chief of the Kriminalpolizei Nebe? People who opposed the regime were put up against a wall and shot. You must know that. What *could* I have done? In those circumstances . . . "

"You could have been shot," Elliott suggested.

"That is quite true," Schöller agreed with a short laugh. "But, you see, I was not yet ready to die . . . " He shrugged apologetically for this failing. "Save himself who can. No? It is human nature."

"If you're clean," Dulles said, "what do you want from us?"

"I am in your 'automatic-arrest' category because of the nature of my job. It can take years to be processed and cleared. Frankly, I do not look forward to that. We are none of us getting any younger."

"What's on your mind?" Quantregg said.

The official cast of Schöller's face relaxed into a universal expression denoting the approach to business. He was assessing the situation carefully and weighing his words before committing himself to speech.

Dulles bècame impatient. "If you've got a proposition to put to me, make it fast."

Schöller's demeanor was becoming softened by an unusual kind of delicacy. It was like seeing a very heavy man take the dance floor and then begin to dance with unexpected agility.

At last he spoke: "I am a person who—looks to the future. You, as practical men, do likewise, I am positive. It is to be expected. I tell you gentlemen, we can be of use to each other. Not only in the matter of General Wolff, whose life I can save and thereby save your so-called Sunrise. But also in other ways."

"What other ways?" asked Dulles.

"My knowledge, my experience, my skills . . . they are at your disposal, sir." He gave a little stiff Germanic bow.

"What d'you mean your 'knowledge' . . . ?" Dulles demanded softly.

"I am in possession of certain files—for instance."

"What files?"

"Files, Mr. Dulles, with special information about prominent people in the Reich. Very full and detailed files, you understand."

"All the dirt?" Quantregg said.

Schöller shrugged. "I am also in a position," he said, "to provide names of covert agents and informants used by various departments of the Reich security services . . . including the Gestapo. The details of their past activities would give a potential employer a strong hold over them. . . . "

"That isn't our way, Schöller," Quantregg said. "We don't work that way. We don't blackmail people into working for us . . . we don't have to. . . . "

"Naturally. Naturally," Schöller said quickly. "I was only meaning to point out that if you know who these people are, it neutralizes their usefulness to the other side, if *they* chose to blackmail these people into working for *them*."

"What do you want from us? What are you asking

for, Schöller?" Dulles demanded in his most business-like voice.

"An arrangement. Immunity from prosecution. A safe-conduct for my family. An undertaking that my personal affairs will not be—uh—looked into too closely."

"Not a Chinaman's chance," said Quantregg.

"That is exactly General Wolff's present predicament."

"Understand this," said Quantregg. "Our terms for all you guys is unconditional surrender. That means what it says—no deals. You give yourself up, you cooperate with us, and it'll notch up points in your favor. How much good it'll do you? Who knows? Depends what War Crimes has got on you."

"I have already told you. There is nothing against me."

"That I want to see."

"What d'you have in mind when you say your personal affairs shouldn't be probed?" Dulles asked.

"The pay of a Reichskriminaldirektor is not very much. Even so, as matter of prudence, one manages to put aside a little here and there, in this way and that. Naturally, since the Reichsmark has little value—we are men of the world, gentlemen—I may speak freely? Swiss francs are the only currency worth having in Europe. No?"

"So you got a little secret nest egg here," Quantregg said.

"A man must provide for his family."

"What are you asking *exactly*?" Dulles inquired in a a softly coaxing voice which contrasted with Quantregg's harshly offensive tone.

"That you ask no questions. The same terms that have been granted to General Wolff. An arrangement between . . . fellow professionals."

Dulles beckoned Quantregg and Elliott to join him in the far dark part of the room, and they went into a huddle, their backs to Schöller and Wirth.

"What do you think?" Dulles asked in a low voice. Quantregg examined the von Thedieck confession.

"This could be a forgery. None of us knows von Thedieck's handwriting."

"We can check on that and he knows we can," Elliott pointed out.

"He could be bluffing," Quantregg insisted.

"Wolff *has* been recalled by Himmler," Dulles reminded him. "We know that independently."

"If he's bluffing, he's going to be found out ultimately," Elliott said, "and then he could hardly rely on an understanding, could he?"

Dulles said, "Unless he has some other plan, and all this is just a cover for it. How come he's willing to trust us anyway?"

"Maybe he's got no choice," Elliott said.

They all turned and looked at Schöller standing by the door. He had lit a cigarette, and was looking the other way with a rather comical air of not wishing to give the impression of eavesdropping. But despite himself, his big ears were cocked, and even if he could not make out their words, he sensed the atmosphere in the room.

Quantregg swung round, anger fomenting in him, looking for some excuse to hit out with his clenched fists. But Schöller was not giving him any excuse. Head nodding up and down fast, palms sliding against each other as if preparing his hands, shoulders twitching to make the Colt .45 sit more easily in the shoulder holster, Quantregg went up to Schöller, very close.

"This could be a forgery," he said, brandishing the carbon copy of von Thedieck's confession. "How do we know it isn't?"

"If it was a forgery," Schöller replied quietly, "how would I have got the circumstantial details correct? The names of the Allied generals who attended the secret meeting at Ascona, Lemnitzer and Airey? They arrived in Switzerland disguised, with false names. They were not introduced by name to General Wolff— how would I know that? Unless it was from von Thedieck, who was present."

"*You* ordered the arrest of Wolff's family?" Dulles said quietly.

Schöller gave a little nod of agreement. "It is the

normal procedure in such a situation," he explained.

"You claiming you broke down von Thedieck in a couple of days?"

"He was a weak character. It was forty-five hours, to be exact."

"You torture him?" Quantregg demanded accusingly.

"No, I did not. I do not use torture."

"Is that a fact."

"I am not the Gestapo, as I have already told you. I am a policeman, like you. You are a former FBI man, no?"

"You know who I am?"

"How could I fail to know you, Mr. Quantregg, a man who has been close to the great J. Edgar Hoover?"

"What do you know about that?"

"Everything. Naturally."

Dulles interrupted sharply, putting an end to these divergences from the issue. "You are asking me to buy into this proposition blind."

"I can take my trade elsewhere."

"We might just let you do that," Dulles told him.

"It is up to you, sir."

"All right, we'll let you know, Schöller."

"Time is limited," Schöller said. "My assistant has instructions that should I fail to be back by noon on the twelfth, he is to open my document safe and act in accordance with whatever he finds there."

"You don't have to tell me," Dulles said curtly. "I am familiar with the way you people operate."

Late on the afternoon of April 10, Dulles and Quantregg were in the Herrengasse, discussing what to do about Schöller.

Dulles proposed: "Let us consider our options . . . one by one. Suppose we say to Schöller—*no deal*. What happens? He goes back, lays von Thedieck's confession before Himmler, which puts an end to Wolff. Result— Wolff is replaced by some fanatic. Some dumb ox like Kaltenbrunner or Dietrich, who will do what he is told and fight to the last man. If Vientinghoff is suspected of having even contemplated a surrender, he'll be 'extinguished' too. The consequences . . . ?

75

The Germans will fight on, with renewed vigor. They have got more divisions in northern Italy than we have, and if they get in a tight defensive knot west of Venice, under the Alps, they can hold out a long time. With Switzerland back of them, supplies coming in by Swiss railways which we can't bomb, they're in a fortress situation. Completes the defensive circle of the Alpine Redoubt."

"Right," Quantregg said.

"Now what does that mean? It means Tito's partisans get to capture Trieste, and if they're in before us, we're not going to get 'em out—Tito wants Trieste for himself, and Trieste is the key to the whole damn Adriatic. There'll be Soviet troops coming across from Hungary. They'll establish a Soviet-controlled belt across Southern and Western Europe, which could be the base for the Communization of France and Italy."

"It sure looks that way," Quantregg agreed.

"The Soviets are fighting in the center of Vienna, and we are going to let them take Berlin by themselves because Eisenhower won't accept the casualties for what he considers purely political objectives. Stalin is going to end up with all the marbles, and by the time we've woken up to that and start to holler, it'll be too late. The whole of Europe will be under the Soviet heel."

When Dulles talked like this, Quantregg knew he was in the presence of a man whose vision was global, who was not concerned simply with some immediate gain or loss but with the course of history.

"Agreeing with all that you say," Quantregg said, "aren't these questions for Mr. Roosevelt and Mr. Churchill and the Joint Chiefs of Staff? It's their baby, isn't it, sir?"

"Surely," Dulles agreed with supreme reasonableness. "But there are two points about that. One. Churchill thinks the same way I do. A few days ago he sent a mesage to Eisenhower, once more impressing upon him the importance of—I quote—'shaking hands with our valiant comrades of the Soviet Union as far as possible'! My second point is . . . Roosevelt is a giant of a man, but he's a tired giant, and he let

76

Stalin bamboozle him at Yalta. Now, dammit, we don't want to let those boys in Washington make any mistakes they'll be sorry for later—if we can help 'em not make those mistakes."

"Can we?"

Talking to Quantregg helped Dulles to clarify his thoughts. He liked to use Quantregg as a sounding board, because his mentality was that of the general public, and if *he* grasped the need for a certain course of action, it indicated that ordinary people would also understand and go along, and all political action involved carrying the ordinary people with you. So while Dulles did not have a very high opinion of Quantregg's intelligence, he attached some importance to his reactions.

"All right, all right," Dulles said. "Let's consider another scenario, Dick. We saw what happens if we tell Schöller, 'Go to hell.' Now let's suppose we say to him, 'OK, it's a deal.' Even though, God knows, it goes against the grain. All right. We send him back. Wolff is in the clear. Better still, we have the Reich Special Investigator to protect him against any other charges that may be thrown at him by Kaltenbrunner or Müller, who are also on to him. With luck, Vientinghoff agrees to an immediate surrender, and we're off to the races. We get to Trieste at least the same time as Tito, which means we've got a foot in the door and can't be dislodged so easy. Tell me what problems you see. List them for me, Dick."

"Point one. Say Schöller double-crosses us."

"He's got to play it straight. Hell, there's no other damn way for him to play it. He's in our hands, isn't he? *Afterwards.* He tries any tricks and he's not going to collect. He knows that. *He's* got to make the pitch, he's got to make us want *him*. Isn't that right? OK then. He's got no motivation to double-cross us."

"What do we do when he comes for his payoff? It'll come out, it's bound to, that we set up the getaway of Himmler's Special Investigator. That we made a deal. After we had been told loud and clear from a very high level, the highest . . . "

"When the time came," Dulles said quietly, "we'd

have to make damn sure that Schöller wasn't an embarrassment to us."

"I'll buy that," Quantregg said. "*Yes*, sir."

"Let's see how it plays, Dick. Way I see it, it's a straight OSS operation. Schöller has got these files that we want. So we go along, as if we were going to deal with him . . ."

"A straightforward operation in the field."

"No political angle. No connection with Wolff. Nothing to do with any surrender negotiations . . ."

"Right. Right."

"No intelligence organization can afford to turn down an in-place volunteer, even if the visitor is uninvited."

"That's basic tradecraft," Quantregg agreed.

"We are obligated to pursue such an offer to see what it may yield."

"Oh I would say so, sir. Certainly."

"Of course, the defector may eventually redefect, in which case neutralizing action would have to be taken."

The cook had come in with coffee and a plate of sugared egg-fingers. Dulles was fond of dipping them in his coffee until they had become soggy and were on the point of disintegrating, whereupon—at the very last moment—he withdrew the coffee-soaked biscuit and popped it in his mouth. There was a kind of art in judging the right moment when the spongy biscuit was tastily soft and heavy with coffee but still solid enough not to break messily upon the chin. Dulles was dipping in the biscuits and swallowing them down with great rapidity and perfect timing as his excitement mounted. His eyes glistened. Already half a plate of sugared egg-fingers had disappeared, with only a few coffee-loaded morsels adhering to the white mustache.

"We send in an agent," he declared suddenly in a high fervor of creative planning.

"An agent. For what?"

"That's the way to play it. *We send in an agent.*"

"Into enemy territory?"

"That's right."

"What would be the objective?"

"See the papers are hidden somewhere in the future

American zone. We have got to make sure of that. And that they're genuine."

"Are you suggesting we can penetrate the Reich Main Security Office?"

"With the Reich Special Investigator as cover, why not?"

"The Prinz Albrechtstrasse must be as soft as a fairy's asshole right now," Quantregg said, warming to the proposition.

"Exactly. They're all so busy trying to get out and save their skins they're not going to bother about anybody coming in. Especially not under those auspices."

"It's a high-risk operation, all the same," Quantregg said. "For whoever goes in."

"That may be so, that may be so," Dulles conceded, "but it's good, it's good." He was pursuing his line of thought, eyes almost closed, licking the egg-fingers from his mustache. "See, we insert an agent in target—at great risk—and it's clearly a field action, not a negotiation. It's expensive, I'll admit, and we don't know the long-term dividend, but in the short term it solves a lot of problems for us."

"It's a nice little operation," Quantregg agreed. "He wouldn't have to be in place longer than a few days."

"A few days, that's all. And putting an agent into the Prinz Albrechtstrasse doesn't contravene any instructions I've had from Washington."

"Nobody could say you weren't entitled to send in an agent on your own responsibility to get those files . . . "

"You're right, Dick. *Absolutely*."

"It's good, it's very good," Quantregg said, getting enthusiastic. "The agent we send in keeps tabs on Schöller."

"That's right. And when the time comes, we have got a man in place to prevent Schöller from embarrassing us," Dulles added.

"It's a lulu of an idea, Mr. Dulles," Quantregg said admiringly.

"I like it," Dulles admitted modestly.

He stopped suddenly. The sugared egg-fingers were

all gone, the plate empty. The coffee in his cup was cold. Good as an idea sounded in the full flush of creative thinking, it was always necessary to subject it to a destruction test.

"Let's you and I sleep on this, Dick," Dulles proposed. "Turn it over in our minds."

"Right, sir."

"See what it looks like in the morning."

"Schöller wants an answer, fast."

"He'll have to wait until we are good and ready."

"Will he wait?"

"Oh, he'll wait, if he thinks there's half a chance he's going to make a sale. Get a good night's sleep."

"You too, sir."

"See you tomorrow. This is a big play—there's a lot at stake. We better get this thing right."

· 12 ·

After sleeping solidly for fourteen hours, Schöller took breakfast in bed in his room at the Bellevue.

There was no point in getting up. Before ordering breakfast, he had gone to the door and checked that his Swiss shadowers were still outside in the corridor. They were—the men were different, but there was no doubt of their function.

Getting back into bed, he lit a cigarette and noted with satisfaction the feminine luxury of satin coverlets, quilted headrest, soft silk upholstery. Opening off his room was a pink marble bathroom. Not bad. Not bad. He gave a grin. He rubbed the stubble of his face contentedly.

When the breakfast was brought in, Schöller told

the room waiter to open the curtains. While he ate hard-boiled eggs, cheeses, cold sausage meat, rolls and butter, and drank his coffee with cream, he looked out across the city of Berne, of which he had a perfect view from his bed. The curve of the river. The low and high bridges. The ancient rooftops. Not bad at all. Not a bad place in which to spend one's retirement, he reflected. Of course, it was necessary to have money . . .

He stayed in bed all morning, waiting for the phone to ring, reading the papers, dozing off from time to time. At twelve, when there was still no phone call, he rang the American legation and asked for Quantregg. After some delay, he was transferred to another number by the operator.

"Good morning, Mr. Quantregg," he said cheerfully. "I trust you slept well. Myself, I slept wonderful. You would be amazed what a difference it makes, clean sheets, a soft mattress, and not expecting to be blown to bits in your sleep. Well, sir. I hope you have some good news for me."

"Good and not-so-good, Schöller."

"Please tell me."

"We're considering your proposition. There are a lot of angles. Can't give you an answer yet."

"When, in that case?"

"I don't know. You'll have to sit tight."

"There is a time limit."

"I know, I know. It's the best we can do."

"All right, all right. I wait to hear from you?"

"Yuh—you do that, Schöller."

After putting down the phone, Schöller thought for some minutes. He rubbed the beard of his face, and with a shrug went into the bathroom and ran a deep bath while he shaved. He spent half an hour lying in the soft green water, lathering himself richly with the delicately perfumed little round French soap provided by the management.

Shortly after one o'clock he went down to take lunch on the hotel terrace above the river, followed by his two Swiss shadowers. He drank a bottle of red wine with his food, and at the end of the meal asked for the cigars and chose a Havana to smoke with his brandy. By the time he had finished and signed the bill it was three o'clock. He went to the reception and asked if there had been any phone calls for him, and upon hearing that there had not, he went out through the revolving doors for an afternoon stroll, followed by his shadowers.

The Americans had not spent such a leisurely morning. When Quantregg arrived at the Herrengasse soon after nine, Dulles told him, "Bill Donovan has ordered me to come to Paris."

"That can't be good, with Schöller here."

"Not just Schöller, Dick. We've got another volunteer. Kaltenbrunner's man, Höttl, has turned up. Also looking for a deal. I've sent somebody to see him. Somebody who knows nothing about Sunrise."

"You think General Donovan has found out about Schöller?"

"Could be. Could be. I know what he's going to say. He's going to say that whatever advantages there might be in a quick German surrender, it is not worth antagonizing the Soviets and running the risk of breaking up the Alliance . . . at the eleventh hour. That's what he's going to say, only stronger."

"And what are you going to say, sir?"

"I? I'm going to say that—notwithstanding my own views—I will naturally abide by the President's instructions."

"And what do I say to Schöller?"

"You say to him—to wait."

Shortly after seven-thirty in the evening Schöller came into the American Bar of the Bellevue, smooth-faced after his second shave of the day, and dressed for once in a suit that had some temporary shape to it, since the hotel valet had given it a sponge-and-press in the afternoon.

As he sipped his drink at the rounded end of the oak bar, he identified the other professionals in the room from their quiet alertness and the quickness of their eye movements whenever doors opened and somebody new came in.

Schöller gave the impression of a man killing time.

His eyes were wandering vaguely; his movements were slow and indecisive; once or twice he looked at his watch, and then undecidedly clinked the ice around in his glass before ordering a refill. It was in this evidently purposeless frame of mind, and after quite a number of refills, that he became aware of a young woman sitting by herself in a green leather banquette, and after an exchange of looks went over to her.

The Swiss watching Schöller knew the girl well; she was an attractive Rumanian refugee, a baroness by marriage, now a widow, who made a living as a part-time prostitute and translator. She also, occasionally, sold to anyone who wished to buy them small items of information acquired in the course of her work. She was known to everybody in Berne as the Baroness, and when approached by a strange man, regularly went through a protracted charade of turning him down while not exactly sending him away.

When she eventually did come around to giving herself, never less than three or four hours after the initial approach, she first gave a touching account of her financial plight as a widowed noblewoman stranded in Berne, and the man usually felt embarrassed to offer her less than three hundred francs.

Schöller sat down next to her and she at once began to talk nonstop about her life, her former houses and servants in Rumania, her highborn friends and cousins, her connections with the famous . . . a long and well-rehearsed monologue.

After listening to all this for about three-quarters of an hour, Schöller suggested they go somewhere else, and then somewhere else. They ended up in a night-club, where they sat for an hour in a dark alcove, opposite another dark alcove occupied by two Swiss who, getting pretty bored by now, had stopped ordering orange juice and were drinking cognac instead.

Just before midnight, Schöller and the Baroness left the nightclub and took a taxi to her apartment. The Swiss shadowers followed in their car.

Once in her bedroom, the Baroness began to embark on an even more intimate account of her financial plight, at the same time undoing her bodice, and puffing at her cigarette anxiously, as if trying to steel herself to make a request that was frankly beneath her. It was a good and practiced performance, but her visitor hardly seemed to be listening. Perhaps he was too drunk. This sometimes happened. It was one of the mishaps liable to occur as a result of the prolonged preliminaries in the bars and nightclubs.

Her new friend seemed to be more interested in looking out of the window than at her.

The two Swiss had got out of their car and were checking the apartment building. Satisfied that there was no other way out, they parked in front of the entrance, switched off the motor and the lights, and settled down to wait.

Schöller saw matches being struck in the dark of the car and the red glow of cigarettes. Quietly he opened the window. The cold blast of air shocked the Baroness, who was by now undressed, and an incredulous look came over her face as she saw her new friend swing one leg over the sill. Even though she knew there was a window box immediately outside, she had a sudden fear that this drunken madman was going to throw himself out of her window and cause a scandal.

But one thing became clear to her as he swung the other leg over the sill; whatever else he was, he was not drunk. He was moving with great sureness. He had placed a finger to his lips and was cautioning her to remain silent. There was something very commanding, even menacing, about the way he did this, and it made her keep quiet. She did not want to make any fuss that might attract the attention of neighbors and bring the concierge to her door asking questions. So she held her breath and kept absolutely still as Schöller flattened himself against the wall of the building, immediately above the car with the two Swiss. Wrought iron window boxes ran all along the front—in summer they were full of geraniums. With surprising agility for a man of his build, he raised one foot over the ornamental railings, lifted it across the gap, brought it down in the next window box, and balancing himself against the wall, pulled the other leg after him.

In this way, he stepped from window box to window box until he reached the corner; he turned it, holding on to a drainpipe while edging along a coping, and with a penknife pried open a window that gave onto stairs. He climbed in, ran down three flights, and left by the entrance of the apartment building adjoining the one in which the Baroness lived.

Walking with the lightest of steps, he made his way back to the corner and looked around it. The car was still in front of the other entrance. A faint self-satisfied smile on his face, he began to walk through the dark streets, looking at parked cars. When he saw a Horch or a Mercedes or a Wanderer, he tried to open it with one of the keys from the huge bunch he had with him. After a number of tries, he was successful in unlocking a Wanderer. Releasing the handbrake, he pushed the car along the street for about a quarter of a mile with its lights off. Then he got in, tried various keys in the ignition, and eventually found one that fitted. Still he did not start the engine. The road was sloping very slightly downward at this point, and he allowed the car to roll another half-mile in darkness and silence before switching on the engine.

He drove without lights for several miles, watching the road behind him in his mirror, and only when he was absolutely sure that he was not followed did he make his way onto a main road and put on the car's sidelamps.

Following the course of the River Aare, Schöller continued looking in his mirrors, which most of the time remained dark. There was little traffic about at this time of night. At Thun he drove alongside the lake and then made a sharp turn and took a rising road.

As he got higher, he lowered a window and let the hard bite of the cold air counteract any proneness to sleep. Some of the bends were tricky, but he was at home in the night. The dark suited him; in his line of work he had got to know it intimately and was able to move about in it with sureness and certain vision.

On the climb by the Simmental the gradients became steeper, reaching 1 in 7, and once or twice the car slithered on hard ground frost; coolly, he corrected the skids, but did not diminish speed. He had a timetable to keep to.

He was feeling the altitude in his ears now. Four thousand feet.

He drove at more than sixty miles an hour through a succession of silent mountain villages, bouncing over railway crossings, spattering shop windows with road slush. A church with an open bell tower. A *Gasthof*, rococo picture frames painted around its windows. The *Post*. Sports shops. An *Apotheke*. A baker. A grocer. Here and there, snow on the ground. One village was much like another.

It was two A.M. when he arrived at the high mountain pass known as the Col des Mosses. It was scarcely even a hamlet, just a collection of shuttered cafés and restaurants, and one or two Hôtels du Col. He left the car where it would not be seen behind a ramshackle hut and made his way on foot along a narrow track that rose steeply upward. There were a few Alpine houses built into the slope of the mountain, looking stranded with their drives all covered over with snow. The higher he climbed, the greater were the distances between individual houses, and finally the track ran for about five hundred yards with nothing on either side of it.

At the very end of this road stood an old mountain inn of wooden frame construction, blending in with surrounding trees, its balconied windows affording extensive views over the entire vicinity. The place looked run-down and deserted. The timber boards had rotted in places, and the resulting gaps had been plugged in a makeshift way with straw and stones. The roof had lost many of its tiles.

Schöller walked up to the inn over snowy ground that bore no footprints or tire marks.

In the courtyard he saw a rusting car body without wheels, stacked lumber under the roof overhang, an old wooden handcart, a large snow shovel.

Schöller's watch showed three-thirty as he knocked on the front door with his fists, the sound echoing harshly in the stillness of the perpetual snow on the surrounding peaks. He knocked again and again, roughly, peremptorily, with no compunction about the hour: someone accustomed to inflicting rude awakenings on people. It took several minutes of continuous knocking before a shutter on the first floor was opened and a befuddled face appeared at the window. Schöller stepped back so as to show himself, at which the disturbed sleeper closed the shutters and the window, disappeared inside, and some moments later there were sounds of locks being turned, bolts being pushed back, and an iron crossbar being lifted.

When eventually the door was opened, a voice said, "Well, look who's here! Look who's here! Of all the people in the world. *You.* I wouldn't have believed it. *You!* What are you doing here? Are you paying me a social visit? In the middle of the night? The night was always your time, wasn't it? One way or another." He laughed.

"You don't ask me in?" Schöller inquired with uncharacteristic deference to the prerogatives of the householder.

"Of course, of course."

"It's a business visit, actually," Schöller explained as he accepted the innkeeper's invitation to enter.

"Business? Am I hearing correctly? You have business with me? In your line, you have business with me? If this were Germany, I might be afraid to hear that."

Schöller took it as a joke and laughed, making an expression of reproof at such an idea.

"You know you never had anything to fear from me," he said. "On the contrary. Hmm?"

"You are right," the innkeeper conceded. "It was only my little joke. Come in, Ernst. Come in. Sit down somewhere. I know, I know. It's a bit of a mess here. But you find somewhere to sit down. I'll bring us a beer. Or a schnapps?"

"Schnapps."

The innkeeper went off to rummage in the kitchen for the alcohol while Schöller quickly looked around. The place was in a terrible state, musty, smelly, damp, dirty. Windows that had been broken were boarded up. Gaps around the frames had been stuffed with old rags and newspapers. Water trickled down the walls from different places. Plasterwork was crumbling.

The innkeeper came back with a bottle of schnapps and filled their glasses. Schöller raised his. "To business," he said.

The innkeeper inquired, "How is it you are here? At a time like this. You have . . . left?"

"No, I have not left. But I will be leaving soon. It is in that connection I have come to see you. . . . Tell me, how is the hotel business?"

"As you can see." The innkeeper spread his hands to indicate the state of the place. "I'm no man to run a guest house. Not my line, Ernst. When Rosalie died, it all started to fall apart. You know how I am. I can't chat to people. Not good at it. And sometimes I have a few drinks. People stopped coming, and then there was no money for repairs, and so even fewer people came—and so finally it got like this. We've been closed for the past two years."

"What you need," said Schöller, "is a partner. One with determination, energy, and the business sense to make a go of this place. Of course, he'd need to have capital. Quite substantial capital. To do the place up, to pay staff. . . . What would you think of me as your partner?"

"*You*—running a guest house!" It seemed a grisly joke.

"Why not? I will need to do something. My old skills may not be much in demand."

The innkeeper's disbelieving chortle was cut short as he realized the seriousness of the proposition.

"This is a valuable property, you know," he said quickly. "It may not *look* in very good condition. But structurally it *is* sound. Sound as a rock. And the situation! The views! People come here for the views. Magnificent mountain scenery. Clear air. The air is lovely here, Ernst. For convalescence it's perfect. Only we would need a proper road. Still, we were not doing so bad—hikers, mountaineers, you know. Then my cook left. You have to have a good cook, because you must provide full pension. We are too far up for people to go all the time to the Col to eat, though it's only a little more than a mile and a half . . . perhaps two miles."

Schöller stopped him.

"This place isn't worth much because of the state it's in. But to me that is an advantage. Because it means that nobody comes here. You follow me? And then there's you. You also are an attraction of this place. Not just because you are a friend whom I can trust, but because you are such an ugly old bastard. With peculiar habits. Not seeing anybody. Never going out. Never receiving visitors. Just living by yourself in this . . . this filth. Am I right?"

The innkeeper began to protest, fearing that Schöller was seeking a pretext for bringing down the price.

"You exaggerate . . . a bit of a cleaning-up, a couple of lads from the village, for a few francs . . . " the innkeeper began, but Schöller stopped him.

"Nothing must be cleaned up. Nothing must be changed. Nobody must be brought here. You understand? How often do you shop?"

"I go down to the Col about once every ten days with my handcart and I load up."

"Do that, but no more."

"I understand you, Ernst."

"I will pay you one hundred thousand francs for a half-share of this place. If you agree, you get one-third immediately. But you must not spend any of it—yet. Otherwise you won't get the rest when I arrive. If I don't arrive, you've made thirty-three thousand francs. There will be nothing on paper."

No question, this was a most generous offer. It was at least twice as much as he could have got on the open market, and to find any buyer for a mountain inn was not easy at a time like this.

"I like to settle things quickly," Schöller said, throwing a thick envelope on the table. "That is why I am offering you much more than this place is worth. Well?"

"All right—considering everything—you're getting a bargain, you know. I accept." Quickly, as if fearing it might be yanked away from him like a joke purse on a string, he reached for the envelope, opened it, and counted the bank notes. Schöller grabbed the innkeeper's trembling hand and shook it vigorously, by way of sealing the transaction.

"Now, if you don't mind, I want to inspect our property," said Schöller.

He found that the remainder of it was in even worse condition than the downstairs, but he noted with satisfaction that the main entrance had two sets of heavy doors, and that the solid window shutters were functioning. Most interesting of all, at the back of the inn there was an annex. It was built right on the edge of the thickly wooded slope, which became steep within fifty yards and almost perpendicular soon after. Because it was built on rising ground, from the top of it he would be able to see over the roof of the inn and observe anyone approaching, while remaining concealed himself. In an emergency, he could disappear in the thick woods behind the annex before anyone coming to the inn had got to the top of the steep approach track. Using these woods should also give him a roundabout way of entering and leaving the annex without being seen.

He had remembered the inn's layout and situation from a brief holiday there eight years earlier, and he was glad his memory had been so accurate, for the place was, as he had thought, perfect for his purposes.

· 13 ·

Schöller took his time driving back from the mountains; in the Aare valley he stopped the car and smoked a cigarette while he watched the early morning anglers. Then he continued in the direction of Berne. He reached the suburb of Muri just before nine A.M. and parked in the car park of an old wooden chalet-style hotel, the Sternen. He got out and went round to the front of the hotel, where he climbed the steps to the veranda and went into the breakfast room. He ordered coffee, fried eggs, cheese, and rolls and butter, and dawdled an hour or more over his meal, idly glancing through the Swiss newspapers.

A little after ten he paid his bill and went outside. Leaving the stolen car in the car park, he walked a few dozen yards to the streetcar stop and waited five minutes until the streetcar to Berne arrived. He got on it, and at ten-thirty was at the Bellevue's main entrance, where he found Quantregg furiously pacing up and down in squeaking crepe-soled shoes.

"I have kept you waiting, Mr. Quantregg?" Schöller inquired innocently. "You have news for me?"

"Come on," Quantregg said. "Mr. Dulles wants to see you."

He took him by the arm, rather like a cop making an arrest, and led him out.

"Where are we going?"

"You were not in your room last night," Quantregg accused, leading Schöller along the road toward the Casinoplatz.

"I was out—searching for entertainment," he said with an air of man-to-man confidentiality.

"You gave the Swiss the slip."

Schöller grinned. "The Swiss do not need to know everything."

"You left the Baroness's apartment as soon as you got there. Climbing out along the window boxes."

"The Baroness . . . at the last moment did not appeal, unfortunately."

"Why all the Tarzan stuff on the window boxes?"

"A man feels freer to look around without a tail on him. Perhaps I have special tastes." He gave Quantregg a broad wink. "The Swiss are a puritan lot. One does not want to corrupt those fine young men from Intelligence by leading them to *louche* places."

"You are not playing it straight with us," Quantregg said. "You left the Baroness's apartment before one A.M. It is now after ten-thirty. That's more than nine hours. Where in hell have you been, Schöller? What did you do in those nine hours?"

Schöller gave a shrug of such worldliness as to shame the most curious inquirer. His eyebrows rose, mocking the naïveté of this line of questioning.

When they reached the bridge, the high Kirchenfeldbrücke, Quantregg took Schöller's elbow and urged him down the steps that led to the riverbank far below. Trees and shrubs hid them from any spying eyes as they descended.

At the halfway point, instead of going all the way down to the river, Quantregg led the way along a level stretch of embankment until they came to the Fricktreppe. The American looked around to see if anybody was following. Satisfied that nobody was, he started up the covered wooden steps in bounding leaps.

The steps curved so that anyone going up them was soon out of sight of those below.

The ancient wooden structure creaked in response to every footstep. By pausing to listen, you could hear if anyone was following. It was impossible to creep quietly up those steps, however light your tread. Stopping from time to time to listen, Quantregg led Schöller almost to the very top.

They passed a succession of back entrances. At an unnumbered wooden gate Quantregg pressed a bell, and in reply to a questioning voice spoke softly into the iron grille, behind which a small panel had opened. They were admitted at once and went along a garden path under a dense trellis of grapevine to a rear door.

The cook took Schöller's hat and coat and hung them up, and the two men climbed the carpeted stairs.

Dulles was sitting upright in a straight-back chair, his left leg extended rigidly and resting on a footstool. The table next to him was untidy with papers. On it there was a small tray with a jug of water, a glass, and various medicine bottles. He waved Schöller into a chair, and while continuing to glance through his papers, said matter-of-factly:

"I'm not here to pass judgment on anyone—that's for others—I'm here to do business. But I have to be satisfied I'm not being cheated. We don't know you, and you are asking us to take a hell of a lot on trust. . . ."

"On the contrary," Schöller said, "you need give me nothing—except your word—until after I have delivered. It is I who must take things on trust."

"That maybe is how it looks to you, but it isn't how it looks to us. Before we go any further, you have to extend the time limit. Nothing can be agreed that quick."

"You are playing for time. I cannot agree to that, sir."

"Then there's no possibility of us reaching any arrangement, and I will bid you good-bye."

"How much extra time do you need?"

"Today is the twelfth. Say—till the fifteenth?"

"That is too long. I cannot be away that length of time. Inquiries will be started. I can give you until tomorrow to decide, Mr. Dulles. I will contact my office and instruct them not to open the document safe for another twenty-four hours. That is the best I can do, sir."

"All right. I'll give you my answer within twenty-four hours."

It was only a short walk from the Herrengasse to the Bundesplatz, past the Parliament buildings, past the Kantonal Bank, to the Commercial Bank of Berne, a pale green building with eight fluted pilasters separating its two-story-high windows. This time Schöller made no attempt to throw off his shadowers.

He went in by the great wrought iron doors and walked rapidly through the marble hall with its high pillars and lofty galleries rising in circular tiers to a coffered dome with a lantern of stained glass windows. His footsteps made discreet clinking sounds, which were immediately swallowed up in their spiraling echo.

From the mezzanine gallery he saw his shadowers in the hall below. They saw him, too, and pretended to be looking elsewhere. He smiled broadly, and went up another flight of stairs to the Special Accounts Department. At the counter he filled out a slip on which he wrote the number 93 80017 LR, and underneath "To see Dr. Behr."

He had to wait less than a minute before Dr. Behr, a small plump-cheeked individual, emerged. He had the manner of someone engaged in daily service to the wealthy—he might have been taken for the head-waiter of a very fashionable restaurant or a high-class jeweler. His tie was silky gray and boasted a pearl stickpin; his jacket was dark, his hair sparse but brushed to a thin lacquered layer which gave off a whiff of expensive hair lotion. His eyes possessed the worldly tolerance of one who has in the course of his life come to have a deep knowledge of people's most intimate financial affairs.

Seeing the Reich Special Investigator before him, Dr. Behr put aside all personal feelings—a banker like a doctor had a professional code of conduct to adhere by—and spoke with meticulous courteousness.

"Ah! Good day to you, Herr Reichskriminaldirektor, good day to you! I trust you have had a safe journey. I am happy to see you. Kindly step inside." He lifted the flap of the counter and with a little formal bow invited Schöller in.

The banker's office, with its dark wood wainscoting and its one narrow window of leaded quarries throwing a diamond pattern high upon the opposite wall, had about it the dim secrecy of the confessional. As he seated himself behind a clear desk, the banker bestowed his benedictory nod upon the proceedings about to unfold, and with a priestly gesture of his plump hand indicated for Schöller to be seated.

"Well, Herr Direktor, in what way can I assist you today?"

"I wish to make a withdrawal," said Schöller.

"Of course." He reached into a drawer and withdrew a plain unheaded slip of paper with a short line at the top followed by the dateline 19——. Then came a line saying simply No.——, followed by a line that said nothing at all and a final short line that likewise was devoid of instructions.

The banker pointed formally to the slip, and said, "Please, if you will be so kind: the date, the number of the account, the amount required, and your signature." He proffered his own gold fountain pen.

Quickly Schöller filled in the details and returned the slip. Dr. Behr studied it for a moment, he pursed his lips slightly, his fingertips pressed together and separated delicately. He gave a somewhat stiff smile.

"Four million francs," he said, reading out the amount in an expressionless tone.

"Yes," said Schöller.

The banker hummed to himself briefly before reaching down and unlocking a drawer of his desk. From it he withdrew a tooled leather volume stamped with the bank's name in gold. He looked up something in it, wrote down a number on a scrap of paper, and pressed a buzzer which brought his secretary to the door. He gave her the scrap of paper and said, "Immediately."

While waiting for the secretary's return, both men sat in silence. The Swiss banker smiled occasionally and tapped his fingers on the clear desk top.

"It will not be very long," he said after two long minutes of silence had elapsed, and then added, "You are staying for a few days in Berne . . . ?" and cut himself short immediately, telling himself that such a question directed to the Investigator might be considered indiscreet.

Fortunately, at this point, the secretary returned with the file, which she placed very precisely in front of Dr. Behr. With the little nervous cough of someone beginning formal proceedings, the banker opened the first folder, and peering down through his half-lenses, studied the typewritten notes. When he spoke, it was in the somewhat singsong voice of a court clerk reading the oath.

"You will recall the procedure when amounts in excess of one hundred thousand francs are to be withdrawn . . . "

"Very well. I devised it myself."

The banker looked slightly annoyed at this interruption, and went on reading rapidly: "The twenty people listed here below are entitled to make withdrawals . . . " His eyes scanned the list. "You are one of the twenty," Dr. Behr stated formally, "and therefore that condition is met. Now . . . " His eyes were racing ahead while he mumbled the banker's jargon that preceded the relevant passage. ". . . Now here we are." His voice slowed down to read out the key phrase with slow exactitude.

"Where amounts in excess of one hundred thousand francs are to be withdrawn, a minimum period of ten days shall elapse between the request for payment and the payment being made. In this period, the bank shall, at its own discretion, obtain the signatures of two additional people on the list of twenty in authorization of the withdrawal, and payment shall not be made unless and until such signatures have been obtained. It shall be left to the bank's sole discretion . . . "

He paused and repeated this phrase since it struck him as being of importance. "It shall be left to the bank's sole discretion as to which of the persons on the list of twenty are approached for their signatures of authorization, and the bank shall under no circumstances discuss with the withdrawer, or divulge to him, the names of those on the list of twenty being approached for their signatures." The banker looked up. "This is not a procedure that is common," he remarked.

"I devised it," said Schöller, "in order to eliminate any possibility of the Reich being defrauded by any individual or conspiracy of individuals."

"Quite so, Herr Reichskriminaldirektor. It is an excellent system, if I may say so, but it does present certain difficulties for us at the present time."

"Oh?"

"This list of twenty names was given to us when the account was opened by your good self in 1942, and has been amended only twice. Once in 1943 and once in 1944. At such times as the present we have no way of knowing which of the persons on the list are still alive or can be reached. Some of these addresses . . . " (he spread his hands apologetically for having to put it so crudely) ". . . no longer exist."

"It is only necessary for you to reach two, Dr. Behr. Any two. That should not be beyond the resources of a great Swiss bank."

"We shall naturally do our best, Herr Reichskriminaldirektor. This is not an insignificant matter. Four million francs is not at all an insignificant matter. I shall give it my personal attention and see that everything is done . . . that no stone is left unturned to find these signatories. . . . " He stopped short, realizing that the stone metaphor was perhaps indelicate in view of the present state of the German capital.

Schöller said, "I am willing to obtain the signatures for you."

Dr. Behr considered this, and then shook his head. "That would not be in accordance with the provisions laid down," he pointed out.

"Since the provisions were made by me in the first place," Schöller said, "we can surely vary them to a small degree."

"That would not be in order."

"How will you obtain the signatures, in that case?"

"I will have to find out if it can be done through the good offices of one of the neutral embassies still in touch with the German government. You will have to leave the matter to me, I shall do my best."

He rose and escorted Schöller to the door. Before opening it, he hesitated a moment as if not exactly sure how to phrase what he was about to say.

"You will forgive my asking you this, but this withdrawal is with the full approval of the German government . . . we shall not encounter any difficulties in obtaining the signatures?"

"Naturally, I am acting at the behest of the German government. There will be no difficulties about the signatures."

"I merely wished to make absolutely certain of that point," Dr. Behr said, opening the door for his visitor.

"Understandable."

"Good day."

"Good day."

Only when the Reich Special Investigator had disappeared from view did the banker permit himself to shudder.

· 14 ·

On the afternoon of April 12, at Warm Springs, Georgia, where he had gone for a period of rest on his doctor's advice, President Roosevelt was having his portrait painted.

The artist was striving to capture the curious luminosity of the President's features—the skin had become parchmentlike and was aglow with an intensely burning brightness that came from deep inside the exhausted man at work on his papers. He began to frown as he felt the start of a sudden sharp pain in his head, and one hand moved up toward his brow but did not quite reach it. In mid-movement Roosevelt suddenly slumped forward on his desk, his head hitting the wooden surface.

When his secret serviceman rushed in, having been summoned by the artist, the President was unconscious. A few hours later he was dead of a cerebral hemorrhage.

The news of the President's death reached Dulles late that day as he was packing his bags to leave for Paris. Four of his closest aides were with him, having assembled to receive last-minute instructions before their chief's departure. Dulles broke the news to them and spoke a few words in tribute to Roosevelt's greatness. After that he sent his aides away, all except Quantregg.

As soon as they were alone, he said, "See if you can get Schöller here right away."

"He wasn't expecting an answer till tomorrow."

"I know. But maybe we can get this settled before I leave."

Schöller was in his room at the Bellevue, and when Quantregg told him on the house phone to come down toot de sweet, he came—fast.

Five minutes later he was standing somewhat breathless before Dulles, who was in his overcoat, hat in hand, ready to leave.

"This is what I'm prepared to do, Schöller. I'm ready to give you the personal undertaking you ask for if you lay off Wolff. But I need to be satisfied that you are going to keep your side of the bargain. That means I have to send somebody in with you."

"To keep an eye on me?"

"Yes. And to make sure that the von Thedieck confession is destroyed and that the files you spoke about are put someplace where we can get hold of them— that means within the American zone."

"This person you are going to send back with me . . . ."

"I will make you responsible for his safety. On that would depend your safety, Schöller."

"He is American?"

"Yes, but his German is fluent and he knows Berlin. We can supply him with papers."

Schöller was weighing up this proposal.

"While he was with me, this person, he would probably not be questioned. But on his own . . . all movement within Germany is highly restricted. He could not move without me, he would be tied to me absolutely. If I did not get out, neither would he."

"He'll just have to cross that bridge when he comes to it."

"He is aware of the risk?"

"Men in our line of business are obliged to take such risks."

"He is someone who can be relied upon not to lose his head? Not to panic. Under highly difficult circumstances. You understand, we would be in each other's hands."

"I don't know," said Dulles. "He is a young man and inexperienced in this type of work. But there is nobody else with the necessary qualifications. We shall have to rely upon you, Reichskriminaldirektor, to . . . look after him."

Schöller laughed.

"It is reasonable," he said. "I accept."

"Work out the details with Mr. Quantregg here. You should be able to tie it all up by tomorrow."

"All right . . . but who's the guy we put in?" Quantregg said when they were alone.

"Elliott."

"Elliott!"

"His German's perfect, and he knows the whole operation."

"He's had no mission training—none. He's a complete greenhorn."

"He's got the Reich Special Investigator to protect him. There's nobody else, Dick. We can't bring anybody else in."

"What are you going to tell General Donovan?"

"I'll play it by ear. Bill Donovan is basically on our side, and we have one thing working for us— Roosevelt never told the Vice President a damn thing.

It'll take Mr. Truman a little while to find out what goes on in the great big world outside Missouri."

• 15 •

Elliott was awakened by the ringing of the telephone. When he picked it up, it was with a sense of foreboding that might have been carried over from an unfinished dream. He heard the voice of the night porter on the line. Someone was in the lobby to see him.

"To see me?" He looked at his luminous wristwatch. Two A.M. The date aperture showed 13. "Who wants to see me?"

"A Mr. Quantregg, from the American legation."

"Oh! Ask him to come up, please. Or does he want me to come down? He'll come up? OK."

What the hell did he want this time of night? Elliott put his face under the cold water tap of the washbasin to wake himself up. Must be some urgent message to be encoded or decoded. He was thinking fast. He hadn't much time to get his bearings, since Quantregg always came up steps three at a time.

A nominal knock, followed by the rough peremptory entry.

Quantregg was wide awake and burning up energy at his usual high-combustion rate.

But as he came into the small hotel room, the terse orders were not immediately forthcoming. Instead, he gave the calculated if spiky smile of a superior officer setting out to put a subordinate at ease. It had the opposite effect. Elliott lit a cigarette. Quantregg said nothing about any coding job as he dropped down

101

into the only armchair and coiled up like a spring. Fanning cigarette smoke from his immediate vicinity—Quantregg was a nonsmoker by conviction—he said something very unusual:

"You been a great help, Elliott. Mr. Dulles is well pleased."

"Glad to hear it."

Words of praise from Quantregg were rare; he regarded the people who worked in the code room as a bunch of eggheads who sat around all day long in a nice clean, warm room, playing leisurely mind games among themselves, while others did the real work.

"This is a tricky business, you know. *Schöller.* What you make of him?"

"I expected him to be different."

"In what way?"

"In your mind you build up a picture of somebody like that, and I suppose it's larger than life. And then what you see is someone trying to save his own skin, and it's different."

"Right. I guess you know 'em pretty well."

"No. I don't *know* them. I lived there. I saw things. I was there during the *Kristallnacht.* I took it in, sure, like anybody."

"How's your German?"

"It's all right."

"Must be pretty damn good. You went to school there. I should think you'd be fluent. I should think you'd speak it like a lousy Kraut."

"Well . . . " Elliott began modestly.

"And you know Berlin?"

"Yuh—sure. We lived there."

"How long?"

"Off and on . . . ten years maybe."

"And you took an interest, didn't you? I mean, you'd be familiar with their way of operating. The protocol. All that stuff."

"I don't know too much about all that."

"You knew about Schöller. And the internal setup of the Main Security Office."

What did Quantregg want? He usually didn't bother

102

to lead up to things—but just blurted out whatever he was after.

"There's something we need done," Quantregg admitted. "We need somebody who's clued in on the whole situation there . . . who knows the scene."

"A rush job?" Elliott had occasionally prepared briefs-in-depth on some aspect or other of the German situation.

"We need somebody to go in."

"Go in. Go in, Mr. Quantregg? Where?"

"Berlin."

"While the war is on?"

"Right. You got it."

Elliott coughed and started to laugh, but then his face froze against his will and he covered up by doing a mock movie double take.

"You're asking *me* to go in," he said, swallowing hard in an exaggerated way.

"Right."

He took a deep breath, and then let the air out slowly.

"You are not kidding me, I suppose?"

"I am not, kid."

"No, I didn't think you were somehow."

"Right."

"I wouldn't want you to think me unwilling or anything like that," Elliott said, "but you ought to know I've had no training in anything like this. I've never gone in anywhere."

"You learn as you go along. Doing it generates its own momentum, you'll see."

Elliott began to shake his head negatively.

"Frankly, Mr. Quantregg . . . I . . . I don't think I'm cut out for this kind of . . . uh . . . thing."

"Don't give me that. You're fit. You play an above-average game of tennis. You ski. You're an all-round sportsman, I hear."

"Well, that is not exactly . . . "

"Look . . . " Quantregg stopped him. "You want to be somebody, don't you? Your father is somebody. Quite somebody. What are you going to be . . . ?"

"I hadn't got around to . . . "

Quantregg came up to him and looked him in the eye, a straight-from-the-shoulder look.

"Look here, kid," he said, "there's always a future for someone who has distinguished himself in the service of his country. Mr. Dulles is not someone to overlook a good man."

"But this is crazy—I'm not a spy. . . . I just happened to be in Berne and I was asked to work in the code room and . . . "

"That's right, you've had a nice easy war so far . . . you just happened to find yourself in a comfortable safe place like Berne when the borders closed. Right. So you didn't have to join the army. No need to do any of those unpleasant, dangerous things other people have to do in a war. Like kill people. No. Still, that wasn't your fault. It was just circumstances, wasn't it? And now that you *can* choose, I have no doubt that like any other patriotic young American boy, after an initial sense of modesty—of asking yourself 'Can I do it?'—you will come to the conclusion that you *have* to do it, for your country. And for yourself. Listen, kid, it's simple. You go in and you go out. That's all there's to it. You keep an eye on Schöller. And you check some files, that's all."

"That's all."

"Right. You stick with Schöller. He's the Reich Special Investigator. Who's going to touch you while you're with him?"

"Our bombers won't know I'm with him."

"Listen, a brick can hit you on the head outside the Tea-Room Wölfli. You take a risk with everything you do."

"I'll think about it," Elliott said.

"If you're thinking of saying no," Quantregg said, "I have to tell you that I am not able to accept that."

"With something like this, I thought you can refuse."

"In the movies."

"You can order me to go in and do this?"

"I don't know if I can or not, but I tell you this: we sure would be sore as hell if you didn't volunteer freely, and we'd throw everything we could find at you, and that's not kidding."

"I know you don't kid, Mr. Quantregg."

"Right."

"But I might prefer the worst you could do to being dead, which is the likeliest outcome of the harebrain scheme you've proposed."

"You might prefer it," Quantregg conjectured, "and again you might not. Who knows?"

Elliott laughed wryly. In no time at all your life changed. One minute you were leading an ordinary uneventful existence, thinking about where to have a drink or meet some girls, and the next, somebody wanted to send you into the sea of flames, and if you didn't go . . . then what?

"We'll give you a way of getting in touch with us if Schöller shows any sign of welshing on the deal," Quantregg said.

"And if he does?"

"You let us know."

"And what then?"

"You let him have it. You let the son of a bitch have it."

"How do you suggest I do that? In his position he must have some experience of people trying to bump him off."

"Use this."

He took a small hard object out of his pocket and threw it to Elliott, who just managed to catch it. It was a Boy Scout knife. The kind of knife that small boys are always so keen to have. In addition to the usual blades, it had a screwdriver, a pair of nail scissors, a bottle opener, a corkscrew, and a nail file, a range of useful implements.

"Press the little catch at the back," Quantregg advised.

Elliott did so, and from the bone handle of the knife a long thin blade jumped out, a murderer's weapon. Elliott felt the point of the blade; his lips puckered in a contemplative way.

He thought about killing the Reich Special Investigator. Cutting his throat. It was like those childhood games of trying to imagine the worst thing you could. If you were on a lifeboat in the ocean, and there were three people in the water, your mother, your father, and your little sister, and only room for one more on the raft, who would you save and who would you let drown? Sometimes standing in front of the mirror you said the worst thing that you could think of, just to hear how it would sound, and to hear yourself saying it . . . unspeakable things, crimes, perversions, bestialities.

"You think I could do it with one blow of this?" Elliott inquired. It was like saying things into the mirror a long time ago, just to hear it in your own voice.

"Well, if you get the vein here, the external jugular, one should be enough. But even if you miss that, if you get in one good blow, he'll be in no state to do anything much about the second or third or fourth." He paused, taking in the change of heart that had apparently occurred in the young man. It was crazy. Sometimes the thing you expected would be hardest to make someone swallow turned out to be the easiest. "I'm getting your papers already. We'll have a final briefing this afternoon. You'll be leaving tomorrow. Early. OK?"

"OK, Mr. Quantregg."

Is that me saying this, or am I just saying it to the mirror? In a minute, he thought, I'll realize what I've agreed to and I'll want to get out of it, and it'll be too late. It's still not too late. For Christsake think of something. Think of something. Some out. Anything. Quantregg was going to the door. He had opened it. Stop him. Stop him. Say something. Stall. Argue. Refuse.

At the open door, Quantregg had stopped, as if suddenly remembering something. He came back into the room.

"Oh, just one other thing. I need to know this. It's a formality. Next of kin . . . in case anything happened to you, who d'you want informed? Parents? A girl someplace?"

"Just my parents."

"Address same as in your PRQ?"

"My father is in Paris now. At the Ritz. Or care

of SHAEF. My mother—she's in England. The address is in the Questionnaire. They are not together. They would have to be informed separately."

"See you tomorrow then. Get a good night's sleep."

"Right," Elliott said.

"These are your papers and money," Quantregg said, handing a thick brown envelope to Elliott, who was dressed in the German-made clothes supplied by Technical Services. A dark brown suit of coarse material of wartime manufacture. It was a standard fitting and too large at the waist, worn with elasticated suspenders. A long double-breasted overcoat with wide lapels. A slouch hat—the kind plainclothes policemen invariably wore in movies. He felt uncomfortable and rather ridiculous in these strange ill-fitting clothes, like a child dressing up for some stupid party game he was being made to play by the grown-ups.

Quantregg proceeded to acquaint him with the details of his assumed identity, and to outline procedures.

"You're Albert Haften, a personal political assistant of Schöller's. Rank of Kriminaloberassistent. That's roughly equivalent to a second lieutenant. You're plainclothes, and you have no corresponding rank in the SS. Schöller's staff weren't given SS ranks. You come under the Reichskriminalpolizeiamt, subsection PP II J Foreign Political Police Forces, and you've been attached to General Wolff's staff in Italy as a police observer, in other words a spy for the Special Investigator. It's their usual setup. Vital statistics same as your own. Born and educated Frankfurt—they can't check that, on account of it's in our hands, right? In Italy you were attached to SS-Colonel Dollmann's staff, to make political appraisals. Dollmann is in on Sunrise, he's been briefed and will bear out everything. That's basically your setup. Questions?"

"Sounds OK," Elliott said.

"Now—objective. Your job in Berlin is to safeguard Sunrise by any means, and I mean *any*. Destroy von Thedieck's confession. See you get all copies. The rest is watching Schöller, seeing he doesn't welsh on the deal, and if it looks like he's going to, you take whatever measures are needed, including using your Boy Scout knife. Right?"

"I get the gist."

"Next. The files. Check for authenticity. And check for contents—we're interested in their secret apparat. We want those names. Arrange for the evacuation of the files to a safe place in the American zone, and watch out for tricks. He's a bargainer, Schöller, and we don't want to put extra cards in his hand."

He placed a scrap of paper before Elliott.

"Item. Berlin telephone number and address. Memorize and destroy. Item. Wristwatch, German make. Give me yours, wear this. Inside the back lid is a manufacturer's number . . . that's your password when you ring the Berlin telephone number. The guy's a watchmaker. He has radio contact with us and will be in the picture.

"Your code words are based on parts of a watch. Wolff is the main wheel in this operation, OK? Mr. Dulles is the center wheel, I'm the third wheel, and you're the escape wheel. Schöller? Let's say he's the mainspring. If we need to get a message to you, or you to us, through the watchmaker, that's the terminology we use. Is that all clear?"

"It's clear."

"Final point. Schöller's a Kraut, and you know the only kind that are good ones. Your mission is completed once Wolff is in the clear and out and you've made arrangements about the files. After that, it's everybody for himself. Get out fast. I think it may pay you to stick with Schöller, but if it doesn't, don't.

On most matters—at any rate before mission is accomplished—you ought to do what Schöller says, unless you have reason to suppose he's double-crossing us. Because, remember, he's making the big play, and he's got the background and experience to know how to handle it, which you haven't. At the same time, if you see fit, you can overrule him at any time, and he knows that. We're talking within the framework of the deal. If he dumps that, you're on your own and there aren't any rules."

Quantregg stopped and a strong encouraging smile spread over his face. He slapped Elliott's right arm and at the same time gave his left bicep a powerful squeeze.

"I think you're gonna do fine," he said, "and we sure do appreciate your spirit of patriotism in volunteering for this. By the way, I'm going to need a signature from you to that effect. Right?"

"Right."

He pushed a batch of forms toward Elliott and proffered his own open fountain pen.

"One here, and here, and here and here . . . " He indicated the various places on the different forms where signatures were required. Elliott signed without reading what he was signing.

"Good, good," Quantregg said, pleased with his agent's unquibbling spirit. "One last thing. A personal piece of advice, Elliott. Like Mr. Dulles says, in our trade you've got to be ready to talk to the devil himself, right? But look out for yourself—huh. Keep a clear head. What I'm saying, kid, is: you're going to have to do some things together, you and Schöller . . . whatever they are . . . but that doesn't mean you're obligated to him. In any way. Understood? So you better make up your mind in advance and be ready to use your Boy Scout knife anytime."

"Check."

• 17 •

Leaving Switzerland on April 14, the Reich Special Investigator and the young man with him, identified at the border as his political aide (Italy), Albert Haften, proceeded northward along a hilly road that rose from the Bodensee and wound through the wooded foothills of the Allgäu to Kempten.

Though the First French Army was now past Pforzheim and across the River Enz, and the Russians were in Vienna, this was the widest part of the corridor between the eastern and western fronts. At its nearest point, the front line was seventy miles to the west.

They passed formations of Tiger tanks and armored troop-carriers going in the direction of Stuttgart, but most of the traffic was heading the other way, long columns of refugees, many on foot, some in horse-drawn carts piled high with personal belongings, or in rickety old farm trucks, a few on bicycles, all trying to get as far as possible from the battle zone.

If he could, Schöller kept to narrow minor roads. When they had to follow main routes, they came across blazing vehicles, the dead quivering in the heated air.

Nearing Munich the sky darkened with smoke palls from half a dozen target areas. Airfields, ammunition and storage plants, ordnance depots, and railway yards had been hit during the night's raids.

From the moment of entering German territory, Elliott had felt apprehension, but at the same time he was in a strangely keyed-up state in which hellish scenes carved out of rain and mud, framed by the

110

clearing action of the windshield wipers, seemed to be happening at some distance from him.

By the side of the road lay the dead and dying, where they had fallen from hunger and exhaustion. Women, children. Old men. Some were covered with dirty rags of clothing, or a tarpaulin sheet, but mostly they had been left just as they were, eyes staring fixedly, bodies frozen brittle and stiff.

It was even more horrifying to see the living. Motherless children, a dull kind of terror etched on their faces. Old men hardly able to walk, who would soon be corpses too. Women striving desperately to keep their family groups together.

They hardly reacted at all as Schöller drove through their midst, bespattering them with the mud and filth of the road.

He did not seem to see them. He was driving hard, alert all the time for significant changes in the condition of the terrain, often looking up at the sky and at the surrounding countryside. His eyes were like the flickering needle of an instrument, registering everything accurately, coolly, without feeling.

"This weather is good for us," Schöller said, indicating the low rain clouds which covered the whole sky in a dense gray-black mass, devoid of openings. "Discourages your compatriots from coming down after us. For the time being."

Elliott was slumped back in his seat, face white and glistening. His palms left moist patches wherever he touched.

Schöller shot occasional concerned glances at him. "You suffer from nerves?" he asked eventually.

"Car sickness," Elliott said.

Schöller grinned, and made a sympathetic gesture.

"The condition of the roads. It is a bumpy ride, I apologize. You must breathe in deep. Regularly, *like this*. Keep your eye on the horizon, something not moving." He added, as an afterthought: "There is some cognac in the glove compartment. It will settle your stomach. . . ."

With the first couple of gulps Elliott felt his mind begin to close. He took another long gulp and as the alcohol burned in his throat and chest, his awareness of things became less sharp, less burdensome.

He looked at Schöller. Solid trunk of neck. Ever-alert eyes. Big ears. Big shoulders, a strong man. *If it came to a fight, I have twenty years on him, and I'm pretty fit,* Elliott considered, *but this is his home ground, and he knows his way around, and he'd be a man fighting for his life. Would have to take him by surprise. A sudden lunge. From behind. Only way to make sure.*

"Your stomach better?"

Why is he so concerned about my damn stomach? Damn him! It disturbed Elliott, this determination of Schöller's to be friendly. *He's trying to get me to like him. It's grotesque. Does he think he can bamboozle me to that extent? Does he really consider me such a novice, so easy to handle?*

Quantregg had said—if it comes to it, you just do it, things sort of generate their own momentum. But could he kill Schöller, if it should have to be done? He couldn't envisage himself doing something like that. Suppose nobody could. Yet people killed all the time. Better not to think about it. Might never arise. But deep inside his pocket he held the Boy Scout knife in his sweating palm to remind him that the situation could arise, had been planned for.

He studied the heavy, crafty face. How many crimes did he have on his head? You couldn't do that job and keep your hands clean.

Abruptly, as if reading Elliott's line of thought, Schöller said, "What I said in Berne is true. I know you do not believe me, but I was not involved in any of those things you have heard about . . . just ordinary police work."

"Police work—huh?"

"Yes. I cannot convince you to believe me, Mr. Elliott. But in your country a person is innocent until proven guilty. Is that not the case?"

"Yuh," Elliott said, "but we're in your country now, and there the opposite applies. Isn't that right?"

Schöller laughed self-deprecatingly.

"That is called turning the tables on me? Like in

your films? I understand. It is considered being a 'wise guy'—no?"

"Something like that. . . . Look, Schöller, we don't have to make conversation. Let's just get on with what we've been told to do—right?"

"I understand."

As they traveled northward along the corridor, Schöller discovered how drastically it had become narrowed in the six days since he had left Schloss Rudolphstein. Bayreuth, through which he had passed on his way south, was on the verge of falling to Patton's Third Army. So it was necessary to swing round east of Nuremberg and make toward Weiden and from there go along the Czech frontier to Bad Elster, and then find out what roads to Berlin were still open.

By noon Schöller was beginning to feel hungry, and something about the countryside they were passing through seemed to have increased his appetite.

"The food situation gets worse the nearer you get to Berlin," he said. "But in the country you can sometimes get a decent meal. I remember a place around here. Yes, yes, there was a place near here that was good."

He was making a detour to find this place, taking his bearings from long, low farmhouses, a railway line, twists of the road, open fields, a church. He was entirely preoccupied with finding this place where he had once eaten well, and each vaguely familiar sight along the road caused him to utter delighted cries— "Yes, yes, this is the way, I am sure of it. We are going right. We are going in the right direction. . . . I would swear it."

When after half an hour of searching they turned a corner to see ahead of them a run-down farm laborers' tavern, Schöller was triumphant. He pulled up the car and rubbed his hands. They got out and he led Elliott through a dim outer room where a couple of old men sat drinking silently and into a small dining room in which thirty or more farm workers were crammed together at long trestle tables, eating noisily. The air was thick with the smell and smoke of sizzling pork, and Schöller went in sniffing like a dog for his dinner.

113

Throughout the meal the smell of frying pork meat almost made Elliott vomit and he ate hardly anything at all, whereas Schöller ate not only the portion with which he had been served but also everything that Elliott left. He tore at the bread and stuffed huge pieces of it into his mouth, washing them down with long draughts of beer.

"This is my part of the world," he told Elliott between gulps. "It's where I come from. I come from people like these. They're my sort. Peasants. Peasants. That's the stock I come from, and I'm not ashamed of it. Common. Common as earth. What you intellectuals call the lumpenproletariat. You know? Well, I'm not such a lump." He tapped the side of his large nose knowingly. "Instinct," he said. "I know a thing or two. I know some things the intellectuals don't know. I know my trade . . . and I know how to use my elbows."

The beer had made him talkative.

"You understand, I was never one of them, never one of the *Herrenvolk*. No, I was an ordinary Munich Kriminalinspektor. I dealt with criminals, pimps, prostitutes, murderers. . . . I used to round up the Nazi louts before '33, I used to give them bloody heads. Mind you, we also rounded up the Bolsheviks. We gave them a rough time too. Me and 'Stapo' Müller. That's funny, isn't it? Him head of the Gestapo, me Reich Special Investigator, and we both were marked down as politically unreliable. Because we used to give those brown-shirted louts bloody heads.

"When the Austrian house-painter took over, we realized we were in for it. Heydrich came down, called us in one by one. He had *Fingerspitzengefühl*, that man, he could tell about somebody in the tips of his fingers. Called me in, *der Chef*. Called me in. Looked down a long list. Always had a list of one sort or another. 'Schöller,' he says. 'Ernst Schöller.' 'Yes, sir,' I say. 'It says here,' he says, reading, 'enemy of the regime, self-seeking, untrustworthy. Potentially disloyal. Not a Party member. Politically ignorant. To be dismissed without pension rights.' Then he looks me in the eye, hard. He had small hard blue eyes. 'True?'

he demands. That was his great cleverness, you see. 'True?' 'No, sir,' I said. 'Then this must be another Schöller,' he says. 'Must be,' I say. 'Good,' he says, 'then I can count on you?' 'I'm a good policeman,' I said. 'I know that,' he said. 'That's why I knew all those things written down here couldn't be about you. I need good policemen. I've got enough ideologists.' Then he looked me over and he said, 'How are you with a gun and with the ladies?' lumping them together, and I said, 'Not bad,' answering for both, and he said, 'Good, I need somebody who is a good shot with both weapons. . . . '"

Schöller gave a coarse chuckle and drank down more beer. "*Der Chef* had an appetite for the low life, night after night, from one low dive to the next. 'Do you know who I am?' he shouted at the girls if they were not immediately submissive. Women didn't like him, though he was a handsome man, blond, striking appearance. We got to be quite close on those nights. It was different during the day. Then he was *der Chef*, who never went anywhere without his escort of motorcyclists, everybody 'Heil Hitlering' all over him. But at night he put his life in my hands. Any of those whores could have stuck a knife in his throat. I had to watch out for that, or somebody putting a bomb under his ass. He relied on me. He knew I was a police marksman, that reassured him. He knew I knew police work backwards. And if we went in a place and I didn't like the look of it, he took my advice. When he was drunk, he'd call me his shooting arm and he'd tell me he loved his shooting arm. But I knew he wouldn't have hesitated to cut off his shooting arm, if it had paid him to."

After the heavy lunch and all the beer, Schöller's driving was erratic. His lumpy eyelids drooped, he lolled forward, and once or twice it seemed he might go off the road. But he would recover with a sudden start, and shaking himself like a wet dog, endeavor to refocus his eyes. The clouds had lifted. They were passing through hilly countryside.

"Beautiful, isn't it?" Schöller said. "What a beautiful country this is! I was brought up here. Yes. In this region. I know it—beautiful, beautiful. In summer . . . "

He undid the top button of his trousers to ease his full belly. His eyes had become vacant with some beery recollection. How easy it would be to kill him now, Elliott thought, as he wallows in his sentimental memories. How unguarded he is. I would not have supposed that the Reich Special Investigator would be so unguarded. . . .

One village was like the next. Each one had its bulbous-towered little church, its half-timbered farmhouses, a few stores, fruit trees in full blossom. The weather had cleared, and the sun was shining down on a spring scene. They went over a humpbacked railway bridge and then along a winding road enclosed by sparse clumps of trees, which broke up the sunlight into innumerable dazzling segments.

As they emerged into the open, there was the clatter of a train on their left. At this point the railway line ran parallel with the road for a short distance before entering a tunnel.

They were going through open country between wide horizons, keeping up with the train a mile or so away on their left; on their right there were ploughed fields, a few huts, a farmhouse or two, before the ground began to rise again, becoming hilly and wooded in the far distance. Birds could be heard in this country stillness. Schöller's eyes closed from time to time and as a result his driving took them on a rather zigzag course.

They were right in the middle of this open space when Schöller suddenly drove off the road, sending the car bumping and bouncing over cultivated land. Next thing he knew, Elliott was being violently pushed against the door on his side. It burst open and before the car had come to a halt, he was falling out and Schöller's massive form was on top of him, moving, rolling him over the hard earth and into a ditch. Elliott felt his face being pressed down into the ground.

He couldn't breathe. He struggled to take a gulp of air and saw above the hills two fast-moving specks growing rapidly in size. The British Mosquitoes were coming out of the sun, flying very low, just above the tops of the fruit trees with their masses of pink and white blossoms. The planes cleared the roofs of the low farmhouses and the telegraph poles, their pointed shadows racing ahead of them, growing gigantic, laying their winged form over the two men on the ground like a shroud.

Again Schöller forced Elliott's head down, partly burying his face in earth. Both felt the air above them quiver violently and then heard the cannon fire.

Elliott felt the knot of dread slip undone. The planes were past. They were going for the train. Earth was spouting up all around it, Elliott saw. Dense clouds of steam rose from a punctured boiler. The engine driver was putting on speed, he was trying to get to the shelter of the railway tunnel about a mile ahead. The train was being raked by gunfire: carriage windows and doors were blown to pieces like moving targets in a fairground range. People were screaming. Some threw themselves from the fast-moving train.

The planes were wheeling, climbing rapidly for the next attack as Schöller pulled Elliott to his feet. They shook the hard earth from them as they ran back to the car. They could see the train. It looked like a long-tailed fox running from the hounds. Could it get to its hole in time?

Schöller had succeeded in restarting the car and was driving it back onto the road, the vehicle shaking and rolling wildly as it went over the furrowed ground.

The Mosquitoes were momentarily poised, glittering in the sun as they reached the zenith of their climb and began their downturn for the next dive attack. Detached, Elliott watched for the outcome of this life-and-death game being played out between planes and train. Helmeted faces at windows. Uniforms. A troop train? A legitimate target. The enemy. Out of the sky, the planes came screaming down, chasing the tail of the train as the locomotive entered the tunnel. The last two carriages were shattered, but the train continued on, dragging its wreckage after it.

As soon as they were back on the road, Schöller put his foot down hard and sent the car hurtling along,

117

at the same time he watched the sky to see what the British pilots were going to do next. But they evidently had decided not to waste their gunfire on a solitary vehicle and were climbing steeply, becoming specks again. All the same, Schöller kept a wary lookout for them as he drove on. Only when ten minutes or more had gone by and the planes had not returned, did he relax his attention somewhat.

"For a man full of beer you acted pretty fast," Elliott said. He removed some of the hard earth from his hair and face. "For a moment I thought you intended to suffocate me back there."

"Mr. Dulles told me I must look after you," Schöller explained. "I am responsible for your safety. I must see nothing bad happens to you, or something bad happens to me. There was not time to explain what those little dots in the sky were. Now you will know too, and keep a lookout. Hmm? We must help each other. For the time being at least, whatever you think of me, Mr. Elliott. Isn't that correct?"

"Yuh."

They drove on in silence, Schöller turning from time to time to take a look at the young American. When he saw, after about fifteen minutes, that some color had at last returned to Elliott's face, he said wryly, "You get used to death in the end, you get to know the ugly old so-and-so. He's not so bad. There's no arguing with the old bastard, but he's not such an ogre as some people think. He's got his work to do too." He gave a laugh. "I know him—I know him. I've seen him come to a lot of people. We know each other, him and me."

"I bet," Elliott said.

"Not what you think, Mr. Elliott. Just in the ordinary course of police work."

"Police work, huh?"

"You know the old saying," he chuckled. "Plan for old age, and live every moment as if it's your last. That's the only way. Some things you can't do anything about. So—you concentrate on the work, and you take a bottle of cognac to bed at night, and when

118

you get up in the morning you take a hair of the dog, and get on with it."

"That's how you do it, is it?"

"You shouldn't judge what you don't know," he said, for the first time allowing a touch of rancor to enter his voice. "What do you know? You know it all from books. Intellectuals! You don't know anything. Take it from me. Things happen slowly, you get used to everything in the end . . . bit by bit by bit. . . . "

"You did. Speak for yourself."

"No? You don't know. People go mad. I was near one of those places once, you know what I mean. . . . ? It was twenty miles away, but you could smell it in the air. Over the whole area. The burnt flesh. . . . It was a rancid sort of a smell, very disgusting. I saw some of them. The Chosen People . . . not the Europeans, the Europeans are different, they look like us. No, the others. Sometimes I had to investigate if there were some of our high-ups doing illegal dealings in appropriated Jewish property. That was the only connection I had. . . . About the other things, there was nothing I could do."

"Like all the others—nothing you could do."

Schöller's face became withdrawn; he drew in breath sharply through flared nostrils; evidently he was occupied with thoughts he could not, or would not, communicate. Presently he emerged again from the hiatus, he stroked his chin, his eyebrows rose up acknowledging the undeniable.

"To a man's nature there is nothing that is out of the question. *Believe me.* You understand?"

They all sought to justify themselves, Elliott thought. Sickened he turned away from the demanding eyes.

From time to time, they saw the horizon on their left lighten up with heavy artillery fire, and the farther north they traveled the closer it got. It was like driving into a slowly closing jaw.

Just before dusk they ran into a Feldpolizei patrol who warned that if they carried on in the dark, they might wander into the enemy lines, the fronts were that fluid.

"Watch out for the laborers from the East," one of

119

the field policemen said. "They broke out of a big factory near here, smashed up their compound, killed their wardens and bosses. They are roaming about armed with kitchen knives and pickaxes. They'll cut your throat for a piece of bread."

Schöller chose an abandoned house in which to spend the night, and for mutual protection moved the beds to opposite ends of the room, so that if one of them was attacked in the dark, the other could come to his aid. He himself slept with his small Mauser automatic next to him under the blankets.

"Don't worry," he told Elliott, "you can sleep soundly." He smirked. "I can sleep with my eyes open. . . . I see and hear everything."

"*Naturally*," Elliott said, turning on his side. Notwithstanding the sarcasm in his voice, he felt a degree of reassurance having the policeman there, guarding the door, and he slept soundly and deeply without stirring until Schöller woke him up in the morning and said it was time to be going.

Continuing in a northerly direction, they saw everywhere the signs of total collapse. Roaming bands of armed deserters, living as bandits. SS patrols checking everybody's papers, particularly those of soldiers on the move, in case they should be moving in the wrong direction, away from the fighting.

Elsewhere they came across Ministry officials and technicians supervising the mining of bridges, industrial installations, water supplies, electric power stations, telephone exchanges, factories, in accordance with Hitler's scorched-earth order. Nothing was to be left intact, even if the population starved as a consequence.

Many roads were blocked as a result of enemy action, or because of the breakdown of army vehicles, some of which had simply run out of gas. Field ambulances and troop carriers, hastily adapted for the purpose, carried the badly wounded away from the battle zone, but where they were going nobody quite knew, since the battle was being joined on all sides now.

Lines of exhausted soldiers dragged their weapons through the road mud. Horses on their last legs drawing field guns. Staff cars full of high-ranking officers driving fast in all directions. And the continuous to-and-fro of dispatch riders.

Every couple of miles, there was a detour—for a check of travel authorizations, or because a particular stretch of the road ahead was being mined, or trenches dug, or tank obstacles erected.

The hard driving was burning up fuel at an excessive rate, and every time Schöller stopped to refill the tank from the supply of gas in the trunk, he was anxiously working out how far what remained in the jerry-cans would take them. It was not something that could be calculated with any exactitude, there being no way of knowing what further detours and obstacles lay ahead.

In the middle of the afternoon they were brought to a halt by a troop train that stood immobilized on a railway crossing traversing the street. Schöller, in a bad temper, shaking his head, muttering about gas, got out of the car and went to find out what the situation was. Elliott followed.

The last two carriages of the train had been badly shot up. This must be the troop train they had seen being attacked by the British fighter planes. So it had got this far, before finally breaking down.

Searching for somebody who might know how long the train was going to be stuck there, they looked over the couplings and saw bodies being carried from the carriages and laid on the ground between two parallel sets of railway tracks. The uniforms of the soldiers from the train hung on their small frames. The rifles came up to their ears. *Children!* These troops were not men at all but children, some of them no more than twelve or thirteen.

On the adjacent track stood another train, to which some of the wounded were being transferred, while at the windows young women of the Women's Auxiliary Anti-Aircraft Force, big, heavy-bodied German farm-girls with ruddy complexions, were calling out to the child-soldiers in a variety of country dialects and giggling coarsely among themselves.

Some of the child-soldiers had got down from their train to urinate, and the girls were shouting down at them, "Is that all you can do?" and such things. One or two of the Anti-Aircraft girls had got off their train and were also squatting down by the tracks, relieving themselves.

There was a good deal of crude badinage as the young women and the child-soldiers shared the improvised urinal between the two railway lines. And when a ruddy-faced Anti-Aircraft girl, in response to some dare from her mates, gave a derisory tug at a child-soldier, a mock battle ensued, in which streams of urine were directed all over the place with screams of hysterical hilarity, and underclothing was torn and finally in several places child-soldiers were mounting Anti-Aircraft girls from front or rear and jerking about on the ground in a messy melee of limbs. This went on no more than a dozen feet from where the dead and the wounded lay on the ground.

Schöller shook his head at the sight. "They're children."

Elliott said, "Looks to me like they are old enough."

Schöller turned away in disgust and returned silently to the car. He started the engine, and with a violent gear change reversed away fast from the blocked roadway.

He did not say anything for the next twenty minutes.

"One thing I would never stand for, that was the violation of children. If I ever caught one of those filthy pigs, he didn't have to wait for justice. We gave him justice straightaway. Medical treatment, psychiatrists, quieting-down drugs. . . . " Contemptuously he cleared the phlegm from his throat and swallowed.

"I will say this for Himmler, and every policeman will tell you the same, he let us get on with the job, instead of bothering with court orders and warrants. *Warrants!* For perverts who molest children! We rounded them up after '33, and we didn't send them to any cozy treatment centers. We sent them to camps. . . . "

"Yes, I heard about the camps," Elliott said.

"You don't know what it means to have a child. You are not a father," Schöller said. "You don't understand."

"You going to teach me?"

"You think you know it all," Schöller admonished. "You'll see."

It was getting dark; it was necessary to spend a second night in an abandoned house on the way. The date was April 15.

· 18 ·

Earlier that day Dulles had returned from his meeting with General Donovan in Paris, at which it was again laid down that official policy ruled out negotiations with Nazi leaders.

Once more Dulles had stated his view that rigid adherence to the principle of unconditional surrender played into the hands of the Soviets, allowing them to take large areas of Europe. But though Donovan sympathized with this view, he said categorically that Truman was going to keep to the policies that Roosevelt had agreed to with the Russians.

Dulles was mulling over this conversation as he sat in his apartment, alone for once, eating a trout *meunière*. He was enjoying the fish and complimented the cook. After his lunch, he decided to have a brief nap on the divan. The cook asked if she could go out to post some letters, and he said yes, surely.

There was a mailbox in the next road, but she did not go to that one. Instead, she walked up to the Casinoplatz. Once or twice she glanced at her watch. She spent some minutes looking in shop windows, and then, seeing what the time was, hurried to post her letters.

At the box she made a last-minute check that the

envelopes were all correctly addressed and stamped, and that each one had a sender, and then began to push them through the slot one at a time. A man behind her, becoming impatient at this, leaned over her shoulder to post his letters. In the course of doing so, one of the letters that the cook was about to drop in the box found its way into the impatient man's fingers, and a bulky foolscap envelope that he was on the point of posting was snatched by the cook and put in her shopping basket.

The cook and the impatient man then left in opposite directions.

Fifteen minutes later, at the German legation, Counselor Werner was reading the following: "In the course of the past week Mr. Dulles has had these visitors ..." There followed a list of somewhat uninteresting names and some vague descriptions. Virtually no conversation had been overheard, since Dulles was careful about closing doors, and the doors were soundproof. It was a somewhat feeble report.

The final paragraph read: "Twice on April 12, once in the morning, once in the afternoon, Dulles had a visit from a German, shabbily dressed, who looks like a policeman. Fingernails dirty and fingers tobacco-stained. Initials E.S. in hatband. An old trilby hat from Ka-We-De, Berlin."

Counselor Werner called in his assistant and asked, "Who of our people have the initials E.S. and dirty fingernails? There is the Ambassador's secretary, Baron Erwin Sorber, of course, but the Baron pays regular visits to a manicurist."

After some thought, the assistant suggested, "There is Kriminaldirektor Ernst Schöller. He has been in Berne incognito, staying at the Bellevue."

In his daily report to Chief of Foreign Intelligence Schellenberg, Werner mentioned the presence of the Reich Special Investigator in Berne and the fact that somebody with his initials, and bearing some physical resemblance to him, had visited Dulles in the Herrengasse.

The report was encoded and radioed to Berlin. It was on Schellenberg's desk at five P.M. on the fifteenth.

He immediately placed a phone call to Ernst Kalten-brunner, Chief of the Reich Main Security Office, who was in Innsbruck.

On hearing of Schöller's visit to Dulles, Kalten-brunner—an ox of a man, seven feet tall, with a face as rough as the bark of a tree—roared drunkenly down the phone: "Never trusted Schöller. Never trusted that peasant. A traitor, I knew it. I knew it. A swine. A swine of the first order. Trying to save his own neck. A traitorous swine."

"Will you inform SS-Reichsführer Himmler or shall I?" Schellenberg asked.

"I will," Kaltenbrunner said. "I shall enjoy doing so."

When he had hung up, Kaltenbrunner yelled to his orderly to bring another bottle of brandy. As soon as he had got himself going with a couple of large drinks, he rang for his aide and gave him a message to send off immediately to Himmler at his field headquarters. It read:

IN LIGHT OF INFORMATION RECEIVED THROUGH MY SOURCES IN SWITZERLAND REQUEST IMMEDIATE CONFRONTATION WOLFF/SCHÖLLER/MYSELF IN YOUR PRESENCE IN ORDER TO INVESTIGATE CHARGES OF THE UTMOST SERIOUSNESS. AM LEAVING BY ROAD FORTHWITH AND WILL BE WITH YOU WITHIN TWELVE HOURS. SUGGEST THAT WOLFF'S AND SCHÖLLER'S ATTENDANCE SHOULD BE ENSURED BY WHATEVER MEANS NECESSARY.

I END BY CONGRATULATING THE SS-REICHSFÜHRER ON THE GOOD OMEN OF THE WARMONGER ROOSEVELT'S DEATH.

KALTENBRUNNER

• 19 •

As they got farther along the ever narrowing corridor to Berlin, the skyline on their left was constantly pulsating and glowing with artillery fire, and there were even more dispatch riders speeding to and fro. In the big OKW staff cars the generals looked as gray as their uniforms.

Now many roads were closed to all except military vehicles, and with the many enforced stops and detours that they had to make it was early evening of April 16 before Schöller and Elliott finally reached the outskirts of Berlin.

From a distance the city glowed like an enormous coal fire, with sudden leaps of flame in places, and thick black smoke twisting and curving upward. In the light of the fires, the skyline took on the aspect of an architect's blueprint; domes and towers and roofs were reduced to their skeletal structures. Seen through the prancing flames, the rooftop statuary seemed to be in motion, on the march, led by the equestrian generals, an army of the dead.

As they entered this hellhole, the night cast a dark cloak over the destruction, but it could be smelled. The smell of burning mixed with the fumes of escaping gas to create an indescribable stench.

Tautly alert, Schöller negotiated a precarious course through this maze of ruins. Every few yards there was an impasse of one sort or another, a burst water main, a bomb crater, a collapsed building, a felled telegraph pole, an uprooted tree (still encased in ornamental ironwork). Glass and rubble everywhere. The wind was tearing at the still-standing ruins, ripping out window frames and bringing down roof slates and bricks and masonry, which fell on the car in a continuous hail. An entire building suddenly collapsed before their eyes.

Great baroque façades with stone maidens supporting tall pillars on their heads turned out to be no more solid than a house of cards. Tall modern apartment buildings stood like groups of eyeless giants, their windows dark blanks.

It seemed impossible that anyone could find a way through these ruins. Most of the familiar landmarks and sights had disappeared, leaving a city of dark tunnels without ends. But Schöller, steering by sounds and shadows and looming burnt-out hulks, found a way—between cast-iron columns supporting overhead railways, along unimaginable alleyways, down here and through there, twisting and turning, sometimes sending the car whiningly over mounds of debris. He came out at the bottom of the Kurfürstendamm.

Much of that long broad avenue was on fire, and there were massive gaps on both its sides where there had once been cinemas, theaters, cabarets, restaurants, apartment buildings, dressmaking salons, showrooms, hotels.

At the top the Gedächtniskirche was a truncated tower. Farther on, they heard the bellowings and screechings of the zoo's terrified animals and birds. A horse, its tail and mane ablaze, was charging down the center of the street between the streetcar tracks, making a fearful neighing sound.

In the Tiergarten most of the trees had become charred stumps, and the air was thick with floating ash which fell over everything like a black snow. On the Charlottenburger Chaussee, before the Brandenburg Gate, route of the triumphal march-pasts down the great east-west axis of the city, the ornamental bronze lamp posts had become gibbets from which hung black-faced, swollen-tongued bodies with elongated necks, bearing placards that said, "I am a traitor and deserter" or "I am a coward who wanted to abandon his country."

127

Schöller said nothing. He continued to steer his grim course through the city, noting closed roads and obstructed ways.

Dense smoke was rising from Unter den Linden, and beyond it in the eastern sector long tongues of flame shot up out of the golden domes of palaces, the pillared museums and libraries, and from the cathedral.

On the corner of the Pariser Platz and the Wilhelmstrasse, the Hotel Adlon, though damaged, was standing. Schöller drove past it and down the long street of the Reich Chancellery and the principal ministries. Most of them had now been evacuated after sustaining heavy damage, but here and there faint lights showed around the edges of blackout paper as the last of the officials worked into the night dispensing the rubber stamps of their authority.

Past the huge plain Air Ministry building, standing solid and intact still, Schöller turned right into the Prinz Albrechtstrasse and pulled up by what had formerly been number 8, Gestapo headquarters, but was now like so many other buildings in the street, no more than a baroque façade behind which the five stories of floorless interior were open to the sky.

Schöller had driven the car right to the edge of a deep crater, and now with lunatic proficiency he negotiated its circumference until he came to what seemed like a steep slide into the earth itself, a chute into the dark interior. Down it he drove, holding the car back by the foot brake. That this could lead anywhere seemed highly improbable, but in a moment the headlights revealed a kind of cave entrance held up by iron girders, and just inside there was a gate manned by black-helmeted SS guards with submachine guns.

They opened the gate immediately upon seeing the Reich Special Investigator, and the car went down a constructed ramp that in a series of spirals took them even deeper, until they came to an underground garage. A large number of special police cars and wagons as well as emergency supplies of oil and gas were kept here.

Schöller left his car with one of the mechanics and rapidly made his way across the cracked concrete floor, with its dark oil puddles and shimmering blue gas reflections and dirty rags, to an iron door. At his approach, the door guard rang a bell and a peephole was opened from inside and Schöller's face was scrutinized, after which the sounds of locks and crossbars and bolts were heard and finally the door, hinged to open in an outward direction (so it could not be battered down), opened and Schöller passed through, followed by Elliott, who felt his body heat drawn out of him by the cold damp walls.

Schöller walked fast and purposefully, his shoulder brushing the exposed pipework, his head little more than an inch or two below the tightly bunched courses of new cables and wires. Electric light bulbs in metal shades left a succession of yellow pools on the stone floor.

The entire underground structure vibrated faintly from the movements of unseen machinery; the same stale body odors were continuously being repumped through vents and chutes.

The functionaries who manned key points all seemed to be in a permanent daze and everybody breathed heavily, took pills, and smoked in contravention of the No Smoking signs.

In addition to the regular thump of a power generator and the crackling of an open public address system, there were other, less definable sounds as they got deeper into these subterranean passages. These sounds might have been caused by the rush of air through narrow air shafts or by the sudden rise in water pressure in old lead pipes, or could they have been human? Choked screams like singing pipes?

At central points comprehensive lists of department sections provided some guidance through the maze. Wall plans and arrows and other indicators gave directions, but even the people who worked here day in day out were wandering about looking lost. They took secret swigs from medicine bottles, or unwrapped little pieces of chocolate inside their jackets when they thought nobody was looking.

One of these secret chocolate-eaters was the functionary in charge of the waiting room (or space) out-

129

side a door that said: DETENTION UNDER PROTECTION OF PEOPLE AND STATE ORDINANCE (1933). In a kind of deep niche in the corridor wall something like thirty weary-looking people were sitting squashed together on hard wooden benches. They had bundles of sandwiches with them and had obviously been waiting for hours if not days. A note pinned on the door of the DETENTION OFFICE said: CLOSED UNTIL FURTHER NOTICE, but still these people waited.

As Schöller passed along the passage, several people got up from their seats and rushed after him, before the somewhat stupefied functionary could stop them.

Imploring hands grasped at the Investigator's sleeve, and even at his assistant's.

"Please, sir. Can you do something? It's my son, sir. My boy. He's done nothing. He's innocent, sir. He's a good boy. He's not a defeatist, sir. He always says the Führer is Victory . . . "

"I can do nothing," Schöller said, walking on. By now the functionary had roused himself sufficiently to drag away the importuning petitioners.

On the left, Room 172, was Amt III (Abteilung II/2, Spheres of German Life) but for some reason next to it was Room 86, Amt IV D (Greater German Spheres of Influence), and after that came IV A, Specialist Desks; IV B, Country Desks; IV C, Frontier Police; and then IV A 1, Left and Right Wing Opposition; IV A 2, Anti-Sabotage; IV A 4, Jews and Churches; IV A 5, Special Cases; IV A 6, Protective Custody . . .

Walking past all these offices, they arrived mysteriously at Room 3 (Technical Emergency Organization). The continuous process of amalgamating some departments, expanding or subdividing others, creating new ones, closing old ones down, had played havoc with the intricate numbering and indexing system.

One of the rooms they went by had its door ajar and as they passed, Elliott had a glimpse of a high wooden chair with flat armrests to which were attached broad leather straps with buckle fastenings; similar straps were attached to the high back of the chair and to the legs. On a low table nearby stood an object that resembled a carpentry tool, a sort of horizontal vice, with an adjustable screw.

Seeing the direction of Elliott's look, Schöller said, "We are all rather on top of each other here. Lack of space." Another turning and they found themselves at Room 199. The card in the metal holder on the door said: Amt IV K (Reich Special Investigator).

Schöller opened the door and went into a general outer office where half a dozen people sat at desks, occupied with clerical work.

At once principal assistant Kriminalrat Kummerl got up and shuffled up to them, his face a picture of catastrophe.

"I congratulate the Reichskriminaldirektor on his safe arrival," Kummerl said, his eyes expressing a mixture of astonishment and dismay at this miracle. "SS-Reichsführer Himmler has been in constant communication and asks that you attend upon him immediately at his field headquarters for consultations of the most urgent nature."

The effort of saying all this had left Kummerl quite breathless.

"Don't fuss so much, Kummerl," Schöller said. "I cannot receive Reichsführer Himmler's orders if I have not yet arrived, can I?"

"Absolutely not," Kummerl agreed dully.

He had once been famous as a seducer of women, a man of considerable charm and social aplomb, whose appeal lay in a combination of high polish and power. As the Reich Special Investigator's principal assistant he had been someone to fear and cultivate. The highest in the land were anxious to know him and to entertain him in their houses. It suited Schöller that his assistant should aspire to such connections, it made the assistant dependent on the Investigator's favors. But now the power and influence that had gained him such special treatment just placed him higher up on the War Crimes list.

He looked a wreck. He, whose cheeks had glowed with scented astringents, now was gray-faced, his sculpted neck and jowl marred by shaving cuts, the bleeding from which was stopped by little scraps of toilet paper.

His eyes were sunken and the eyelids thick and red. And worst of all, he smelled. A rank odor of bad teeth and bad bowels clung to him. Only the splendid blond head of hair had remained impervious to the general deterioration. From a distance he could still have been taken for one of the *Herrenvolk*, which made the ruined features, when seen, more of a shock.

"Pull yourself together, Kummerl," Schöller told him. "All you can lose is your life, and how much is that worth?"

"Nothing, Reichskriminaldirektor."

"Exactly."

Digging into the sagging pockets of his jacket, Schöller pulled out a ring of heavy keys, selected one, unlocked his private office, and went in. Elliott and Kummerl followed.

"You know Haften," Schöller said, indicating Elliott.

"I do not believe so," Kummerl said, his eyes vacant.

"Political department, Italy," Schöller said.

"Ah yes, ah yes. Honored, I'm sure . . . "

It was cold in the inner office and Schöller kept his coat on. Shivering, Kummerl inquired, "Shall I have the paraffin stove lit, Reichskriminaldirektor?"

"Later. Later. And stop shivering, man."

"Yes, Direktor." He at once stopped, as ordered.

Schöller held out his hand for the MOST URGENT folder. The first three sheets were teletypes from Himmler demanding Schöller's immediate attendance upon him; the fourth was a record of a telephone conversation with the aide Grothman to the same effect. The fifth sheet was a message from the secretary, Brandt, saying that General Wolff had now arrived at field headquarters and was holding himself in readiness for questioning.

Schöller flicked quickly through these sheets. He glanced disinterestedly at the summaries of various investigations that were in hand, and then turned to the list of Arrivals. He made a disbelieving expression and then frowned when he saw the name of Dr. Behr

132

of the Commercial Bank of Berne. Booked in at the Hotel Adlon. Due April 16.

"Dr. Behr," Schöller said.

"My apologies, Direktor, I do not know Dr. Behr."

"The Swiss. The Swiss banker . . . so-called. . . ."

"Ah. In this respect, I am, with regret, uninformed, Direktor."

"What would a Swiss banker be doing in Berlin? *At this time.*" He shook his head. "No good, you can be sure. No good. Upon arrival he is to be placed under round-the-clock surveillance. Reports to me every half-hour. Transcripts of all phone calls. If he attempts to contact anyone . . . I want to know whom. Such contacts to be prevented from taking place by any means, pending my orders to the contrary."

"Certainly, Direktor. At your command, Direktor."

When the principal assistant had left, Schöller went straight to a large, free-standing, heavily armored safe, and again taking out the huge bunch of keys he carried everywhere with him (this was why all his pockets sagged so badly), selected one and inserted it in the keyhole. There were three definite smooth unlocking sounds. He dialed the combination number and opened the safe with a half-turn of a wheel at the front. He pulled back the heavy door and reaching inside took out first a bottle of French cognac and glasses and then a worn leather-bound volume, devoid of any print on spine or covers. He closed the safe again, put the black book in his pocket, and filled two glasses with cognac.

"Drink up," he ordered Elliott, setting the example by knocking back his cognac in two rapid swallows, after which, rattling his keys again, he selected a long iron one and with it unlocked a bulkhead in the floor. He put on a light switch and began to climb down the iron ladder that led into an even deeper underground chamber.

Elliott said, "You were to give me von Thedieck's confession to destroy, together with all copies."

"It is not here," Schöller said from the ladder. "It

133

is in Rudolphstein, where von Thedieck was arrested and interrogated."

"I was not told that."

"It is not important."

"On the contrary . . . "

"Nobody will remove it from my safe, without my authorization."

"We will have to get it later."

"As you wish." He added, "It would be easier if you trusted me. It would save time. For the moment nothing can be done about the confession, so we better get on with what we can do. . . . The files *are* here. You can check them."

· 20 ·

Elliott followed Schöller into a low-roofed tunnel. The walls and ground glistened. The exposed pipes were heavily encrusted with rust.

Its rounded shape gave this place the appearance of a disused culvert. With another key, Schöller now opened a wooden box mounted on the wall, and inside turned off a number of Bakelite switches. He made sure that the red warning light was off, which meant that the explosive charges would not be automatically detonated when the first filing cabinet was opened. He handed Elliott the index.

"This is the key to the whole system. It gives the names, with the numbers under which they are filed. Without the index, there is no way of finding a particular file. *With* the index, it is simple. . . . Now I will let you carry out whatever checks you wish to make. You see, I leave you free. I hide nothing from you."

"OK, Schöller."

Left alone in this damp cold hole, Elliott began at random pulling out filing cabinet drawers and running his fingers over the densely packed folders. So much moldering paper. All the dirt, carefully filed away, set out in pompous police officialese, on thousands and thousands of sheets of yellowing paper.

Where to start? Into whose life to look first? Hitler's? Göring's? Whose guilty secrets should he lay bare at the pull of a drawer. He felt rather powerful, having all this dirt at his fingertips, the accumulation of years and years of laborious ferreting and filing. *OK, let's start with the Reich Special Investigator. Let's start with you, Schöller. The real lowdown.* He ran his finger down the thumb index to the letter S, found Schöller's name and his file number. In a minute he had out his file. First a card giving basic details:

Schöller, Ernst
born 21.1.1900; Criminal Police Inspector, Munich Police, 1924;
Section Chief Kriminalpolizeihauptamt, Berlin, 1933 (Special Duties); Head of Special Investigations, Kripo, 1934;
Reichskriminaldirektor and Generalleutnant der Polizei, 1937;
Reich Special Investigator and Chief of Amt IV K RSHA 1939—

This card was attached with a rusty paper clip to a sheaf of typewritten notes.

Elliott began reading the first sheet.

"1933. HQ of Munich/Upper Bavarian Nazi Party. Schöller not Nazi Party material though a 'Most violent opponent of Communism, who at times will disregard legal rules and regulations.' This attributed to personal ambition rather than identification with Party aims. Political assessment is that Schöller would act with equal ruthlessness against right wing, if it served his personal ambitions. It is noted that Schöller's contributions to Nazi Party funds are derisory. (Contribution for Eintopfspende 40 pfennig!) A regular churchgoer! Member of the Bavarian People's Party. Pre-1933 showed himself a vigilant persecutor of National-Socialists in order to curry favor with his superiors.

"In this action supported by his close colleagues Senior Inspector Fritz Kamitz, and criminal police Inspectors Johan Gustav Waldbrunner, Heinrich Müller, Karl Peter Kremer."

Elliott leafed through the sheets, scanning the pages rapidly. Much of the material was of this nature. A chronicle of minor misdemeanors and vague suspicions. Failure to lend his presence to Party functions in support of this or that. Accusations that he had insulted high Party functionaries. Allegations that he had used his official position to seduce young girls, or to obtain financial benefits for himself. All rather vague and unsubstantiated.

Some pages further on, Elliott came to a note, which was headed: "SUMMARY OF AMT IV INVESTIGATION OF REICHSKRIMINALDIREKTOR SCHÖLLER. Dated 2.5.1937." So this was Müller of the Gestapo investigating his colleague Schöller of the Kriminalpolizei.

The summary began: "Our inquiries reveal that Reichskriminaldirektor Schöller has engaged in a persistent and calculated campaign of publicly and privately defaming his colleagues of the Gestapo and misrepresenting their activities. In this connection he has been supported by Chief of the Kriminalpolizei Nebe, and the possibility of a police clique conspiring against the supreme authority of SS-Reichsführer Himmler requires investigation.

"Calculated lies by Schöller and Nebe that the Gestapo uses its power under the February 28 1933 Protection of People and State Ordinance in an unlawful manner are inappropriate coming from the criminal section, which exercises identical powers on much larger scale, including arrest on suspicion, house searches without warrant, listening-in on telephone conversations, and the opening of letters in the public mails. More specifically, Kriminalpolizei Chiefs Nebe and Schöller have blatantly used the February 23 1937 Order of the Chef der Deutschen Polizei for the Preventive Detention of Anti-Social Malefactors and Habitual Offenders Against Morality in order to unlawfully detain 28 valued agents and helpers of the

Gestapo. Full list attached, and immediate release of those named herewith demanded."

As he dug further into the file, he found that these animosities had developed out of initial friendship. There were frequent references between 1933 and 1937 to the quartet of Munich police inspectors, Heinrich Müller, Johan Gustav Waldbrunner, Fritz Kamitz, and Ernst Schöller. From the way their names were constantly linked, it seemed they had been pals in the Munich days and had maintained their links as they rose within the Nazi police echelon. Until around 1937, which was when the breach had evidently occurred.

The file contained some mildly disreputable details about Schöller's rumored associations with various women and there were a few vague charges of accepting bribes, but on the whole the dirt on Schöller did not amount to much.

Elliott put away the file, and by way of comparison got out Arthur Nebe's.

This, too, referred to his early career as a Munich police inspector, though it did not link him directly with "the quartet." Some years older than Müller and Schöller and the other two, he had probably been in a superior position to them and therefore not one of their intimates.

The material on Nebe was interesting to Elliott mainly because of how much more damaging it was than anything he had found on Schöller. Nebe had been executed only a few weeks earlier for his part in the July 20 plot on Hitler's life, so it was hardly surprising to find in his file the details of his associations with suspect men like SS-General Count Heinrich Wolf von Helldorf, Police President of Berlin, and with the anti-Hitler plotters Gisevius and Olbricht. But there was also a mass of highly incriminating material on Nebe as Commander of Einsatzgruppe B in Russia in 1941. Enough to have got him hanged by the Allies had the Nazis not already done the job.

Elliott was beginning to see that the work of the secret police was like the slow spinning of an invisible web. At the beginning, the subject under close observation was not aware of it—had no reason to be—

but all the time his remarks, his habits, his associations, no matter how innocent, were being noted down and filed away. And then one day this person woke up to discover that he was bound by the strands of the invisible web, and no longer a free agent.

In building up a dossier that would finally be capable of destroying a man, if the need arose, the strongest single factor that could be used against anyone was suspicion of Jewish blood, though homosexuality and other sexual misdemeanors were also powerful dirt. Elliott found a packet of photographs showing Goebbels in indecent postures with various film actresses. Other prominent Nazis were photographed in homosexual acts. Globocnik, SS and police chief of Lublin concentration camp, was charged with putting money in his own pocket after an audit of the camp's accounts had shown up missing funds. The dossier on Göring set out his many secret business connections, and the payoffs he received, amounting to millions of marks a year.

But the worst offense remained Jewish blood. Himmler himself had a suspect cousin named Heymann. He was said to be "an obvious Jew," whose family had enjoyed the SS-Reichsführer's protection for many years until he finally consigned them to a concentration camp too. In Halle lived a man named Heydrich, considered by the Gauleiter a possible Jew, and the possible father of the then Gestapo Chief Heydrich. So it was whispered in Halle. Alfred Rosenberg had a Jewish mistress. His love letters to her were filed as evidence. And then there was the matter of Hitler's grandmother, Matild Schickelgrueber. She had been an unmarried servant girl at the Palais Rothschild in Vienna at the time she became pregnant, which suggested the quite unspeakable possibility that Hitler himself . . .

Much of the "evidence" in these files was of this order. But it was all painstakingly collected and filed. Rumors. Gossip. Anonymous denunciations. Information derived from undisclosed sources. Speculation. Conjecture. Suspicion. It all added up, and finally suspicion and guilt became one and the same thing.

Elliott slammed back a filing cabinet drawer. The old metal rollers made a grating sound which echoed through the low culvert. He felt totally spent, worn out by the journey and these delvings.

One final check. Individuals marked down as covert Gestapo agents. He picked out six names so marked from the index and looked them up in the files. It checked out. The men concerned held positions and jobs unconnected with any of the security services, but were sending in regular reports on their colleagues and superiors.

OK, Elliott decided, *that's it. I've had enough.* He had a filthy taste in his mouth, he was cold, his head was spinning, and he was very very tired.

Heavily, he climbed back up the ladder.

• 21 •

"Well, are you satisfied? You have been down there long enough. By now you must know the dirt on all the big shots," Schöller said.

Seeing how Elliott was shivering, he poured out a cognac and pushed it toward him.

"Drink up," he commanded. "Warm yourself at the stove. It's cold down there—hmm? You are too conscientious. What were you looking for all that time?"

Elliott drank the brandy and warmed his hands over the paraffin stove, and when his teeth stopped chattering, he said, "Your own file is very sparse."

"Naturally," Schöller said with his massive shrug.

"What is it you don't want us to know?"

Anger showed in Schöller's face. "The arrangement was that you check the authenticity of the files, assess their potential value—and agree where they are to be hidden. Not to check up on me. . . . "

"I did that on my own account."

"It is not part of the arrangement."

"You keep saying you're in the clear. If that's true, why take stuff out of your file?"

"You don't understand." He was becoming exasperated by the young man's wholly inappropriate delving into matters of no relevance in the present situation. Trying to control himself, he said, "You have to know how to read a file. You must know how to assess the material. . . . No point putting unnecessary things in your mind."

"What things, Schöller?"

"You must understand," Schöller said, his patience sorely tried, "they—the chiefs—they do not feel safe unless they have got something on you, so one allows certain material to go into the files for their benefit. To make them feel safer. A man entirely in the clear would get nowhere. There must be something to be held against him, a Jewish cousin, a taste for young boys, some fraudulence in his character. Some dark deed in his past. Something that will bring him down, if it should be necessary."

"Are you saying that you planted false evidence against yourself?"

"It is better than giving them the real thing. No? Like that, you give them their feeling of security, and if they try to use this dirt—well, it is usually easier to disprove *false* evidence."

"You know your trade," Elliott said.

"Naturally," Schöller said, taking the remark as a compliment.

"Still," Elliott said, "took you a long time to get onto Nebe. Eight months after all the other conspirators had been executed?"

"Arthur Nebe was a friend from Munich days."

"You had the evidence, and you did nothing . . . is that what you're saying?"

"Evidence is a matter of interpretation. Who a man sees, when, how often. It has to be looked at in the light of given circumstances. . . . "

"You were awaiting the outcome, before deciding which side of the fence to come down on."

Schöller shrugged. "A secret policeman has got to sit on all sides of the fence at once," he said.

"In the end, Nebe got his too. Friend or no friend."

"I had no choice in the end," Schöller said. "Müller also had the evidence by then. I therefore had to make mine available first, to clear my own position."

"One way or another you are pretty damn good at putting yourself in the clear."

"Like you have said, I know my trade. And now . . . there are things I must do. I think you should stay in this office. If you go out of here, you may start asking questions. And we can't afford that."

When Schöller had gone, Elliott looked around the room. A desk. With three telephones. A few chairs. A large padlocked cupboard, made of steel. On the walls, various charts and maps, and a notice board covered with orders, directives, instructions.

He walked slowly to the desk. Every inch of space was taken up by papers and files. At the top, looking incongruous here in this bare cellar, a huge marble inkstand. Next to that, rubber stamps, suspended from rotatable circular holders. Elliott removed one and, inking it, made its impression on a sheet of plain white paper. The symbols of authority and terror of the Third Reich appeared in black. *Reichssicherheitshauptamt.* Office of *Reich Special Investigator.* The words were embellished with the ubiquitous Nazi eagle, bearing a wreathed swastika in its claws.

Elliott looked at some of the papers on the desk. Lists. Lists of people to be placed under surveillance. Lists of people to be held in protective custody. Under house arrest. Lists of those whose travel authorization was to be revoked. Lists of others whose authority was rescinded. . . . All these lists.

He lit a cigarette. He felt very tired. His head was beginning to swim. His chest moved as laboriously as a hand pump. He looked at the nearest wall and saw a large-scale map of the city, marked with different colors to indicate buildings and areas destroyed, roads blocked, routes that no longer led anywhere. His eye followed the yellow lines of open routes winding tortuously through the destruction. These slender threads were his only exits.

Schöller returned briskly. "We must go," he said. "You will spend the night at my home. It will be the safest place for you."

He went to one of the telephones, picked up the receiver, and pressed a button. A light came on in its base, and Schöller said, "Give me the night duty officer." When he was through to him, he said, "Schöller speaking. Let me have the picture."

He held the phone between his chin and shoulders while making various new markings on the wall map. "And the estimated time of arrival over Berlin? The projected flight path?"

He mumbled acknowledgement as he received the answers to these questions. Then he replaced the receiver and studied the wall map, making calculations.

"Come." He acted fast now, closing up his office and marching Elliott out through the twisting corridors to the underground car compound. This time he selected a police squad car.

With its big supercharged engine it took the steeply winding ramp and the makeshift road out of the crater with ease. Emerging in this way out of the earth, they found the city eerily still, despite the many fires, as if it were uninhabited.

Following the route he had worked out in his office, and checking with the latest information coming over on shortwave transmissions, in code, on radio Mio, Schöller made his roundabout way out of the center of the city.

Once when the car engine stalled, the city was so quiet that you could almost hear its fearful breathing in the dark. Only the occasional swishing sounds of bicycle tires or hurrying footsteps indicated that there were still some people about, making their way to one of the underground stations or a community air raid shelter.

From time to time Elliott glimpsed some outline that restored, briefly, his sense of orientation. After leaving the Prinz Albrechtstrasse they had made a number of convoluted detours to get around the almost totally destroyed area of the Potsdamer Platz, had entered the Tiergarten, crossed the east-west axis of the Charlottenburger Chaussee, and then driven for a time along the banks of the Landwehr Canal before turning left and wending their way down through the district of Charlottenburg to cut across the Kurfürsten-damm at its lower end, where it ran into the Grune-wald. They had just reached the comparative safety of Berlin's green fringe when the second air raid alert of the night sounded and the sky at once became a crisscross pattern of searchlights with little puffs of flak caught in their beams. The radio transmitter giving the minute-by-minute flight path of the bombers con-firmed Schöller's original calculation.

"We shall be all right where we are going," he pre-dicted. "They are going for the center again."

The drive through the outer parts of Dahlem, skirt-ing the Grunewald, was much faster, there being less major damage here. They began to pass pleasant de-tached villas with gardens, clustered around the little boating lakes at the edge of the woods. Grunewald See. Schlachten See. Nikolas See. And then at the point where the Havel widened and split came Wann-see, with its Strandbad and its beach, a place, at one time, for Sunday outings. Here the nabobs of the Third Reich had built themselves summer houses with balus-traded roof terraces and parapets lined with neoclassical statuary. Stone lions guarded the great iron entrance gates. There were riding stables and boat houses within their grounds. Most of these places now were pad-locked and boarded up, and some doors in addition were sealed with red sealing wax, a notice of seizure attached by the Gestapo, or Ministry of the Interior, or whatever other body the former high-up householder had fallen afoul of.

The big houses occupied the best positions close to the river, but behind this front there were more modest establishments, pleasant suburban villas, with little gardens, a few trees, some shrubs, and flower beds. Outside one such place, with iron handwriting spelling out number One Hundred, Schöller pulled up. It was a snug low pink place, of modern construction, with a blue front door approached by a short crazy-paved path, a patch of lawn on either side of it. Two dark figures in slouch hats and long double-breasted overcoats sat on a cast-iron garden bench amid the blooming forsythia. They rose as the car stopped, picking up their submachine guns, but relaxed when they saw who it was.

"We are here," Schöller announced. He nodded curtly to the bodyguards, who withdrew again into the foliage. Quickly Schöller strode up to his front door and unlocked it with another key from his huge key chain. The corridor was narrow and dark. With routine caution Schöller did not switch on any lights but called softly, "Lo-li-lo, Lo-li-lo," in an intimate singsong, grinning a little sheepishly at using such a private pet name before a stranger. It crossed Elliott's mind, however, that the endearment was not without practical value: a kind of code word. Someone lying in wait for the Reich Special Investigator would not know the correct answer to the call of "Lo-li-lo, Lo-li-lo." Only when he heard his wife's unmistakable reply—"Ernst? Ernst, is it you?"—did Schöller switch on the light.

The middle-aged woman who emerged from the kitchen was long and thin and bosomless with mannishly cut short hair, wearing a long embroidered skirt and a white blouse with a cravat. She peered along the corridor with a nervous frown.

"We have a visitor, Lilli," Schöller told her. "My political assistant, Italy, Haften. You've heard me talk of him."

"No."

"You have forgotten."

There was a thump, followed by a patter of feet, and a slight wan dark-eyed child of about six, in pajamas, appeared from behind the woman and rushed down the corridor calling "Papa, Papa, Papa." Schöller hugged and kissed the little boy, holding the soft-cheeked child against the coarse stubble of his beard.

"Oh, this is my best moment, Papa." The child's chest was heaving with excitement, his eyes were wild, and he started to cough. Air whistled down his trachea

144

in desperate gasping inspirations and then stayed locked up in his tight lungs, to be exhaled only by means of choking convulsive effort. His face had gone purple, his lips struggled for speech.

Schöller did something quick and exact, holding the child's head and back at a fixed angle, at the same time saying firmly, "It's all right. It's all right. Calm yourself. Breathe naturally—easily." To his wife he said, "Open the windows and bring the inhaler." With the gust of night air, the child's breathing became immediately less violent, the heaving of his chest reduced to a slower rhythm, and when the inhaler was placed under his nose, the seizure began to subside, the struggle for air lost its raucous desperation; the child became calmer.

When he could speak again, he said, "I'm sorry, Papa," and Schöller said, "It's not your fault. You're a good boy, I know."

"He's asthmatic," Schöller said to Elliott. "All right for long periods, and then something . . . something brings it on again."

The child was white and drawn and his eyes were full of dark guilt about his choking illness.

"What have you got for me, Papa?" he asked.

"I haven't brought you anything," Schöller said, clearly somewhat abashed to have arrived empty-handed. "I didn't have time."

Almost hesitantly, he asked, "Can you make us some scrambled eggs for now, you think, Lilli? We are both tired out from traveling and we haven't eaten a thing."

"The egg powder is finished," she said.

"The sardines? There is some bread?"

"Yes."

"Bread and sardines will be all right for you, Haften?"

"Yes."

"It is fine, Lilli. Make us a little rice, too, with some cheese. You have some cheese? I'm starving, Lilli. We haven't eaten all day."

"I'll go and do it," she said, sullenly.

"It is good of you," he said.

145

They all moved along the corridor, into the kitchen. The fluted glass doors to the dining room were open. The woman, given her task, began to move about preparing the meal. From somewhere about her scant person she produced a half-smoked cigarette, lit it carefully, and with the smoke curling up into her watering eyes, began to wind back the top of the sardine tin with a slotted key.

"We will get out of your way," Schöller offered vaguely.

"Yes," she said, "yes. Sit inside with your assistant, and let me get on." She was bent and busy. Schöller grinned and gave her a peck on a smoky cheek, at the same time bestowing an intimate husbandly squeeze to her behind, which she chose to ignore completely.

"We must not disturb her when she is cooking," Schöller said. "You know how women are about that." And he led Elliott into the dining room and sat him down at a round table covered by an embroidered and tasseled tablespread that reached down to the ground. A green silk-fringed lamp of adjustable length hung low over the table, the light from a solitary bulb— the other six were dead—casting a gloomy circle over the child, who sat up tense-faced and straightbacked as if being taught his table manners.

A paternal frown spread across Schöller's face at the sight of the child's paleness and dark-ringed eyes.

"You don't get enough sleep," he said rebukingly. "And you need fresh air. When was the last time you were out? Days, I bet you. When was the last time she took you out, Mutti, hmm? When? Well? Answer me."

The child said nothing.

"Was it today? Yesterday? When, in that case? When was the last time you breathed some air into your lungs? Hmm?"

Still the child did not answer; his eyes had grown large and afraid.

"You are afraid to answer me?" Schöller said, becoming impatient. "A simple question. You don't want to tell me the truth? What are you hiding from me?"

A note of suspiciousness had entered Schöller's voice.

"When you go out with your mother, where do you go?"

"We don't go out, Papa," he said. "We don't go out. Ever."

"Is that true?"

"Yes, Papa. It's the truth. It *is* the truth. Mutti says it is too dangerous to go out."

"Doesn't she go out?"

"To do the shopping, yes."

"How long does it take her to do the shopping?"

"I don't know, Papa."

"Well, think what you do while she is away. . . . "

"I play, while Frau Schmidt is cleaning."

"What do you play?"

"I play policemen, Papa."

"How do you play policemen?"

"I arrest people. And I line them up against a wall and I shoot them. . . . " He mimed the shooting.

"If they have done something wrong . . . "

"Only if they have done something wrong, of course. If they are Jews or criminal characters or cowardly defeatists. . . . "

"You should find some other game to play."

"But I like it."

"You should play something else. You should play something that will improve your mind. Something educational."

The child stood rebuked, head hanging, silent.

"Why don't you say something?"

"I don't know, Papa."

"Playing at policemen . . . what sort of a thing is that to do with your time?"

"You're a policeman."

"You know you have to pass exams to be a proper policeman. You have to know things. It takes a lot of learning. It was a good position to have, when I became a policeman. You had a smart uniform, and you were regarded as somebody. Not just anybody could become a policeman, you know. You had to be strong, and truthful. Policemen mustn't tell lies, you

147

know. So don't let me catch you telling any more lies about going out or not going out."

"Mutti told me not to say . . . " He stopped, biting his tongue at having been trapped into this indiscretion.

"Not to say what?"

"Nothing. Nothing."

"You think I don't know. *Papas know everything.* Do you know that?"

"Yes, Papa."

"Go on, go to bed." He pulled the child close to him and hugged him strongly. "You're a good boy," he said. "It's for your own good that I get the truth out of you. . . . "

"Yes, Papa."

"Go on then. Off with you. Sleep well, my son." He ran his hands through the child's hair and kissed him strongly, gave him a playful smack, and sent him scampering off to his bed. Turning to Elliott, he added, "As far as one knows, hmm? What man can say for certain he is the father of his own child? What man can be so sure?"

Schöller stood up, and breathing deeply with tiredness, went to the sideboard and got out a bottle of French cognac and two glasses. He filled both, with a somewhat unsteady hand, spilling some of the alcohol, and then slumped down in his chair again, the joints of which creaked and moved upon receiving his formidable weight. Schöller swallowed the first glass of cognac with a couple of quick backward head movements, emitted a long *aahhhh* of satisfaction, and at once refilled his glass. He rubbed his eyes through his lowered lids.

"Life is not easy," he confided. "But what can you do? Who can you complain to?" His chest was rising and falling steadily. His eyes closed. He remained in this posture for two or three minutes, sitting-up half asleep.

Elliott looked around the little dining room. On the shiny light-wood sideboard, serpentine-fronted, there was a wedding picture of the Schöllers. Ten years ago she had been a beauty, with a thin dark elegance, eyebrows plucked down to delicate arches, hair lying in a formal kiss curl on the white forehead. Her lips were strongly outlined by lipstick, her fine hands displayed for the camera around a posy of flowers that she held severely to her breast. Her hair, as now, was parted on the right and cut short, almost as short as a man's, which emphasized the length of her neck and the long narrow slightly concave body with its flat chest and straight hips. Her expression was curiously suspicious, considering the occasion. What was most noticeable about the bridegroom was his evident discomfort in the tightly buttoned suit that pinched him under the arms, either because of the thickness of his chest or the contents of his breast pocket. Could he have been carrying a gun at his wedding? Ever careful not to be taken unawares? Was that why he bulged out there by the armpit? There was a certain provincial awkwardness about him as he stood bulkily next to the bride, undisguisable pride of ownership in his eyes. His hair was thicker then, combed in a wave at the front and cut razor-sharp around the large ears.

Of the other framed photographs on the sideboard, one was recognizably of Schöller's parents. The father was a big heavy man with a bald skull, in a checked suit and wing collar, patterned tie with tie pin, and open jacket which displayed the gold watch chain and fob across the stomach. He wore eyeglasses with thick dark rims and sat with legs somewhat apart, trousers creased. The mother had straggly gray hair, a thin face, thickly veined hands, and a high dark dress buttoned up to the neck and reaching to her ankles. They sat close together on a cane settee in the porch of a Bavarian farmhouse.

Schöller's eyes opened abruptly as he came out of his doze.

"You are interested in my family?"

"Farmers?" Elliott asked.

Schöller nodded minimally.

"Your wife . . . she comes from quite a different background, I would guess."

"You guess good," Schöller told him, but offered no more information. "Better stretch out five minutes on the bed," he said. "I'm suddenly dog tired. You too?"

Elliott nodded.

"Come, then."

In the bedroom there was a dressing table made entirely of mirror glass. Twin beds whose bedspreads were embroidered with golden sun rays. A lacquered wood wardrobe. Schöller threw himself down on one bed, not bothering to remove his boots. In a moment he was asleep.

Elliott stared at the thickly flowered wallpaper, the toiletries in their elaborate glass bottles; and breathed in the secret smell of somebody else's bedroom. A green onyx clock showed half past eleven. The fragrance of a woman's face powder hung in the air.

Suddenly restless, Elliott sprang up from the bed and returned to the dining. room. The door to the kitchen was closed, the woman occupied at the cooking stove.

On the sideboard there was a framed photograph he had not noticed before. A group of five grinning men, with arms linked, standing outside what he recognized as the Munich Police Praesidium. They all looked very young, Schöller couldn't have been more than twenty-two or twenty-three then, a big-eared lad with a large bony face, not yet filled out. They all looked in high good spirits, for some undisclosed reason. Had they all been promoted? Was that the occasion for the celebratory photograph? Like a school graduation picture. Each of the policemen had signed his name. Elliott made out three signatures—Heini Müller, Fritz Kamitz, and Ernst Schöller. The others were just scrawls. This must have been 1922–1924, judging from the clothes styles and their youthful looks.

In the kitchen Frau Schöller had finished cooking the rice. The door opened and she brought in the steaming casserole dish and plates. She called out, "Ernst, Ernst, food is on the table. . . . "

Somewhat refreshed by his fifteen-minute snooze, Schöller came out of the bedroom stretching and yawning. He was in trousers and suspenders and had removed his collar. He inhaled the aroma of cooked

150

rice and as soon as he sat down began to heap his plate. He took a large piece of cheese from the plate and cut chunks of it into the rice. The sardine tin, its top wound three-quarters back, had been put on a saucer. Schöller extracted a silvery fish and placed it on top of the rice and cheese. He poured oil from the sardine tin all over his food and began to eat hungrily.

Sweat appeared in droplets on his forehead and skull where the hair had begun to thin, and lay in the creases of the neck, which was like the thick frayed rope used for tying up ships. The large neck artery filled out with the pressure of his rising blood. Cut through it, Elliott considered, and the Investigator would spout like a fountain.

"Frau Schöller," Elliott inquired politely as he helped himself to rice, "you are from Berlin?"

"No. From Munich," she told him, rejecting the opportunity of enlarging the conversation.

"From Munich," Schöller agreed, with mouth full. "Like me. But what a difference. Hmm? Me, I came from the bottom, out of the dirt. She came from the top. You should have seen her apartment. Sideboards with ivory handles. White carpets on the floor. Her clothes. Pure silk underwear. On the walls she had modern paintings. You couldn't tell whether it was meant to be a human being or a dog's dinner. That was the fashion then. Before the Austrian house-painter had it all condemned. . . . "

She gave him a sharp cautioning look for allowing himself such indiscretions in front of a subordinate. "It's all right," he assured her. "Haften is very close to me. I have no secrets from him—eh, Haften? He knows enough about me to have me hanged ten times over. Mind you, what I know about him could have him shot twenty times." He chuckled. "My wife is a very careful woman," he explained. "Always was. Thinks twice, even three times, about everything. Me, I'm the opposite. I know immediately. I can decide without thinking. I knew the moment I saw her— that's for me."

151

"Is that supposed to be flattering to me?" she said sarcastically.

"A manner of speaking," he said. Eating all the time he was talking, he continued, "She wouldn't look at me, I can tell you. I came once to her house. There had been a robbery. Some jewels stolen. She treated me like all those sort of women treat a policeman, like her servant. I wanted her though. She was so . . . finely made. Very fine. I said to myself, she won't have such a superior look on her face one day. I made a vow to myself."

"You forced your way in. Again and again, with tricks," she reminded him.

He chuckled and gave his wife's face an affectionate pat, his eyes warmed with recollections of his trickery in the cause of love. "I used to come to tell her what progress we were making, finding her jewels. She didn't even let me in. Stood at the door talking to me. To get rid of me quick. Had to return to her dinner guests, you see. Or perhaps her lover. I could imagine. I could imagine. I wasn't on her level, you see, Haften. One day I came to her door, and I said, 'I have some good news for you, Madame, I found your jewels.' She was astonished. 'After all this time?' she said. This was '33 now. She was really thrilled to get them back, they had sentimental value for her . . . love gifts, you see."

"You stole them yourself," she accused, "to get to me. . . . "

"I told her that once for a joke, and now she believes it."

"It's the sort of thing you would do."

"Anyway," he said, "she offered me a reward. For finding her jewels. If that was allowed. Yes, I told her, but she might not want to give me the only reward I was interested in. What was that, she asked, what reward did I want? A kiss, I said. She laughed, and offered me her mouth. You know, like a forfeit. . . . Lovely. After that it was plain sailing, once you're in, you're in. Eh, Haften?"

"The methods of the secret police," she said.

She had hurt his male vanity with that remark; in

a moment the sentimental good humor was wiped from his face and replaced with a flash of pure murderous hatred.

"A man uses what weapon he has," Schöller said.

"You think everything is weapons."

"You forget. You did not look at me before."

In the silence that followed, a whole succession of charges and countercharges passed mutely between them. Schöller was first to extract himself from the entanglement with past things. He smiled. "But Haften does not want to hear our matrimonial quarrels," he said to his wife.

"Since you feel free to talk about our private life in front of . . . " she began.

"It is not for you to tell me what I may or may not say," he said to her, angrily. "You forget . . . I am not nobody now."

She laughed contemptuously at his high office.

"You know what I think of that. You want me to say it? In front of him?"

"You will behave as I tell you to, Lilli."

"You think you can frighten me, like you frighten everybody else. Once, yes. Perhaps. But it is a long time since I was frightened of you, Ernst."

"There was a time when you preened yourself on being the wife of a Reichskriminaldirektor."

"Before I knew what your work was."

"What did you think was my work? Helping old ladies across the road? You asked me for plenty of favors. For your lovers. You think I didn't know they were your lovers?"

"If you thought that, why did you grant them?"

"I liked to give you things," he said simply. "I was a big fool."

"Love gifts?" she said mockingly.

With an effort he controlled his temper, knowing how she would go on and on with her sharp-tongued taunts until she caused him to explode. That was her victory, to make him lose control of himself. But he was not going to let it happen tonight. He had a knack of disengaging himself from situations. His face became resigned with a man's knowledge of women.

"You see, Haften, how it is. Wives. Always complaining about something. Eh? Eh? Now it's enough, Lilli. I want to go to bed."

She started automatically to clear the plates. He said, "Leave that. I have important matters to discuss with you."

"I cannot leave dirty plates," she said and continued to clear.

Schöller raised an eyebrow in an expression of helplessness and turned to Elliott.

"Help me open the settee."

When she had swept up the last crumb from under the table, and pushed in its extending flaps, Frau Schöller brought out fresh sheets and pillowcases and placed them on the converted settee.

"We have to leave a light on in the corridor. For the child," she told Elliott. "He is frightened of the dark. We leave our bedroom door open slightly . . . so we can hear, in case he has a seizure in the night." Elliott nodded. "Good night, Herr Haften."

Elliott knew he was not going to be able to sleep, despite his great tiredness, which had become a spreading numbness behind the eyes. He began to walk up and down in the little dining room. The silver-framed photographs on the sideboard kept drawing his attention. The wedding picture. The parents. The grinning Munich detectives. He studied their faces, looking for some indication of what these men were to become. But all he could see was five young men, in high good spirits.

The drone of the returning British bombers had been followed by the all clear, and as that came to an end, a profound suburban stillness settled over the little villa. Elliott discovered that he could hear bits of what was being said in the bedroom.

"Don't argue with me, Lilli. Do you know what people pay for such papers?"

"I don't want to spend the rest of my life hunted from one place to the next."

"In Bregenz you will be in the American zone. You and the child will be safe . . . "

Elliott slept intermittently, waking up with a succession of night starts every half-hour or so. The last time he woke in this way, he found himself looking into Schöller's face.

"We must leave," he said.

"It's still night."

"It is necessary that I come and go at different times in my position."

As Elliott dressed, Schöller sat very still in the dark room, a little way back from the open window, observing the houses opposite. He knew where his own men were and could place each one from small movements and sounds. It was his custom, before leaving any place, to spend some minutes watching for the glow of a cigarette or a sudden movement, listening for the clearing of a throat or the stamping of cold feet, anything that might indicate the presence of somebody not supposed to be there. Next he checked the small Mauser pocket pistol and slipped it in his overcoat pocket.

Elliott was ready. Making a sign to him to go ahead, Schöller stopped at the door of his son's room and for a moment or so looked tenderly at the sleeping child.

Out in the street Schöller walked rapidly to the police car, and releasing the handbrake pushed the car a short distance with its lights off. When the car was rolling, he jumped in and gestured for Elliott to follow suit. The engine was then switched on, but not the lights. Only when the car was traveling at some speed did he put on the dimmed headlights.

As they approached the center of the city, people were beginning to emerge out of the dust and rubble, clambering over heaps of things, dragging their feet like very old men. The women had raw-boned faces and pale lips and the children were scampering scavengers, quick as rats. They were all blinking dazedly at the first light. They resembled the debris out of which they emerged: a second skin of masonry dust covered the exposed parts of their bodies and their clothing.

Women street sweepers, soldiers' caps tied to their heads, were at work, pushing the rubble into mounds

155

to make twisting pathways through the destruction. On a circular pavement billboard a poster for the film *Die Grosse Liebe* had been covered with a sticker proclaiming, "The Führer *Is* Victory."

There were no cars to be seen—just a few people on bicycles, making their way to work. Queues were beginning to form outside food shops.

As the police car came closer to the center, the smoke from burning buildings, twisted downward by the wind, blocked certain streets with a thick suffocating wall.

Jolting and bouncing and twisting as Schöller sought to steer around the larger pieces of fallen masonry, the police car made its way along the Wilhelmstrasse and from there into the underground offices below the Prinz Albrechtstrasse, where Kriminalrat Kummerl had become a ghost. Such was the impression created by his unshaven face, his beard being entirely white, whereas his hair remained improbably blond. His head trembled violently as he pointed to somebody on a wooden bench in the outer office.

"General Neuss has been waiting since five A.M."

The Waffen-SS general yawned and stretched himself, and slowly stood up. He was a heavy rough-faced man. Three of his men, armed with submachine guns, appeared out of a room across the corridor.

"SS-Reichsführer Himmler's compliments," General Neuss said, getting to his feet. "He sent me to fetch you. To make sure you arrived safe and sound."

Schöller nodded. "That was thoughtful of him."

"He's like that," General Neuss said, "as you know."

"Yes, I do know."

"Who is this?" Neuss said harshly, examining Elliott.

"This is Haften, my political assistant, Italy."

"He'd better come too," Neuss said. "Reichsführer Himmler wants to get this Italian business settled. All right. Let's get going."

"There are one or two matters. . . . "

"You'll have to deal with those some other time, Schöller. The Reichsführer is waiting. And you know he doesn't like to wait. It makes him nervous and tired." He stood up, his hand resting lightly on his pistol holster.

"As you say." Turning to Kummerl, Schöller said, "If there are any urgent developments in the Behr situation, you will contact me at the Reichsführer's field headquarters."

· 22 ·

On arriving in Berlin on April 16, Dr. Behr had been collected at the railway station by a car from the Swiss embassy.

Fires were raging in many parts of the city, and the air was full of the choking dust of falling buildings.

Dr. Behr was bewildered. Whole neighborhoods had vanished—the ruins stretched for acres. An ocean of desolation in which a few familiar sights appeared through the dust like ghost ships.

The Swiss embassy car passed under the one archway of the Brandenburger Tor that still remained open (the other archways having been barricaded with paving stones) and into the devastated Pariser Platz. Dr. Behr gasped at the sight of the destruction. The camouflage netting draped over the length of the great axis of the Charlottenburger Chaussee and Unter den Linden created an eerie sense of permanent twilight. So many of the buildings had disappeared that Dr. Behr had no sense of where he was; so much was destroyed . . . the French embassy, the Frielanders' mansion, the corner houses built by Schinkel . . .

Looking around, he could not conceive of any kind of life still existing under these conditions. Having come to this conclusion, he attributed his first glimpse

157

of the Hotel Adlon to some sort of momentary hallucination, a memory of the past that his overwrought mind had conjured up to protect itself against the shocks to which it was being subjected. But as the car slowed down and the vision persisted, Dr. Behr saw that the hotel was still there, mysteriously preserved, its richly decorated façade scarcely damaged. He got out and stared up in amazement. It was the old Adlon he knew so well, and yet it was not the same. A protective wall had been built around it, reaching from the ground to the second-floor balconies. It concealed the former main entrance, with the lanterns on either side, and gave the hotel an alien, inhospitable appearance.

Dr. Behr made his way in by way of a heavy steel door and found himself in the old entrance lobby, to which no daylight now penetrated because of the wall. Peering over his half-lenses, the Swiss banker had the impression of a concourse of shadows. There was a great deal of activity and movement in the permanent gloom of the great hall, but everything had the insubstantiality of scenes in a dream.

As he was standing about trying to see where he was, a page boy came forward, curiously dressed, considering the times, in the regulation uniform, white waistcoat, white gloves, buttons of his jacket polished bright. He took Dr. Behr's suitcase and steered him toward the reception desk.

As he became more accustomed to the light (mostly provided by candles and electric light bulbs of low wattage), some of the shadowy figures took on more definite shapes . . . he saw young Luftwaffe officers in noisy little groups. They were drinking champagne, and laughing and fondling the attractive women who were with them. Other people were standing on their own, staring blankly at nothing in particular.

Dr. Behr also saw another type of person (the sort that would not have been admitted to the Adlon in former times), lurking by the square marble pillars, watching everybody. These men in their badly made suits, not the tailcoated assistant managers, appeared to be giving the orders to the hotel staff.

At the reception desk an unknown person with an offensive manner checked Dr. Behr's name against a list of arrivals, and then cross-checked with a card index.

When all the formalities had been completed to his satisfaction, Dr. Behr was issued a three-day ration card, and another white-gloved page boy took him down into the basement, through the barbershop, and into the air raid shelter, where he was shown the cell-like space allocated to him.

It was now almost six o'clock and since he had eaten very little during the past thirty-six hours, Dr. Behr washed and then went straight to the dining room.

All the tables were occupied, and he was obliged to sit with another hotel guest, who introduced himself as the actor Paul Egner. He said the Adlon was now the only place to live. It had its own independent electricity generator, and hot water; and although the food was no better than anywhere else, the wines were superb. Despite his own determined efforts, the Adlon's great cellar was by no means depleted.

The food, for which the waiters demanded coupons, which they cut from the ration card with scissors attached by a little chain to their belts, was vile. The meal began with a kind of green pea soup that in neither taste nor coloring remotely resembled the green vegetable, and was followed by a pancake made of colored potato starch which contained a filling of some sort of tinned fish, and ended with a pudding filled with desiccated oatmeal, covered in a substitute fruit sauce. Ghastly though the food was, he ate it, feeling in need of nourishment after the nightmarish and exhausting train journey from Switzerland. The train had been attacked twice from the air. The second raid had immobilized it and killed a number of passengers. Dr. Behr and those others with a high-priority designation had been transferred to another train.

After the meal he went to his room, lay down on the bed, and without meaning to, fell immediately asleep. He must not have heard the air raid alert, because what awoke him was the continuous mellow sound of a gong being beaten somewhere in the hotel.

He rushed to the window. The sky was as brilliantly illuminated as a stage set. He could see the British bombers: a huge single organism spread out across the sky, its different parts pinpointed by the searchlights. Across the city a moving wall of flame followed the bombers. Dr. Behr watched mesmerized. The fire was all around. He was in the center of an inferno.

The gong was still sounding. Agitatedly, Dr. Behr ran out of his room and along empty corridors and down stairs, into the basement, through the barbershop, and down steps to the deep shelter.

Though it was under several feet of concrete, the shock waves of the explosions, each one stronger than the last, made the earth move like a ship at sea.

Looking around him, Dr. Behr saw that his companions were SS generals and high Nazi officials. . . . It was all quite unbelievable, and ghastly.

But clearly it had been his duty to come to Berlin. Four million Swiss francs was no small matter. It was the bank's responsibility to ensure that all the conditions for the payment of such a large sum had been met. Not to adhere strictly to the complicated procedure laid down by the depositor would constitute a breach of Swiss banking ethics, and possibly of the law.

If the bank paid the money improperly, it might be liable for the entire amount. If the bank wrongly withheld payment, it could be sued, and its reputation damaged.

Of course, Dr. Behr didn't doubt that these Nazis were extremely evil men. Bloody-handed murderers. But a banker's obligations were akin to those of a medical man or a priest. Like them, he had to fulfill his role. Otherwise society would disintegrate. If a person could not have complete trust in his bank, what could he trust?

And then there was also the other matter. There was also that.

After a terrible night in the Adlon shelter, Dr. Behr managed to get two or three hours' sleep in his room. The following day he rose early, took a hot bath,

160

dressed, and not bothering with breakfast, set to work.

From his briefcase he took out a list of the twenty names from among which he would have to obtain two signatures. There were penciled notations against some of the names: Heydrich (assassinated Czechoslovakia, 1943); Nebe (believed executed); Admiral Canaris (executed for treason, 1944).

Some others simply had the words "whereabouts unknown" beside their names. A few of the officially deceased had been replaced by other names. The Chief of the Reich Main Security Office, Ernst Kaltenbrunner, had been added to the list, and so had one or two others. Allowing for these additions, the net result was that the list of twenty was effectively reduced to about nine people thought to be still alive and reachable. They included SS-Reichsführer Himmler; Chief of the Gestapo, Heinrich Müller; the Führer's SS Liaison Officer, General Fegelein; SS-General Stallermann, Chief of Budget Administration SS . . .

Dr. Behr always considered it advisable to start at the top, and so he asked the Adlon telephone operator to get him the Prinz Albrechtstrasse. The connection was virtually instantaneous, and Dr. Behr told the operator, "Kindly connect me with Herr Himmler's secretary, Dr. Brandt. This is Dr. Behr of the Commercial Bank of Berne."

The voice on the telephone said automatically, "Reichsführer Himmler has moved to new field headquarters."

"And where are they?"

"That information cannot be given without authorization."

"How can I obtain authorization?"

"You must apply to Amt IV of the Main Security Office."

"Amt IV is Müller, isn't it?"

"It is."

"Then please connect me with Herr Müller."

"SS-General Müller is not accepting calls. If you wish to see him, you must come here and fill out an application for an interview, stating the nature of your business. You will then be informed, in due course, if the interview can be granted."

"My business is most urgent, there is no time. . . . "

But the line had gone dead. He consulted his list, and then asked the Adlon operator to get him the office of the SS Personnel Chief.

The voice that answered the phone said, "The Head of Department is not available. . . . "

"In that case, perhaps I could have a word with his secretary or assistant. This is a matter of the greatest importance."

"His secretary and assistant are also unavailable."

"Would you do me the courtesy of explaining," Dr. Behr said allowing his exasperation to express itself in his voice, "why they are all unavailable?"

"They were killed last night in the air raid."

Dispiritedly Dr. Behr replaced the phone and again looked down his list. Since Berlin was in such chaos, perhaps the best procedure was to try and contact Kaltenbrunner, who had been moved to Innsbruck to oversee defense operations in the south. He gave the operator the number of the Innsbruck headquarters, and some minutes later a distant voice answered.

"This is Dr. Behr of the Commercial Bank of Berne," he shouted into the phone. "I am speaking from Berlin. It is a matter of the utmost urgency that I speak at once with Dr. Kaltenbrunner, or one of his senior aides. . . . "

"Just one moment." There was a short wait and then the faint voice said, "Dr. Kaltenbrunner has left for SS-Reichsführer Himmler's field headquarters. But I can connect you to his secretary."

"Ah!" Dr. Behr said, and heard a slight click. He listened. He called, "Hello, hello, hello . . . " Again the phone had gone dead. When he got the Adlon operator back, he said, "The line was cut."

"It happens sometimes," she said vaguely.

"Please try and get it for me again," he said.

After several minutes she came back to him and said, "There is a temporary interruption of the connection with Innsbruck. You are advised to try later."

Depressed by this foretaste of the difficulties he was

going to encounter, Dr. Behr decided to go down for breakfast, and start telephoning again immediately afterward.

He was drinking his coffee substitute and chewing on the curious tasting bread-biscuit that was served with it, when he saw a familiar face. Ferdy von Niesor! As impeccably dressed and as handsome as ever. With cane and hat, naturally.

"Ferdy!" Dr. Behr called out, his spirits rising at the sight of his old Berlin friend.

· 23 ·

Himmler had made his latest field headquarters in a pillared *fin-de-siècle* mansion of turrets and spires and belvederes situated in a spruce wood 150 kilometers north of Berlin.

Even though the SS staff car taking Schöller and Elliott drove as fast as conditions permitted, often forcing other traffic off the road, it was early afternoon by the time they arrived at the headquarters.

There was little sign of activity at the approach to the gated drive, somewhat casually guarded by half a dozen youthful Waffen-SS in field gray. They opened the gates hurriedly for SS-General Neuss, and the car drove through and stopped by the steps going up to the main door. A large truck was being loaded with crockery, bed linen, blankets, cooking utensils, and other household effects, suggesting that another change of headquarters was under way. SS drivers stood by their long cars, smoking, chatting to each other. They gave no indication of expecting to have to move in a hurry.

General Neuss led the way up the steps, into a long hall hung with flags. Nobody about. Nobody at all.

"Where is everybody?" Schöller asked.

"Film shows," Neuss said, checking with his watch. "They are showing *Kolberg* again. It is very popular with the men. I have seen it four times myself. Ach— we showed that syphilitic Napoleon how German soldiers fight! To the last man. You have seen it?"

"No."

"There is another showing after supper. Try to see it if you can. It will make you proud to be a German."

"A dead German?"

"I trust that is not intended as a defeatist remark, or I should have to report it."

"Like the Führer," Schöller said, "I am confident of ultimate victory."

They passed the ballroom where the film was being shown, and through the partly open door heard the thunder of French cannons and caught glimpses of the tidal wave of Napoleon's army sweeping down on the small German garrison. On the screen the eyes of the German soldiers waiting for the end were shining.

"I would not mind seeing the end again," Neuss said. "I am not ashamed to say that I weep when I see the bravery of our men, but first I will let SS-Reichsführer Himmler know you are here."

He took them to a waiting room, where about twenty men sat around with an air of having been there a very long time. One or two looked up briefly, warily, at the new arrivals, and then looked away again. The rest were half asleep, or conducting whispered conversations in defiance of a sign that said "Talking Forbidden." Some also ignored the Smoking Forbidden sign and chain-smoked, dropping their butts in little piles on the stone floor, since ashtrays were not provided. From time to time somebody got up to stretch his legs and went out into the corridor. After walking up and down for a few minutes, he'd put his head in inquiringly, in case he had been called.

One of the SS generals began to snore loudly, mouth

agape, whereupon his neighbor gave him a savage nudge.

"What? What? Am I called?"

"No—no. Nobody has been called for forty minutes."

Neuss sat down next to Schöller and Elliott.

"I've told them you're here," he said. "Brandt says he'll tell Reichsführer Himmler the moment he finishes talking. . . . You know he does not like to have his train of thought broken."

"Who's with him?"

"Wolff and Kaltenbrunner."

Neuss disappeared to see the last bloody minutes of *Kolberg* for the fifth time.

After fifteen minutes had gone by, one of the double doors at the end of the room opened a fraction and Dr. Brandt's head emerged between the sentries; eyes were raised. One or two of the waiting men remained looking down, hands tightly clenched together. The disembodied head of Himmler's secretary swiveled as he looked around the men seated against the walls. He gave Schöller a minute nod of recognition that meant: Wait a moment. The head was retracted and the door closed. Almost immediately it opened again and Brandt made a summoning sign, at which Schöller got up and went in under the secretary's arm, which held open the door only just wide enough.

Elliott saw a large room, with a huge stone fireplace, and a man of middle height, his breeches rather too voluminous at the seat, his face of a spongy consistency; he was pacing, his ceremonial dagger getting in the way of his movements.

Of the others in the room, the handsome hook-nosed man must be Wolff, and the very tall one Kaltenbrunner. The door closed again.

Schöller entered deferentially—Himmler expected that. Even Heydrich, whose arrogance was notorious, had bowed and scraped before Himmler when it was necessary. Best not to take chances. So Schöller stood rigidly still by the door, next to Brandt, waiting to be formally noticed.

Eventually Himmler said in his mild, somewhat

165

prissy schoolmaster's voice, "Ah Schöller. You are very late."

"The conditions on the road, SS-Reichsführer. We came with all possible speed. . . . "

"In view of your lateness, Reichskriminaldirektor, let us not waste any more time on excuses," Himmler curtly said. "General Wolff has returned from Italy to answer questions. We shall proceed."

Wolff stood very tall and straight, shoulders, neck, and arms glittering with silver thread.

Kaltenbrunner, towering over the others from his seven-foot height, the sixtieth cigarette of the day hanging from his lower lip, opened the proceedings.

Taking out of his breast pocket an envelope on which were a few jottings, he said, "On March 19, General Wolff left his headquarters in Fasano, wearing civilian clothes, and traveled by train to the Swiss border. He was allowed across by the Swiss authorities without any trouble, and later that day, at a villa in Ascona belonging to the traitor von Gaevernitz, Wolff met Dulles, together with Allied generals Airey and Lemnitzer, who had entered Switzerland in disguise and under false names."

Kaltenbrunner stopped and stared through the cigarette smoke in which he had enveloped himself during this recitation of the facts.

Himmler's wire-frame glasses flashed as his head turned in quick short movements from man to man.

Wolff was not flustered. Though pale, he spoke with calmness and dignity.

"I was aware that your spies on my staff, Dr. Kaltenbrunner, would most certainly inform you of my movements. I therefore saw no pressing necessity to do so myself."

"You did not see fit to inform me either," Himmler said with that abrupt temperature fall in his voice that people knew to be an ominous sign.

"What I did," Wolff said, growing paler, but maintaining a matter-of-fact tone of voice, "was in accordance with the Führer's personal instructions to me, on the occasion of our last meeting, to keep a door to the West open. . . . "

"Did the Führer authorize you to save your own skin, Wolff?" Kaltenbrunner shouted out, his face growing violently red, spittle flowing from his mouth and hanging in long spidery threads from his chin.

"My actions were in accordance with the honor of an officer and gentleman," Wolff said.

"You had at least six meetings with Dulles," Kaltenbrunner shouted. "That isn't keeping the door open, that is treason and conspiracy . . . to save yourself. I have proof. The meetings with the Allied generals. They would not have come to Switzerland, in disguise, on false papers, for mere chitchat. My sources inform me there was a definite undertaking to deliver a surrender to the Allies in return for your own neck. . . . "

"I wish to hear from the Reichskriminaldirektor," Himmler said, turning to Schöller.

Schöller stood with his hands deep in his sagging pockets, jingling his keys.

"My own findings support Dr. Kaltenbrunner's," he said. "There is evidence of the meeting in Ascona, and of the other meetings with Dulles. There is also evidence of an approach to Kesselring to involve him in the surrender as Commander-in-Chief-West. . . . "

"Kesselring too," Himmler said hoarsely.

"There is no evidence that the Field Marshal was willing to lend himself to the plot," Schöller said, "but an approach was made."

"Well?" Himmler demanded, turning his flashing eyeglasses on Wolff.

"My conscience is clear," Wolff said with resignation.

It was now nearly six P.M., a time of day when Himmler began to get very tired. At his field headquarters, as all his residences were known, no matter where they were situated in relation to the battle, he rose at eight A.M., rested for three hours after lunch, and retired utterly exhausted before ten.

On a particularly trying day, such as this one, when he was required to pass judgment on an old and previously trusted associate, the exhaustion began earlier. Sometimes it impeded his speech. In the morning and in the early afternoon he was capable of long tirades, of abstruse digressions, historical flights, and great

167

bloodthirstiness, but as evening approached, he became increasingly cryptic and shorter of breath, and sometimes he choked on his words as he felt the shadow of the long night ahead.

Now his eyeglasses flashed from man to man, the basilisk eyes told nothing of what he was thinking.

"If the corruption were in my own body," he said, "I would not hesitate to burn it out. . . . You understand, Karl?" There was a finality in his voice. He had come to the end of his day's energy.

Himmler was on the verge of making a decision thereafter never to be revoked, when Schöller said quickly, "It would be instructive to see the record of the last occasion when General Wolff was questioned on this subject."

"For what purpose?" Himmler demanded, his weariness closing in on him.

"To compare what was said then with what has been said now," Schöller said. Wearily, Himmler motioned to Brandt to get the records, though in a manner that suggested he could see no point in such formalities.

At the open door, he stopped his secretary.

"Surely we all recall what was said last time," he said.

Everybody thought about this.

"Yes, but the exact words would be instructive," Schöller said.

"All right, Brandt. But be quick."

While the door was open, Elliott again saw inside. What he saw gave an indication of the way things were going. Wolff, palely solemn, seemed to be swaying on his feet, quavering before his accusers.

Himmler—those peculiar hips. Hindquarters of a bull. Half man, half beast. Glass lenses flashing to and fro. The antennae of some eyeless intelligence.

Elliott thought quickly. A secret policeman had to sit on all sides of the fence at once, right? If things were going against Wolff in there, Schöller would not hesitate to break the arrangement and add his evidence against Wolff in order to put himself in the clear. He'd done as much, by his own admission, in Nebe's case, and Nebe had been hanged. *If he reneges on the deal, sells Wolff down the river, then he has to kill me. I am a threat to him however it goes after that. If he gets out of Germany or if he doesn't. He has to kill me. If Wolff comes out of that room under arrest, it means I'm done for. What do I do then? Make a run for it?*

He got up and walked out in the manner of someone going to stretch his legs. In the corridor he lit a cigarette. Walking up and down, smoking, he studied the layout of the ground floor, trying to formulate a plan of escape.

As he stood looking through a tall glass window into a small inner courtyard below, working out where it was in relation to the car compound, he heard the regular clunk of steel-heeled boots on the cobblestones. Four uniformed men, the woven silver braid on their epaulets indicating positions of some rank, were being marched out under escort. One of them was about Elliott's own age, hair the color of dirty straw, rather long, and falling over his eyes as he walked with arms stiffly at his side, so that he had to keep tossing his head in order to be able to see something that he was holding inside his upturned palm. The four men were put up against a wall at the end of the courtyard. Two officers went from one to the other tying hands and securing them to large rusty iron rings in the wall. When it was the turn of the young officer with the straw-colored hair to have his hands tied, what he had been holding in his palm fell to the ground—a snapshot. It lay by his feet. He continued to stare down at it until the moment they came to tie the blindfold, and even afterward the tilt of his head indicated that he was still looking in the same direction. A placard was hung around his neck on which was scrawled: "I am a dirty defeatist pig and deserve to die." Next to him, a stocky man of about forty-five, not yet blindfolded, reading this message while craning his neck, began to open his mouth repeatedly, as if about to start arguing with somebody—but who? As he too was blindfolded, and felt the placard being hung around his neck, his mouth was opening and closing very rapidly, without any words or sounds emerging. His trousers became a viscid mess, the man next to him turned his head away, and still the argumentative officer—struck dumb only by the circumstance of his present position—was vainly seeking someone to whom his irrefutable argument could be put.

The officer in command of the firing squad had now returned to his men, who were sullenly unslinging their rifles. There was no drumroll, no ritual: just the quick raising and dropping of a hand. It was all done in a rather slovenly way, the men discharging their rifles individually, without bothering to take careful aim, and after the first volley the mouth of the argumentative man was still opening and closing in an expression of strenuous disagreement, and the young man with the straw-colored hair was still looking downward at the fallen snapshot that he could not see through the blindfold. The other two men were dead, hanging forward from the rusty iron rings. Angrily, the commanding officer shouted something at his men and dropped his hand a second time, and a second volley was fired, which finally ended all of the stocky man's arguing, and made the young man with the dirty straw hair swing from side to side on his cords.

Elliott was seized by a spasm of shivering.

"You are not used to such sights?"

The words were spoken mockingly by an exceptionally handsome man in his mid-thirties who was studying Elliott with a kind of scholarly curiosity.

"It is cold here."

"You are used to the warmer climate of Italy?"

Who was this man? He was wearing the uniform of a Major General in the SS, and it was apparent from his whole bearing that he was someone who expected to be known. Elliott recognized the type: clever, good-looking, good family—one of the elite. The arrogance of the brainy schoolboy still shone in his face. He had the smirk of the know-it-all. Nobody could contradict him because he was always right. But who was it? *Who?*

"You're Schöller's man, aren't you?"

"Albert Haften, political aide, Italy, Herr General."

"I have not seen you here before. Where are you from?"

"Frankfurt am Main."

"Frankfurt? I can nearly always tell a person's origins from his voice inflection. You were not brought up in Frankfurt."

"I have spent much of my life in Berlin, Herr General."

"But it is not the true Berlin accent either. There is a trace of something else. . . . " It was said casually, but Elliott felt the implicit threat.

"An American inflection perhaps, Herr General?"

"Yes, yes—now that you mention it. Perhaps."

"It is quite possible," Elliott said. "For the past two years my responsibilities have included monitoring American broadcasts. Like you, Herr General, I have a very keen ear for accents. I pick them up almost without noticing."

The SS-Major General suddenly reached out and gripped Elliott's wrist in his hand, a long finger finding the pulse.

"I thought you were about to faint," he said, "you suddenly looked so pale. Your pulse is extremely rapid."

"I have not slept for three days and nights. We have been on the road the whole time. The journey was extremely difficult—exhausting. But I am not going to faint, Herr General."

Elliott's wrist was released.

"I did not know Schöller went in for using your type . . . I thought they were all roughnecks." Of course! Now it clicked who this was. Otto Ohlendorf, Chief of the Inland SD. One of Himmler's cronies.

"There are sections of the Special Investigator's department that are unknown even to the Chief of the Inland SD," Elliott said.

"I believe you," Ohlendorf replied, easily, and then added in a confidential tone, indicating the courtyard where the bodies of the executed men were now being removed: "We are not feelingless oafs, you and I, people of our background. Such sights. . . . Even Reichsführer Himmler is obliged to steel himself. . . . "

"So I have heard."

"Perhaps we shall see you later, Haften. At supper?"

"Yes, Herr General. Perhaps."

"Do you play chess?"

"Yes, Herr General."

"Perhaps we can have a game, later. There is not much to do here. Except wait. Are you good . . . at chess?"

"Quite good."

"Then we must definitely have a game. If you stay on."

"Yes, Herr General."

Ohlendorf left, and Elliott saw that the cigarette in his fingers had become a column of trembling ash. He dropped it on the floor. Lit another cigarette, drew the smoke deeply in. He turned and walked slowly down the corridor, back toward the waiting room. When he had finished his cigarette, he sat down again on the hard, polished pine bench—to wait.

In the silence after Brandt had left, Wolff drew himself up, and although very white and swaying a little, said in a strong voice, "I am ready to accompany anyone in this room to the Führer to lay before him explanations of our conduct, and leave it to him to judge our actions."

The bluff had been delivered with aplomb, and for a whole minute nobody in the room was prepared to accept it or able to find a convincing reason for rejecting it.

Then Kaltenbrunner said, "It is not for the Führer to deal with the detailed evidence of criminality. The Reich Special Investigator is entrusted with the task of investigating such charges, and passing his conclusions to higher authorities to act on."

"That is correct," Himmler said. "General Wolff will give any explanation of his activities to the Reichskriminaldirektor."

Wolff took a deep breath, and resigning himself to his fate, spoke over the heads of those who accused him, addressing himself, stiffly, to a tapestried wall of Teutonic knights and through them to history.

"My purpose in Berne," Wolff said, "was to create a situation that would lead to a breach between the Anglo-Americans and their Soviet allies. It is my frank assessment that only in such an eventuality is there any hope for Germany to find an honorable way of ending this war. I calculated that if evidence were to reach Stalin of a secret deal between us and the Americans, whereby we would open our lines to the Anglo-Americans, allowing them to advance to the East ..." He paused, breathing hard, momentarily lacking the breath to go on, and looked from face to face to see to what extent this story was believed, and found no sign of hope for himself. Nonetheless, girding himself for a final effort, he continued.

"Already this maneuver has been attended by some success. There have been bitter accusations from Stalin against the Americans ... if the full extent of Dulles's plotting comes out, there will be a breach with the Russians. And then Russian will be fighting against American and Englishman. . . . The offer of a surrender to the Anglo-Americans had to appear to be genuine. I see it has also taken in those of you who accuse me now. That was a risk inherent in the maneuver. I was prepared to take that risk for the sake of the German people."

Having made his statement, Wolff turned away; he now was above all of them, already mounted on his hero's bronze horse in some provincial square.

Himmler's eyeglasses were flashing again as his head moved in its rapid jerks from one person to the next.

"Clever lies, clever lies," Kaltenbrunner said.

"What does the Reichskriminaldirektor have to say?" Himmler demanded.

Schöller shambled forward and slowly removed a hand from the depth of his pocket in order to scratch his unshaven jowl. Though restrained in his manner, he had an authoritative air.

"Yes," he mumbled thoughtfully, "yes, yes . . . " His eyes were sharp, assessing the situation with fractional exactitude before speaking.

"The evidence against General Wolff is full, very full. Remarkable for its fullness. So much so, it bothers me."

"Bothers you, why?" Himmler demanded.

"In my experience, SS-Reichsführer, as a policeman, you understand, not as a politician—I am not political, as you know, Reichsführer—but, as I say, as a policeman, I have found that where there are secret dealings of a treasonable or conspiratorial nature, what comes to light is always incomplete. The case of Nebe, for instance. Very fragmentary evidence really, but convincing in the end, convincing. In the present case, the fragments fit together perfectly—to form a total picture. Too perfectly." He shook his head. "The Russian agents in Berne are not that good, not of the first order. Not by any means. But they also got the complete picture. Everything. All the details of how Kesselring was opening up the West to the Allies in return for special terms. Those Russian agents in Berne, I know them, Reichsführer, they aren't that good. . . . "

Seeing the drift of Schöller's remarks, Kaltenbrunner interrupted violently: "I think before we go any further, the Reichsführer should be informed that you too, Schöller, have had secret meetings with Dulles."

Schöller said quietly, "I am not the only person in this room, besides Wolff, to have had contact with Dulles. . . . " Himmler looked at Kaltenbrunner, whose massive face seemed to shatter like thick glass; he began to splutter, more spittle dropping down his chin.

"What are you talking about?"

"Höttl," Schöller said, "has been in Switzerland to seek a meeting with Dulles on your behalf, Dr. Kaltenbrunner. He saw one of Dulles's senior aides in Zurich. . . . "

"It was necessary," Kaltenbrunner said, foaming rabidly, "to get to the bottom of this whole *Schweinerei.*"

"My own view—exactly," Schöller said. "It was why I, too, felt it was necessary to see Dulles."

"And your conclusions?" Himmler said, tired out by these complexities and wishing to be done now.

"My conclusion is, Reichsführer, that the Russian agents are not competent enough to have got hold of this secret pact unless it was given them on a plate. Planted. Therefore I am inclined to accept General Wolff's explanation that he acted to drive a wedge between the Allies."

Once again the flashing eyeglasses described a series of rapid circles back and forth, back and forth, and then Himmler said exhaustedly, "Well? You are satisfied, Kaltenbrunner?"

"If you are, Reichsführer."

Himmler said, "I am obliged to take a great many burdens upon my shoulders, and I have never shirked any of them. But this is a matter for the Kriminalpolizei—they have the technical expertise to assess the evidence of crime. Therefore, in this instance, I will be guided by the Reichskriminaldirektor. Good night."

· 24 ·

It was too late to return to Berlin that day. Schöller and his assistant were shown to quarters in the castle. Neuss informed them that they could take supper in the great hall where the SS-Reichsführer, if he was not too exhausted by his day's work, sometimes joined his senior officers. If that should happen tonight, it was as well to know that once he began to speak, he expected the entire table to listen. A man who went on talking while Reichsführer Himmler was talking was liable to get in his bad graces, which was not advisable.

When the SS-General had gone, Schöller turned to

Elliott and said, "Well, I've kept my side of the bargain. I saved that pompous fool Wolff from dancing at the end of piano wires."

"Then Wolff's in the clear."

"He is for the moment."

It was cold in the dining hall; the heat of the log fire in the enormous hearth did not quite reach the officers seated in high-backed pigskin chairs down the sides of the long oak table.

The highest chair, at the end, was vacant. From its oaken spikes was suspended a silver gorget with the Death's Head emblem; the Nazi eagle, its wings outspread, formed a kind of canopy.

The first course was being served by tall blond SS orderlies in white tunics and white kid gloves.

Schöller and Elliott took their places. They were about to be served when everything stopped and a sudden hush that had begun at the head of the table spread along its sides, silencing one man after another.

Himmler was approaching, accompanied by Wolff and Kaltenbrunner. The officers all rose to their feet and only resumed their places when the SS-Reichsführer and his guests were seated. Thereupon the meal continued but in a noticeably more subdued atmosphere.

Himmler appeared to have recovered some of his strength. He was solemnly in command of himself now, and his puffed-out cheeks moved rhythmically as he carefully masticated his baked meat, potatoes, and peas. Wolff looked withdrawn and exhausted, barely able to get through the meal, whereas Kaltenbrunner talked nonstop, spraying everyone in the vicinity with his saliva, eating almost nothing, but drinking all the time.

Ohlendorf had not come down to dinner, Elliott was relieved to see. The proposed chess game was something he was dreading. To be scrutinized at such close quarters. For hours! Anything could give him away. Some mannerism. Ohlendorf wasn't the sort to miss a thing.

He ate with silent gravity, scarcely looking up, so as

not to invite conversation. Fortunately, the presence of Himmler at the head of the table discouraged all but the most perfunctory exchanges.

From time to time, as he lifted food to his mouth, Elliott looked toward the man with the constantly flashing glasses, slumped in his throne-like chair, sipping dandelion tea for his digestion after each profoundly masticated mouthful of roast meat. The Beast himself, struggling to suppress the air that was forcing itself out of his distended organs. Once or twice he gave well-mannered burps behind his white linen serviette.

The monster gave off none of the expected emanations. Elliott had an impression of tight muscles strangulating his movement, making them all formal and stiff, like those of a man reading a carefully rehearsed speech. There was a rigidity of the jaw that had a long history; something unbudging about the face. Evil could be as simple as that. The unwillingness to move an inch. An awful certainty of being in the right.

Toward the end of the meal Dr. Brandt came to the head of the table and stood waiting to catch Himmler's eye. The Reichsführer was finishing his dandelion tea and chose not to notice the hovering secretary, who coughed once or twice without success.

Finally, summoning up his courage, Dr. Brandt spoke in a low voice: "If the Reichsführer will forgive the intrusion . . . "

"What?" He had no wish to hear whatever fresh piece of bad news Brandt was bringing.

"A Dr. Behr of the Commercial Bank of Berne has been on the telephone, and requests to speak to you most urgently on a matter of the greatest importance. . . . "

"I do not know any Dr. Behr. . . . "

Halfway along the table, Schöller, who had heard this exchange, began to sweat. He was about to say something when Himmler, ignoring his secretary, began to address the entire table.

"When we came to power in '33, the police force was a pitiable organization, tied hand and foot. Whenever police officers arrested a criminal, they had to take care not to fall foul of the law themselves. You bear me out, Schöller?"

"The SS-Reichsführer has stated the truth of the matter."

"The criminals got off scot-free," Himmler said.

"All too often," Schöller agreed.

"We, the National Socialists," Himmler said, wagging a schoolmasterly finger at the whole table, "set to work to put that right. From the outset I worked on the assumption that it did not matter in the least if our action was contrary to some paragraph of the law ... " His voice trailed off. Murmurs of approval came from both sides of the long table. Himmler was looking straight ahead, his face covered by a film of perspiration, his eyes swimming behind the thick lenses of the pince-nez with the agitation of a hooked fish. Had he finished what he was saying or was he only beginning? His mouth was still open and moving as if he intended to continue, but no words came out. Yet it would be foolish on that account to assume the SS-Reichsführer had finished. Everybody was waiting for a more positive sign.

Sometimes exhaustion strangled Himmler's vocal cords, rendering them incapable of fulfilling the commands of his brain. He was not necessarily aware that this was happening. He might suppose that he was making a speech when he was speechless. Such things befell the SS-Reichsführer these days. And then, too, there were times when—perhaps in midsentence— he simply disappeared into himself, vanishing somewhere behind his glittering glasses, leaving only his effigy behind to be reviled or dreaded, as the case might be. He was quite accomplished at this disappearing trick, and many of his duties had been conducted in this way, in absentia.

My dancing partner was Fraulein Buck from Kempten. Yes, yes. A charming girl, I accompanied her home. She did not take my arm, which, in a way, I appreciated. I cracked jokes, talked, and talked. The upshot is—I am becoming a phrase-monger and chatterbox and lose energy and get nothing done. And disgust myself! If only there would be fighting again, war, departing troops. This kind of frivolity wastes my time. . . .

"When they talked abroad of the police, and therefore the state, being in a condition of lawlessness, they did not know that only by acts of great ruthlessness could the fatal taint be removed from our lifeblood."

Mysteriously he had found his voice again; noises of approval came from those around the table.

"If we ignored the law of the petty bourgeoisie, it was to act in accordance with a superior law, the will of the leadership, which, whatever is now said, history will legitimize. . . . "

Now he was completely exhausted and sank back in his throne-like chair, breathing hard beneath the spread wings of the Nazi eagle.

Dr. Brandt was still there pestering him.

"Reichsführer, if you will forgive me. . . . The Swiss banker . . . "

"You think I have time for Swiss bankers, Brandt?"

"It is in connection with the special Swiss funds . . . "

"The Swiss funds? That is something Schöller deals with, why should I have to do everybody else's work, Brandt? Do I not have enough burdens?"

"I will deal with the matter," Schöller offered.

"Then shall I tell Dr. Behr you cannot speak to him, Reichsführer?"

"Yes, yes, yes, Brandt. Do I have to say it a thousand times?"

He rose, and scarcely able to drag his feet along for tiredness, made his way to bed. It was 8:15 P.M.

Next day Schöller and Elliott set off before dawn, and after another difficult journey, arrived at the Prinz Albrechtstrasse around noon.

Once again Kummerl had had almost no sleep; he was visibly disintegrating. He made his report in a failing voice.

Three two-ton trucks would be needed to evacuate the Department's "special" files. He had prepared the requisitions for these vehicles, if the Direktor would sign them.

179

As he was doing this, Schöller asked, "And what of Dr. Behr?"

"Full details of his attempted phone calls are on the Direktor's desk. So far he has not succeeded in getting through to any of these people. However, at breakfast at the Adlon he ran into an old acquaintance, Ferdy von Niesor. As the Direktor is aware, von Niesor knows everyone. It is his sole claim to distinction. If I may be permitted to express a personal point of view, I have always regarded the man as a downright snob. If the Direktor does not agree, I naturally withdraw the aspersion."

"Get on, get on. What happened with von Niesor?"

"Well, the Swiss moaned about the impossibility of getting in touch with anyone in Berlin, and von Niesor, being the insane socializer that he is, immediately offered to see what he could do."

"*See what he could do.* What does that mean?"

"He is giving a . . . a *soirée* for Dr. Behr this evening."

"A *soirée*," Schöller repeated, letting out a guffaw of disbelief.

"Yes, Direktor. He has undertaken to invite some of the people that Dr. Behr wishes to see but has so far been unsuccessful in contacting."

Schöller's face darkened. "What a blunderer you are, Kummerl."

"Our man could not prevent it," Kummerl said feebly. "It was a stroke of chance. The two men ran into each other and were in conversation before anything could be done."

Ferdinand von Niesor, after breakfasting with Dr. Behr, had returned to his house in the Steinplatz, a man inspired. It had come to him as the concept of a great picture overwhelms the artist.

Yes, even with the bombs raining down and the pagans at the gate, he would demonstrate before the eye of history what was meant by the von Niesor style. And if one of the British bombs should be directed by fate onto the house in the Steinplatz, what more fitting way for Ferdinand von Niesor to take his leave of the world than with a party!

In the marble-pillared hall of his house, he took off his overcoat with the astrakhan collar and his hat, and gave them to a very old footman, his one remaining servant.

Opening the high cream-and-gold double doors, he entered the master bedroom, which now had also to serve as his reception room. In the thirty-room mansion only two other rooms were still habitable—his daughter's bedroom and old Albert's. The life of the household, such as it was, centered on the master bedroom, dominated by a four-poster bed. Propped up in this bed by silk cushions, Ferdy made his phone calls, wrote his letters, and received callers.

After pouring himself a large early-morning cognac from the bottle on the little Louis Quinze table that served also as a bedside stand for his medicines, he dialed the telephone number of the Countess Schörner.

When he told her he was giving "a little last supper" tomorrow night for a few of his friends, the

Countess emitted a shout of delight; Ferdy's suppers were always so entertaining. The English bombs did not bother her in the least. "The only way I should hate to die, my dear old friend, is naturally."

Ferdy had said to everybody, "Come the same time as the British," which meant eight o'clock, the usual time for the first raid of the night, but the guests started to arrive before the bombers.

"Perhaps they do not intend to honor us tonight," Ferdy speculated, giving a coy upward glance at the bright moonlit sky.

It was not easy to get to the house in the Steinplatz. Much of the surrounding area was destroyed and in the ruins there were deep puddles of stagnant water.

Old Albert stood outside the front door with a flashlight showing the party-goers the best way to approach the house, while Ferdy and his beautiful daughter, Maritza, received the guests in the master bedroom.

"Ah! What a great pleasure, my dear Count. . . . How honored we are that you could come, Herr Minister. . . . Baroness, it is far too long that we have not seen you . . . it was most adventurous of you to accept my invitation. . . . "

"You know, Ferdy, that I am an adventuress at heart."

"I shall hold you to that, my dear delightful friend."

A smell of mothballs intermingled with that of French perfumes. If a sequined evening blouse lacked some of its sequins or a diamanté-studded cape its rhinestones, and black lamé and silk organza bore the deep creases of having lain in bottom drawers or cabin trunks, such things were not noticed, and everybody told everybody else how marvelous they looked.

"Ah . . . General. Good of you to come. We are flattered that you could find the time. There is champagne. There is caviar. There is pâté de foie gras. Or grouse, if you prefer . . . tinned, of course. We had a little put aside for a rainy day. You will have to help yourself. My footmen are all in the Gestapo, listening at keyholes, of which, I may say, they have much experience. As well as an infallible memory for any unsavory details overheard. So tonight it must be self-service in accordance with the *Zeitgeist*."

The arriving guests filed past Ferdy to squat down on the floor or sprawl on the bed. Most kept their overcoats on, since the paraffin stove standing in the middle of the Aubusson did not really provide sufficient heat.

On the ceiling the trompe l'oeil clouds had become darkened from the smoke of the stove, and flaked in places, and there was only a dark cavity, where formerly a circle of light bulbs had created the illusion of sun rays suffusing the sky.

The main illumination was provided by one or two utilitarian table lamps with bulbs of a low wattage, supplemented by thick night candles in saucers. In this mixed lighting, faces had a tendency to deathly pallor and eyes looked even more sunken than they were, which, however, did not inhibit flirtations.

Ferdy, in crimson velvet smoking jacket—his crest in gold thread on the left breast—cravat, and patent leather shoes, welcomed each guest with some delicate compliment.

At nine o'clock Schöller, pockets bulging as always, arrived with a young assistant.

Ferdy received them as effusively as the others.

"Ah . . . my dear Reichskriminaldirektor. What an unexpected pleasure. I am most flattered that our little occasion should interest the Special Investigator. It sets the seal on it, so to speak. And it is so very time-saving to know that one has no need to invite the Special Investigator, that he will come of his own accord if he is interested in doing so."

"My political adviser, Italy, Haften," Schöller said.

"Honored. Please make yourselves at home, gentlemen. But then that is something I have no need to say to you, Reichskriminaldirektor. You always do in any case, without requiring any urging."

Turning to another guest who had just entered, he exclaimed, "Ah . . . there is General Fegelein! What news from the bunker, General? Is it true the Führer is about to become your brother-in-law?"

"What is this? What is this?"

"It is not true? I heard the Führer is going to marry Fräulein Braun?"

"As usual you have the latest gossip," Fegelein said evasively. He was a short wiry man, somewhat bow-legged from his former occupation of jockey.

"And how is life 'down there'?" someone asked him.

"The Führer is optimistic about the ultimate outcome," he said.

"How very original of him."

"The Führer still has certain secret weapons in reserve," Ferdy said. "He thinks that when the Russians see our defenses, they will die laughing."

When Dr. Behr arrived at nine-thirty, having finally managed to get a lift in the Swedish ambassador's car, the party was in full swing, with about thirty people packed into the bedroom. Blinking over his half-lenses, the banker saw highborn ladies sitting on the floor, licking the caviar off their fingers, while their over-exposed bosoms were being ogled, or worse, by leaders of the nation, who squatted next to them, drinking champagne straight from the bottle and helping themselves to grouse from the open tins on the carpet.

He saw an aged satyr thrust a thickly veined hand into the cleavage of Countess Schörner's black satin evening gown; he observed Baron Cleve sitting on the four-poster relating smoking-room stories in mixed company.

"Ah, my dear Bernard. How happy I am that you inspired me to this little occasion," the host called out by way of welcome.

"It was I?" Dr. Behr said in astonishment and horror, noticing an old colleague, the onetime President of the Deutsche Credit Bank, patting the thigh of a young SS officer.

"Of course, of course," Ferdy said. "We had all sunk into a state of apathetic self-pity, and then your arrival stirred us out of it."

"I don't know what to say, Ferdy. I am honored, but really this kind of party . . . is hardly . . . hardly appropriate at such a time."

"A little frivolity is not amiss before the portals

of the nether regions," Ferdy observed, and then with the discretion for which he was renowned, quickly changed the subject and led Dr. Behr to one side. "I must show you the clock I bought last week, Bernard. A Louis the Seventh long-case clock, in superb working order. It was an incredible bargain. There . . . look!" Proudly he pointed to where he had placed his most recent acquisition. "You can pick up some absolutely fantastic stuff these days," he confided, "for absolutely nothing."

Dr. Behr wondered if the dreadful march of events had perhaps unhinged his old friend's mind. Certainly there was a look of inappropriate elation in Ferdy's eyes. Dr. Behr addressed him sternly, feeling an obligation to bring him back to reality.

"I am most concerned, Ferdy, that you continue to live in Berlin. The situation gets worse every day. Every hour. I had no idea that things were as bad as this. You must allow me, as one of your oldest friends, to arrange through the Swiss embassy to obtain an exit visa for you. You have friends everywhere. In Switzerland I shall be most honored to accommodate you, and you have other friends who would be equally willing to share in that responsibility. . . . "

"Even if it were possible, which it isn't, I wouldn't dream of it, Bernard. This is my house. I have no intention of becoming dependent on the hospitality of others at my time of life. . . . No, no, no. When the Russians come, I shall offer them a glass of champagne and my best remaining caviar. . . . If they choose to behave badly, that is their concern. *I* shall have behaved correctly. Should they prove too tiresome, we of course have our little capsules. In this respect the government has been uncharacteristically foresighted, and laid in an ample supply. But enough of these gloomy prognostications. You see that I have got hold of SS-General Fegelein for you."

At this news, Dr. Behr's face lit up. "Fegelein! Perfect. Perfect. You are a genius, Ferdy. An absolute genius. I don't know how to thank you. How did you manage it?"

"Oh, we have known Fegelein a long time." Ferdy

185

dropped his voice slightly. "Used to send Maritza to him to learn horse-riding when he was running his school. Let me introduce him to you. Come. We had better go to him. At one time one only needed to snap one's fingers, and his sort would come running. But now that he is married to Fräulein Braun's sister . . . well, you can imagine." He threw up his hands. "*C'est la guerre.*"

Gingerly stepping between the sprawling, and in places intertwined, bodies of his guests, Ferdy led Dr. Behr to where SS-General Fegelein was being pressed for news by a group that had formed around him.

"Ah, my dear Fegelein!" Ferdy called to him. "A moment of your time, if you would be so generous. I want you to meet Dr. Behr of the Commercial Bank of Berne. He has a business matter to discuss with you, I believe."

SS-General Fegelein was by no means uninterested in talking business with Swiss bankers; mustering what raffish charm he could, he bowed to those in his vicinity and detached himself. He shook Dr. Behr's hand warmly, a stiff smile concealing the sudden excitement he felt at the thought that this encounter could turn out profitably for him.

"I am very pleased to have found you," Dr. Behr said. "You can have no idea what problems I have been experiencing in getting through to *anyone.*"

"Your business must be of great importance, if it has brought you to Berlin at this time," Fegelein said, carefully steering the banker away from anyone who might be able to overhear their conversation. Having found an empty corner, he made a sign that he was all attention.

They had been talking intimately for about ten minutes when they were interrupted by the sudden appearance, from behind a column, of the Reich Special Investigator.

"Well, Fegelein," he said, "you and our Swiss banker friend look thick as thieves."

"Oh, not at all," he began to protest, "we were merely talking about this and that."

"You have come all the way to Berlin, Dr. Behr, at this time, to talk of this and that?"

"You know very well why I am in Berlin, Herr Direktor."

"I never imagined you would wish to settle your business here in person, Dr. Behr."

"There is a matter that I have taken the liberty of raising with General Fegelein."

"Oh?" Schöller said, and succeeded in putting so much suspicion into the single syllable, implying such a range of possible crimes against the State (all of them punishable by death) in which a Swiss banker and the SS Liaison Officer to the Führer might be conspiring, that Fegelein actually began to shake.

"Nothing of any significance, Schöller. A simple inquiry, isn't it so, Dr. Behr?" Fegelein said quickly, and by way of proving the unimportance of the matter, began to withdraw. Dr. Behr sought to detain him. "We will talk another time," Fegelein said vaguely.

"Could we make an appointment? As you know, the telephones are not to be relied on."

"If I can be of some little service to you, Dr. Behr, I shall be glad to see you tomorrow at eleven o'clock in my office in the Reich Chancellery."

"I am indebted to you, General."

"Not at all. Not at all."

Elliott had become separated from Schöller shortly after their arrival.

At the Special Investigator's side nobody heeded the assistant. He was just the other man's appendage. But now he was someone who had to be separately dealt with.

By looks and secret nods and significant eye movements the knowledge of his presence was passed on from person to person. Elliott could sense the mixture of distaste and fear with which he was regarded. It made him feel strange—not himself.

Who would have guessed he could be so convincing in this role? How completely they seemed to accept him as the secret police.

187

He could tell from the way they made him feel—not human.

Oh, what the hell! He should be feeling bucked up it was working so well. They were scared of him, OK, great. *I'll breathe down their necks and make them shiver.* Since it was not really *him* doing it, he could obtain some mordant satisfaction from scaring the bastards.

They were walking about, chattering, flirting, indulging their heavy German sense of humor.

Intruding into one group, he heard them talking about the performance of the Berlin Philharmonic a few days ago. A woman with a reconstructed face (nothing but powder and lipstick and eye shadow and mascara) remarked that she considered it in doubtful taste to have opened the concert with the finale from *Götterdämmerung.* As soon as Elliott was noticed, the conversation came abruptly to an end.

He tried somewhere else. This circle were talking about their hairdressers, which of them still existed.

"But I thought Alphons' was destroyed weeks ago."

"He has reopened in the cellar. I may tell you, his prices are an atrocity. . . . "

Elliott kept walking around in circles. Nobody spoke to him. People moved away as he approached.

He felt his face stiffen, and his eyes grew harder. This was required. It would be incorrect to smile too readily. Instead, he drank. It helped with his face and his general demeanor. The alcohol froze his features in a suitable mask.

It was very strange to be feared in this way, to find people edging away as he approached. He wondered how he would have felt had it really been *him* they were afraid of.

He looked at these people with a cold official eye. They were behaving as if they did not know they were all done for. But he could see they were just walking death masks. This made him smile with the superiority of the living, who have drunk a little too much.

The only one alive in this whole room was the daughter. He kept looking at her. She was beautiful. He wanted to touch her, just to have some brief contact with another living person. If he could just touch her.

Of course, it was smarter to keep himself to himself, talk to nobody. Less chance of giving himself away. As soon as he opened his mouth, there was danger. Once or twice, becoming conscious of him staring at her, she held his look briefly and he thought he saw some interest in her eyes. Her look warmed him, when he was beginning to feel as deathly as officialdom.

He made another futile circuit of the room, bumping into more zombies. Their shrinking touch made him feel like them—done for. He could get no restorative warmth from such sources. Only this girl . . . There was a feverish vitality flowing through her, he could see. She was smoking continuously, drawing in smoke and exhaling, as if in a hurry to finish this cigarette and start the next. Everything about her was hurried. Laughter. Glances. Movements. She gave the appearance of not having enough time.

He just had to talk to her. He took another swig of champagne, straight from the bottle, like the others did. Filled with Dutch courage, he started toward the girl. Stupid, stupid, he told himself, but went on. All right, he thought, give it a try—see if I can carry it off. . . . He did not know what he would say to her, but as he got so close he could no longer turn back, he began acting his part. He told her a joke, an anti-Hitler joke. It was not very funny and he told it badly, but she laughed, and so he said—another joke—that she was reckless to laugh at such jokes, since it was forbidden to do so, and was she always so reckless? In other ways too?

"What makes you think I was laughing at your *joke*?"

The character he was supposed to be, said, "I know all about you."

He did not know what he meant by that, but he thought it was perhaps a way of getting close to her, of quickly entering her life before too many obstacles were put in his way.

"You people know everything about everybody, don't you?"

"There are some advantages in that," he said, with an effort at lightness which he did not quite achieve.

She looked at him. "You are with Schöller?"

He affected a flirtatious mysteriousness. "What do you suppose?"

"Anyone can see what you are," she said. "It's written all over you."

"In what way . . . ? You must tell me."

"Why *must* I? Will you force me to? You have an air of knowingness," she said.

"In that case," he said, "permit me to tell you what I know about *you.*"

"What do you know about me?"

"That you are beautiful, and reckless. Laughing at jokes that are disrespectful to the Führer—an offense which carries the death penalty." He smiled. "From which I conclude that you put yourself in the power of others, and are prepared to pay the price of that."

Since he was not himself, he was free of the ties of his own nature.

"You don't know anything about me."

"I want to know everything about you."

She laughed and looked sharply at his hand still resting on her arm.

"The other thing that marks out your sort . . . you are always detaining people against their will."

"You are free to go," he said, at once taking his hand from her.

"Oh, you are too generous."

"I did not mean . . . *Of course*, you may go. I was only talking out of . . . out of . . . "

"What? You are like your chief, you get in where you can."

"I am not at all like him," he said. "Not in the least."

"You think you have entrée everywhere," she went on with her accusation. "Because of your position."

"Professionally," he said, "it is necessary."

"You even think you can get in with people like us."

Elliott looked around in some consternation, unable to place exactly the cause of her anger with him. He had done nothing. Just talked to her. He saw Schöller moving freely among the guests, and she followed his glance.

"You see how he makes himself at home here, your boss."

"Yes, he does have the air of a regular visitor," Elliott agreed. "Though it's not exactly his milieu."

She let out a peal of ironic laughter. "No, it's not his milieu," she agreed. "Do you know what it meant, once, to be asked to this house? It was an accolade. Prominent writers, musicians, diplomatists, politicians, they all waited—eagerly—for an invitation. And now any common police ruffian can come and march in with his dirty boots . . . They make themselves big and important, with a finger in everything. Travel passes. Exit visas that never materialize. Or they can get you gasoline. Or cigarettes. Or extra food. Or the release of a brother or a father or a daughter from Plötzensee or the Lehrter Strasse. Take somebody off one list and put him on another."

"He used his position with you?" Elliott demanded with a sudden queasiness. "Schöller?"

"He uses his position with everyone, doesn't he? Like you all do."

"You allowed it?"

"One learns what one has to do in order to exist."

She was looking about her, viewing with distaste the many opened tins and empty bottles and the drunken figures on the floor. With no servants to clear the place, for all its Louis Quinze, was quickly coming to resemble a pigsty.

"I've got to get out of here," she said suddenly.

"Out of Berlin?"

"Out of Berlin," she laughed. "Who can get out of Berlin? I meant out of this room. It makes me feel sick."

"Where is there to go?"

"There is the rest of the house."

"I will come with you."

She gave a shrug as if it was no concern of hers if

he wished to follow her. Outside, on an unlit landing, a staircase curved dimly upward. Moving through rubble, feeling his way, he asked, "Is it safe?"

"I don't know," she said. "Does it matter?" And added, "You don't have to follow me."

But she kept looking round to see if he was still following, and if he seemed to hesitate, peering too long, or feeling around in the dark, she let out a mocking laugh that drove him on, made him reckless too.

He caught up with her at a room on the top floor.

As they looked around, both, at the same time, became aware of two people on the Louis XV bergere, the silk of which was ripped in several places, the horsehair spilling out. They were covered with an army greatcoat, but the rough movements were on the point of dislodging it. As it fell away, female legs, suddenly contracting like a mechanical claw, closed around male buttocks. The wild jerkings made the fragile piece of French furniture shake as if on the point of coming apart.

As they went out again, he suddenly reached toward her, wanting only to take her arm, but she pulled away. The next room was so badly damaged it was open to the sky and let in moonlight. She stood very still. He watched her breathing as if he had never seen anybody breathe before. She was alive, and her anger was welcome, since it was not directed at him, only at this person he was supposed to be. He was unexpectedly happy. He smiled at her and tried to get closer to her, craftily kicking bits of debris about, until he was almost touching her. He knew that if he could just kiss her, it would make him feel like a living person again.

He said, "Look, look—do you think . . . " Abruptly stooping down, he kissed her on the mouth, roughly, since it was done with whipped-up courage. She struggled and pulled away, and reluctantly he let her go.

"Because you barge in everywhere, you think you can barge in with me too. You think I'm to be taken like some servant girl in the dark. . . . "

192

He said, "Sorry . . . I . . . I made a mistake."

He lit a cigarette, and then apologizing for his forgetfulness offered her one; she accepted and he lit it for her, cupping his hands together so as to keep them from shaking. He smiled at her, to show he had meant no harm.

"You are diffident suddenly," she said, examining him with cool eyes. "When force does not work, try trickery? Aren't you going to offer to save my life? Like they all do. Papers to get out of Berlin. If I will just lie still, open my legs. What does it cost me, after all? Such a little thing in return for being allowed to go on living. Just a few moments in the dark . . . hmm?"

"Stop this," he said, hurt by her scorn.

"A member of the secret police so sensitive?" The ironic tone was not quite as confident now. She was puzzled by him.

"You can't see that I am not like those others?" he asked.

"I see no difference."

"Look at me, look at me. . . . "

"I see no difference," she said with finality.

He was shocked. Wildly he began, "You talk about papers, papers to get out of Berlin. All right. All right. I will get them for you." His eyes shone; he was elated by his promise to her.

"*You* will?" She began to laugh.

"I will get them for you."

"You think I have not heard that before. I'm twenty-two years old. I've lived through six years of war. . . . "

"I told you I'm not like all the others."

"You have drunk too much champagne," she said. He had an intoxicated look in his eyes—though he seemed steady enough on his feet.

"I know what I'm saying."

"You will get me papers." She laughed at him again. "How will you?"

"Through Schöller."

"Through Schöller!" This seemed to increase her bitter mirth. "Why do you suppose he would do it?

Out of the goodness of his heart? I was not able to get them from him. . . . "

"I will be able to."

He was so certain, like they all were—in his profession.

"Oh you have some hold on him," she said. "That is how the system works, isn't it? Everybody has something on somebody else. But I tell you . . . whatever you have won't be enough. I know Schöller. It's too late now."

"He will do what I say," Elliott said. "He has to."

"He has to? *Has to?* Who are you?"

"It does not matter."

· 26 ·

At quarter to eleven Fegelein said that he would have to go; the Führer did not like immediate staff to leave the bunker for too long. He was apt to become suspicious if he asked for someone and that person was absent. But you couldn't stay "down there" all the time.

Ferdy saw him out. The British bombers had not come yet, and in the blackout the city seemed to be barely breathing, some huge stricken beast mortally wounded, lying in the hollow of the dark, waiting for the death blow.

The SS-General started rapidly across the rubble, in his rather waddling jockey's walk, going toward his waiting car. Moonlight coming through gaps in burntout buildings fell with the formal effect of stage lighting on puddles, piles of masonry, the tangled mesh of ironwork, fallen statuary. A massive Third Reich eagle, from the top of a public building, lay shattered on the ground, a relic of the past.

"Fegelein!"

The SS-General swung round to find Schöller a short distance behind. How they crept up on you, these swine!

"A word with you, Fegelein," Schöller said.

"Here?" Fegelein was about equidistant between the house and his car. His driver had got out, carrying a submachine gun.

"Yes," said Schöller. "This will do."

"Well?"

"Greenland," Schöller said thoughtfully. "Why *Greenland*?"

The little ex-jockey experienced an uncontrollable twitching of his upper lip, the result of an attempted smile that was going wrong. He thought better of it, and scowled. There was sweat on his upper lip.

"What are you talking about?" he said, mustering all the brute authority of his position.

"Of all the escape plans I have uncovered these past weeks," Schöller said, "yours is the most . . . *schoolboyish*. But I suppose it had *some* chance of working. With Werner Steincke to fly you there from northern Norway in the seaplane. I see you have laid in a good stock of supplies. Rifles. Faltboats. Skis. Tents. Hand grenades for fishing. A good supply of tinned and dried food. Medicine. It could work, provided you have a taste for the life of the Eskimo."

Fegelein was getting panicky in his breathing. His eyes were going wildly from Schöller to the driver-bodyguard.

"To order your man to shoot me will gain you nothing. All the evidence is in my safe. Besides, I am also armed, and probably a better shot than he is. So calm yourself, Fegelein, and listen to me."

"Contingency plans," Fegelein said, having to some extent regained control of himself. "In case the Führer should wish . . . "

"But the Führer has made it quite clear he does not intend to go on living in a world that has shown it is not worthy of his greatness."

"I have merely provided for the possibility . . ." Fegelein began.

"That you may be able to slip out when he's not looking? I think he wants company on his last journey. He will want to have all his family with him."

"If you are arresting me, Schöller, I must tell you . . ."

"What makes you think I am arresting you, Fegelein? We are just having a private talk."

"Yes?" Fegelein said with a look of noncomprehension.

"The trouble with Greenland," Schöller said, "is that you can't live there forever. Or you might *just as well* be dead. Of course, hiding out there for a time in one of these deserted ice-bound fiords makes sense. Later, fly the seaplane to Spain or Portugal. And from there, a boat to South America. . . . Yes, yes. It is schoolboyish, but just possible. Only you would need money. To obtain transport to South America and an entry visa with no questions asked. I know the current price and you don't have that kind of money, Fegelein. Do you?"

"I will not argue with you, since you seem to know such a great deal about me."

"These are times," said Schöller, "when people like us, Fegelein, must stick together. Am I right?"

"You are right, Schöller."

"Each for himself, yes. On the other hand, if we can help each other . . ."

"I could not agree with you more."

"If the Führer and the rest of that lot want to perish in the flames, it is not for us to spoil their fiery end. But we don't have to break our necks rushing to follow in their footsteps."

"That is also my own opinion," Fegelein said, wary of the Investigator, suspecting that he might be acting as agent provocateur to trap him. But there was nobody here to listen to their conversation, and why would he need to trap him when he already had so much evidence, all the details of the escape plan?

"I want to help you, Fegelein," Schöller proposed.

"I am—naturally—glad to hear that. Only . . ."

"Since we agree then, the details of your plan will remain in my safe, and you will not be stopped when you make your escape bid."

"It is friendly in the extreme. . . . I will not forget such . . . "

"I know you won't. I will do more. You will need money. And friends, if you succeed in getting out. The man married to Eva Braun's sister is bound to suffer from a certain amount of public interest. They will be looking for you. They may even think of looking in Greenland. You must not stay there too long. I will see that two hundred thousand Swiss francs are paid into your bank account in Switzerland."

Fegelein did not know what to say. He was not a particularly bright man. Some people said that in his years as a jockey he had fallen too often from horses.

"One does not, after all, abandon comrades in their need," Schöller said.

"I venture to say that I have always shared such sentiments entirely."

"Yes? My study of your file has shown me that you also possess a healthy sense of self-interest. Marrying Fräulein Braun's sister was a good move at the time. How could you have foreseen the disadvantages? Considering everything, I am sure you will take a realistic view of the little favor I am going to ask you. A matter of a signature."

In his panic, Fegelein had up till this moment totally failed to connect Schöller with what Dr. Behr had begun to tell him. But now even he understood.

"Tomorrow when Dr. Behr comes to see you, you will sign his piece of paper, won't you? And let the poor man return to the bosom of his family, before he is blown to pieces."

"But that would be participating in a colossal fraud," Fegelein protested, finally seeing what this was all about.

"Yes," Schöller agreed mildly. "I can rely on you then?"

Fegelein began to splutter nervously, his rather slow mind trying to grasp the ramifications of what he was letting himself in for.

"But if it is found out," he said.

"You will be in Greenland by then, or where it will concern you even less. Fegelein, stop thinking! You're not good at it. I can tell you, you have no choice. If you refuse the signature, I shall consider it my duty to place the evidence of your escape plan before the Führer."

"I do not refuse, Schöller. Please don't think I am refusing. No, no. Not at all. In fact, since you put it in this way, I would go so far as to say I agree. I agree. Yes. There you are, I agree. . . . " He appeared surprised with himself.

"Good. Good. But let me just warn you, should you change your mind, even if you got out of the Chancellery, every roadblock out of Berlin would have orders to arrest you. Our defenses against the Russians may be virtually nonexistent, but there is an iron web around the city to prevent our own people escaping."

"I have agreed, Schöller. Haven't I said so?"

"The money will be paid into your Swiss account UL 959 K 32? I have it right?"

"As always."

"The other matter Dr. Behr wishes to discuss with you, what is it?"

"The special prisoners."

"Yes?"

"They include, as you know, two relatives of Churchill."

"As well as Léon Blum, Schuschnigg, et cetera."

"Exactly."

"What is Dr. Behr's interest?"

"Some of his shareholders, he tells me, are concerned for the lives of these men. They fear we may have moved them to Niederdorf in order to hold them as hostages. . . . "

"Not a bad guess. What does he want?"

"Some reassurance, *for his shareholders*, that these men will not be harmed."

"Otherwise?"

"His shareholders and directors are at present considering an official request from the Allied powers to freeze all German accounts opened in Switzerland during the war, pending investigation of the sources of these special funds."

"Hmm. Dr. Behr is not quite such a fool as he looks."

"Evidently not."

"You will do your best for him, won't you, Fegelein? We wouldn't want those special funds frozen."

"No, no, of course not."

"Then our business is settled?"

"Settled."

Unthinkingly, the automatic concomitant of avowals and bargains, Fegelein's hand shot up and he cried, "Heil Hitler!"

"You will have to try and get out of that habit," Schöller said.

· 27 ·

SS-Major General Oswald Stapplemann, Head of Budget Administration SS, was a chubby-cheeked man with virtually no neck, his large, round, pink head resting like a boulder upon the stiff collars of his uniform. He was an orderly man, and even at a time like this he made it a principle not to let the paperwork pile up. No matter how it mounted, he sought to keep pace with it, working long hours and taking two bulging briefcases home with him every night.

No man was better versed in the intricacies of SS administration work. This was no trivial accomplishment, for every day new orders and regulations were issued superseding old ones. He had to be able to decide how valid an order was if, for example, the person who had issued it was later executed for one of the many crimes against the State that were punishable by death. Execution did not always invalidate the order, only in certain circumstances.

Stapplemann knew all about such matters. Official papers poured down upon him in a daily deluge, requiring his signature and stamp of authorization, without which money could not be paid out, whether it was for transporting Jews or refurbishing one of SS-Reichsführer Himmler's castles.

But though Stapplemann was familiar with hundreds of different kinds of requisitions, authorizations, special budget allocations, secret fund expense chits, and the like, he had never seen anything like the piece of paper that had been placed before him by the Swiss banker, Dr. Behr. A withdrawal form for four million Swiss francs, signed by the Reich Special Investigator, Ernst Schöller, and below that the signature of the SS Liaison Officer to the Führer, SS-General Fegelein. There was a dotted line where another signature was required. His, apparently.

But how did he know that he was the proper person to authorize this? He had been shaking his head disapprovingly for the past three minutes as he examined the piece of paper before him, turning it over again and again with finicky fingers, as if there was something positively unclean about it.

It was not the amount of money involved that disturbed him. Over the years he had authorized the expenditure of many millions of Reichsmarks without a quiver, as long as the cash demands were on the correct forms and were countersigned by the relevant department chiefs in the regulation manner. It was not his job to go into the purpose for which the money was required, only to make sure that the various departments were keeping within their budget or, if not, that they had obtained special dispensation to exceed it.

It was also his job to ensure that departments of the SS were not swindled, either by being overcharged for goods or services or as a result of somebody's putting money in his own pocket. Stapplemann had an eagle eye for spotting an excessive profit or an inadequately explained cost in a budget.

Looking up at the Swiss banker, Stapplemann said at last, "I regret I am not familiar with the procedure to which you refer. I shall have to obtain further instructions."

"By all means," Dr. Behr said. "But I trust that will not take long . . . time is pressing."

Stapplemann threw up his hands as if to say that nobody could know these days how long anything might take. He frowned and again studied the piece of paper. Of course, it was not advisable to keep the Reich Special Investigator and the SS Liaison Officer to the Führer waiting. They might consider him to be failing in his job if he did not know how to deal with something like this.

Who could he ask about this? Reichsführer Himmler might be highly annoyed to be consulted about an administrative matter at the present moment of destiny. To waste his time was an offense against the State, insofar as it obstructed the defense of the Reich. He forgot whether being an obstructionist was or was not punishable by death, but it was quite serious. Still, all his bureaucratic instinct told him that this matter must not be dealt with too quickly, in case something was not correct. The thing to do was to delay. When in doubt, that was the only thing to do.

"If you will leave this form with me, Dr. Behr," Stapplemann said, "I shall deal with the matter at the earliest possible moment."

"If I call tomorrow morning . . . "

"Tomorrow morning?" Stapplemann said, appalled at being subjected to such pressure, and then he sighed wearily, a man used to being overburdened. "Very well," he said, "very well. I will endeavor to have some information for you by then. But I can promise nothing."

When Dr. Behr had left, Stapplemann slipped a Prevetin tablet in his mouth to give him extra energy to cope with this problem. It was clear he would have to obtain instructions from someone. Without instructions, Stapplemann felt lost, at the mercy of wild and contradictory emotions and thoughts. He resolved as a first step to have his secretary bring in all the rules and regulations, with amendments, relating to Special Funds *Ausland*.

I shall take it all home with me, he decided, and study it tonight.

There was a knock, and his adjutant put his head in to say that the Reich Special Investigator was outside and wished to see the Head of Budget Administration at once.

"Very well, very well. Ask him to come in," Stapplemann said, deciding it was inadvisable to deny the Investigator's invariably exigent demands—and perhaps some elucidation would be forthcoming from such an interview.

As Schöller came in, Stapplemann got up and gravely gave the Hitler salute, and asked, "In what respect can I assist the Reich Special Investigator?"

"Sit down," Schöller said, taking a seat himself. Stapplemann sat down too.

"You've had a visit from the foreign manager of the Commercial Bank of Berne. Dr. Behr."

"As always, the Special Investigator is remarkably well informed."

"Did he succeed in settling his business with you?"

"Not entirely."

"What does that mean?"

"It is necessary for me to ascertain that I have the required authority for what he has asked me to do."

"You have, Stapplemann."

"I must satisfy myself that I have."

"I'm telling you that you have. I myself put your name on the list of twenty people who could authorize withdrawals from the special fund."

"I had no knowledge of it."

"There was no need for you to have knowledge of it."

"But if I am required to authorize such a matter ... the withdrawal of four million Swiss francs, I must know that I have the authority to issue such an authorization," he argued with pedantic logic that seemed to annoy the Investigator.

"You are wrong."

"I do not follow the Special Investigator's exact line of thought," Stapplemann protested academically, wondering at what point it was customary to forgo talk and resort to "physical pressure." His own armed bodyguard was outside, his adjutant carried two loaded pistols, his secretary was armed, and so was Stapplemann himself, but it was hard to know at what point the Reich Special Investigator was going beyond his authority and at what point he was still within it . . . one might be beaten up quite legitimately, in which case it would be illegitimate to offer resistance. On the other hand . . .

"I am authorizing you to sign this authorization," Schöller said brusquely.

Stapplemann pondered this.

"You have my signature," Schöller said, "and you have the signature of the Führer's SS Liaison Officer. That should be enough."

"If the Special Investigator will forgive my reminding him, it is a general principle that where an authorization requires more than one signature to be effective, the superior signatory cannot validly order the inferior to sign."

"Like hell he can't."

"If the Special Investigator says so . . . "

"I do."

"Since there appears to be a difference of opinion as to the correct way of proceeding, I shall have to consult Reichsführer Himmler on this."

"That is not necessary."

"I beg to differ."

"I advise against telephoning him, or contacting him in any other way. His health is not good, as you know, and this matter is bound to upset him."

"Why should it upset him?"

"He may have his own plans for using the money."

"But in that case," Stapplemann said, horrified that anyone could think of going against the SS-Riechs-führer's wishes, ". . . in that case the money can on no condition be withdrawn by the proposed withdrawer."

"Reichsführer Himmler's state of health means he can't take all the decisions that need to be made at this time. So I am taking some of them for him. You understand?"

"But there is absolutely no precedent for . . . "

The Special Investigator was every moment becoming increasingly impatient with the Budget Administrator's pedantry.

"If I order my assistant outside to take out his pistol and shoot you, Stapplemann, for being an obstructionist, that might be unprecedented too, but you would be dead all the same."

Schöller threw open the door and indicated his young henchman seated on the polished pine bench, wearing a long brown double-breasted overcoat and slouch hat, a little pile of cigarette ends between his feet, notwithstanding the Smoking Forbidden sign. Blue-gray clear eyes. A mere youth. The Budget Administrator had never seen him before. Not the usual type of killer. Not the usual ruffian. Open face—deceptive, of course. The stiff features and the unwavering cold eyes spoke tellingly enough of his vocation.

Elliott looked the Administrator straight in the eye and felt in his breast pocket for the cigarette packet.

Schöller closed the door again.

The Administrator was shaking.

"Such an act would be entirely . . . entirely without legitimacy." The chubby-cheeked Administrator's face was red with agitation, his chest was heaving, his excessive flesh bulging and pressing against tight buttons and cross-belt. His jaw became locked in the expression of a stubborn unbudging child, lips tightly compressed, face rigid.

"I am appalled . . . appalled, I may say . . . to be subjected to such illegitimate and unauthorized terrorization. Anyone would think that the Reich Special Investigator wished to steal the money. . . . "

"You've understood, Stapplemann, at last."

The Administrator could not believe his ears. Was

this the Reichskriminaldirektor himself, proposing that . . .

"You will correct me if I am wrong, but I thought . . . "

"You are not wrong."

"You are asking me to authorize a criminal act."

"You'll get your cut."

"I fear the Special Investigator has made an error. I am not a dishonest man. . . . "

"What do you think is going to happen to your family when you are hanged, Stapplemann?"

"Hanged?"

"What else do you suppose the Allies will do with you? Pay you a retirement pension? You're the man who paid for the concentration camps, among other things. Your signature is on the checks."

Stapplemann's mouth hung open stupidly.

"I'll refresh your mind," Schöller said, reaching inside his briefcase and taking out a file. He laid it on his knees and quickly flicked through the pages.

"Here, for example," he said. "March fifteenth, 1943, to C. H. Kori, makers of heating equipment. You wrote to them as follows, on that day:

" 'While it is acknowledged that four furnaces supplied by you for Dachau and five for Lublin have given full satisfaction in practice, I must point out that the Didier Works of Berlin have submitted tenders for the Belgrade camp substantially below yours. Didier have proposed for putting the bodies in the furnace, a simple metal fork moving on cylinders.

" 'My office is faced with ever-mounting costs, and is obliged to exercise the most stringent economies.

" 'For these reasons, I ask you to consider if you can bring down your price to a minimum figure, if necessary by using a simple method of disposing of the corpses (human labor could be used for this purpose in place of mechanical machinery, if this will bring down costs). Failing this, I will be obliged . . . '

"Et cetera, et cetera," said Schöller. "Signed Oswald Stapplemann, Head of Budget Administration SS." He looked up. "That's just one letter out of hundreds, all bearing your signature. There is enough here to hang you twenty times. Of course, this whole file *could* accidentally fall into a deep drain. I am sure you have already taken care not to leave any other correspondence around. With no *specific* evidence, you could try telling the Allied war crimes investigators that you had no exact knowledge of what was being supplied by these heating firms. You thought it was heating equipment, to keep the inmates warm during the cold winter months. Sign Dr. Behr's form and you can have this file. Also, there will be some money for you in Switzerland, to take care of your family if the worst comes to the worst."

The Budget Administrator's neck had sunk even deeper into his collar, the tabs of which became obscured by the thick flesh under his chin. He had the expression of a shame-faced child wishing to disappear through the floor. His face burned red, and he fidgeted about in his chair. The concentration camp correspondence. He had always felt uncomfortable about that. But had felt obliged to steel himself to deal with this disagreeable matter. Surely the Allies were not so barbarous as to hang a man for having written a few letters and signed some checks. He had never even been inside a concentration camp. Never.

"I'm a family man, Herr Investigator," Stapplemann began to explain, "and I have always prided myself on having a sense of duty. I have four children, aged eleven, eight, four, and three. My wife has a phlebitis of the left leg. The children are entirely dependent on their father's support, there is no one else. . . . My little ones are very dear to me, Herr Special Investigator . . . "

"As a good father, Stapplemann, which I am sure you are, you must make some provision for them. Hmm? Sign Dr. Behr's paper and there'll be two hundred thousand Swiss francs for you in a Swiss bank account . . . in your wife's name, if you wish."

A distant explosion somewhere in the city made the Administrator start; an unexploded bomb going off, or perhaps a gas main igniting.

"In the circumstances, I shall abide by the Special Investigator's instructions."

"Go ahead then. Sign."

"Dr. Behr took the form with him," Stapplemann said. "He is returning in the morning. I will sign the paper then."

"All right, Stapplemann. In the morning. But no slipups, mind."

· 28 ·

Schöller said nothing to Elliott during the drive back to the Prinz Albrechtstrasse. He drove even faster than usual, and in the car compound got very quickly out of the car and then half walked, half ran to the entrance of the underground offices. He was impatient at the length of time it took the inside guard to slip back the bolts, and shouted abuse at him. In the underground maze he went a different way than before, through humming and vibrating passages that all looked the same to someone not intimately familiar with their subtle differences of dampness and discoloration, and ended up outside one of the many locked doors. Here, again, there was a ritual of knocking and a peephole opening before he was admitted with his assistant to the telephone interception room, manned by some dozen or so operators wearing earphones and equipped with tape recorders.

Schöller went straight to the superintendent sitting in a small glass cubicle.

"Stapplemann: who has he phoned in the last ten minutes?"

The superintendent quickly consulted his pad for exactness though he had the information in his head.

"He has attempted to place a telephone call to

Reichsführer Himmler's field headquarters. He was connected by the telephone operator, but we cut him off, as per instruction."

"Continue as instructed," Schöller said.

Not by the smallest facial expression did the superintendent question the legitimacy of an order to prevent a senior SS officer from being able to make contact with the various police and security departments of the Reich.

If the superintendent had been ordered to intercept the Investigator's calls, he would have carried out that order just as unquestioningly.

Schöller returned hurriedly to his own office, seated himself behind his desk, and opening the Budget Administrator's file, let his eye run down the summary of basic details: age, status, address, etc.

"That pompous idiot," he said, "has found out about Sunrise."

"How?"

"Accident. I have put a stop on his calls. But that is only temporarily effective. If he succeeds in getting through to anyone and tells what he knows, Sunrise is finished. And so are we."

"What do we do?"

"We have to kill him," he said without looking up from the file.

Elliott stroked his upper lip like someone examining the beginnings of a mustache. His fingers continued around his mouth and along his jawbone and came together at the chin, as if tracing the line of a future beard. He said nothing. The logic of Schöller's conclusion appeared irrefutable.

"It will have to be done tonight," Schöller said. "Stapplemann usually works late at his office, until about seven-thirty P.M., and then is driven home in an SS staff car. He gets there just about the time the first air raid alert is sounding. In the car there is an armed driver. The car is armored and has one-and-a-half-inch bulletproof glass windows. He lives in a special compound for high SS officials and their families. Guarded. If he gets home, there are people he can talk to on the internal telephone system. That's probably what he is planning to do."

"Then it will have to be done before he gets home," Elliott said.

Schöller nodded. "His office is out of the question. As he is leaving? Very difficult. The entrance is strongly guarded. No unidentified person is allowed to wait in the vicinity. It will have to be on the road . . . on his way home. He travels in convoy. The funk train— the nightly exodus of the bigwigs to the safety of the outskirts. They have an escort of SS motorcyclists."

"A sitting duck he is not," Elliott said.

"It has to be done," Schöller said and stood up. "Come with me."

Once more they went along the damp passages and past locked doors. Schöller's peremptory knock on one of these doors resulted in an inset grille being opened and their faces examined. They were admitted —this time to the armory.

Schöller strode along the length of the firearms rack, where a range of light weapons was held by metal spring clips. He took down an MP-40 and gave it to Elliott, who grasped it somewhat awkwardly.

"You ever handle one of these?"

Elliott examined the crude weapon made largely out of stamped sheet metal components, with a folding steel frame stock. He shook his head.

"Simple enough to use," Schöller said. He came forward, took the gun in his hand, and proceeded to demonstrate the action, sliding back the bolt and then turning the small handle inward to lock into the slot in the barrel. He took a thirty-two-round magazine and clipped it vertically into the corrugated housing, under the barrel, forward of the butt and trigger.

"It's a fierce little weapon, hang onto it tight. It's not very accurate, but the range we're thinking of, that won't matter."

"What range are we thinking of?"

"Close," Schöller said. "Very close. Has to be."

"Have you worked out how?"

"Not yet, but I will."

For himself Schöller selected a Sturmgewehr, which

was capable either of fully automatic fire or, if more accuracy was required, of single-shot rifle fire.

After signing the duty's officer's book for the items taken, he led the way back to his office.

"Six o'clock," he said. "Half an hour's rest, then we go. You take the bed. I can sleep sitting up."

He sat down in the chair behind his desk, slipped forward in the seat so that his head was supported at the back, and closed his eyes. He opened them again almost immediately to look at Elliott, who was staring up at the ceiling.

"Rest," Schöller told him. "Don't think. You agree it has to be done, don't you?" Elliott gave an uncertain shrug. "Then forget about it. You will see, it is easier to do than you think. Something takes over . . . you will see." He closed his eyes again and in a moment was in a light sleep.

Damn him, Elliott thought. *With all he has on his head, he's the one who can sleep. By what right? What right has he to sleep?* He was alarmed by the waves of panic he felt as he thought about what he was going to have to do. *I'll just go to pieces if I'm like this, I'll blow it. Take it easy, take it easy,* he counseled himself. *Keep calm. It has got to be done, hasn't it? Don't think about it. Empty the mind. Mindlessness—yes, yes.*

Quantregg had given him clear instructions. Go along with Schöller, he's making the big play—he's got the experience. You can overrule him on your own judgment at any time, but the implication was: Don't unless you're pretty damn sure, because he knows and you don't.

He couldn't empty his mind, didn't have the knack like Schöller of being able to do that. Still, even worse than having to do this killing, cold, was making a mess of it, getting jittery when the moment came and blowing it. On account of some stupid visceral nervous reaction.

Listen, he told himself, *the guy's an SS-General, he's the lousy money man of that whole lousy stinking outfit, he paid for everything, it's his signature on the lousy checks. You don't need to have any compunction about killing a rat like that. And it's necessary for Sunrise to work. Which is going to save the lives of American boys in Italy, apart from all those future benefits for the free world that Dulles sees. It's for an ideal and it's for the future. Get that straight in your head. Relax. You've just got to steel yourself and do it. Got it? Don't think. Empty mind. Think of something else.*

He thought about the German girl. About how beautiful she was. That calmed him a little. He thought about kissing her and that eased something in him. Yes. It would have rested him. The soldier's rest. He tried regular controlled breathing to achieve calmness.

Still he couldn't empty his mind, all those other images out of gangster movies kept intruding. And he was the gangster. In the slouch hat, with the gun ... Only it wasn't like that because this was for the good of the world. *Get that clear in your head. Right?*

He thought about his father. Last time he'd seen him was in the restaurant at Basel Bahnhof. He'd been wearing the old trilby hat with the crooked rain-soaked brim. December '41. Dad had finally got out of Berlin, and he was going to go across Vichy France to Lisbon, and from there take the Clipper to New York. Wanted me to follow. I didn't and then in '42 the borders closed. If I had followed him back to the States ...

Dad, that time, was so amazed about all the lights in Switzerland, and the food, those two-inch-thick T-bone steaks we ate. Fifty-three separate dishes on the menu. He couldn't get over it. We drank old-fashioneds. And we had one of those railway station talks. That's when I was always closest to him, when he had time for me, waiting for a train, or a plane. He'd talk then. It was a little like listening to one of his broadcasts, but he was saying it to me. What was it he said that time? "Howard, the lights are going out all over Europe ... "—yuh, that's right, that's right—and he said, " ... it's going to be dark a long time. But I'm an optimist at heart, I believe that the mess human beings get themselves into they can get themselves out of again. In my lowest moments in Berlin, when I'd get pretty damn blue, I can tell you, and feel everything was lost, I'd cheer myself up with an old German folktale that's a favorite of mine, about the Baron sinking in the bog? When he's up to his neck and about to go under, he just up and grabs himself by the hair and hauls himself out. That's the way I see it, being the perennial optimist I am. Civilization has got to grab itself by the hair and pull itself out, and it will—it will. I have faith in that. We Americans are going to have to come into this war sooner or later, we're going to have to throw our strength into the struggle against Hitlerism and all that means. . . . "

"You've rested? It's time."

Schöller had awakened and was ready to go. Elliott got up; he must have moved too abruptly, for the blood did not rise quickly enough to his head and for an instant he blacked out. Swaying, he gripped himself at the wrist and in his clammy palm felt his blood race.

Seeing his condition, Schöller poured him a medicinal dose of brandy.

"Drink this. For your stomach." He watched him drink and then said, "I have worked out something. I will tell you at the right moment." He gave the queasy young American a sharp look and said, "Take the bottle with you if you like."

Elliott picked up the flat three-quarters-full flask and stuck it in his side pocket. With his other hand he picked up the MP-40. Doubly armed, he was ready.

"I'm ready," he told Schöller.

"We go then."

On their way out, Schöller stopped again at the armory. It was only for a minute or so. To collect something, he said. Elliott waited outside.

They drove in the police car to the SS administrative offices, which were housed in a Ministry building at the top end of the Wilhelmstrasse. He parked close enough to the main entrance to be able to recognize Stapplemann as he came out, but not so close that the Budget Administrator or the guards could make out the faces of the men inside the dark car. Both wore their hats pulled down low over their foreheads and had their coat collars turned up.

As the high-ups left their offices to go home, the dusk was turning rapidly to darkness. A fixed routine was followed. Before somebody came out, his driver was called by his individual code number on the car radio. The car so summoned then crept forward along the curb at the regulation five miles an hour until it was directly outside the main entrance. An SS guard checked that the driver was known, and when he was satisfied, gave a signal, whereupon the high-up came quickly out of the building and got into the car, which immediately drove off at speed. Any unidentified car following at the same speed would have raised the alarm.

Schöller watched this departure procedure repeated again and again. It was after seven-thirty now and getting dark. Seven-forty-five. Still no sign of Stapplemann. He was working even later than usual, signing those all-important checks, a man dedicated to his work, evidently. If he stayed much longer, he'd get caught in the first night raid. At ten minutes to eight a large gray Mercedes started to creep slowly forward—it was the last one, must be Stapplemann's. It stopped right in front of the entrance, and the driver got out, in readiness for opening the rear door. Still no Stapplemann. Probably some last-minute matter that had demanded his attention.

The driver was beginning to pace up and down, from time to time looking up at the sky, which was getting darker every moment. He was obviously nervous. He looked at his watch and then started to walk toward the parked police car some twenty yards away. Elliott watched him approaching. He was an awkward gangling youth, with uniform untidy, gun belt sagging. Pistol holster in the wrong place. He bent low and rapped on the window. Elliott opened it slightly and the youth practically stuck his face inside. A freckled face, with glasses.

"What is the time, please?"

Elliott told him, avoiding showing himself.

An explosive shout from the entrance of the building. Stapplemann was waiting by the car. Whirling round, almost tripping over his own feet in his confusion, the driver started running back. He opened the car door for his passenger, and then had difficulty closing it properly. He got into the driver's seat, and had trouble starting the car. It kept stalling. He was not exactly the highly disciplined supertrained automaton, this one. A clumsy fellow. They must be using third-category call-up groups now as drivers, which was just one category before cripples and mental defectives.

Eventually he did get the car to start, and it moved off with a violent forward jerk.

Schöller remained unmoving in the police car. Not until he had allowed three full minutes to go by did he switch on his engine and move off slowly, going in the opposite direction to Stapplemann.

In reply to Elliott's questioning look, Schöller said, "They rendezvous in the Nürnbergerstrasse, and then they go out in convoy, through the southern districts, and out through Tempelhof. We'll pick them up past the airport."

Clouds moved rapidly across the sky, from time to time covering the large, perfectly rounded yellowish moon, which was like some big baleful eye in the sky watching everything. Lit up like this, the city looked unearthly.

The first few splashes of rain fell in heavy blobs on the windshield, drawing strange maps in the masonry dust. The rain seemed on the verge of becoming a downpour, but still continued to fall in large isolated drops with the regularity of a slow heartbeat.

Schöller was taking a southerly route out of Berlin, keeping roughly parallel with the convoy. They spotted it once or twice at intersections, several blocks away on their left. They were able to overtake it without much trouble, and then, putting his foot down hard, Schöller pulled far ahead on the Reichstrasse 96. By the time the airport had been passed, he was several minutes ahead of the "funk train."

Having chosen the spot with care, he drove the car off the road and into the shelter of a small copse. He switched off his lights and the engine and said, "Listen carefully."

From under his seat he produced the object for which he had returned to the armory. A one-inch-bore single-shot signal pistol. He handed it to Elliott. "When

I tell you, fire this out the window up into the air. Aim forward slightly. Certain things will happen, you'll see. Stay close, and do exactly what I say. You'll want your MP-40. Now relax. The timing is vital."

Elliott reached in his coat pocket and pulled out the brandy bottle, and took a long swig. The liquor burned inside his chest. He waited for the effect, and was gratified by the quick dulling waves that spread through his veins to his head. Soon only a small bright ring of concentrated awareness remained. He took another long swig and everything became easier. He wiped his palms on his trousers. Schöller gave him a hard look. Fortunately no great accuracy was needed to carry out what was required of the sweaty-palmed young American.

On the Reichsstrasse 96, the first dimmed half-lights of the motorcycle escort had become visible, faint as night-glowing insects. Then came the sound of car engines.

Schöller turned on the ignition and gently revved the car. He waited until the two motorcyclists, traveling about a hundred yards ahead of the first car in the convoy, had passed, and then pulled out into the gap behind them, at the same time switching on the police siren. At once the motorcyclists swerved and slowed until one was on either side of the police car. In accordance with established drill the first car of the convoy had slowed down, keeping well back.

Schöller wound down his window, pointed up at the sky, and shouted out, "Night marauders. Mosquitoes. Get a move on! Looks like the British got wind of this route. Five kilometers ahead, take the Nuremberg direction."

The SS motorcyclist acknowledged the instructions and roared off, giving the signal to the lead vehicle in the convoy to increase speed. The police car, siren still going, slowed down and pulled into the inside lane, allowing the other cars in the convoy to pass it.

Schöller let five cars pass him in this way, and then a sixth—Stapplemann's. It was the one before last. Four SS motorcyclists brought up the rear. As the Budget Administrator's gray Mercedes went by, Schöller, accelerating hard, swung out, forcing the car that was following Stapplemann's to brake sharply.

Through the rear window Elliott saw the thick flesh at the back of the Administrator's neck, below his cap. He was looking from side to side, through one window, then the other. He leaned forward, probably to ask the driver what was the meaning of the police siren, the sudden increase of speed.

Schöller was staying very close behind him.

"Now," he said.

Elliott stuck the signal pistol through the open window. Cold air whipped around his fingers and up his sleeve. He pointed the gun upward at an angle of eighty degrees and pulled the stubby trigger. The faint report was completely drowned by the continuous howl of the police siren, with its agitating pitch.

Schöller was braking gently and positioning himself on the inside lane clear of the car behind, in anticipation of what was going to happen next.

As the flare burst, an area about a quarter of a mile in diameter was brilliantly lit up.

Everything within the area of illumination was starkly defined—the pandemonium of abruptly braking cars, slithering and skidding over the wet asphalt, the motorcyclists going into violent wobbles.

The flare suspended from a small parachute was floating slowly down. The light became fiercer. It showed an open expanse of farmland and far back, at the periphery of the intense brightness, the dark and dripping pine forests. Furrowed land. A ditch. A clump of small trees. In the distance, some huddled farm buildings. A tractor. No shelter nearby. But there was more chance in spreading out than in remaining clustered together on the crown of the road, and passengers were getting out of their cars before they had come to a full halt, and were starting to run across the fields, eyes wildly searching the sky for the planes.

Blinded by the flare, they saw nothing and ran without knowing where. Some were calling out to each other as they stumbled across the unlevel ground, men not accustomed to great physical exertion: "Where are they?" "Do you see anything?" "Where?" "Where?"

Schöller had pulled up just off the road, and with car door open and automatic rifle on his lap he watched Stapplemann as he ran for his life, like all the others. A dozen yards behind him came his driver. The police siren howling continuously drowned out all sounds. All the cars had been abandoned: there was nobody left on the road.

When Stapplemann had gone about fifty yards, still clutching his two heavy briefcases, Schöller and Elliott got out of the police car and started after him.

"Fire over their heads. When I fire."

At a range of sixty yards, Schöller raised the automatic rifle to shoulder level, sighted carefully along the barrel, and fired a loud burst. It cut down the Budget Administrator and made all the other running figures throw themselves flat, cover their heads, and try to dig themselves into the ground with their bare hands.

Elliott was firing burst after burst in the air. The fierce piece of machinery in his hands seemed to pull him along with it as it fired without stop, becoming hot to hold. Schöller was still firing as well. Shots continued to pierce the fallen body of the Administrator.

The gunfire had ripped open the briefcases, scattering their contents over the fields. Seeing this, Schöller signaled to Elliott to stop firing.

As the flare burned out, everything became dark again.

Schöller said in a low commanding voice, "Get back to the car. Turn it round, have the engine running, ready to go. . . . "

And then he was gone into the dark, searching the ground for something. Elliott could not imagine what. Where was the necessity for this delay? He could see Schöller only very faintly now, the sole moving figure (the others were all still flat on their faces, expecting the next blinding flare and strafing attack), every so often stooping down and picking up pieces of paper.

Elliott ran back to the car, turned it around as instructed, and then waited with engine running, door open, submachine gun on his lap. The beady-eyed moon was covered over again, and all he could see was vague movements in the dark—evidently one or two people were taking advantage of this lull between attacks to find shelter.

Where the hell was Schöller? What was he doing? What the hell was he doing? All these movements. Voices.

For an instant the clouds opened like a camera shutter, a yellow beam of light fell on a bulky shadow— Schöller bent over the Budget Administrator's body, going through his pockets—and then the shutter had closed again and Elliott saw no more, just the blackness of a closed box.

Supposing somebody else came out of the dark, not Schöller. What do I do then? Let him have it. Whoever it is. Sure. That's what I do.

He heard a single shot, followed by low questioning voices. What did it mean, that single shot? It occurred to him that if Schöller had been killed, he, Elliott, was alone in this hellhole. Flashlights. They were being shone over the ground. Others were wondering about that single shot too.

Elliott was nervously over-revving the car engine. How long do I wait here? Supposing he's been killed, supposing they're coming for me now. Come on, Schöller, damn you. Come on, be alive, you bastard. If you are alive, what are you doing, what are you doing? Any moment they were going to catch on that there were no fighter planes. And then? Apart from the driver-bodyguards, there was the motorcycle escort. Six or seven of them. I'll give him another minute, Elliott decided, and then I get the hell out.

He was getting ready to fire a burst into the thick darkness that was rapidly becoming a tangible form when he saw it was Schöller. Running. Keeping low and running hard. He scrambled in, panting, and Elliott got going before the door was slammed shut.

"What the hell were you doing there? What was going on? What was that shot?" Elliott's voice was jittery and angry and wild, and he did not recognize its sound.

"Concentrate on the driving," Schöller said.

Elliott was driving fast and recklessly with only the dimmed lights on, which gave the minimum of illumination on the road. He was driving much too fast for the distance he could see ahead.

"Take it easy. Easy," Schöller said again. "For God's sake, watch the road . . . !"

The delayed downpour came at last. It was so heavy and sudden that for a moment there was no vision at all and the car slid all over the road until Elliott had succeeded in finding the wipers switch on the unfamiliar dashboard arrangement; even with the wipers on, it was only intermittently that the way ahead could be made out with any degree of clarity, the rain was so thick. But Elliott continued to drive at the same speed, something had got into him, preventing him from slowing down.

"There is nobody after us, we got away with it," Schöller said, trying to get him to slow down. "Slowly. You'll get us killed this way."

He was talking with interruptions, still breathless from running. He got the brandy flask out of Elliott's coat pocket, put it to his mouth, and took a long drink. He had blood all over him, on his hands and coat sleeves and coat front, Elliott saw.

"What happened there? What was the damned rifle shot?"

Schöller took another long drink of brandy.

"The driver," he said, wiping his mouth. "Stapplemann's driver. The idiot. Stumbled onto me . . . "

"And?" Elliott said, dangerously taking his eyes off the road to look Schöller in the face.

"Keep your eyes on the road," Schöller warned.

"And?"

"I had to kill him," Schöller said.

"You had to kill the driver? That category-three specimen?"

"He was pulling his gun out. . . . "

"Pulling his gun out. He couldn't pull his cock out to piss."

"I couldn't risk it."

He had got his breath back, and with that his authority.

219

"All right," he said firmly. "Slow down progressively, not too fast. And pull up where you can, I'm going to drive before you get us both killed."

Elliott did as he was told. As Schöller walked round the car to change seats, he raised his face up and let the rain wash him.

After they had been driving some time on the road back to Berlin, he evidently felt the need to say something to Elliott, who had fallen into a slumped daze.

"It's all right. It's done. You did all right, better than I expected. You didn't panic, you did what you were told, and you see . . . we did it, and there's nobody after us. Look in the mirror. I've been watching. Not a glimmer." He seemed in good spirits now, elated even.

To his surprise, Elliott found Schöller's words gratifying in some way. So he hadn't exactly disgraced himself. He too was beginning to feel elated now that the killing of the Administrator was behind him.

· 29 ·

The air raid alert was sounding as they entered the city, and they heard the huge antiaircraft batteries of the Zoo flak towers open fire in remote-controlled unison. Switching to the coded broadcasts on channel Mio, Schöller noted the details and rapidly worked out the flight path of the bombers.

"We'll wait here," he said, pulling up into a side street in Wilmersdorf. "We'll be all right here."

They saw the flames shoot into the sky as the bombs fell some three miles to the north of them.

A smell of wet clothing and of something else filled

the car. Schöller's long overcoat had become badly bloodstained while he was searching the Budget Administrator's body . . . then the rain had soaked him, and now the blood and the rainwater were drying out together in this confined space.

Elliott saw that somehow blood had got onto him too: on his trouser cuffs, the hem of his coat, his boots. It had even got onto his hands, under his fingernails. Taking out his pocket knife and opening the file blade, he began to scrape under his fingernails.

Meanwhile Schöller was examining himself in the driving mirror. He had a dark growth of beard. His hair was wet and plastered down. He began to comb it. He straightened his clothing. Seeing the bloodstains on his overcoat, and as it was also very wet, he took it off and threw it in the back. After that, he got Elliott to lend him the knife, and opening out the nail scissors, carefully cut away the bloody rims of dirt.

The British were going for the big marshaling yards and warehouses in the northern part of the city, the Moabit area. Some major munitions dumps were sited there, and as they went up, the sky around the edges of the explosion became white.

After an hour, even though the all clear had not sounded, Schöller checked with channel Mio and judged that it was safe to proceed to their next destination, in the eastern part of the city.

The damaged camouflage netting that covered the Charlottenburger Chaussee had been ripped loose by the wind and was being blown about. Burning pieces of it were drifting all over the city. Unter den Linden was deserted. Driving fast along the central avenue, only slowing to swerve around felled trees or blocks of fallen masonry, they were soon in the Alexanderplatz.

In the network of streets that spread out from the great Platz, workers lived in dense concentrations, layers upon layers of humanity, piled one on the other in the high tenements. It was an area with a reputation for vice and petty criminality as well as poverty, full of hole-in-the-wall shops, narrow dark rooms.

"I used to work here," Schöller said. "They didn't move me to the Prinz Albrechtstrasse till '39. September '39. Up till then my department was at Police Headquarters. Right here. It's a good place to teach you about human nature. That it's dirty. Human nature is dirty. Oh, if you've got the money, you can cover it up, put nice white wall-to-wall carpets over the dirt. But you can't get away from it. Here you saw it out in the open. No pretense. Use and be used. Buy and sell. Anything and everything. It's all right, it's what people are. You can't complain. Who can you complain to?"

Schöller was examining the succession of exactly similar arched entrances along the front of a huge workers' tenement until he found the number he was looking for. "Come on," he said, pulling up and getting out. Elliott followed automatically. He no longer inquired where they were going or for what purpose. The street was cobbled, streetcar tracks ran down one side of it. As they went in under the arch, they smelled the dog piss.

A bare stone-floored passage led past a number of half-glazed front doors, with dirty net curtains behind. They all had bells that were rung by giving a brass handle a half-turn.

Outside number 379b Schöller stopped and gave the handle several turns, as if impatiently winding up a clock, and a disproportionately tiny *burrrrh* came from inside. When the door was not immediately answered, Schöller continued to turn the handle, evidently exasperated by the feeble ringing. He supplemented it by banging with his fists on the glass pane. Eventually a woman's thin old hand drew aside the net curtain sufficiently for her to see out.

Distant eyes examined the callers with suspicion. "I want your son. Your son," Schöller shouted through the glass. The woman was shaking her head with the incomprehension of the very old. A moment or so later a plumpish middle-aged man, in elastic suspenders over a collarless shirt, came to the glass and also peered out. When he saw Schöller, he frowned at first, as if not quite sure if this was who he thought, and then realizing that it was, became quite agitated at having kept the caller waiting and quickly started to unchain and unbolt and finally unlock the door, and as he opened it shooed his old mother away with a secret urgent wiggle of his hand.

"Good evening, Herr Direktor. Good evening. Heil Hitler!" he added as an afterthought. "To what, may I ask, do I owe the honor of this . . . visit?"

"Not everyone finds a night visit from me such an honor." The collarless man went pale. "But," Schöller added quickly, "in this case you have nothing to fear. Can we come in?"

"Of course. Of course. You must forgive my great rudeness in not asking your Excellency in of my own accord . . . but I must admit to having been dozing, and I am only just waking up properly."

The front door gave directly onto the main living room and kitchen, after which there was a tiny hall with two small bedrooms off it. The old woman had returned to her corner and was sitting in a rocking chair, stroking a mangy black cat.

"Perhaps your bedroom," Schöller said. "Where we can be more private."

"Yes, yes. By all means." He coughed with distress. "I hesitate to offer your Excellency refreshments . . . in view of the poor quality of what I should be obliged to offer. . . ."

Schöller cut him short. "We require nothing. My assistant will wait outside."

With that, the two men went in.

Elliott had got used to waiting outside—it was evidently what assistants did. Though sometimes they were called in, for one purpose or another. He did not ask himself what Schöller was doing here in this shabby smelly apartment. He had stopped asking questions of himself and others. Events simply had to be got through.

He sank into a broken-down old armchair whose springs squeaked protestingly on receiving his weight. He was still wearing his overcoat and hat. He felt enormously tired and closed his eyes. When he opened them, he found the old woman staring at him. Her eyes were full of foreboding, as if she knew or had sensed who he was. Perhaps she had seen the bloodstains on his trouser cuffs.

He smiled to assure her that no harm would come to her or her son, but realized that he did not know this for certain, and he saw from her face that his smile did not convey reassurance. For the old woman seemed to have become more afraid. In his state of being both highly keyed up and utterly exhausted, he must have given the wrong sort of smile.

The bedroom that Schöller had entered, though small and poorly furnished, was very neat and tidy. Everything in place. The walls were decorated with cutouts from magazines, pictures of great Party rallies, triumphal march-pasts, victory celebrations.

"You've done good work for the Party and your country, Braun," Schöller said.

"Thank you, Herr Direktor. I have endeavored to do my best."

"Over the years, you must have done dozens of jobs for us. Hmm?"

"Over one hundred, Herr Direktor."

"As many as that? Always through Amt IV, counter-documentation?"

"Yes, always, Herr Direktor."

"I don't suppose you always knew for what purpose we required the graphological copies that you made for us." He chuckled.

"Naturally enough such things were not divulged to me."

"The three or four times that you have done work for me, I was highly satisfied."

"I am flattered you should say so, Herr Direktor."

"Your skill—in reproducing handwriting—is uncanny."

"It is a gift one has," the official forger said modestly.

"A great gift, Braun."

"You are much too generous, Herr Direktor."

"There is a small service you could do for me, Braun. A few minutes' work for a man of your great skill."

"Yes?"

"You have heard of the death of SS-Major General Stapplemann? No? Killed in an air raid. Yes. Night marauders." He pointed upward. "They come out of nowhere, those swine. I have to confide in you, Braun, we're in an awkward mess. All sorts of papers of his were destroyed, and as you well know, in Germany nothing moves unless there is a proper piece of paper to say it can do so."

The forger laughed as required.

"Now the point is, Braun, we require the Budget Administrator's signature for certain interdepartmental movements of funds. Otherwise we shall be entangled in endless red tape. I have brought you some specimens of his handwriting. You think you could oblige me?"

Braun was blinking rapidly. Without saying a word, he put on spectacles and examined the various pieces of paper with Stapplemann's signature. He held the sheets very close and moving his glasses up on his forehead examined the handwriting with the naked eye. Then with glasses back on his nose he examined the writing from further away. He passed his fingertips over the signatures. He scratched his head and rubbed his eyes. His expression was doubtful.

"Well," Schöller said. "Can you do it?"

"Oh, I can do it," Braun said. "It is simple enough to do." He hesitated. "If the Herr Direktor will forgive my saying so, I have never before done a job for him *privately* . . . that is, without a Q seventy-two authorization."

"The forms have all gone up in flames, Braun. I am giving you a verbal Q seventy-two."

"That would all appear to be in order then. If I may ask, since the order is verbal, how will I be paid?"

"In cash. Immediately. One thousand Reichsmarks, as it is such a rush job."

"That is all in order then," Braun said, beginning to flex his fingers.

He went to a wall cupboard built into the recess to one side of the chimney flue, opened the double doors, and cast his eye over the shelves with their dozens of different pens and ink bottles. He felt the

225

nibs of one or two of the pens against his thumb, and finally selected an ordinary wooden penholder with a cheap broad-tipped steel nib, and a bottle of black ink. He took them to a table with a large blotting pad and a rounded desk blotter. Opening the ink bottle, he carefully dipped in the pen and then tried the Budget Chief's signature on a plain sheet of paper. He did this half a dozen times, after each attempt comparing his work with the specimen signatures before him. After each signature he carefully used the desk blotter.

"He uses—*used*," he corrected himself, "rather a lot of ink on his pen." This time Braun kept the steel nib longer in the bottle and examined the adherence of the ink before signing. He appeared more satisfied with the outcome and held it up for Schöller's inspection.

"Perfect."

"Shall I do it now?" Braun asked.

"If you are ready. It must be right the first time, you understand. There is only one form."

"If the Reichskriminaldirektor will give it to me, please."

Schöller handed it to him, folded down the middle, so that the part with the name of the Swiss bank and the nature of the transaction was not visible. All that Braun could see was the words "In authorization of the above," and the signature of SS-General Hermann Fegelein, SS Liaison Officer to the Führer, and then the blank space where Stapplemann's signature was required.

Braun picked up his pen, dipped it in the ink, and began to unfold the form, spreading it out. As he did so, Schöller leaned over him and placed his hand over the top part of the paper, as if to hold it more firmly in place.

"I suppose," Braun said, pen poised, not looking up, "that there can be no question of . . . of illegality in carrying out the orders of the Reichskriminal-direktor?"

"No question at all," Schöller assured him.

Braun looked down; he exercised his fingers for a moment, like a concert pianist before embarking on a tricky composition. Then he picked up the pen, dipped it in the ink bottle, and signed in a quick continuous hand. He waited a moment before carefully blotting the signature with the desk blotter.

He looked up. Schöller lifted his outspread hand from the top part of the form, and in the instant before he picked it up and folded it again, Braun read the name of the Commercial Bank of Berne and saw—though he could not have sworn to this—the figure of four million Swiss francs written below.

· 30 ·

The whole northern sky had become reddened with the fires of the marshaling yards as Schöller and Elliott left the forger's apartment.

As they drove toward the west end, the all clear was just sounding. The first raid of the night over, people were emerging from shelters, looking around dazedly to see what, if anything, was still there. In the streets behind the Kurfürstendamm faint frames of light were coming on around the blackout paper of a few night bars. Here and there people were ringing bells, knocking on doors, finding out what places were still open.

Schöller was looking out the window, and slowing down by some of the places he knew.

"There are some nights when I cannot sleep," he said.

Elliott nodded. A harsh light blazed in his head, dazzling him like an interrogator's lamp. He knew he would not be able to sleep either. He was feeling strange, not himself. *It was I who went with Schöller and assisted in the murder of the Budget Administrator and his driver. I did that. That was me.* The sudden exploding light of the flare. The running men falling to the ground. The hot metal in his hands as he fired over their heads. It *had* happened.

"Why don't we get the hell out?" Elliott said. "Right now."

"Impossible. There are things that still have to be . . . arranged. Besides, Wolff has an appointment with Hitler tomorrow. If it does not go well, I may be required to step in—again."

"Can we get a drink somewhere?" There was no brandy left, and the wispy electric outlines around the windows of night bars drew him insistently with their suggestion of some sort of life still going on. What was the alternative? To lie in a dark room, alone, unable to sleep, trying to achieve mindlessness unaided.

"Extase," Schöller said.

"What?"

"It's a cocktail they serve. Some kind of poisonous rotgut mixed with a thick sweet grenadine syrup. Completely foul. But don't worry, I have a little influence, you know. We don't have to drink that filth. For me, they keep something special. You see," he said, "I am some use . . . "

"I could use a drink," Elliott repeated.

"I join you, I join you," Schöller offered. "It is done now—what had to be done. We have saved Sunrise. It is something to celebrate."

"Celebrate? Oh Christ! *Celebrate!*"

"Why not, if you have the chance? When you haven't the chance, you can't."

"Any more of that folk wisdom of yours and I'll throw up."

The first bar they stopped at was a long dark underground room, with Cubist murals that could not have helped the focusing of the eyes after two or three shots of Extase. It was surprisingly crowded.

"I saw you disappear with Maritza," Schöller said as he knocked back his first so-called cognac.

"You see everything."

"Naturally."

He chuckled, rapped the bar counter for a refill, and said, "She is good, our Maritza. No?"

"*Our* Maritza?"

"One can't be too exclusive with someone like her."

"Oh, you don't mind sharing her?"

"Not at all, with my political assistant, Italy."

"Big of you. Except it wasn't like that."

"You missed your chance?"

"Yes. That's right. You never do, I suppose."

"Not if I can help it."

"You know she despises you, don't you?"

He laughed. "That what she said? She despises me? Is that so?"

He did a rapid tut-tutting sound with his teeth, a smug obscene knowingness on his face. It was an expression which denoted the possession of inside information on everything and everybody, in this case the life and thoughts and passions of Maritza von Niesor. He spoke to Elliott now in a low intimate voice.

"She is a great snob, our Maritza. Like her Papa. Ferdy. But the truth is, our Maritza has . . ." (he lowered his voice to the appropriate level for the exchange of such male confidences) ". . . low tastes. The type that can't get enough." He banged the counter for another refill. "Loves it, oh yes. The dirtier the better. I could tell the moment I set eyes on her, I always know. You can tell. Something in their eyes. That sort of empty blank craving, no? You know what I mean? When I come in, she says to me, 'Wipe your shoes.' Wipe your shoes! Imagine. To the Reich Special Investigator. A snob, an undoubted snob. Doesn't take my hat or my coat. Nothing. Doesn't ask me to sit down even. I did just the same. Dropping names all the time to put me in my place. How Herr Speer comes all the time to the house, and what a close family friend Herr von Ribbentrop is . . . and von Rundstedt, all that. But then . . ." Again he banged the bar to have his glass refilled, and went on. "But then, you see, when I was going . . ." He came even closer, his mouth was practically against Elliott's ear, his voice had become a hoarse whisper. "Listen. Listen to this. As I'm going . . . " He put his hand on Elliott's arm to gain his total attention. "As I'm going, you see, I say to her, 'Thank you, gracious lady,' very polite, and take her hand, kiss her hand, you see, which she didn't expect. And then . . . " His eyes sought out Elliott's to engage them in man-to-man rapport. " . . . Knowing the type, I don't let go of her hand, you see, but instead pull it down, pull it down, make her put it on my cock, you see . . . "

"You are a lying pig, Schöller."

He laughed delightedly. "I tell you, it was as if an electric shock went through her. I wouldn't let go of her hand, made her keep it there till I was like a bar of iron. She pretended to be horrified. Naturally. Oh, but she liked it, she liked it. Excited her. The higher class they are, the better they like a bit of crudity. In the end, she took me in her bedroom. She wanted it, all right. And not the usual way either. 'Vaseline,' she says. 'Use the Vaseline.' The other way, you see. That's how she wanted it."

"That's your dirty dream."

"I tell you—human nature *is* dirty. Believe me, I have seen enough to know."

"*That* I'm ready to believe."

"Tell me something—you're a fine upstanding young man, I know, I know. An idealist. I can tell. Tell me, that never appealed to you, what I just told you? It didn't cross your mind ever? With someone like Maritza von Niesor. . . . Wipe that superior look off her face, drag her down a bit. . . . "

"I don't share your tastes, Schöller. And in any case, I don't believe you. About that or about anything else. And while we're on the subject, there's something you should know. I promised that girl something."

"Then the encounter was not altogether so uneventful?"

"I promised her papers. Exit papers. To enable her and her father to leave Berlin."

"Her and her father! You are very generous. Her and her father!" Schöller laughed.

"Listen to what I'm saying."

"Everybody promises papers," Schöller said dismissively. "She is used to that, I assure you, I assure you. . . . "

"But unlike the others, I meant it."

"Some people become very gallant when they have had too much to drink. I understand."

Elliott was incensed by Schöller's casual cynicism. "I meant what I said."

"You are drunk now?"

"I am not drunk."

"Then explain to me how you propose to get her these papers. Tell me."

"I'm not going to get them. You are."

"I am! What do you think I am? Jesus Christ?"

"You'll get her the papers," Elliott said, quietly and forcefully.

"It is impossible," he said. "It's impossible in any case, and it's doubly impossible in the time we have."

"We don't leave until you've got her the papers."

"We'll talk about it later," Schöller said, judging that Elliott was probably in an overwrought state after the experience he had been through, and in no fit condition to discuss things rationally. "You must relax," he told him. "You must not be so tense, or none of us will get out."

They found another place to go to that was even more crowded, and after that another, and another.

A cadaverous comic with long false eyelashes and red painted lips was performing in one of the cellar cabarets. A friend of his had ordered a suit from his tailor. He was arrested on a charge of willful destruction of Germany's timber reserves. Wild laughter. It was a rotten joke? Why should jokes be different from everything else? Applause and laughter. This one was so rotten it didn't even qualify for the death penalty. What sort of joke was that? He used to have first-class jokes, in the death penalty category, but all his joke writers had been shot. Laughter. Why hadn't he been shot? Bureaucracy. Who could get what they wanted these days! Laughter and applause. The other day he had bitten on his potassium cyanide capsule. Like

231

everything, ersatz . . . all it did was make him fart. Hysterical laughter, wild applause.

From one place to another. Schöller and Elliott slithered and staggered down dark stairs into half a dozen more or less suffocating holes, becoming only very slowly drunker, since the alcohol was everywhere watered. But they kept on. Another drink, and another. Somewhere or other the real stuff would be found and the blank mind finally achieved.

At three A.M. Schöller pulled up outside a heavy wooden door with a large bellpull, under which a brass plate said, "Ring for entry." The unlit neon script above said simply "The Night." Below, the large window had its steel roller shutters down. The place appeared to be closed, but when Schöller rang the bell, the door was opened immediately.

"Good evening, Herr Direktor. Good evening. It is an honor to see the Herr Direktor."

Firm hands steered them through the hot smoky dark. Dusty velvet curtains were pulled aside for them; people moved chairs to let them pass; their shoulders brushed against quilted walls from which came a smell of old scent, dust, and stale body odors. Feeling for direction and support, Elliott was turned by guiding hands and pressed downward. He made the motion of sitting, and—much to his surprise—found himself seated. The strongly breathing bodies he sensed around him, without actually seeing them, appeared to be watching something, and only as he turned in his chair toward the light source did he realize that a couple was copulating a few feet away on a large circular bed that served as a kind of apron stage.

"There is some entertainment provided with the Extase cocktails here," Schöller said. "I trust you are not prudish." They appeared to have come in at the end of the act, for the couple rolled apart, like circus tumblers, and for a moment held their fixed posture, as if waiting for applause. There was none, either because it was not considered appropriate here, or perhaps because the pair had not been very good.

Over the loudspeaker system came an amplified whisper: "Friends of the night—welcome to The Night.

232

Where we bring you the final solution of the sexual question. Total sex. The liquidation of the mind. Friends of the night, I wish you good enjoyment, much pleasure, and a total erotic experience, with Lulu and Anton."

The two named performers came on, she in bordello corsets, he naked, and rolled about on the bed, the man's body more or less obscured by the girl's, presumably to conceal his unaroused state. Both looked rather serious-faced and underfed.

At this point a small man, his face boldly made up with greasepaint, stopped at their table and produced a bottle of cognac from under his jacket.

"For the Herr Direktor," he whispered, "naturally only the best." It was the same whisper that had been heard previously, announcing the couple now on the bed, but without the mechanical amplification it was rather flat and world-weary and gloomy.

His large painted and shadowed eyes fixed despondently on Lulu and Anton. After the initial rolling about, she was now lying across his belly, her lips descending in a series of swoops upon the slack member, which her hand supported at the base. Between hand and lips, she succeeded in drawing it out to some semblance of erection. She was working very hard, with determination. The member was stiffening a little, without being yet in any reliable state for entry.

The little master of ceremonies sighed and poured out drinks for the two men and himself.

"The food," he said glumly, apologizing for his performer. "The lack of vitamins in the diet. We see that he gets the best food, but without meat, what can you expect?"

He kept refilling their glasses and wincing with shame and embarrassment at being so let down by his performers. Ah, but this next one . . .

Another girl had come on. She was very beautiful—a Nordic princess, blonde as a forest naiad. The top part of her body was clothed in yellow and white flowers, the lower part naked. She got down on all fours, and then reared up, pretending to be a horse. The room was going round and round as Elliott sought

233

to keep the erotic vision in view. Sometimes she was very close, and then his eyes, playing their drunken tricks on him, removed her again and made her appear quite far away, ascending the wall like a bat.

"I may be sick," Elliott informed Schöller.

"Not over the girl, I hope," Schöller said. She was, indeed, that close now. Squatting, her rear to the audience, her fingers deliberately parted her flesh, first the one opening, then the other. Offering. Offering. Submission. A black violent entry. The liquidation of mind. Anything. Anything. A dark electric shock of excitement passed through Elliott like a convulsion that transforms thought.

Schöller had leaned very close to him, blowing alcohol fumes in his face, talking above the music. "She is good, that one. Good value. Hmm? It appeals to you? She comes from a good family too. Almost as good as Maritza. And she is less trouble. I can arrange it. I promise you, she is exceptional—an exceptional whore of the first order."

Perhaps it was the alcohol, or Schöller's words, but Elliott began to see Maritza's face superimposed on this whore. Dream logic. Elementary wish fulfillment. The high brought low. The low raised up to power. The dirty dream of man.

"Got to get out," he said, abruptly getting up. "Going to be sick." And as he started to his feet and began to push out of the hot, closely packed room, he called back to Schöller, "I'm overruling you, Schöller. You understand. Overruling you."

"We talk about it in the morning," Schöller said, to calm down the American since he was clearly overexcited as well as about to be sick.

Somehow he succeeded in getting as far as the police car before vomiting violently. After the first spasm he straightened up and tried to walk. Stepping back, he veered unexpectedly right. Schöller caught hold of him and in doing so lost his balance, and both of them stumbled the other way like inexperienced entrants for a three-legged race. They performed a series of wild zigzags, in the course of which they were obliged to embrace for mutual support.

As they were holding on to each other in this way, Schöller suddenly looked Elliott straight in the eye and said, "You despise me, I know. Think I'm a swine. I know, I know."

"I don't know you. Don't know you."

"Liar! Liar! You think I'm a swine. Don't you? *Don't you?*"

They were performing a kind of two-step during this exchange.

"How do I know what you are? Half your file is missing." He giggled at this logic and added mysteriously, narrowing his eyes for concentrated brain effort: "I know you, I know you, Schöller. Don't think I don't know you, Schöller!"

"You don't know your ass from your elbow," Schöller said with disgust. "Listen. Listen . . ." He steadied himself carefully. "Listen . . . I was a God-believer, and still am. Yes. Yes. Inside. In here." He rapped his chest with a violent forefinger. "They made me sign a piece of paper. Renunciation. Had to. Comp . . . compulsory. Couldn't get promotion otherwise. Had to renounce God. On the proper official form, naturally. Naturally . . . " He began to laugh wildly.

• 31 •

When Dr. Behr called at the offices of the SS Budget Administrator in the Wilhelmstrasse, on the morning of April 20, he was told that Stapplemann had been killed in an enemy air attack on his way home the previous night. However, he had left an envelope on his desk, addressed to the Swiss banker. Dr. Behr was given it, and tore it open anxiously. Having no wish to remain in Berlin any longer than was necessary, he was extremely relieved to find the signature of the Budget Administrator below that of the SS Liaison Officer to the Führer.

Dr. Behr allowed himself a modest smile of satisfaction. Despite all the difficulties, he had settled his business in Berlin. The matter of the withdrawal could now be expedited in accordance with the laid-down procedure. It was, of course, unfortunate that Stapplemann had been killed last night; not that Dr. Behr wasted any of his sympathies on that type of man, but he did not like to have to rely on a dead man's signature. Still, there was nothing in law to invalidate a signature if the signatory subsequently died.

He asked if he might be allowed to see some recent documents signed by Stapplemann, and when these were brought, Dr. Behr compared the signatures on them with that on the withdrawal form. Dr. Behr was no novice at this; in his position he often had to compare signatures in order to rule out the possibility of forgery, and he was indeed something of a handwriting expert. As he examined the precisely formed letters of Oswald Stapplemann's name, there was no doubt in his mind that all the signatures matched perfectly.

Pocketing the now completed withdrawal form, he returned to the Adlon and proceeded to make arrangements for his immediate departure. When he had succeeded in getting through to the chargé d'affaires at the evacuated Swiss legation, Dr. Behr was advised to proceed immediately by road to Schloss Gross Wudicke, to which the legation had been removed for safety. They were in contact with Berne, and Dr. Behr would be able to give his instructions from the Schloss. The legation still had some diplomatic facilities in Berlin; they would send a car to fetch him.

Dr. Behr packed his suitcase and went down to pay his bill and wait.

In the lobby he was informed that he did not have to pay for his room, the hotel having that day stopped presenting accounts to its guests.

The great reception hall with its clouded marble

walls and its Chippendale furnishings had become a field dressing station, and the seriously injured and the dying had been laid down on tapestried settees and velvet sofas and the rest on the big Constantinople carpet. When fresh casualties were brought in, they were taken down to the barbershop, which had been turned into an emergency operating room. The bodies of the dead were removed and laid out in the Goethe garden, and covered with hotel blankets.

Dr. Behr was greatly distressed by these sights and by the fact that he had not been asked to pay his bill. A most ominous sign. Seeing Schöller coming toward him did not make him feel any better.

"You have concluded your business?" the Special Investigator asked.

"Yes."

"Then everything is in order?"

"It would appear so, but the final decision will have to be made in Berne by my directors." He paused. "I may tell you, they are greatly concerned about the fate of the Niederdorf prisoners, as I have already informed General Fegelein."

"Your representation on their behalf has been heeded," Schöller told him. "Certain action has already been initiated to ensure the safety of these prisoners. I have taken steps to see that this action is not countermanded."

"I am relieved to hear that," Dr. Behr said.

"I trust we will be able to conclude *our* business quickly then."

"I trust so, provided everything else is in order."

"It will be, I shall see to that," Schöller told him. "How do you intend to return?"

"I have made certain arrangements."

"If I can do anything else to assist you, Dr. Behr," Schöller offered. "I am concerned for your safety."

"I understand your concern," Dr. Behr told him dryly, "but I believe that the protection of the Swiss embassy might be more useful than yours at this time."

The page boy came up to say that his car had arrived, and Dr. Behr quickly removed himself from the disturbing presence of the Special Investigator.

As the long limousine, flying the Swiss pennon prominently from each mudguard, made its tortuous way out of the city, Dr. Behr was feeling quite sick in his stomach from the escaping gas and the stench of the uncollected garbage. The dust made him choke. He could see that the city was coming to a stop. The streetcars did not appear to be running anymore, and many of the shops had not opened today. People were no longer waiting to use the public telephones, an indication that they were not functioning. Those food shops which had opened had nothing in their windows except the standard papier-mâché sides of ham and cuts of meat and bottles filled with colored water— "for decoration only."

The only signs of life were around the special food distribution centers, where notices said, "Extra Crisis Rations Here." The Ordnungpolizei supervised the distribution of food to the waiting women. Dr. Behr saw one woman being dragged off by police as she bitterly threw the handful of dried lentils, with which she had just been served, onto the street, screaming something about her children.

At some street corners there were sights that made Dr. Behr turn away his head: the corpses of men and women dangling from the lamp posts, with placards around their necks saying, "Deserted my country and people" or "I am a filthy defeatist pig" or "I am a rat who abandoned his post." Some of them had been daubed with dog excrement.

Their staring eyes bored into the orderly mind of Dr. Behr and filled it with thoughts of a kind that he did not normally entertain: about the ultimate fate of all living things, the decomposition of the flesh, the fact that in the end the story must turn out badly . . . badly.

He would not easily be able to forget these sights: "From dust to dust." As he looked about him, the Biblical prophecy appeared to be in the process of fulfillment. Seen from a rise in the road, the entire city seemed to have become one enormous dust heap.

Below the Prinz Albrechtstrasse Schöller and Elliott

were bent over topographical maps, deciding where the Department's "special files" were to be taken. In Berne Elliott had been shown the secret plan to divide Germany into Soviet, American, British, and French zones, and it was his task to ensure that the files were hidden in what would be the American zone.

It was decided, as a precautionary measure, to split the files into three consignments and to send each to a different destination in the same area. One lot was to be taken to a "safe house" between Miesbach and Bad Tölz, south of Munich, that Schöller had used in the past. The second army truck was to be sent farther south to the Alpine resort of Garmisch. And the third to the southeast of Munich, to the Tegernsee, where the files were to be hidden in a boathouse between Gmund and St. Quirin.

Schöller produced large-scale army maps on which he marked the hiding places and Elliott also committed the exact locations to memory.

And finally, Schöller showed Elliott that he was putting the file index, the indispensable key to finding any particular name among the thousands, in his leather briefcase. It had a combination lock which Schöller set in front of Elliott, but without allowing him to see the number settings.

"You don't trust me?"

"It's not that."

"What is it then?"

"It is foolish to put all your eggs in one basket."

Kummerl was called in and given instructions in Elliott's presence on the dispatch of the files to the agreed destinations. When the principal assistant had noted down all the details, Schöller told him, "The guard on General Wolff's family is to be withdrawn, and the order restricting their movements rescinded. Have that put into effect immediately."

"At your command, Direktor."

"What's the military situation?"

Kummerl gave the situation report in a flat voice, having evidently reached the dead end of his panic: "The latest confidential communiqué from the Berlin Commandant's office says that Russian tank columns are eight miles from the outskirts of Berlin. High Command headquarters at Zossen are being abandoned. It is expected to fall to the Soviets within twenty-four hours."

"The land corridor to the south?"

"The land corridor was open at the time of the last communiqué, Direktor."

"All the way down to Switzerland?"

"At the time of the last communiqué. Yes, Direktor. The American bridgehead across the Elbe at Barby, southeast of Magdeburg, is holding. But the Americans are not moving. This is in accordance with our intelligence reports that Eisenhower has ordered them to halt and let the Russians take Berlin."

"Still," Schöller said, "nobody would be foolish enough to try and get out, would they? Considering the penalties."

"Nobody would be so foolish," Kummerl agreed.

Schöller went to the wall map on which a forest of colored arrows showed the forces converging upon Berlin. The ring was almost complete. In the light of the latest information, he put another red arrow just outside the eastern suburbs of the city, pointing toward Treptow. He extended a red arrow, farther south, obliterating Zossen. From these main thrusts he drew dotted tentacles ending in question marks outside Teltow and Zahlendorf in the south and Spandau in the northwest, and a further one that reached out from Konev's First Ukrainian Army at Muskau to end in a series of question marks along the eastern side of the Elbe, around Torgau and Strehla.

Standing back, he scratched his head and studied the effect of these latest projected advances. The corridor out of Berlin, at the top, looked rather like a long twisted swan's neck, all the way down to Chemnitz and Meissen. Lower down it widened, but the neck itself couldn't have been scrawnier.

"Like getting a sailboat down the neck of a bottle," he said wryly.

"Exactly, Direktor."

"They do get sailboats into bottles."

"Ah yes, quite true," Kummerl said with the vagueness that had overtaken him lately.

When Kummerl had left to carry out his instructions, Schöller said, "Well, you heard. We must get moving."

"You forgot something, Schöller. The papers for the von Niesor girl and her father."

"No way of getting them in time," Schöller said, busying himself at his desk. He had a lot of last-minute matters to deal with; provisions had to be taken for the journey: food, firearms, gas.

"They have to be got in time."

"Impossible. Besides, you have heard the situation. They would never make it." He was putting papers in drawers and locking them.

"We are going to make it."

"That is because you have got me, because I know my way, because I have some practice in these matters . . . " He picked up the internal telephone.

"I know it's only a chance," Elliott said, "but I'm going to see they get it."

"I cannot issue the authorizations. They have to come from the Berlin Commandant's office."

"You got them issued for your wife and child."

Schöller put down the internal telephone without speaking into it. "They left on the seventeenth. Today is the twentieth. Those days make a difference," he said.

"Still, you can fix it, since you can fix everything."

"It is completely out of the question."

"Look at it this way, Schöller. If they don't leave, neither do I. And if I don't get out, your understanding with Dulles becomes inoperative. So—think of it as saving yourself. That, I am sure, will stimulate you to think of something."

Schöller stared at Elliott in silent astonishment that anybody could act so stupidly over a girl he had not even slept with. He tried to assess whether Elliott was bluffing. He could not believe that he would really jeopardize Sunrise because of some girl. But you never knew with these innocent young Americans.

"You are completely mad," he said, but he was no longer arguing, he had evidently accepted the situation

241

and was saving his breath. "I shall see what can be done," he said.

"I knew you would, as soon as you looked at it in the right way."

· 32 ·

On April 20, in Washington, the Joint Chiefs of Staff had finally decided that Dulles's intrigues and plots were too costly in terms of the possible breakdown of the alliance with the Russians, and sent off to him a triple priority signal that gave him unequivocal orders to break off all negotiations with the Nazis.

The cable from Washington read:

1. BY LETTER TODAY JCS (JOINT CHIEFS OF STAFF) DIRECT THAT OSS BREAK OFF ALL CONTACT WITH GERMAN EMISSARIES AT ONCE. DULLES IS THEREFORE INSTRUCTED TO DISCONTINUE IMMEDIATELY ALL SUCH CONTACTS.

2. LETTER ALSO STATES CCS (COMBINED CHIEFS OF STAFF) HAVE APPROVED MESSAGE TO ALEXANDER STATING THAT IT IS CLEAR TO THEM THAT GERMAN COMMANDER-IN-CHIEF ITALY DOES NOT INTEND TO SURRENDER HIS FORCES AT THIS TIME ON ACCEPTABLE TERMS. MESSAGE CONTINUES: ACCORDINGLY, ESPECIALLY IN VIEW OF COMPLICATIONS WHICH HAVE ARISEN WITH RUSSIANS, THE US AND BRITISH GOVERNMENTS HAVE DECIDED OSS SHOULD BREAK OFF CONTACTS: THAT JCS ARE SO INSTRUCTING OSS: THAT WHOLE MATTER IS TO BE REGARDED AS CLOSED AND THAT RUSSIANS BE INFORMED THROUGH ALLIED MILI-

Grimly, Dulles showed the message to Quantregg.

"But they can't do that," he said, "when we've got it all sewed up."

"They can," Dulles corrected him. "They sure can."

"What do we do?"

"Well, one thing is pretty clear. I can't afford to have Schöller show up in Berne, expecting to collect on the deal. Besides," Dulles added, "if Schöller got to hear—and he may through his sources—that Sunrise is off, Elliott's life won't be worth a row of beans."

"What do we do?"

"We've got to act before Schöller does." He paused to think, and then said, "Get a message off to Elliott through the Watchmaker. Say the goddamn watch has stopped. Tell him the mainspring's defective. Has to be taken out. You briefed him on that?"

"Yes, sir."

"You think he can handle it?"

"Frankly . . . I don't know, sir. He's had no training."

"Well, let's hope he may have learned something these last few days."

• 33 •

It was eleven P.M. when Schöller came in from the outer office, carrying some papers in his hand, and said to Elliott, who was lying on the iron bed, smoking: "Well, it's done. I've got you the papers."

Elliott leaped up from the bed and in a high state of excitement examined the exit authorization, signed by the Berlin Commandant, the top priority travel passes issued by the Ministry of the Interior, and the special police clearance document bearing the stamp of the Reich Special Investigator's office. This last had been signed by Schöller.

"You're a damn magician, Schöller," Elliott said.

"Naturally."

"How'd you do it?"

"I thought of something."

"I knew you would, given the incentive."

"You have learned something, since you have been with me."

"I'm a quick learner," Elliott said.

"I had an idea you would want to give these papers to Maritza yourself. A police car will take you there, and wait for you. It must not be long, you understand. We leave as soon as you return."

Elliott had got it all worked out. All the time lying on the iron bed, waiting, he'd been working it out. He'd knock at her door, say, "You don't remember who I am. You thought I was drunk. You didn't believe me . . . thought I was shooting a line. Well, here you are."

Yes. That was the way to do it. Like a Van Johnson scene. "I got you the papers, Fräulein."

There was an air raid going on when he came up out of the ground. It was odd how you hardly thought about that down there. The shaking of the earth was something you got used to and accepted as normal. But out on top, in the open, you noticed it all right— the sky ablaze. It was the southern periphery of the city that was being battered tonight. Sealing off the escape route. They were laying off the center, since almost everything was already destroyed there.

Outside her front door he composed himself. Casual. Casual. You didn't want to act too pleased with yourself. Just a normal civilized—platonic—gesture from one human being to another, Van Johnson style.

She opened the door herself. And recognized him at once, even in the blackout.

"It's you," she said, as if she'd been expecting him. She didn't ask what he wanted, but stood back a little from the door to let him in. He hesitated, having prepared himself for more antagonism, which he would then have demolished with, "I got you the papers, Fräulein."

He went in, and she watched him with dull eyes.

"We better close the door," she said. "The blackout." He closed it and leaned against it. It was cold in the unheated hall. She was wearing a man's quilted dressing gown, knotted tight for warmth.

Concealing as best he could the sense of triumph he felt, he handed her the envelope. He didn't say anything. She quickly got out the papers and looked through them. She examined them carefully at the light, page by page, section by section. The highest priority travel pass, issued by the Ministry of the Interior. The official authorization to leave Berlin, signed by the Berlin Commandant. The police clearance, signed by Schöller.

Finally, she said without softness or gratitude in her voice: "Why? Why have you brought me these?"

"I said I would," he said. It was not working out as he had expected: she seemed to be resentful of the fact that he had kept his word. Or, at any rate, suspicious.

"A man of his word," she mocked. "A secret policeman with a sense of honor."

"Why can't you just accept it, that somebody wants to help you. . . ."

"*For nothing?* Or because you want . . . ? These papers are worth a fortune. There are women who will give themselves for a package of cigarettes."

"It's not like that," he said.

"What do you want then?"

"Nothing."

"Nothing? I don't believe you. Everybody wants something. You want to feel good," she said with sudden understanding. "Even in the concentration camps sometimes they will pick out one person to be nice to, and save. So the guard can feel good. Human . . ."

He shook his head, miserable at not being able to tell her who he was.

245

"I have to go," he said.

"You are not in love with me, are you?" she asked.

"Yes, I think so."

"But you are going?"

"I have to. There is a car waiting for me outside. I have to leave."

"I will not see you again?"

"That's right. Unless you want to. I can give you a phone number. If everything goes . . . all right. Where you can call me."

She nodded her head, her throat tight, but said nothing, and watched him write a number on a scrap of paper.

"It's in Switzerland," he said.

"And if I lost it, or if anything . . . ?" Her voice had lost its mocking inflections.

"I'll find you, if you want me to."

"Yes, I think I want you to." The words were spoken against her better judgment and sounded strange to her.

The police car outside was honking sporadically, reminding him there was no time to lose.

"Try to make your way south," he said. "As far south as you can. Try to get to the Bavarian Alps. That'll be the safest place . . . it'll be the American zone."

He moved awkwardly toward her, meaning only to touch her, afraid that if he tried to kiss her again, she would pull away like the last time. He put his hand on her arm to say good-bye. She looked up at him questioningly. Applying the lightest touch to her other arm, he found rather to his surprise that he was holding her. She raised her mouth, a token of gratitude, and kissed him.

Out of a sense of obligation, she said quietly, "You can stay."

He said, "But I *must* leave."

She shrugged and said, "Suit yourself," turning away, having done all that she felt obliged to do.

He caught hold of her and held her inside his thick overcoat, kissing her. They stumbled, as if tied together, to the side of the stairs, and he found he couldn't let her go. Standing her against the ironwork of the stairs, he was undoing the dressing gown and drawing up the thin garment underneath, and she placed herself one knee drawn up so that it was possible for him to come into her, whereupon all his fear and whipped-up courage and longing flowed out of him at once. To her astonishment—since the whole act had been so perfunctory, a quickly rendered service—she too found herself carried to a peak of extraordinary intensity. She did not understand this at all, but when he started to mumble about not having intended to force himself on her, she stopped him, took his hand tightly in hers as they separated, and said, "I don't want to lose you now," frowning a little as she spoke the words, since they sounded so unlike her.

She led him by the hand, which she continued to hold tightly, into the bedroom, and there he seemed to just fold up, from the release of tension or whatever it was, and collapsed onto the bed, where he lay still for a moment, avoiding her deeply puzzled scrutiny. She was on the point of asking him something when she saw that his eyes had suddenly closed and that he had fallen into a deep sleep, like a child at the end of an overfull day.

She was studying his face when he woke up as abruptly as he had fallen asleep. The police car's hooting was continuous now. She saw the agitation return to him, following the brief respite: he was getting up from the bed and going toward the door. She came after him, unfolding the crumpled scrap of paper with the Swiss telephone number, staring at it and then at him.

"Is this all?" she asked.

He nodded silently, mouth clenched tight, turned, and left.

Schöller looked up from beneath the several layers of old overcoats with which he had covered himself on the narrow iron bedstead in his office.

He stared balefully at Elliott, and then throwing off his coverings, swung his legs down onto the stone floor. He had kept his shoes on, indeed had been sleeping fully dressed.

Rubbing the thick coarse stubble of beard on his face, he reached for the cigarettes, and lit one.

"A fine time for . . . for womanizing. A fine time."

He stood up and walked heavily to his desk. He made an abrupt hand gesture to Elliott indicating for him to look at something, and then with a stabbing forefinger pointed at Berlin on the map. He took a thick red pencil and drew an almost complete circle around the capital.

"The Russians have got Berlin totally surrounded except for this one section on the southwest, approximately between Spandau and Teltow, which is still open . . . or *was* ten minutes ago."

"We had better get going then," Elliott said.

Schöller took a thermos flask from his desk, poured hot coffee into two paper cups, three-quarters filling them, and topped up with cognac. He made a motion for Elliott to be quick.

As they were drinking, the telephone rang. Schöller answered it. He listened and a doubtful expression came over his face. After a moment's hesitation, he turned to Elliott.

"The man asks for you. He says he is your watchmaker."

He held the phone away from himself, awaiting an explanation.

"It's the procedure," Elliott said easily. "For Dulles getting in touch with me."

Schöller nodded, considering this answer carefully. Then he said, "Take it on Kummerl's phone. I'll switch it through."

"I'll take it here," Elliott said, coming forward and taking the phone from Schöller's hand. "Hello. Haften speaking," he said into it.

Schöller was making for the door.

Elliott held the phone threateningly over the cradle.

"Stay where you are, Schöller. Where I can see you."

"I was only going to the toilet," he explained innocently.

248

"Hold it. Or would you rather I didn't take the call?"

Schöller considered this, then said, "Go ahead. Speak."

"Haften here," Elliott said.

In the Wilmersdorf cellar, the watchmaker slipped a fresh magazine into the automatic rifle and said, "About your watch, Herr Haften. It has stopped completely. The mainspring. It will have to be removed. You understand?"

Elliott said, "I see. Well, I'm glad you've let me know. The only thing is, you see, I'm leaving right now. . . ."

In the Wilmersdorf cellar, the watchmaker frowned and shot a quick glance at his assistant, who was connecting a slow-burning length of fuse to the inside of a stick grenade.

"Can you have the watch seen to where you are going?" he asked. "Or would you prefer me to see to it for you? I could be with you in—three-quarters of an hour."

"But we are leaving immediately," Elliott said. "No, I think it will be more convenient if I have it seen to where I'm going."

"As you wish, Herr Haften."

Schöller was staring at him dangerously as Elliott replaced the receiver.

"A code message from Mr. Dulles," he said. "Everything is all right. Wolff's family has arrived safely on Italian soil, so Wolff's free to act now. He's back in Fasano. So we can get the hell out."

"I'm so glad to hear it," Schöller said after a moment's reflection.

· 34 ·

There had been a dawn bombing raid. The all clear was just sounding as they came up the steep ramp in the police car, headlights on full for the winding ascent in the subterranean dark. They did not know if the exit to the streets would still be open. A new avalanche of rubble had descended on the crater, partly blocking the iron causeway that spanned the distance between the entrance to the underground offices and the street.

It was necessary to drive off the iron tracks and force the car, its engine screaming, up the last few yards of the crater's side. The spinning of the wheels in the debris added to the dust. It was impossible to see anything for several hundred yards, and Schöller had to drive blind, relying on his uncanny ability to interpret shadows and degrees of darkness to find a way out. When a break occurred in the dust pall, the light of the burning city reflected by the clouds made the sky itself seem to be on fire. Making their twisting and turning way through the destruction, they saw people walking about with the vacant expressions of lunatics.

The route they took brought them out into the Potsdamer Platz. As they drove past the gutted dome of the Kempinski Kaffeehaus, they heard something new. It sounded like the earth cracking open, and all over the Platz people suddenly died, their lungs burst by the blast of the exploding shell, their bodies pierced by thousands of pieces of shrapnel.

"God in Heaven," Schöller said, "the Russian artillery have started shelling the city."

The blast had thrown the car a dozen yards off the road and onto the pavement, but the 1½-inch-thick armor plating and armored glass had protected them against the worst of the explosion. Five seconds later another shell landed a little further away, and five seconds after that a third.

As the screams of the injured and the dying filled the air, a new dread could be seen on the faces of those left alive. This was the end now. The Russians were at the gate, and nobody in the city had been left in any doubt as to what that meant. The Propaganda Ministry had made sure that the stories of rape and indiscriminate slaughter of men, women, and children were known to everyone.

Schöller drove like a guileful madman, across pavements and through the rubble of buildings. No radio Mio to give the path of destruction—these shells fell at random, with only a wild whistling, like that of an express train out of control, to warn of the imminent impact. It came every few seconds, this wild whistling, and in the open streets people who heard it for the first time instinctively sensed what it meant and ran panic-stricken for shelter and were torn to pieces as they ran.

Schöller had worked out a plan, taking into account both the Russian pincer closing on the city, and the SS control points in the one segment that still remained open.

With both dangers to consider, he had traced an intricate route that depended on his knowledge of where the main defense positions and control points were situated. Under present chaotic conditions there was no guarantee that these units would be where they were supposed to be, and there were also the mobile street courts, with their summary justice, to contend with, but it made sense to keep to the plan until events dictated otherwise. So having crossed the Potsdamer Platz, he now worked his way westward through the Tiergarten to the point where the Kant Strasse and the Kurfürstendamm converged. As they passed the zoo they heard the bellowing of wild animals being slaughtered by their keepers, and saw stray horses charging through empty streets.

Parts of the center of the city were totally deserted. Either everybody was dead, or they had all taken up full-time residence below ground, in deep shelters, underground stations, cellars and basements, and in the sewers.

The picture changed from one street to the next. Suddenly, the police car had to make its way through hordes of fleeing people, carrying bundles of belongings on their backs, wheeling prams and handcarts loaded up with household utensils, mothers on bicycles with babies strapped to them . . . These people all had wasted, wild faces encrusted with dirt and dust, and there was a look of hopelessness and incomprehension in their eyes.

"Where are you heading, where are you heading?" Schöller shouted at them, his hand continuously on the car's horn. Sometimes he had to switch on the police siren to clear a way through these refugees.

"You—you! Where do you come from?"

"From the east. The Russians have broken through at Fürstenwalde."

The next group at which Schöller shouted the same question called back, "We are heading east. Fürstenwalde. The Russians have broken through in the west. . . ."

Schöller continued down the Kant Strasse to the Adolf Hitler Platz and from there past the Reichssportfeld to the northern end of the Havel lake, where a battalion of Hitler Youth had dug in to hold the Pichelsdorf Bridge until the expected arrival of General Wenck's army.

It was not excessively difficult for Schöller to persuade the Hitler Youth leader to let them cross the bridge; the habit of obedience to such authority as the Reich Special Investigator's had been deeply inculcated in the youthful commander.

On the other side of the lake, Schöller swung southward, driving parallel with the Havel, going around Gatow and Kladow. Seeing from his map that units of the Ninth Army were in position at the lower end of the lake, and judging that their officers might be more difficult to handle than the Hitler Youth commander, he made a wide detour around Potsdam and then headed in the direction of Wittenberg.

It was cold for late April once the burning center of the city had been left behind. Great black storm clouds were darkening large sections of sky, hanging low over the landscape in dripping shifting masses. In the distance an ominous luminosity indicated where the weather was clearing.

Astonishingly, the road was packed. Every kind of private vehicle had been pressed into service by the fleeing populace. They must have been hoarding gas for this final emergency. Many of the cars had already broken down and were blocking the road.

The police siren and the flashing light gained for Schöller a degree of priority, but even so the first hundred miles were slow going and it was late afternoon by the time the traffic lightened in the vicinity of Wittenberg.

A few miles farther they saw why. Barbed wire barricades. Tank obstacles. Warning signposts in English and German. DANGER MINEFIELDS. FORBIDDEN TO GO FURTHER. Schöller kept on, in the knowledge that the German defenses were better equipped in warning signs than in actual mines. Minefields would not have been laid to the rear of German troops, unless Himmler had gone totally insane.

Outside Wittenberg they were stopped by a detachment of mobile field police of the Waffen-SS. Men carrying submachine guns surrounded the car. An officer began to shout and wave his hands about. Hadn't they seen the signs? What were they doing here? Didn't they realize they were within five miles of the front line?

Schöller identified himself: "Reichskriminaldirektor Schöller and assistant Haften . . . "

The SS-officer was unimpressed.

"All military and defense personnel were ordered to head north. Anyone heading south is to be regarded as a deserter and traitor. We have orders to shoot any-one heading south . . . "

He had pulled open the car door and stuck one hand inside to drag out these running rats and dispense to them the summary justice that such scum deserved. The Waffen-SS Colonel had little reason to suppose he was going to be alive in twenty-four hours, so he couldn't see why these "golden pheasants," with their connections and their women, or young boyfriends, should be allowed to get away. A shooting would pass the time and ease the general tension. His authority was clear. Anyone heading south was a traitor and was to be shot.

"Out. Out," he called, at the same time signaling to his men, who were unslinging their weapons, their haggard faces gaining a flush of life at the prospect of some grisly sport. Schöller got out of the car.

"You imbecile!" Schöller's voice had the unmis-takable rough abusive ring of authority. Turning to the Colonel's men, he ordered them, "Place this man under arrest."

"On what authority?" a junior officer inquired un-certainly, looking from his Colonel to the man who had just got out of the car.

Schöller thrust his impressive badge of office under the junior officer's nose. To the Colonel, he said, "So you are aware that only northbound traffic is autho-rized? Explain to me, in that case, why you have allowed dozens of traitors and deserters to pass through, heading for the Swiss frontier. . . . " The Colonel began to shout. Schöller shouted back, louder. This went on for some time and nobody could hear what either man said.

Finally, when the Colonel had been shouted down, Schöller was heard to say, "You say you have not allowed them through. In that case, why do you sup-pose I have been ordered by Reichsführer Himmler to go after them? Are you saying the Reichsführer is a liar, or misinformed?"

He turned away from the browbeaten man and gesticulated impatiently to the junior officer.

"Anyone else who delays me will be answerable to

Reichsführer Himmler." He got back into the car, started it, and roared off toward the barrier, which was hastily raised as he approached.

From there on, all traffic was military. They had entered the battle zone. Twenty miles to the west, the battle for Dessau was raging, with SS troops giving fierce resistance to the Third U.S. Armored Division.

Farther south, Halle and Leipzig had fallen. And lower down the corridor, on the direct north-south route, all organized resistance had ended in Nuremberg. The Americans were conducting mopping-up operations there and starting their main drive for Augsburg and Munich.

In the continuous rain the road had become a miasma of oil and mud and water. The heavy army trucks moved in clouds of rising wet, their wake slopping against the police car's windshield, turning it opaque between the up and down stroke of the windshield wipers. In the watery landscape, greens and browns and yellows ran into each other and the all-enveloping gray wetness gave a spectral suddenness to the appearance of objects, a farmhouse, a tank, a gun emplacement on rising ground.

The gusty winds blew the rain in all directions and caused the army trucks to swing about on the road in zigzags, their canvases and flags flapping.

Just beyond Wittenberg, Schöller crossed the Elbe, and thereafter they kept to the west bank, more or less following the course of the river, knowing that the Americans were at varying distances to the right.

Most of the villages they passed through were silent and empty, with only the occasional abrupt movement behind a curtained window to indicate the presence of a terrified villager.

At one point, some way past Torgau, the road rose, affording a clear view across to the east bank and they saw that for an area of about half a mile the ground along the shore was covered with the corpses of civilians, men, women, and children. They saw overturned farm wagons and dead horses. Suitcases, clothing, shoes, hats, feather pillows, clocks, framed photographs, and other small personal possessions were strewn everywhere.

Nothing moved. Whoever was responsible for this massacre had gone.

By the time they had passed Strehla, it was getting dark. It had taken nearly twelve hours to cover just over a hundred miles.

The necessity of keeping headlights dimmed would make night driving very slow going, and even a faint speck of moving light might draw gunfire. Moreover, the chance of blundering into either a Russian or SS patrol was infinitely greater in the dark. Taking these considerations into account, Schöller decided to stop for the night and was searching the countryside for somewhere suitable. In the last faint daylight, he saw a low-built farmhouse in the middle of fields, reached by a twisting farm track. It was about a quarter of a mile off the road, and from the way its front door was blowing open and shut Schöller concluded that the place had been abandoned.

It had got dark as he swung the car onto the bumpy dirt track. In places there were deep ditches at the side, and he drove slowly, without lights, little faster than a man walking. Approaching the house, he pulled out his Luger and placed it carefully on the top of the instrument ledge. He indicated to Elliott to get the submachine gun from under the seat.

He stopped the car a short distance from the farmhouse, and they continued on foot. Not a sound was coming from the house, with the exception of the regular noise of the front door blowing open and shut, open and shut. There was no light to be seen through the uncurtained windows, not even a gas flame or the glow of a cigarette or the flicker of a wood fire. Schöller listened for sounds. Nothing. He picked up a stone and threw it against the swinging door. No response. He took a second stone, a heavier one, and lobbed it at one of the windows. The glass shattered noisily. No other sound or movement followed.

"Come," Schöller said, going first. "Stay ten paces behind, and cover me."

Luger in one hand and a flashlight in the other, he

walked up to the front door, kicked it open, and after a moment's hesitation went in. From outside the door Elliott saw the cone of light moving over walls and furniture. He came closer, until he stood just behind Schöller.

The light beam had reached a long table: it picked out a loaf of bread, a bottle of wine, plates, a soup dish, the remains of a meal, and then as Schöller jerked the flashlight upward and sideways, a man's face was illumined, and then another and then another.

In a spasm of nervous reaction Elliott began to fire wildly from the hip, smashing the uncleared plates and dishes with his first burst. Schöller was calling "Stop, stop," and when Elliott stopped, there was still no sound or movement from the people around the table. On its continuing path the cone of light fell on a woman's face and a child's and another child's. Schöller's nostrils were twitching at the air. Elliott had still not understood.

"They're all dead," Schöller said. "Cyanide." He directed the beam of the flashlight upward, lighting up the high wooden back of a pine settle. Held by the table in front and the seat back behind, they had died seated upright, at the end of the meal, and remained in that position. The moving lightbeam revealed several more bodies, this time on the floor, two dogs, a boy of twelve, a baby, an old woman, a middle-aged man.

"This will do," Schöller said. He returned to the car and drove it into the barn attached to the farmhouse. From the trunk he took out cans of tuna fish, bread, and a bottle of cognac. Elliott followed carrying the submachine gun and blankets.

They picked their way past the bodies on the ground floor and went upstairs, where there were several bedrooms. Schöller looked briefly into each of them, shining the flashlight around, testing the bedsprings with his hands. As he was doing this, it occurred to Elliott that this was a good time and place to remove the mainspring.

Schöller had turned round abruptly: "We sleep in the same room. I am a very light sleeper. The slightest sound wakes me up—so you are safe with me. Nobody can surprise me in my sleep."

After they had eaten, Schöller made up a bed with the blankets from the car. "Small farmers," he said. "Filthy people. We don't want to get their lice." As he stripped off the used sheets, indicating for Elliott to do likewise with the other bed, he kept talking. "You are lucky you are with me. Do you know that? How do you suppose you would make out on your own? Hmm? How far do you think you would get? Not very far. Not very far. You see, I am useful. I know a thing or two. Is that correct? We are protected because," he chuckled, "we are like lovers—we need each other. It is a good arrangement that Mr. Dulles made. I must look after you, and you . . . and you know that without me you are a dead duck. So we can both sleep soundly."

While talking in this way, half humorously, shooting periodic glances at Elliott, he had been taking his coat and jacket and trousers off, but he kept the shoulder holster with the pistol, and swaddling himself in one of the blankets from the car, he lay down on the larger bed. Within two or three minutes, judging from his stillness, he was asleep.

Elliott moved on his bed, and the squeaky bedsprings made a noise like an alarm going off. Immediately Schöller's eyes flickered open and then closed again, a half-smile on his lips. Elliott tried to move more lightly, but the smallest movement made the bedsprings howl.

Elliott felt bound to conclude that this was not after all the right time or place to carry out his orders to kill the Reich Special Investigator. Apart from anything else, he was so tired he couldn't keep awake another minute.

· 35 ·

Willy Höttl was one of those bright young careerists to whom the Gestapo had offered opportunities for rapid self-advancement. He had shown himself a resourceful man, capable of carrying through schemes of an unconventional character, calling for a very particular kind of guile.

It was he, for instance, who masterminded the forging on a mass scale of British pound notes and American dollars and unloading them through agents in Switzerland and Italy. And it was he who carried out the rescue of the disgraced Italian Foreign Minister, Count Ciano, from a Rome prison. The resourceful Willy had found out how much it would cost to induce *all* the carabinieri to look the other way at the same time, and being rich in forged bank notes, had bribed the entire police force of the jail.

On April 10, 1945, Höttl had arrived in Switzerland on his most important mission of all. Ernst Kaltenbrunner, second only to Himmler as chief of Germany's security forces, had sent Höttl to see Dulles and try to negotiate terms.

Dulles already was in trouble over his negotiations with Wolff, and this was a couple of days before he was due to give an explanation of his activities to the OSS Chief, General Donovan, in Paris. So Dulles had decided it was not the right moment for him to have a meeting with Höttl. But he was very interested to hear what Höttl, speaking on Kaltenbrunner's behalf, had to offer, and he sent one of his senior aides to meet the Gestapo man in Zurich.

On returning from Paris, he had received a full report of the meeting. Höttl's offer was certainly interesting. Kaltenbrunner had been appointed to take charge of preparing the defense of the so-called Alpine Redoubt. In return for his life, he was ready to surrender this last fortress.

Of course, it was politically impossible—especially after the instructions he had received in Paris—for Dulles to negotiate with a major war criminal like Kaltenbrunner. On the other hand, the Alpine Redoubt was an extremely strong card in the hands of the Nazi leaders. Allied military experts were of the view that if Hitler withdrew his remaining divisions and armor into a strongly fortified ring of mountain defenses in the Austrian and Bavarian Alps, he could hold out a very long time. And the longer the war dragged on, the deeper would be the Soviets' penetration of Europe.

Just a few days ago Churchill had urged once again that the Anglo-American armies should aim to enter Berlin at least at the same time as their Soviet allies. But his view had been rejected by Ike and by Roosevelt—wrongly, in Dulles's opinion. He too saw the tremendous importance, now that Germany was defeated, of creating a front against what he considered the new danger to the free world—the Russians.

Therefore Dulles had not sent Willy Höttl packing. The surrender of the Alpine Redoubt might turn out to be so crucial, in terms of time, to the whole map of Europe, that it would justify dealing with someone like Kaltenbrunner. At any rate, Dulles had not been ready to rule this out, early in April. As a result, Höttl had been kept hanging around waiting for an answer. And he was still in Switzerland ten days later, on the afternoon of Friday April 20.

By now Willy was short of money. He had with him the authority to draw on the special account at the Commercial Bank of Berne. So after a good lunch he strolled from his hotel to the bank in the Bundesplatz and asked for the estimable Dr. Behr. He was told that Dr. Behr was not in Berne at present, but his assistant would be glad to help.

When this individual appeared, Willy Höttl gave

him the account number and showed the special authorization from the Chief of the Main Security Office, entitling him to make withdrawals of up to fifty thousand francs. He had often used this facility in the past and was known at the bank.

The assistant went away and returned after a somewhat prolonged absence. Unfortunately, he said, it was not possible to make this payment, as the account had been closed.

"Closed?" Willy Höttl knew nothing about this. It was a nuisance. He would have to try and borrow some money at the German embassy.

"When was it closed?"

"This morning. Dr. Behr contacted us from the Swiss legation in Germany, where he is temporarily staying, to say that the withdrawal of all the funds in the account had been duly authorized, and the account was therefore closed."

"How stupid that I was not informed," Höttl said. "The entire amount has been withdrawn? There was more than four million francs in the account."

"Yes, that is so."

"Who has made this withdrawal?"

"It is all perfectly in order," the assistant assured him. "The withdrawal has been made by Reichskriminaldirektor Schöller himself, and authorized in accordance with laid-down procedure by SS-General Fegelein and SS-General Stapplemann."

"I was not informed of it," Höttl said, peeved.

After leaving the bank he had a few drinks in a café, and when he paid his bill and saw how little money he had left, he became even more annoyed than he had been before. They might have left *some* funds in the Swiss account. How was he supposed to manage?

Realizing that it was the weekend and he had no money and would have to borrow some at the German embassy, he hurried to get there before it closed.

They made a certain amount of fuss, but eventually gave him enough money to tide him over.

"Really," he said, in a huff, "it is not my fault. They have cleaned out the entire special account, over four million francs. Leaving me without resources."

It was not until the following morning, April 21, that Werner, the special assistant to the German Ambassador, who as the man responsible for intelligence matters had authorized the loan to Willy Höttl, thought there might be something unusual about the withdrawal of four million francs from the special account. Of course, at a time like the present it was not surprising that large sums should be withdrawn for one purpose or another. What surprised him a little was that every last franc should have been withdrawn.

He decided to include details of the closing of the account with the other intelligence messages that were to be radioed to Berlin that morning, Saturday. In any case, he did not have much else to send today. Dulles's cook had been far less productive of late. Sending the details about the closing of the Berne account would at least show that he kept his ears to the ground.

The Chief of the Gestapo, Heinrich Müller, was a man in his middle forties, short and thickset, with a square head, protrusive forehead, a thin, rather handsome nose, and a tight seam of a mouth. His adherence to the Prussian practice of shaving the back of the skull as far as the tops of the ears gave his neck a brutal kind of nakedness. His eyes were the hard gray of beach pebbles. He wore the uniform of a general in the SS.

On the morning of Saturday April 21 he was on his hands and knees on the floor of his underground office, below the Prinz Albrechtstrasse, running an electric flex under the carpet to a time-bomb device in the bottom drawer of his desk. The knock on his door made him straighten the carpet and close the desk drawer. He stood up.

"What is it?" he called out.

His assistant came in and said, "I thought you would wish to see this straightaway," and placed the morning's decode from Berne on the desk. He had put a pencil mark around the matter he wished to draw to his chief's attention. This was a sentence which read:

"The closing of the special account at the Commercial Bank of Berne was affected yesterday, with the withdrawal of the entire sum on deposit, amounting to over four million Swiss francs, on the authority of Reichskriminaldirektor Schöller, countersigned by SS-General Fegelein and SS-General Stapplemann."

Müller sat hunched forward slightly, arms folded, as he read these words, and then reread them.

Picking up the internal phone, he asked to be connected with the Reich Special Investigator's office. He got through to the principal aide, Kummerl, who said that Schöller had left Berlin yesterday morning to supervise the evacuation of the Department's files. His exact whereabouts were not known.

Next Müller telephoned the Reich Chancellery and at the bunker switchboard asked to be connected with Fegelein. He was informed that Fegelein was not in his office, and it was not known when he would be returning, nor did anyone know where he was.

Müller sat thinking. So his colleague the Reich Special Investigator was absconding with four million Swiss francs. The Gestapo Chief was not easily shocked by the venality of men in high places, and he wasted no time or emotion on feelings of outrage. He was a man who kept all his reactions to the practical minimum, whatever the circumstances. His main concern now was to assess the effect of this development on his own plans.

One thing was certain: by now the decode from Berne would also be on Himmler's desk and on Kaltenbrunner's. The SS-Reichsführer might have enough on his mind to prevent him from getting around to this particular piece of bad news for several hours, but it was unlikely that he would still be ignorant of the Special Investigator's decampment by the end of the day. And Himmler was likely to react emotionally, to rage and fume and to demand the initiation of the most ruthless action. He might even come to Berlin to take personal charge of the case. This would not have suited Müller. Therefore the Schöller question had to be settled expeditiously. If possible, before Himmler fully realized what had happened.

The first step was to issue a general order for the arrest of the Reich Special Investigator. All Gestapo sections and out-stations were to receive this order immediately, by teletype. Next, Müller called in the Inspector General of Frontier Police and instructed him to speak personally to the chiefs of all frontier commissariats and frontier posts on the Swiss border and at the Danish and North German ports. The most rigorous measures were to be taken to prevent Schöller's escaping across the borders or by sea.

He next called in the Inspector of the Geheime Feldpolizei, and told him to issue orders to all field police attached to army and Waffen-SS units to keep a watch for the Reichskriminaldirektor and arrest him on sight.

Finally, he ordered that Stapplemann's body be exhumed and an autopsy performed. He had just dismissed his aide when Kaltenbrunner came on the line from Innsbruck. He had just seen the message about Schöller. Though it was not yet eleven A.M., the Chief was already very drunk; curses and wild shouts of abuse came over the line. He had suspected all along that Schöller was a criminal traitor. Had a nose for that sort of thing. Always trusted his nose. Never trusted that pig's asshole, Schöller. An opportunist. But Himmler believed in him. The SS-Reichsführer was going to go out of his mind when he learned what had happened. What was Müller doing about it?

Calmly, Müller informed the Chief of the actions he had already taken; he now requested that similar orders should be issued to those other departments of the Sicherheitspolizei not under his own jurisdiction, including the Kriminalpolizei and the Ordnungpolizei. Kaltenbrunner said the orders would go out at once. He would also speak to Himmler and ask him as Minister of the Interior to inform all Gauleiters and defense officials of the urgent necessity of apprehending the Reichskriminaldirektor. Through the Gauleiters a house-by-house check of the entire land would be initiated.

Having put the machinery in motion, Müller busied himself with other matters. These occupied him until early afternoon, when his assistant came in with the report of the autopsy.

It showed that Stapplemann's throat, lungs, and heart had been pierced by bullets of standard 7.92 mm caliber, of German manufacture, which could have been fired from any number of weapons but probably had come from an MP-43 automatic assault rifle. The bullets removed from the body could not possibly have come from any Allied aircraft. The British night fighters were equipped with .303-inch machine guns. The American planes had .50 Browning machine guns.

So undoubtedly Schöller had murdered Stapplemann to prevent his giving the game away, and then forged his signature on the withdrawal form or, more likely, employed one of the official forgers to do the job.

That was the way he, Müller, would have done it.

It was three P.M. when an official knock on the door, accompanied by the persistent turning of the bell lever, awoke Otto Braun from the stupefied sleep into which he had fallen after drinking half a bottle of schnapps with his lunch. When he opened the door, two plain-clothesmen pushed their way in and started turning the place upside down. The old mother remained in her corner, unmoving, eyes wide with terror.

In the forger's bedroom, the Gestapo men overturned the bed, pulled off the mattress, stripped the pillowcases off the pillows, took down the bamboo swastika and looked behind it. They turned to the writing table. One of the Gestapo men picked up the desk blotter. Examining its base, he saw the succession of almost identical signatures, some of them overlapping, in the blotting paper. Taking a shaving mirror from a hook on the wall, he held it facing the rounded base of the blotter. In the glass the signature of Oswald Stapplemann appeared in half a dozen variants.

Otto Braun was arrested and taken to the Prinz Albrechtstrasse. There, in reply to Gestapo Chief Müller's questions, he admitted that he had forged the Budget Administrator's signature, but insisted this was perfectly legal since it had been done at the request of Reichskriminaldirektor Schöller.

A Gestapo typist took down the forger's confession straight onto the typewriter as he spoke. When it was finished, Braun signed as instructed. After that he was taken to a cell below the Prinz Albrechtstrasse, where he was executed at six P.M., April 21, with a single shot of a Walther PPK 7.65 mm.

At six-fifteen there was a telephone call from Himmler. In reply to the Reichsführer's furious questions, Müller was able to give details of the action he had already taken. One of the conspirators, the forger Braun, had already been found, had confessed, and had been immediately executed. An intensive search was on for Schöller. As far as the third conspirator was concerned, it might be best if Reichsführer Himmler himself were to inform the Führer about Fegelein's involvement.

Fegelein, ever since his marriage to Eva Braun's sister Gretl, had been one of the inner circle of Hitler's court, rarely left the Führer's side and was regarded as one of the family. The accusations against him were therefore not believed straightaway. But when Hitler sent for him, Fegelein was nowhere to be found. He was not in the Chancellery, nor in his normal quarters in the bunker.

Hitler had become a man living in constant expectation of betrayal, and Fegelein's absence aroused his deepest suspicions. He at once sent for the head of his personal police bodyguard, SS-Colonel Hoegl. Hoegl was ordered to form a party of armed men from Hitler's SS Escort and scour Berlin to find Fegelein, and bring him back.

The bodyguard finally found Fegelein in his own house in Charlottenburg, preparing to leave. On being told that he must return to the bunker at once, he tried to persuade Hoegl to join him in getting out of Berlin, saying that he had an airplane at his disposal. But Hoegl could not be persuaded.

When this ploy had failed, Fegelein phoned Eva Braun in the bunker and told her there had been some misunderstanding. Would she speak to Hitler, use her influence to calm him down, and explain that

266

he, Fegelein, would never dream of being disloyal. Eva Braun reacted coldly and refused to intercede on behalf of her brother-in-law.

Fegelein was taken back to the bunker under armed guard. He was brought before Hitler, who told him of the charges brought by Müller. When Fegelein began to protest his innocence, Hitler's eyes became vague.

He degraded the little ex-jockey from the rank of SS-General and sentenced him to death. The bodyguard Escort led him away to the second bunker, where he was held under armed guard.

In the confused events of the next few days, with Russian artillery shells now falling on the Chancellery itself, the order for Fegelein's execution was not immediately implemented. During this time his wife Gretl made no approaches to her sister to get the death sentence lifted, and sometime between April 25 and 29, nobody is sure of the exact date, Fegelein was taken from the second bunker, led into the debris-strewn courtyard of the Chancellery, and executed by a firing squad made up of members of Hitler's personal bodyguard.

Sometime on the afternoon of April 25, Gestapo Chief Müller left the underground office in the Prinz Albrechtstrasse carrying two briefcases and set off in a westerly direction in a small car without official markings.

That same day Berlin was completely encircled, and Russian and American forces met at Torgau, thus cutting the north-south escape route.

· 36 ·

Waking up in the dark, Elliott experienced a moment of disorientation panic. Then he remembered the farmhouse door blowing open and shut, open and shut, and the suicides, and the journey ahead, and what he had to do.

It was beginning to get light. Where Schöller had slept there was an empty space. Some primitive fear of having been left behind made Elliott jump out of bed and rush to the window. Schöller was outside, wearing a heavy overcoat, working on the car—he had already changed the license plate, and now was removing the police lights and siren from the roof.

Elliott dressed and went down. Out, quickly, past the human waxworks at the dining table. The first diffused light of day showed that the farmhouse was situated on high ground. To the east lay the dense vast fir and spruce forests, stretching away toward Czechoslovakia. Far to the south, faint as breath on a windowpane, were the Bavarian Alps. In a broad sweep from west to north, at varying distances, the landscape was dotted with puffs of smoke. At this distance the artillery barrage looked innocuous enough.

It was very still and cold. In places the ground shimmered with frost.

Schöller finished screwing the new number plates in position before looking up.

"Eat something," he said. "We leave in five minutes." He indicated the bread and an open tin of tuna fish. Elliott emptied what remained in the tin onto a large piece of bread, letting the oil soak in. Shivering, he began to eat.

Schöller wiped his greasy hands on some old rags and then threw them down on a little pile of brushwood. Taking one of the jerrycans from the trunk, he poured some gas onto the rags, lit a match, and threw it down. The gas-soaked wood and rags immediately burst into flames. For a moment he warmed his hands at the blaze. Then he took a bundle of papers from inside his coat, threw them onto the fire, and watched the stamps and seals of office and the embossments of taloned eagles shrivel up and become ash.

"The Reich Special Investigator is of no further use to us," he said. "They will be after him by now." He held out his hand. "Your papers." They were tossed into the flames, too.

Before getting into the car, he made sure, by raking the embers with a stick, that not a scrap of official paper remained undestroyed. He started the engine, and as it was warming up, handed Elliott another bundle. "Your new papers. You are now an Inspector of the Ministry of War Production and Armaments, and I am Defense Commissioner Reither. Our job is," he said with mordant glee, "to see that everything is blown up, destroyed, burned. . . . The Führer has decreed that nothing shall be left except ruins."

Schöller drove cautiously along the dirt track to the road, keeping a lookout for patrols.

When he got on the major road, he started to drive fast, his external jugular vein filling out and becoming prominent in the neck. Elliott watched him closely. The Boy Scout knife, with its range of useful implements, was in his trouser pocket.

What a smugly unfearful look Schöller had. Knowing how indispensable he was right now, and with that faith of his in the future usefulness of his skills.

Patches of fog lay in hollows and fields. Dark turbulent-looking clouds low in the sky produced squalls of rain and sleet. Yet all the time they were heading farther south, with the white and pink blossoms of the fruit trees covering the countryside in a continuous froth.

From one of the official radio communiqués they heard that Nuremberg had been taken and that the Americans were advancing rapidly on Munich. It became necessary to veer across to the other side of the corridor and stay close to the Czech border. They were making for Weiden and Cham and the Bavarian woods. It meant a wide circle to the east of Munich, but it seemed the safest way.

They had been following this route for some hours without encountering any military traffic whatsoever when a motorcycle patrol came out of a sheltered side road and was alongside in a moment, ordering them to halt. There was no point trying to make a run; two of the motorcycles, with machine guns mounted on their sidecars, were already ahead. Schöller slowed down and finally stopped.

A sternly handsome Feldpolizei officer demanded their papers.

"Reich Defense Commissioner Reither?"

The Feldpolizei officer had a list, which he began to check through, and long before the officer got that far Schöller saw his name as a red-ink addition at the bottom. The name had an asterisk against it.

The handsome officer opened his leather map case and took out a file of photographs. He glanced through them rapidly, passing over Schöller's in this first quick check-through. But when he had got to the end, he started again at the beginning, more slowly this time, looking at each photograph carefully and comparing it with the features of the man at the steering wheel of the car.

"Look me in the eyes," he ordered. "And take your hat off. And turn down your collar." Schöller did as he was told, looking deeply into the eyes of the handsome young man, who held the look with a stern unflinching intimacy.

"Are you making love to me, perhaps, with those beautiful blue eyes of yours?" Schöller said, grinning boldly. He let his fingers brush lightly against the Feldpolizei officer's gloved hand resting on the lowered window, and as he saw his own photograph come up and the handsome young officer raise his eyes for the scrutiny, Schöller's face became a mask of seductiveness and at the same time his hand closed over the young officer's in an intimate squeeze.

"Would you like to search me?" Schöller said. "I may have something concealed that would interest you." He gave a coarse laugh.

The young Feldpolizei officer blushed darkly, his eyes blazed.

"You should be ashamed of yourself, Reich Defense Commissioner," he burst out with a kind of prim violence, dislodging the offensive hand from his. Before him was Schöller's photograph, a serious full-face dossier portrait.

Grinning obscenely from ear to ear, Schöller said, "Come on, don't be shy, *Liebling*. What about a French kiss?" He put out the tip of his tongue in a pantomime of lasciviousness.

"It is your sort that has brought the nation to its present plight," the young man said.

"Then let's at least enjoy it," Schöller said, eyes gruesomely flirtatious.

"Go on, get going. Out of here!" the Feldpolizei officer said, thrusting the papers back through the window, and not even asking for the young man's, whose function seemed only too disgustingly obvious.

As they drew away from the patrol, Schöller's face was covered in sweat and his grin had crumpled like a papier-mâché clown's mask. He was fumbling in his pockets for a cigarette. Elliott gave him one, and when he saw that Schöller's hand was shaking too much to strike a match, he lit it for him.

They were not stopped again in their wide-sweeping circumvention of Munich, and by early evening had reached the lakeside resorts on the Tegernsee and were turning at right angles toward Switzerland, with the sudden looming presence of the Bavarian Alps on their left, the first range wooded and green, and behind it the glacial ice. The last stage of the journey. In just a few hours they would be at the southern end of the Bodensee, and then Switzerland.

For Elliott the closeness of the border meant that time to carry out his orders was short. There could be no more procrastinating. It would have to be done cold-bloodedly, without warning. With a proffered cigarette, a smile of thanks. Undoubtedly that was how Schöller would do it, being an expert.

"Do you object if we stop briefly when we get to Bregenz?" Schöller asked hesitantly. "I would like to see my wife and child, make sure they are all right."

Oh God, he had to bring that up; had he done it calculatingly? Everything he did had a purpose. Elliott looked closely into his face. The expression on it seemed to denote quite genuine concern, and a worried anticipation of some objection being raised.

Elliott said, "Do as you like."

"So far you were in my hands largely," Schöller said. "It will soon be the other way round—and I shall be in yours. Naturally, I ask your permission. If you advised against it, if you considered it too dangerous . . ."

"Oh for Christ's sake, see them. See them. What does it matter? We have taken enough risks."

"I would like to see them, if you will allow it," he said. "I am very fond of the child. As you know, his health is not good."

"All right, Schöller. All right. I said—all right."

After a brief silence, Schöller said, "I believe I can trust Mr. Dulles, I believe him to be a man of his word. I am right?"

"Sure."

"Major Waibel too. Also an honorable man."

"A very honorable man."

"Both have given their word."

"Then you've got nothing to worry about, have you?"

Elliott wanted to say that a promise exacted by blackmail and threat and double-dealing was not binding. But he knew he must say nothing; words would give away his intent, which must be what Schöller was seeking to discover.

I should do it now, Elliott thought. Why did they want Schöller dead? They must have a good reason. In any case, it was not for him to judge. He'd received his instructions from the watchmaker. Meaning? That Sunrise had come unstuck somehow, and Schöller was an unacceptable liability. That happened. Fortunes of war. Tough luck! He wasn't going to waste his pity on somebody like Schöller. Why was he feeling angry? With whom? *Calm down.* He had to do it. He wasn't going to give Quantregg a chance of saying, "Well, you blew it, kid."

They were driving through farmland and occasional small woods. There was not much traffic. *Next time he takes a piss by the side of the road. I come to join him. A man's very vulnerable taking a piss. . . . In the back, with the Boy Scout knife. In half an hour it'll be dark. Then.*

"I was just thinking," Schöller said. "In case something were to happen to me. You never know—hmm? If something goes wrong. My wife and child, what will happen to them at the hands of the Americans?"

"What the hell do you think we are?" Elliott threw back at him. "What the hell! *Jeezus.* Look . . . look . . . " He was so angry suddenly he could hardly speak. "Look," he said, "Americans don't make war on women and children, no matter who they have the misfortune to be married to, or were begotten by . . . "

"It reassures me to hear you say that. I am naturally concerned—like any father."

"Yuh."

"I meant no reflection on the honor of America."

"OK. OK, Schöller."

When was the bastard going to take a piss? It was hours since he had last gone. But Schöller appeared to have no need to relieve his bladder, for the time being. He was evidently preoccupied with tender thoughts, judging from the uncharacteristic softness of his expression. How come he could look so soft all of a sudden? Was it in anticipation of his wife's embraces that he showed this boyish keenness . . . ?

Elliott decided that if Schöller took a piss before Bregenz, that was when he would do it. *But if not, not. Not yet. Later. Let it rest on that. Let that decide it. The bladder's fullness.*

Elliott said, "I'm bursting, we got to stop."

"All right." He pulled up at the first convenient spot, and Elliott got out.

"What about you?" he said, hands tightly inside his overcoat.

"I don't have to."

All right, Elliott thought, as he directed a scalding stream into a thicket: *After he has seen his wife; let him see his wife and child first. So he has won himself some extra time by his continence. That is all it means.*

They reached Bregenz just after nine, a sprawling shabby garrison town under the wooded mountains. It had been a popular Austrian lakeside resort before the war, but now its proximity to the Swiss border gave it strategic importance. The streets were full of drifting groups of soldiers, calling loudly after girls who passed them on bicycles. Most of the cafés and restaurants appeared to be closed. The one or two that were open had military vehicles and staff cars outside.

Schöller drove through the town's center, along a strand, and past the small harbor full of border police motor patrol boats. They were equipped with searchlights and machine guns. He drove on parallel with the railway track which ran behind a gated crossing across one of the main streets. A little further on he took a sharp turn and entered one of the smaller streets that splayed out from the center. After a hundred yards he stopped the car.

"The place where they are staying is round the corner from here," he explained. "I will make my way there, on my own. You can stretch your legs meanwhile."

Then he was off to his wife and child, as he went straightening his crumpled clothing, and brushing his slouch hat with his sleeve.

Elliott walked down to the cold dark lake. There were patches of mist suspended over its still surface. He observed a border policeboat coming in at the same time as another was going out. Visibility was less than a hundred yards.

The waiting was making him tense, and to ease up he took occasional swigs of brandy, which he had had the foresight to put in his coat pocket. Up and down, up and down, a solitary promenader. Every ten minutes or so he strolled back to the car to see if Schöller had returned.

What the hell was Schöller doing? Must be an hour now. Was he making love to his wife? Elliott had said, "Yes, go and see them," but had not expected to have to wait around for hours. A man of long farewells evidently. He could not help picturing it all, and such a vivid imagination was not a good thing when faced with his present task. Better to have no imagination at all, just a blank mind. Schöller knew the trick of emptying his mind of all feeling.

Now, on top of everything, it began to rain—a cold stinging rain that cut the face and neck. He sheltered in a doorway until the squally shower was over and then went back to the car, fed up with walking about, and peculiarly exhausted.

Schöller was waiting. He had the look about him of a man coming out of church.

"I hope it was not too long a wait for you," he said, with that air of having just received holy communion.

"The child is all right?"

"Seeing me so unexpectedly was too exciting for him. He had one of his choking fits, but he got over it quite well, with the inhaler."

They drove along a road that for a time ran parallel with the railway track and the lakeshore. Once out of the residential districts, they were straightaway in the countryside, passing a succession of ramshackle little farmsteads from which came a strong smell of manure.

"The border is about half an hour farther on," Schöller said.

"They'll have your photograph at the border post?"

"Probably."

"How will we get through?"

"We won't go through the border post," he said.

"Where then?"

"You will see very soon."

He was driving more slowly now, as if searching for a particular place. Through the trees there were occasional glimpses of still water. The mist was drifting inshore, coiling around clumps of reeds in wispy tentacles. The area around here was fairly desolate;

the few simple farmhouses were set well back from the lake. Schöller slowed the car to a walking pace.

Beyond the trees, close to the lakeshore, there were parallel lines of high barbed wire fences, about four yards apart. Schöller consulted his topographical map, with its contour markings and configuration details superimposed. He kept looking out of the car, checking these details against the actual locale, looking for very small landmarks: rising ground, paths, diverging roads, farmhouses, barns. A sudden look of satisfaction indicated that he had got his bearings. Calculating the exact distance by counting the telegraph poles, he drove very slowly for another two kilometers and then turned off the road and pulled up in the shelter of a dense thicket.

He looked at his watch and began to move rapidly. With a suddenly thumping heart Elliott saw how completely hidden they were here, and that Schöller was totally preoccupied with the execution of his plan. The perfect moment. Schöller had gone round to the back of the car and opened the deep trunk and was bending down, getting something out. He was totally unprotected in this position. As Elliott came up behind him, silently, Schöller swung round and threw him wire cutters.

He looked at his watch. "The border patrol passes here in five minutes, so get moving."

While Elliott was cutting through the barbed wire, Schöller had spread out on the ground the emergency pack from a Stuka bomber. He broke the tapes, and at once the rubbery material unfolded and spread open. He felt under a fold for the rip cord and tugged. With a startling sound of rushing air the dinghy began to inflate. When the small life raft was ready for use, he joined Elliott, who was now working on the second barbed wire fence.

"Help me," he said. Together they went back to the çar. Schöller put his briefcase and a bottle of cognac in the dinghy, and the two of them carried it into the space between the fences. While Elliott was cutting through the second fence, Schöller was repairing the first one, rapidly binding the severed wire together again with adhesive tape.

They crawled through the gap in the second fence and dragged the dinghy after them, and Schöller quickly repaired the cut wire, as he had done before.

"Two minutes," he said, after a quick glance at his watch. Running, they carried the dinghy down to the water's edge and threw themselves flat in the rushes as they saw the dimmed lights of the motorcycle patrol.

The border guard in the sidecar had a powerful flashlight which he was shining through the barbed wire, all along the lakeshore. In the dazzling beam Schöller and Elliott both saw a piece of loose black adhesive tape hanging down from the hastily repaired fence. Schöller moved onto his side, took the small Mauser automatic from his pocket, slipped off the safety catch with his thumb, and fixed first one then the other border guard in the sights.

The motorcycle combination, a machine gun mounted on the sidecar, was driving at no more than five miles an hour. It took an eternity to pass the piece of loose black sticky tape. When its rear lights had finally faded, Schöller scrambled up and with Elliott's help lowered the dinghy into the water, where it was concealed amid high rushes. He looked at his watch, made a quick calculation, and said, "Get in." He got in first, a rather bulky man in a heavy long overcoat and slouch hat, carrying a briefcase. He seated himself and waited. Elliott sat down opposite.

"What about the patrol boats?" Elliott said.

"We have to avoid them. I know *their* schedules too," Schöller confided with a smirk. He was sitting absolutely still, looking repeatedly into the dark and then at his watch.

"This part of the Austrian shore juts out," he said. "Switzerland is just over there." He pointed with his head. "In three miles we are in Swiss waters." He had evidently seen or heard something, for he looked at his watch again and raised a finger to his lips. A minute later Elliott also saw the patrol boat. The end of the promontory where they waited was at the apex of the zigzag patrol route. A beam of light fell to one side of them and passed. The boat made a sharp V turn and moved rapidly away. When it had disappeared, Schöller started to pull away, rowing strongly and carefully so that the oars would cut the water cleanly and not make any splashing sounds. Within minutes the shoreline had disappeared from view, and visibility was down to a few yards. Low clouds obscured any light from the sky. It was like being led blindfolded to some unknown place. Schöller was rowing an intricate course, making small changes in direction every few minutes, each time checking with his compass and watch. Once, having noted the time, he shook his head and stopped rowing. Two minutes later they heard the patrol boat ahead as it reached the furthermost point of its zigzag. Its searchlight was sweeping the water in a wide arc whose perimeter came within ten yards of the stationary dinghy. When the sound of the motorboat's engines had diminished sufficiently, Schöller again began to row.

Now? Why not now? Pulling on the oars, Schöller was wide open and vulnerable. Elliott had his hands in his pockets for warmth. He felt the bone handle of the Boy Scout knife, pressed the hidden catch, and inside his coat pocket the blade sprang out, cutting through the lining. He saw the external jugular in Schöller's neck fill out and swell with the physical exertion of rowing.

Schöller was watching him closely with his damned knowing eyes.

"This lake," Schöller said, speaking very quietly, "is tricky." He spoke in a confidential tone, as if imparting some very private information. "Very tricky. Unless you know it well. Mists—it's famous for them, the Bodensee. Easy to get lost. The blackout doesn't help. Nothing to see, except the lights of the patrol boats. Even the Swiss have a blackout along their shoreline. Somebody who didn't know the lake might think he was rowing to Switzerland"—he laughed in quiet mockery of such a mishap—"and end up back in Germany. Four-fifths of the lakeshore is German, you see. Just that little piece in between that is Swiss territory." He paused. "But there is no need to worry.

You won't get lost with me. As a young man I often came here on my holidays. I know the lake, A beautiful spot."

Elliott's hand came out of his pocket and surreptitiously in the dark he wiped the palm on the cloth of his coat.

Seconds after getting out of the little lifeboat and starting to clamber up the wooded escarpment of which the Swiss lakeshore largely consisted, searchlights of a blinding brightness caught them in a web of light.

They were surrounded by polite Swiss border police and politely disarmed, and then driven to St. Gallen police station. There Elliott gave the code word Sunrise and informed a senior officer that he wished to speak to Major Waibel or Captain Wirth. The police officer returned after twenty minutes to say that unfortunately neither could be contacted. In view of this, he was obliged to ask them to remain the night at the police station. They were brought bread and cheeses and beer, and the polite Swiss officer said he was most dreadfully sorry but he would have to lock them up. They would understand, he hoped. They said they did.

Before going to sleep, Elliott went to the washroom. There was a wide mirror above the row of washbasins. For the first time in days he saw himself in a strong clear light, and momentarily he did not recognize his face in the glass. It was very tautly drawn and covered with two days' growth of beard, and the eyes had become deeply hidden within their dark hollows. White debris dust had got into his hair and eyebrows and eyelashes and into the beard on his face, giving the impression that he had begun to go prematurely gray. The corners of his mouth and the crinkles around the eyes and the incipient lines of his forehead were boldly marked as by a defacing scrawler. His teeth, when he bared them, were dull and yellow, like an animal's. He had become a scarecrow, and in some weird way frightening to himself. The most striking change was how the open face had closed and become hidden. I'll see myself differently after I have slept and had a shave, he told himself.

37

In the morning Elliott was provided with a razor and soap and a nailbrush, but still he could not get all the grayness from his skin and hair.

At breakfast he watched Schöller put several spoonfuls of sugar in his coffee and saw him smile sheepishly on being found out in his sweet-toothed greed.

Elliott thought Schöller looked very out of place in this clean Swiss police station, the morning sunlight lying across its waxed linoleum floors and reflected on wall charts under glass; his habitat was ruins and rubble, the underground maze: it was there he excelled in his own brutish way. Here he was just a large man with big ears, big hands, and a shabby suit sagging at the pockets.

"What happens now?" Elliott asked for something to say, out of habit putting Schöller in the position of providing the answers.

"That is not for me to say," Schöller replied humbly. "I'm at Mr. Dulles's disposal. . . . "

Elliott was feeling on edge. He could hardly bring himself to look at Schöller. The bastard ought not to be sitting there now. He had no right to be alive still. Quantregg would say, "Well, you blew it, kid. You screwed it up. Why couldn't you do it? Why couldn't you carry out orders?"

Well, why couldn't he? Somehow Schöller had played him along, from one situation to the next, with his tricks, always getting the moment postponed. How could Elliott explain that? *Maybe I just didn't have the guts to do it.* He was sore as hell with himself, and there was a bad feeling inside him. He didn't know what it was about exactly, but he couldn't get rid of it. Why couldn't I do it? If anybody had it coming, Schöller did. And I allowed myself to be taken in. He felt he'd been used and made a fool of. He was angry with himself and couldn't eat his breakfast.

Wirth arrived at eleven. His plane was waiting at the military airstrip, and they left immediately with him. Elliott noted how all formalities were dispensed with at Wirth's behest. Not even their names had been taken.

"The first thing I must do in Berne," Schöller said, "is pay a visit to the bank. I am without funds."

"I can provide you with interim funds."

"Good of you, Captain. But not required. As soon as I have been to the bank, there will be no problem."

"As you wish."

They were in Berne at twenty minutes to twelve, and Schöller suggested that he be taken to the Commercial Bank in the Bundesplatz.

At the bank he went in through the wrought iron and glass door and walked unhurriedly across the marble rotunda and up the broad marble steps to the second floor. At the desk he gave the number of the account and asked to speak to whoever was deputizing for Dr. Behr. He had been waiting little more than a minute when Dr. Behr appeared in person.

"You are very fortunate to be here, Dr. Behr."

"As you are, Herr Direktor."

"We are both fortunate," Schöller agreed with a wolfish smile.

"I had the good fortune to obtain transport in a Red Cross convoy," Dr. Behr said. "You, Herr Direktor, must have come in some other way. . . . "

"Yes," Schöller said. "Some other way."

"If you will be so good as to come in my office."

In the small room with its one narrow window and dark wainscoting, Dr. Behr seated himself behind his glass-top desk and with great delicacy placed the tips of his fingers together like a man about to pray.

He cleared his throat, coughed a little uncomfortably, and began: "The question of the withdrawal. I assume you have come about that?"

"Yes."

"There have been certain problems," Dr. Behr said. He reached into a drawer of his desk, took out a file, turned the sheets, and studied them over his half-lenses.

"What problems?" Schöller said heavily, his face going a yellowish white and his eyes becoming dead. "The signatures were in order . . . ?"

"Not entirely."

"In what way?"

"They have been repudiated. We have received a communication from Herr Müller of the Gestapo on behalf of the German government to the effect that the signatures are forgeries."

"That is of course a lie," Schöller said.

In the low leather armchair, in which to sit up straight required a certain forward inclination of the body, Schöller had slumped into a round-backed heap.

Dr. Behr spread his hands in a gesture of Swiss neutrality, indicating that he was merely repeating what he had been told and not presuming to take sides.

"Well?" Schöller said gruffly, moving forward to the edge of the leather armchair in preparation for levering himself into a standing position.

"The German government through Müller has sent an official demand that this money should not be paid to you . . . "

"If it is a question of whose word is to be taken, Müller's or mine . . . "

"Yes, yes, it comes to that, I suppose . . . "

"Who are you willing to trust, Dr. Behr? In the matter of the Niederdorf prisoners, for example?"

"Yes? There is no news so far."

"You must regard that as a good sign. Their former guards will have been relieved by now. . . . The important thing is that attention is not drawn to this changeover," and he went on with mounting confidence in this last card of his. "It would be extremely dangerous for the Niederdorf prisoners if Berlin were to discover what is happening. I was willing to refrain from countermeasures. I very much doubt if Müller would be as accommodating to your directors, Dr. Behr."

"Of course," Dr. Behr agreed, "it is extremely difficult at present to know who is, or isn't, the German government. We did attempt to contact Herr Müller to elucidate the matter of the signatures, but he . . . was not available."

Dr. Behr stood up, looking severe.

"We have always made it clear that while the Swiss banking system maintains a policy of the utmost discreetness in all its dealings with clients, we cannot allow the system to be used for the furtherance of criminal activities. On the other hand," he continued with the air of a man who is prepared to allow that every question has many sides to it, "you, Herr Direktor, came to us with this money in the first place, and you are therefore our primary client to whom we owe our first responsibility, in the absence of evidence to the contrary. As there is no such evidence and the proper conditions for the withdrawal have been met . . . therefore . . . " He pushed a small slip of paper toward Schöller. "If you will be good enough to sign here, and here and here, and fill in the amount, I shall fetch the money and that will then close the matter."

Schöller signed where indicated, filled in the amount, and after carefully examining the slip of paper, Dr. Behr, with an air of having reconciled the demands of conscience with fiscal honor, went out for the money. He returned in a short while, followed by a uniformed bank messenger carrying what looked like a rather large hatbox. There were code letters on the box which Dr. Behr checked, then with a little if-you-will-be-so-good hand gesture to Schöller, he invited him to lift the lid. Schöller did so and stared transfixed at the tightly stacked bank notes while feeling the stubble of his upper lip. Inside his mouth his tongue moved dryly over his front teeth. He picked up one bundle of 500-franc notes held in the middle by a brown paper band, and allowed the notes to flick rapidly between his thumb and forefinger.

"You wish to count the amount?"

"It is not necessary."

Selecting the combination number on the lock, Schöller opened his leather briefcase and proceeded to fill it with the bank notes. The case was expanded to its maximum and every inch of space used to cram in the bundles of Swiss francs. The remainder he stuffed in his pockets. Each of his two breast pockets was crammed, making him bulge out at the chest; his voluminous sagging side pockets, normally weighted down with keys, were filled with Swiss francs. Finally his outer overcoat pockets were likewise filled. He reset the combination lock of the briefcase.

"You will need to buy yourself another briefcase," Dr. Behr commented.

"Yes, yes . . . ." Schöller mumbled. He seemed anxious to leave, as if fearing that Dr. Behr might at any moment change his mind and demand the return of the money. Walking a little lopsidedly because of the weight of the money-stuffed briefcase, he almost stumbled on the slippery marble stairs. He crossed the rotunda and went out through the glass and wrought iron doors.

Captain Wirth's car was waiting for him. The driver opened the rear door for Schöller, and he got in.

The limousine moved off with silent smoothness, past the Spar & Leihkasse, with its gold ornamented balconies, turning round the Bundesplatz, past the Kantonal Bank von Berne with its high pillars, occupying one whole side of the square, and then going round the square in front of the Parliament building, took the street in which the Bellevue was situated. It was only a few hundred yards farther along, and the cars drawing up in front of the hotel entrance had reduced the traffic flow to a crawl. Pedestrians were crossing the street, weaving their way between the slow-moving vehicles. A big man in a raincoat was walking by the side of Captain Wirth's car, as if intending to cross behind it, but then recognizing the occupants, he appeared to change his mind, for he opened the rear door with his left hand and got in. As he did so, Quantregg with his right hand took the .45 Colt automatic out of his raincoat pocket and rested it on his lap, pointing at Schöller. At the same time the driver quickly extricated himself from the traffic holdup and swung sharply round by the side of the Bellevue, taking the narrow downward curving road.

Schöller looked at Elliott with a deeply hurt expression.

"That is not necessary," he said, sadly shaking his head and indicating the gun as if it were an object whose vulgarity offended him. "I have come here to place myself in Mr. Dulles's hands—entirely." He got no answer. The car continued downward along the Munzrain and then made a hairpin turn into the Weihergasse.

Schöller said, "Mr. Dulles gave his word."

The car had reached the same level as the river and now gathered speed on the road, which followed the curve of the Aare. They passed under the high Kirchenfeldbrücke and pulled up sharply at the Frick-treppe.

"I'll take that," Quantregg said, indicating the leather briefcase.

Schöller handed it over docilely. "Is it because of the money?" he inquired.

"You opened that account with forged American dollars," Quantregg said.

"Everything," Schöller said with reasonableness, "is open to discussion."

"That's mighty big of you," Quantregg said. He poked Schöller with the gun, motioning him to get out.

"Are we going to see Mr. Dulles?" Schöller asked.

The road alongside the river was used by fast traffic and hardly at all by pedestrians. There were no people in the immediate vicinity as Quantregg prodded Schöller out of the car. The covered steps went from the riverside road to the high Plattform, the cathedral square, and the rear entrance of Dulles's house. When

Elliott had also got out, the car with Captain Wirth in it drove off.

"Where am I being taken?" Schöller demanded. These old broad steps were a structure of creaking timbers with heavy wooden overhead beams, carrying the roofing; it was like being below decks of an old sailing ship.

Elliott went first, Schöller in the middle, Quantregg behind as they started the long climb. The covered steps were not much used these days; further on there was a hydraulic lift that took people up to the Plattform, and there were gentler gradients to the cathedral square by road. Being completely closed in, the steps were dim even in full daylight. After about twenty yards of straight ascent, they curved sharply to the right, past a number of rear entrances with iron grilles and barred windows.

They had gone about halfway up the steps when Quantregg said, "Stop." As they all stopped, the creaking of the timbers stopped too. In the silence Quantregg listened to hear if anyone was coming. He made a quick hand movement to Elliott to step to one side, away from Schöller. Then he took his right hand holding the Colt automatic out of his raincoat pocket. On his bristling brush head a white streak stood out.

Schöller was leaning against the Fricktreppe walls. He was breathing very strongly and rapidly, and sweating.

He said, "Why does Mr. Dulles want me dead?"

"None of your business, Kraut bastard," Quantregg said, raising his arm to aim the gun.

Schöller said, "Can you be sure that what you want is in the briefcase? The index. The money."

Quantregg shot a questioning look at Elliott. Elliott said, "I saw him put the index in the briefcase . . . "

"When?" Schöller asked pointedly. "I could have transferred the index when I went to the bank. This briefcase might be stuffed with old newspapers."

"He's talking to gain time," Elliott said. He too was breathless. He was alert for the sound of footsteps.

Quantregg began to tear violently at the brass catch of the briefcase.

"It's locked," Schöller said.

"Open it," Quantregg ordered.

"You are making a mistake. I can be of use to Mr. Dulles."

"Open it."

"So that you can go ahead and kill me? I make a deal with you. I will open the case in Mr. Dulles's apartment, in his presence. . . . "

"Your days of making deals are over, you lousy Kraut bastard. These locks open with a hairpin," Quantregg added contemptuously, again attempting to force the catch.

"Not this one. It is a special lock, a combination lock," Schöller said.

Quantregg took out a penknife, transferring the gun to his left hand; grasping the briefcase between his knees, he stuck the point of the knife in the leather and began to cut out the lock. It was thick leather, hard to cut through at first, but it became easier as soon as the point of the blade was through and the cutting edge of the knife in use. Quantregg was sweating as he cut, at the same time tensely watching Schöller. He was in a hurry. At any moment somebody might come up or down the steps. Schöller too was conscious of this. He started to edge away, one step at a time, as Quantregg struggled to cut through the leather. He had already cut part of a semi-circle around the lock.

"Stay by him," he told Elliott, tilting the gun up, as he saw Schöller trying to move away. There was ten feet between them.

Quantregg had an expression of satisfaction on his face as he felt the leather give more easily to the cutting edge of the knife. With a powerful circular movement that made the veins stand out on his forehead, he had succeeded in moving the knife in a continuous cut of three inches along one side of the lock when the briefcase exploded in his hands. It was not a big explosion, no more than a detonating charge, but it set off the inner incendiary device, and in a moment the briefcase was a mass of flames and Quantregg's sleeves and coat were ablaze.

Schöller was running heavily up the steps three at a time, making the wooden Fricktreppe shake and sway like a ship on a high sea.

The explosion of the incendiary device had sent pieces of blazing material in all directions. Quantregg was staggering about, arms flailing wildly, like a man who has been attacked by a hornets' nest. His clothing was alight in about a dozen different places, and he was rolling himself against the wall of the covered steps to smother the flames.

Elliott without success was trying to use his bundled-up coat to beat out the flames that adhered like limpets to different parts of Quantregg's body. Useless. The fire spread to whatever came in contact with it, and Elliott realized that it must have been some kind of phosphorus bomb device in the briefcase, because the flames could not be put out. He began to yell at the top of his voice, "Fire, fire!"

Quantregg was trying to tear the burning clothing from his body, tumbling and rolling down the steps, standing up, running crazily from side to side. Rolling down again. People had come out of back entrances that gave onto the steps, and seeing what was happening rushed back in to phone the fire brigade and get water.

By now Quantregg had stumbled, rolled, and slithered to the bottom of the steps. Still on fire in a dozen places, he ran toward the river as if intending to throw himself in. Halfway across the street he collapsed. Cars stopped and people gathered around the writhing form on the ground. Somebody rushed off with a bucket to get water. A man shouted, "Sand. Get sand." But before either water or the sand could be brought, Quantregg's movements suddenly ceased.

When the ambulance arrived, he was dead.

38

Once among the window-shoppers in the continuous arcades of the Kramgasse, Schöller had stopped running. Walking fast, he pushed his way through the leisurely throng. Before reaching the Zeitglockenturm, he turned right into the Rathausgasse and then cut across to the Kornhausplatz, where he saw a two-carriage streetcar about to move from its stop. Its route plate said Berne-Worb-Berne. Via Gotlingen. Schöller ran hard and caught it.

As he regained his breath, he worked out that he probably had half an hour. By the time Dulles had gathered his thoughts, decided his next move, phoned Captain Wirth, Captain Wirth had got through to the right person in the Kantonal police department, and that person had instigated a police search, at least half an hour would have gone by.

Therefore they would place two or three concentric cordons around the area—in case he had already slipped through the first one. They would calculate that the farthest he could have got in the time was fifty kilometers. They would therefore set up the first circle of roadblocks at a radius of fifty-five kilometers from the city center. After that, there would be additional checkpoints every five kilometers, so that if he had slipped through the first net he would be caught in the second or third. They would naturally check all trains and buses and streetcars coming from Berne or nearby.

Telegraphed messages would go ahead to railway and police stations, giving his description. There would be police at all the ticket barriers, while others would board trains and make a carriage-by-carriage check. It was possible to jump off a train while it was slowing down at a signal point, but that would mean continuing on foot or finding some other means of transport.

Having sealed off the area, they would then proceed to search it, street by street. Schöller knew the way a manhunt was conducted.

At Worb he got off the tram. It was 12:45, exactly fifteen minutes since the fire-explosion on the Fricktreppe. By now Dulles would have spoken to Captain Wirth and Wirth would be talking to the Kantonal police. Too early for them to have organized a comprehensive linked system of road checks, but a warning flash giving his description might have gone out to key points. Schöller looked carefully around for any sign of heightened activity, but everything was quiet. He found a taxi at a stand, and told the driver to take him to Thun. He said he had a train to catch in fifteen minutes and he would pay double the fare if they got there in time. The taxi driver put his foot down and reached the lakeside city in twenty minutes.

As they entered the busy main street, Schöller, looking through the rear window, saw police cars pulling up in the road behind and uniformed police waving down the approaching traffic. He had slipped through the first cordon.

He told the driver that he had missed his train, but he'd pay him his double fare all the same for having tried. At the railway station Schöller bought a one-way ticket for Lucerne, paying with a 500-franc note.

He then left the station, tore up the ticket, and dropped the little pieces into a garbage bin. He took another taxi to the main shopping street, the Hauptgasse, and bought himself a green Alpine hat with a little feather. Wearing this in place of his slouch hat, which he rolled up and placed inside his overcoat pocket, he went into another shop and bought himself a rucksack. Two shops farther he bought himself a pair of stout walking boots, thick red woolen socks, and a steel-tipped walking stick.

With these purchases he went into a public lavatory

and inside one of the cubicles took off his own shoes and socks and put on the boots and knee-length red wool stockings. He rolled the bottoms of the trousers tight and tucked them inside the stockings below the knee. Then he rolled up his long double-breasted over-coat and put it with his squashed-up slouch hat and shoes inside the main compartment of the rucksack.

He counted the money he had stuffed into his pockets at the bank and discovered he had nearly 150,000 francs. He distributed this money among the outer pockets of the rucksack and fastened the straps tightly, passing each toggle through the last hole. He swung the rucksack up onto his back, slipped his arms inside the shoulder straps, picked up his steel-tipped walking stick, and went out into the street, where he was quickly lost among dozens of similarly attired mountain hikers.

Settling down to a steady walking pace, he made his way along the lakeshore and out of the town, where he turned right and took the steadily rising road to Gwatt and Latterbach. It was a route that followed the course of the Simme. The gradients were not too steep, a maximum of 1 in 10.

Every half-hour or so he paused at a view to rest briefly and look around. The base of the mountains, above the towns, was thickly wooded, but higher up there were massive expanses of sheer bare rock face, and higher still the glaciers and the perpetual snow.

The winding ascent by the Simmental passed through a number of mountain villages and at one of these he stopped to buy food: bread, cheese, sausages, chocolate, and beer. He ate seated under a covered bridge spanning a torrent. It was becoming colder as the sun began to go down and the altitude increased, and at the next village he bought additional woolen stockings and a woolen scarf.

At one of the views where he stopped to take a drink of beer, he was able to look all the way down to the main road two thousand feet below, and saw the regular blue flash of a police roadblock and the long line of halted cars being systematically checked.

He gave a wolfish grin, threw the beer bottle away, and continued on the climb.

By nightfall he had gone some twenty-five kilometers and was at nearly three thousand feet. As he walked, he searched the surounding slopes, patchily covered with snow at this height, until eventually he saw what he was looking for. On an isolated ridge on his right there was a simple Alpine shelter. Leaving the road, he climbed up to it, and there he spent the night, lying on the wooden bench, wrapped up in his overcoat, scarf around neck and face, extra stockings on his feet, and gloves on his hands.

Next day he started before dawn. He continued the journey, through Zweisimmen and the little resort of Chateau-d'Oex, and by late afternoon he was at over five thousand feet, in the fir woods above the Col des Mosses.

He could see the little clusters of hotels and restaurants and shops far below, and a few farmhouses and mountain inns scattered about the sides of the Col. The most remote of these was the dilapidated Gasthaus Rey, its annex backing directly onto wooded slopes, its balconied rooms affording sweeping views of the entire surrounding area.

Using his stick, carefully examining the ground ahead so that he would not put a foot wrong, Schöller made the steep descent through the woods to the rear entrance of the inn.

• 39 •

After conveying the formal regrets of his government at the death of a senior member of the American diplomatic staff in Berne, Captain Wirth went on to give details of what the police were doing to find the criminal responsible for this outrage.

"The police have mounted a most extensive hunt. They have checked hotels, apartment buildings, rooming houses, hospitals, private sanitoriums, hostels, nursing homes. . . . All forms of transport have been subjected to the most rigorous checks." He threw up his hands. "The trail peters out at Thun Bahnhof. The taxi driver who took him there from Worb identified him from the description. The ticket clerk who sold him a ticket to Lucerne has also identified him. And that's the last anyone saw of him. He has just vanished."

"He must have had some fallback position prepared," Elliott said.

"I don't see how he could have foreseen what happened on the steps," Dulles said.

"He always leaves himself an alternative—plays everything both ways," Elliott said.

"I still don't see how in hell he could have gone to earth like that," Dulles said. "Here in Switzerland."

"It is my opinion somebody is hiding him," Captain Wirth said. "A friend."

"A friend? How come somebody like him has got friends?" Elliott said.

"It must have all been arranged very carefully in advance, worked out to the smallest detail," Wirth said.

"Even so," Elliott said, "it shouldn't be beyond the resources of the whole Swiss police force—and intelligence services—to find one man. One man. It's not as if they've got that much else to do. . . . "

"Now that's uncalled for," Dulles rebuked him softly. "I'm sure the Swiss law agencies are doing their level best to find Schöller and I'm indebted to you, Captain Wirth, for your endeavors. Please convey my respects to General Guisan, and say that on behalf of the American government I accept the condolences of the Swiss General Staff."

When Captain Wirth had left, Dulles said, "You're cut up about Quantregg's death, I know. But no point taking it out on the Swiss. Major Waibel and Captain Wirth have always been most helpful to us." He paused. "I'm very upset about Dick Quantregg's death myself," he said. "It needn't have happened. If he had exercised the most elementary risk estimation."

"I guess he acted on impulse. You know the way he felt about the Germans."

"Yes. Yes."

"It was really horrible—on the steps."

"Awful way to go."

"And that lousy murdering bastard Schöller has gotten clean away."

"As you say, he must have had some fallback position prepared."

"I'd like to have a shot at finding him. I know you think the Swiss are doing their best, but it's just not damn good enough. Is it?"

"I know you feel bad about it, and even maybe blame yourself. Well, now, *that*, I want to tell you, is unnecessary."

"Unnecessary?"

"Flexibility of response is the capability that is called for in our tradecraft. A few days ago Schöller represented a certain kind of problem to us, in the light of which certain solutions were called for. Sunrise had been called off. Now it's on again. They've changed their minds in Washington, and that alters a lot of things. In our new scale of priorities, catching up with Schöller no longer comes so high on the list. We'll get him in the end. Oh surely. But right now there are more important things to deal with. As a matter of fact, there is some advantage in the Swiss *not* finding him immediately. Keeps certain aspects of this business under wraps for the time being. . . . "

Elliott stared back blankly. His mind felt worn down by events to a level of dull compliance. Well, if that was the way they wanted it, OK. He couldn't follow all the ramifications, the twists and turns of their reasoning. One minute they were giving you Boy Scout knives with secret implements and sending you messages about the mainspring having to be removed and all that stuff, getting you whipped up to do something like that, because it was absolutely necessary, for winning the war, for making the world a better place to live in—yuh—yuh! And then the next, it was not really all that necessary, no need to panic. . . . Washington had changed its mind, circumstances were different now . . . *OK. OK.*

"You're pretty tired. You've had a hell of an experience," Dulles told him, seeing the dazed exhaustion on Elliott's face. "Why don't you try and ease up a bit? Take a few days off. We can spare you. Go up in the mountains . . . or something."

But Elliott couldn't bring himself to go away, now that the end was so close, and he couldn't ease up. Things were happening too fast. It was the last phase, and he couldn't just shut off and pretend it was all nothing to do with him, since he had been ready—*almost* ready, anyway—to kill a man in order that Sunrise wouldn't be compromised.

The surrender in Italy was imminent, and then it wasn't. The German military were still against it, while the SS were for it. Soldiers were moving in to arrest Wolff. The SS were moving in to arrest the vacillating generals. Finally, on April 28, came word that Vientinghoff, the German military commander, had agreed to surrender. No sooner had this message arrived in Berne, occasioning considerable jubilation, than it was followed by another which said that Commander-in-Chief-West Kesselring had relieved Vientinghoff of his command and ordered his arrest. Wolff responded by arresting the military commanders, Generals Schultz and Wenzel, appointed to replace Vientinghoff. SS military police surrounded their offices and cut all their communications with Berlin.

The situation was changing from one minute to the next, and in the American legation there were little groups around the code clerks all the time, watching over their shoulders as the latest developments were spelled out letter by letter.

Time had become a vital factor. In northern Italy the Allied troops were poised for a major new offensive. With a surrender supposedly imminent, they were holding back. And while they were not moving, Tito's partisans were going all-out for Trieste, and by April 29 had reached the outer suburbs of Fiume. The German garrison of Trieste was putting up fierce resistance, but their capitulation could only be a matter of hours, or at most days.

On the afternoon of April 29, Dulles gave Elliott a last-throw message to send to Wolff. It read:

SURRENDER MUST BE DELIVERED IMMEDIATELY. ALL OUR TIME HAS NOW RUN OUT.

He said to the group around him: "Once Tito takes Trieste, he'll hang on to it tooth and nail . . . and bang goes the whole goddamn Adriatic."

A code clerk came over with the message that German envoys had set off for Alexander's headquarters in Caserta to sign the surrender.

Another code clerk came with the message that Kaltenbrunner was initiating moves to have the envoys arrested before they reached the Allied lines.

On May 1 came the news of Hitler's death. . . . And then at two o'clock on May 2, German soldiers in Italy finally laid down their arms.

That same day General Freyberg's New Zealand Division raced across the Isonzo and broke into Trieste.

As news of this came in, Dulles was jubilant. Deep inside their cavernous folds his specklike eyes glinted with triumph. His long-range strategy had borne fruit today. The German surrender in Italy, for which he had so strenuously worked, plotted, and intrigued, had occurred just in time to check the Communists as they overran Trieste. Tito was in, but thanks to the surrender so were the New Zealanders.

"At least we've got a foot in the door," he said, pouring champagne for his associates of the Berne mission. "Tito can cut up rough as he likes, and he will, *he will*, but he's not going to get us out of Trieste now we're in."

And since he was a man given to large statements when they seemed to him justified, he raised his glass and declared, "Gentlemen, today we have seen Italy, and some would say France too, saved from the imminent threat of the Communist yoke, and I think I may say without immodesty that we in this room had some part in that . . . yes, I think we are entitled to make that claim."

Next day Elliott decoded a message from Bolzano, Wolff's headquarters, which read:

WOLFF TO ALEXANDER BY COMMAND OF KESSELRING—INSTRUCT WHAT ALLIED HQS TO CONTACT FOR SURRENDER OF COMMANDER-IN-CHIEF-WEST.

While the others were celebrating—letting go after all the tensions of the past months—Elliott was morose and dispirited. He was tense all the time, could not calm down.

He kept thinking about the German girl, Maritza, even though he had difficulty even remembering her accurately—sometimes she seemed like somebody he'd dreamed up. But he was sure that no matter what anybody said, there was something good about her. He had felt that. Been drawn by that. After three or four Jack Daniel's with Captain Wirth in the Bellevue, he'd explain for the umpteenth time: "OK, maybe she was a Nazi at one time. When she was fifteen or sixteen. Maybe. For me she was the only good thing in that stinking graveyard."

Captain Wirth would smile understandingly, but Elliott saw that he did not understand, thought of it as just the usual boy-girl war thing. He didn't understand how close Elliott had been to going to pieces in that hellhole, and that somehow the girl had given him something to hold on to.

Still there was no news of her, even though the capitulation had now come into effect and communications were being restored. She could be dead. Or in a Russian prison. Or safe somewhere, but not wanting to see him. Maybe she felt quite cynical about the whole episode. He had given her papers, and she had given him something else—her body, momentarily, and an image to hold on to during some bad moments.

Just one of those arrangements that people entered into. In a war. . . . Maybe that was all it was.

He could find no peace. He was beset by violent feelings in himself that he could scarcely recognize as his. Sometimes he raged in his mind against Maritza and thought of her as that ungrateful snobby Nazi bitch. He'd saved her life—if he had, *if*—and she couldn't even pick up the telephone and say, "Thank you." But, then, of course, she did not know who he was, thought of him as one of Schöller's henchmen. In which case, wanting nothing to do with him was sort of in her favor. Couldn't she have seen through that impersonation? Had he been really so convincing in the role?

Elliott was getting to look quite ill, eating little, sleeping badly, and drinking too many Jack Daniel's. People told him he should do something—see a doctor, maybe—he was not himself, he was heading for some kind of breakdown if he didn't watch out. But he shrugged it all off. He wasn't sick, he told them, just angry. What about? they asked. And all he could find to say was: the unfairness of it all. All that had happened. The girl and Schöller and Quantregg, and Dulles and his deals—but who could you complain to? Who was there? That's what I'm complaining about, he wanted to say. That there was nobody.

One day coming back to the hotel, there was a note in his cubbyhole and for a moment his heart leapt as he thought it might be a telephone message from Maritza. But it was only from Mr. Dulles. He wanted to see Elliott right away.

When he got to the Herrengasse, Dulles was finishing packing, laying an array of vividly patterned ties over his shirts and pajamas. He grinned at Elliott a little sheepishly, taking in the young man's plain gray knitted tie.

"I have to confess to a weakness for bright colors. When you get to my age, you need a few peacock's feathers. That's not to say I don't admire sobriety, it's an elegant trait."

Dulles was in good spirits; he looked rested, his

skin had a smoother, healthier texture, and he was no longer hobbling.

"Glad to see the gout's better, sir," Elliott said politely.

"Damn nuisance. Comes on at the goddamndest times, but it's not giving me any trouble now." He closed his suitcase, and taking Elliott's elbow, guided him into the other room. "What about joining me in a little drink, Howard?"

"You wouldn't have some Jack Daniel's?"

"I think that can be arranged."

Dulles poured two generous measures over the ice cubes and handed Elliott his glass.

"Expect you know I'm going to Berlin tomorrow?"

"I'd heard."

"Going to take a look around. Soon as it's feasible, I want to move our whole operation out there. That's where the action is going to be now. Be sorry to leave Berne. It's a city I'm fond of. First worked here after World War One—I was about your age then, I guess . . . just about. . . . "

He swirled the ice around in his glass and looked out the window at the river and the rooftops of the old city, nostalgically savoring the past.

"Got my first experience of intelligence work here. Began to find out what it's all about. We Americans are not naturals at it like the Russians are and the Germans. Clandestinity isn't in our natures. Our tradition is for openness. We have to *learn* concealment and the whole tradecraft of deception. . . . "

He paused as if the mere chance drift of the conversation had brought him to this point. "Have you thought about your future, Howard?" Before Elliott could answer, he continued, "Some of those who joined me when the borders closed in '42 are going back to their businesses and professions, but some others are fixing to stay on. . . . "

"I don't have any special plans," Elliott said. "I'd like to see my father. And also my mother."

"That can be arranged. Those trips can be arranged."

"I would appreciate that."

"And after?"

"I don't know. My education was sort of interrupted by one thing and another. . . . I don't know."

"Well, let me say this to you. We threw you in at the deep end and you learned to swim. You know that? It was tough, what we asked you to do, considering you'd had no training in that line, were a complete novice at it. You showed natural aptitude."

"Frankly, sir, I thought I flunked it."

"I wouldn't say that. You safeguarded Sunrise." He paused. "Look here, Howard. America has a pressing need for a cadre of young professional intelligence officers. The Russians are old hands at this game . . . their tradition goes right back to the Czarist secret police. Hell, the Czar's Okhrana had guys tailing Leo Tolstoi around. When the Bolsheviks came in, the system and the men were there. All they had to do was make them over—to their line. They turned it into the most sophisticated and terroristic secret police and espionage system in the world. The MGB and the MVD are the clandestine arm of Soviet state power, capable of carrying out any task that the leadership assigns it, from checking up the meat content of sausages to carrying out wholesale liquidations. . . . They're the masters of kidnapping and murder and duplicity. Those are the people we're up against now. By comparison we're babes in the wood . . . we live in an open system . . . there are things we can't do. But in order to safeguard our system, Howard, there are some things we have got to do. For our self-protection. I'm saying this to you, Howard, because—frankly—I think you're cut out for this work. . . . "

"How do you judge that, sir?"

"How do I judge that? You want to know my criteria? You're entitled to ask that. All right. There's not a lot of money in it and no public acclaim, so it rules out the merely mercenary and the seekers after fame. Who does that leave? Well, it leaves the man who gets his life satisfaction in other ways, by being engaged in something that's important, that isn't routine, and that can bring him in touch with the highest levels of decision-making. Someone with a love of adventure and country, because no question about it, it's exciting. Now I admit there is another kind that you get. Some people thrive on clandestinity or deception for its own sake and get a perverse satisfaction from being the unknown movers of events. . . . I'll use that kind too, if need be."

"Which am I, sir?"

"What do you think, Howard? You know yourself best."

"I had a talk with Captain Wirth once, and he said people *choose* their characters."

"Is that so? Is that what Wirth said? Well, he may be right. If so, it's up to you. . . . I won't pressure you, Howard. Think about it."

"I don't think it's my line. . . . " He laughed.

"Like I said, I won't press you, Howard. But there's one hell of a lot to be done. Don't think because the war in Europe is over, that's the end of it. Now we've got to win the peace."

"There is one thing I would like to do, sir," Elliott said.

"Yes?"

"I'd like to come to Berlin with you, sir."

Dulles thought about this.

"You want to take a look-see before giving me an answer?"

"Yuh . . . you could say that. And I'd like to see if I can get some line on Schöller."

Dulles was thinking, looking closely at Elliott. "I don't see why you shouldn't come with me to Berlin," he decided. "In fact, I think it's a damn good idea."

· 40 ·

Through the dust that hung over the city, a skyline of
skeletal domes could sometimes be made out. Berlin
had become a flatland, dotted with great mounds and
hills and towers of rubble. Here and there a building
remained, dilapidated but standing, mysteriously ex-
empted from the general flattening. But in the center
there were not many such exemptions. Much of the
Charlottenburger Chaussee was gutted. The Tiergarten
had become a blasted heath consisting of lifeless trees
burned down to their trunks and main branches, with
no foliage.

From the back of the violently rocking jeep in which
Elliott was traveling, you could turn and turn and
see nothing but ruins. Nevertheless, people lived here,
like moles, inhabiting cellars and air raid shelters and
the underground railway stations.

In taking the city, the Russian artillery had flattened
what the bombs had left standing. Elliott had not
previously seen the whole map of destruction spread
out continuously before his eyes like this. Smoke,
flames, darkness, and fear had served to limit vision.
Now it was all to be seen, and even the dense swarms
of birds, swooping and turning futilely above the burned
trees, seemed clamorous with disbelief.

As expected, the Russians had scavenged thoroughly
in the ruins and the obvious intelligence prizes were
gone. The Gestapo and Kripo files, if they had sur-
vived the air attacks, the shelling, and the time bombs,
were presumably in Moscow by now.

Through his operatives in Berlin, Dulles had got

wind of the papers of the former Abwehr chief, Admiral Canaris, whom the Nazis had executed for treason. These papers were said to consist of a diary giving a chronology of Nazi crimes from 1933 onward; a card index of files on Nazi leaders kept by the Abwehr; a full secret record of the trial of General von Fritsch; and memoranda of negotiations between the Goerdler anti-Hitler plotters and the Vatican. Dulles had a number of leads on these papers, which he and his assistants began at once to follow up.

Elliott was assigned to a line of inquiry that involved checking into what had happened to a freight train loaded with crates of books from the Royal Bibliothek; this train had been derailed outside Berlin toward the end of 1944. One of the crates supposedly contained the Canaris papers among the tooled leather volumes.

Elliott was being driven to the area where the train was derailed. He told the GI driver assigned to him to go by way of the Steinplatz, saying he wished to see something there. When they arrived, he was astonished to see that the von Niesor mansion was still there. It had taken a bad battering, most of its roof was gone, the parapet statuary had been decimated, the windows were all boarded up, the baroque mask faces of the façade were shattered, the great iron main gate was off its hinges, but the house was standing.

Elliott leaped out of the jeep and picked his way through the debris to the front entrance. The door was gone and wooden planks had been nailed horizontally across the gap. The place looked deserted. Elliott banged with his fists on the wooden boards and shouted. No answer. He repeated the shouts several times, and still getting no answer had to conclude the place was empty. But he decided he would take another look at the house on his return.

He spent a futile day around Spandau. The derailed train was still there; its freight wagons had become a home for a community of bombed-out women and children and a few old men. He talked to these people, asking them about the crates that had been on the train, but none of them seemed to know anything. He went to nearby houses and asked if anybody remembered the derailment of 1944 and what had happened to the crates. One old woman said she remembered that trucks had come to take away the crates, but where to she didn't know.

In the late afternoon, returning to Berlin, he told the driver to stop again in the Steinplatz and once more tried banging on the boarded-up entrance and windows. He was about to go away again when he heard a cracked old voice come from between the boards of an upstairs window.

"What do you want? What do you want? Go away. I am nobody. There is nobody here. Nobody here."

"I am a friend of the family," Elliott called up to the crack between the boards.

There was a prolonged silence during which this claim was evidently receiving consideration. Then the voice said, "You are American."

The old servant, for Elliott was now sure from the aged sound of the voice that it must be he, had obviously seen the American jeep.

"I am not with the army," Elliott called up. "I was a visitor to this house. I have been received here."

"You have been received here?"

"Yes."

"I will be with you at once, sir. At once. I beg your pardon."

As Elliott waited to be admitted, he felt in a strangely suspended state, like somebody coming out of an anesthetic, knowing that shortly he would feel pain again but not yet, not yet—for the moment he still possessed the dull immunity.

A ground-floor window shutter had been opened and a long bony hand was beckoning to Elliott to come in that way. He did as bidden by the old bent servant, whose face looked worn away, like stone exposed to the oceans. Lifting his legs over the sill, stepping into thick glass which broke under his feet, he followed old Albert through inches of masonry dust across the ballroom, over the platform where the gilt chairs for the members of the dance orchestra remained in position, and then out onto some stairs open to the sky.

Old Albert shuffled ahead of him. By this round-about route, they came to what had been the last reception room used by the von Niesors, the scene of that final absurd party. This room was now deep in plaster and debris and glass. The silk canopy over the four-poster bed sagged under the weight of the pieces of fallen ceiling. The telephone from which Ferdy von Niesor had issued his invitations lay smashed on the floor. A circular "conversation sofa" in wine-colored velvet had collapsed—having lost its legs—in the center.

The old footman was standing bent and waiting, his permanently stooped posture preventing him from looking directly at the caller.

"Yes, it was in this room," Elliott said.

"It was the room they used at the end," the old servant agreed.

"Before they went away?"

"Yes. Before they went away."

"When was that?"

"Why do you ask me that, sir?" It was a discreet rebuke.

"*You* didn't go away."

"Oh I stayed, yes, yes, seeing I lived here since I was a boy. Where else could I go? Wasn't—like—the same in my case. The Russians. You understand, sir. They wouldn't harm an old man like me, sir, now would they? Not me. Seeing I was one of them—a working man, you see. It was different for the master."

"Yes, of course."

"Worked for the von Niesors seventy-three years, I have. From when I was just a boy of thirteen. You know that, sir."

"Must have been terrible for you to see this." He made a vague head gesture to the windows and the devastation outside. "At least they were not here for the worst?"

"The worst?"

"I know it was all bad—but the worst must have been when the Russians came."

"Yes, that was the worst. You are right, sir. The shelling and the killing and the rape. That was the worst."

"By then they were gone."

"Gone, yes, yes. Oh Lord, yes. By then they were gone."

"Where did they go? Did they tell you where they were going?"

The aged stooped back heaved under some enormous invisible load of years as it sought to straighten up; the rigid neck pulled stiffly back in a series of jerks; the long downcast eyes became raised to look at this caller, this madman. And the worn-out features took on the kind of disrespectful expression that good servants allow themselves only among other servants, and with a shrug he abruptly stuck out his hand and jabbed a thumb downward, repeatedly.

Elliott did not immediately understand, though he heard the alarms go off distantly in his head and began to feel the first tingle of feeling return to his numb brain. Since he appeared to have misunderstood and was floundering in some kind of daze, or near faint, the old servant felt obliged to make himself clear.

"Dead," he said with a curious forcefulness, considering his age and frail appearance, the face illumined with the smile of the bestower of bad news. "Dead and gone, sir."

"The father and the daughter. Both?"

"Both, sir."

"You are sure of this?"

"I saw them, didn't I?"

"What? You saw them killed?"

"I saw them die, sir," he corrected. He did a quick biting movement with toothless gums. "Us—of our station—wasn't given pills like that," he said. "KCB pills. No, that was for the masters. Quick. Oh, very quick. Not a pleasant sight seeing them die—specially Fräulein Maritza—but it was very quick, I must say."

"Both of them, father and daughter?" Elliott said stupidly.

"Father and daughter together. They were always very close. They dressed up very nice and smart, you

306

know. Oh yes. Yes. He wore his tails and his decorations, and Fräulein Maritza had on a blue dress. . . . "

"Stop it, stop it, you filthy old buzzard."

"You asked me, sir. I thought you knew." He shook his head uncomprehendingly at the ways of the masters.

"Why didn't they leave . . . why did they stay?"

"Leave, sir? Nobody could leave."

"They had papers, they had special papers to enable them to leave."

"Oh, those!" He shook his head and gave a hoarse dry laugh. "I heard about those. There was a lot of talk about them at the end." He shook his head. "Some Gestapo man gave them to her. Well, you know what they are. They're low. Very low. Use any trick or weapon to get what they're after. You understand me, sir?"

"The papers . . . what was wrong with them?"

"They were no good. No good. Out of date. It was an old serial number that had been canceled weeks before. . . . Good for wiping your ass with, that was the only thing those papers were good for."

"Oh Christ," Elliott said. "Oh Christ Jeezus."

He began to shiver violently, his head shaking on his neck.

"Are you all right, sir? Is there something you want, sir? Glass of water?"

With an effort he recovered himself.

"When they found out, about the papers not being any good—what did they do, what did she say? Fräulein Maritza?"

"Say? Do?" The old servant seemed to be mystified as to what information was being sought. "She didn't say anything, far as I can recall. Now let me see. Herr von Niesor come back from the railway station where he'd been to get the tickets and they'd told him about the papers being out of date . . . the date of issue was correct, they said, but the serial number was an old one that wasn't valid anymore. That's right. Well, you understand, it was a trick, they're like that, those Gestapo. . . . Fräulein Maritza? When he broke it to her, gently, you understand, her father, she just laughed. That's right. She just laughed. Laughed and laughed and laughed, sir. You wouldn't believe it, but that's what she did. A mocking sort of laugh, you know, like she had sometimes. More at herself, I'd say, than anything else, if you follow my meaning. . . . "

.

After four days of intensive inquiries the OSS group in Berlin had drawn a complete blank on the Canaris papers. At the same time, Dulles had asked American Army Counterintelligence to check into the arrival of the Schöller files. Units were sent to the Tegernsee and to Garmisch in the mountains, and to the "safe house" near Miesbach, but none of the files had arrived at their destinations.

There were various possibilities; that the trucks had been captured or destroyed; that the drivers had abandoned them somewhere; or—that this was another of Schöller's tricks. That the files had been sent to some other destination, so that he would have an additional bargaining card up his sleeve, if he needed it.

At this point Dulles took Elliott off the Canaris inquiries and told him to see if he could get any line on Schöller's present whereabouts.

It was not easy even to start. The Prinz Albrecht-strasse was in the Soviet sector and the Russians were not willing to let American intelligence poke around in the ruins of Gestapo headquarters, which they regarded as their own preserve and where, in any case, it was unlikely that anything would have been left of use. Police headquarters in the Alexanderplatz were also in the Russian sector, and so the Americans were denied access to police files.

However, the Russians did formally cooperate in the work of the Allied War Crimes Commission, and through this agency Elliott put out a routine request for anything known on Schöller. The Russians responded promptly—with a mass of charges.

They claimed he had been an official assassin for the regime. They had detailed evidence of his involvement in the murder in 1938 of Baron Kettler, secretary of the German Ambassador in Vienna, Franz von Papen. The secretary's bruised body had been found floating in the Danube shortly after he had taken certain papers to Hitler in Berchtesgaden.

These papers were Austrian police files on the death of Hitler's niece Geli Raubal. Years earlier, before coming to power, Hitler had been in love with his little niece and on discovering her sexual infidelities—in one instance with his chauffeur, Emil Maurice—he'd had her murdered, according to the Russians. The police files on the case were kept by the Austrian Chancellor, Herr Schuschnigg, in his personal safe.

Shortly before Hitler's ultimatum to Austria in 1938, these papers were stolen from Schuschnigg's apartment. The Russians claimed that the burglary had been committed by Schöller, with the help of professional criminals, on instructions from Heydrich. The stolen files had then been taken to Hitler by the German Ambassador's secretary.

On his way to Berchtesgaden Baron Kettler had made microfilm copies of the papers, and this was discovered. Schöller was then sent to liquidate the Baron and retrieve the microfilm.

Elliott had heard the rumors about the death of Hitler's niece (who was officially supposed to have committed suicide), though he had never given much credence to them. This was the first time he had heard Schöller's name connected with the case—as the supposed assassin of Baron Kettler.

Finally, the Russian memorandum stated that Schöller was a murderer and a forger. In the last days of the regime he had embezzled four million Swiss francs from a secret Swiss account and to cover up his crime had murdered the SS-Budget Administrator Oswald Stapplemann, and forged his signature.

The upshot of the memorandum was that the Russians wanted Schöller arrested and charged with war crimes of the first category.

Dulles mused over this memorandum for a long time. He was struck by the speed with which it had been produced and the vagueness of the charges, simply repeating old well-known rumors. For years there had been various theories about the murder of Baron Kettler; to state categorically that it was Schöller's handiwork, without offering any kind of evidence, was just facile rumormongering. Of course, it could be true . . . but this Russian memo gave no particular reason for thinking so.

"You'll note," Dulles observed, "that our request for anything known about Gestapo Chief Müller meets with a stony silence, and no word about *his* multifarious crimes. You know what I think, Howard? I think they've got Müller, he's gone over to them by arrangement, with his files. And these charges against Schöller originate with Müller. *Why?* Because if they've got Müller and are proposing to use him, they're afraid of what Schöller might know. Therefore they want to neutralize Schöller. Best way would be to liquidate him, but if they can't get their hands on him and suspect he's in the West, the next best thing is charge him with enough war crimes and have him legally removed. A hanged man can't spill any beans. Of course, that's only my guess, Howard, but in my experience the Soviets never do anything that isn't motivated by self-interest, and they wouldn't be so co-operative just to help us."

"The last part is true," Elliott pointed out. "We did kill the Budget Administrator."

"So you told me," Dulles agreed. "It is also true," he conceded, "that Schöller's briefcase was stuffed with Swiss francs when it blew up. But, you know, such basic facts can be twisted to fit any number of stories. There is no reason why we should believe Gestapo Chief Müller's version."

"There are things that begin to fit," Elliott said. "The visit to the guy behind the Alexanderplatz, after the murder. He must have been the forger. Schöller must have gone to him to get Stapplemann's signature forged . . . "

"It's possible," Dulles agreed.

"Which means . . . we murdered the Budget Administrator so Schöller could lay his hands on the dough."

"Whatever Schöller's motive, Stapplemann would have blown Sunrise. So he *had* to be removed. Schöller was quite right about that. If the war in Italy had

310

gone on just a few days more, do you know how many American boys might have died in a major offensive?"

"Yes, sir, I realize that."

"Still, I know how you feel, Howard. And it does you credit."

There was one other obvious line of inquiry. A request went out from OSS to American Army Counterintelligence to find Schöller's wife. Elliott gave them the name of the street in Bregenz where she had been staying last with her small child. She was found without difficulty, still at the hotel. She claimed not to have heard from her husband, and the hotel keeper confirmed that there had been no telephone calls for her and no letters. But of course, CIC pointed out, a man like Schöller would have arranged a dead-letter drop, and so she might be lying.

"You want us to use a little physical pressure on the Frau Special Investigator?" the CIC man offered.

"Oh, hell, no," Elliott said quickly, angrily. "That's not necessary. I'm sure she's telling the truth."

"OK, OK, but if you change your mind, buster, remember. . . . " He chuckled, and said in Hollywood-German accent " . . . Ve also haff vays off making dese Krauts talk."

"Oh, for Christ's sake," Elliott said, "she's his wife, but *she* hasn't done anything. Lay off her, huh? The kid's ill, you know."

"My heart bleeds."

With no other leads presenting themselves, Elliott decided to pay a visit to Schöller's place at Wannsee. On his way out there he remembered the previous journey through the darkness of the blackout, skirting the blazing city.

The district of boating lakes and Strandbads and pleasure gardens, though desolate now, was clearly once a good place to live and raise a family, and there must have been days when this petty bourgeois comfort represented the height of Schöller's aspirations.

His low pink villa, when they found it in one of the quite residential streets, seemed both smaller and even more conventional than Elliott remembered it. The forsythia around the iron bench in the front garden was in full blossom; the fruit trees were a froth of whites and pinks; lace curtains shielded the interior from the curiosity of neighbors.

Elliott lifted the latch of the three-foot iron gate and went along the path to the front door. It was locked, but he had authority to break in, and did so by knocking out the glass from a ground-floor window. No alarm went off; there either had been none, or electrical failure had inactivated it.

The driver waited outside while Elliott searched around in the house. It had been left tidy and clean, beds made, coverlets smoothed, bolsters thumped out to their full fullness. In the kitchen, cooking utensils and plates were washed and stacked in accordance to size. The house of a house-proud woman.

The cupboard and closet keys had been left in their keyholes. When Elliott unlocked the doors, he found only linen and clothing and personal possessions such as any ordinary middle-class household would have.

Finally he went into the dining room and opened the mahogany sideboard. A canteen of cutlery. Napkins. Tablecloths Tiny liqueur glasses. He pulled out the drawers. Silver and leather framed family photographs. He looked at these again, as he had done the night he spent in the house. Schöller and his wife on their wedding day. The sepia photographs of his parents. Various photographs of the child. And the signed photograph of the Munich police detectives, standing with arms linked, grinning into the camera, outside the Police Praesidium. Heinrich Müller, Waldbrunner, Kamitz, Schöller, and a fifth whose signature he could not make out, perhaps because the name was unfamiliar to him. He studied the face of this fifth man, wondering vaguely who it was.

He clearly remembered that in the files below the Prinz Albrechtstrasse there had been references to "the quartet of Munich detectives"—never any mention of five. Yet judging from this picture, this fifth man had once been very much part of the group, he was between Heini Müller and Schöller, and Schöller had his arms round the fifth man's shoulders. Elliott took the picture to the light and studied the scrawled signature of the unidentified young policeman. The first letter seemed to be a P followed by two K's. The pen had not made a very good impression on the glossy surface and the end of the name had simply disappeared in a meaningless squiggle. The open face was that of—one of the boys. No striking characteristics. Same unformed immature face as the other youthful policemen with their big grins and posing expressions.

Like the others he would look totally different now, more than twenty years later. In the case of Schöller, Elliott could just about see in the young man of the picture the uncompleted outline of the later person, the Reich Special Investigator. Something in the expression—a sort of knowingness, though in a young man this would pass for youthful cockiness.

Elliott put the picture back in the drawer. This was not getting him anywhere. He proceeded to conduct a thorough search of the house, knocking on walls for hollow places, examining floorboards to see if any were loose, feeling pillows and cushions in case things had been hidden in them. But it was just an ordinary suburban house with all the usual things in it. It was clear that Schöller had taken good care not to leave anything behind that might either incriminate him or provide any clues to his present whereabouts.

When Elliott got back to the center of Berlin, he started thinking about the unidentified policeman in the photograph. He remembered Schöller saying how both he and Müller had originally been regarded as unsuitable but had talked their way back into favor. Well, perhaps the fifth cop had failed in this respect. What would have happened to such a man? Would he have been kicked out of the police force? Found another job? A man close to four men so powerful in the Nazi regime would presumably have been found something. Unless they'd all turned their backs on him.

Elliott felt curious about this fifth man in the photograph. Perhaps it was because knowing, roughly, what the other four had become, it would complete the picture to find out what had happened to the fifth. Why had he disappeared from the scene and the records?

On the basis of this vague curiosity, Elliott placed a call to CIC in Munich. He identified himself as OSS. Could they check out something for him at Munich police headquarters? A matter of going through some old records. He wanted to know what had happened to various detectives working in the criminal section before '33. The CIC Captain said he would phone back if he could lay his hands on anything.

Two days later Elliott got a call from Munich. The CIC Captain, whose name was Shulman, said he'd got the records in front of him. He reeled off a string of names. "There was Heinrich Müller—. Then there's a guy called Johan Gustav Waldbrunner, and a Kamitz, a Meisinger, and a Flach, Weiss ... and Kremer ... it goes on. Which are you interested in?"

"Any indication of what happened to them?"

Captain Shulman was flicking through the record cards.

"They moved on . . . various jobs. Except this one. Kremer. His card ends in 1933 . . . Karl Peter Kremer . . . "

"Yes. What's it say about him?"

"Hold on. There's a note. I'm just reading it. . . . Oh, yuh. Seems he got kicked out of the force. Considered unsuitable. Politically untrustworthy. Dismissed from the force without pension rights."

"What happened to him?"

"Doesn't say. But—wait a minute—there's a cross-reference."

Silence as Captain Shulman searched through another card index. Finally he said, "Oh there's nothing much. Just a note that in 1937 the question of his pension was reopened. Says here that after due consideration the Chef der Deutschen Polizei decided to restore the guy's pension, together with back payments, on the recommendation of Reichskriminaldirektor Schöller."

A sudden shiver went through Elliott. He said quickly, "It say anything else about Karl Peter Kremer?"

"No. Just the amount of the pension and the back payment to which he was entitled."

Elliott put down the phone. He felt elated—that feeling of knowing. He knew now, oh yes. No need to think this through bit by bit. He had got it, he was sure. The feeling of sureness was like the sense of being privy to hidden truths, secrets of the universe, that sort of thing. Things other people didn't know about. He felt exhilarated and wanted everything to happen very fast now, so as not to lose the momentum that had begun in him.

He picked up the telephone and placed a call to Captain Wirth in Berne.

"Something important," he said when he got through. "I'd appreciate your help. Can you check for me if a German called Karl Peter Kremer came to Switzerland and took up residence sometime between 1937 and the war? Legitimate. May have changed his name, but if so, it would be all above board. Probably started a business of some sort, which, I guess would have to be registered and licensed . . . right? I really would appreciate it if you could pull strings and get me this as a matter of top priority, because I think it might be pretty damn important. . . . "

"I will see what I can do," Wirth promised.

For a while Elliott sat next to the telephone as if expecting it to ring there and then to give him the answer. Any delay in confirming what he now knew, was like a leash and muzzle on a wild dog. Delay was his enemy. But he knew, of course, that the answer couldn't come through that quickly. For one thing, the telephone connections, though now restored and functioning, were still extremely erratic. For another, even if Captain Wirth dropped everything and everybody else dropped everything, it would still require painstaking searches through stored records in order to elicit the information he had asked for.

Elliott, by such arguments, succeeded in getting his impatience under control. To Dulles and the other assistants he said nothing, although there was something in his demeanor—a kind of knowingness—that they had not seen before, and it gave him a certain forcefulness of manner he had previously lacked.

That night Dulles told the group that they were

returning to Berne. They had drawn a complete blank on the Canaris papers, and it had become clear that war criminals like Himmler, Kaltenbrunner, Müller, and others had succeeded in getting out of Berlin. The net would have to be spread wider, and meanwhile the full-scale move to Berlin organized.

This news of a return to Berne suited Elliott fine. He told Dulles, "I agree, sir, that that's the way to play it."

"Glad you agree, Howard," Dulles said, smiling faintly.

There was one final thing Dulles wanted to do before leaving: take a look at Plötzensee prison. Several members of the German underground with whom Dulles had worked were executed there, and he wanted to pay a last tribute to them.

A low rectangular room. Bare concrete floor. At the back two high arched windows reaching to the ground, barred. Solid iron inner shutters on gate hinges, capable of closing tightly on the windows so as to shut out all light. Whitewashed rough-cast walls. Two electric lamps in gray metal shades hanging from roof beams.

Toward the back of the room, not far from the high windows, the floor sloped slightly to a drain. Above, at a height of about nine feet, a steel girder with nine meat hooks spanned the width of the room. And in front, next to a section of the rough-cast wall that had been tiled white, there was a wooden garrote, with a large wooden screw, and a slab.

The little group of Americans were staring up at the girder with the meat hooks. Spring sunlight coming through the tall arched windows cast the pattern of the bars on the concrete floor. Dulles took off his hat and held it by the crown against his chest and inclined his head slightly, and the other Americans did likewise. They stood in silent homage for a minute.

Elliott, next to Dulles, felt a sob form in his chest and force itself up into his throat; it came out half gasp, half cry. It was a startling and embarrassing sound in the stillness of the Plötzensee execution shed.

The group of Americans were ready to move off

again. Dulles turned to Elliott and looked sternly into his eyes.

"Nothing to be ashamed of, Howard, in weeping for colleagues who have fallen in the field. They're honorable tears."

Turning away nevertheless, Elliott walked out by himself and stood alone in the courtyard under the shadow of the high brick observation tower. He had been keeping busy, concentrating all his attention on tracking down Schöller, but now a feeling of total desolation caught up with him. He was choking. Gasping for breath in the open air.

He took a few shuffling steps and as he walked, he regained some of his composure, remembering that he had, after all, tracked down Schöller. Things would be put right. Things would be put right. The thought of this calmed him. Things had to be put right. Or one could not breathe.

He was finding in himself a deep vein of anger that he had not known of, and it was a source of energy.

Recovering, and catching up with the others who had gone ahead, he allowed himself to reflect whether Dulles would consider it so honorable to weep for a self-murdered girl, who in all likelihood had been a Nazi, if not recently, then certainly at some time in the past.

The train was passing through open countryside. His spirit felt soft and smug and lazy in the absence of danger. He was impatient to be back in Berne and put his certain knowledge to the test.

The scenery was very variable. Sometimes the sunlight, flashing between long single lines of trees, raked the train with its blinding fire. The jagged outlines of destroyed buildings and installations and towns were seen at intervals, already fixed and rooted in the landscape, like ancient ruins.

In the late morning Elliott found himself alone with Dulles. Making a conscious effort to speak casually, he said, "I think I've found Schöller, sir."

"What do you mean you *think* you've found Schöller?"

"I mean: I think I know where he is to be found."

"Go on."

"Well, sir, it seemed clear to me, sir, that Schöller was being hidden by some friend, and I figured a man like that couldn't have that many friends."

"OK."

"Well, sir. I happened to remember that in the files I'd examined in Berlin there were references to the quartet of Munich detectives—there was a bunch of them that were buddies back in '23, one of them was Müller, another Schöller. At Schöller's house in Wannsee there was a photograph of these guys, and there were *five* of them. I checked with Munich and found out that one of these cops in the picture was kicked out of the force, and that years later Schöller got his pension restored. It just struck me there couldn't be that many people Schöller had done a good turn that he could go to if he needed help . . . Well, I checked with Captain Wirth and I heard last night that a former Munich cop, Karl Peter Kremer, came to Switzerland in 1937 and obtained a license to run a mountain inn. It's up in the Col des Mosses, about forty miles from Berne."

He stopped abruptly, voice petering out, wondering if he had perhaps jumped too readily to conclusions, if his detective work was about to be demolished as amateurish and unsubstantiated.

"It's a damn good piece of guesswork," Dulles said at last, having weighed up the facts. "You may be right." He allowed a minute or so to go by while he thought, and then he said, "Dammit, I'll wager you *are* right."

Toward early evening the train was south of Munich, passing through the lovely Bavarian countryside of lakeside resorts and spas. The wooden gables of the inns and town halls and post offices in these little towns glowed golden and blue and red with vivid religious pictures of Madonnas, redemption, self-sacrifice, martyrdom. . . .

In the streets noisy German soldiers wandered about drinking beers, most of them still carrying their rifles and sidearms, waiting to be rounded up. Elliott watched them lolling about, bedraggled youths with spotty skins, big awkward country boys; how extraordinary that once they had inspired terror wherever they went.

Dulles came to join him in the corridor of the train to admire the view. Together they watched several geese flapping low across the quiet water.

"Most pleasant, the Bavarian lakes," Dulles said. "Schliersee. Tegernsee. Bad Tölz. Very agreeable little places. An expanse of water eases the eye. Back home we have a place out at Henderson Harbor. Lake Ontario. You know it at all? Oh, it's great. The bass fishing is great. It's a place for the family, where we can relax. My brother, Foster, is as fond of bass fishing as I am. We play some tennis, do some sailing. And talk politics, naturally." He chuckled. "You never find the Dulleses together not talking politics. It's in our blood, I guess, and part of our heritage. We've had one Secretary of State in the family, and who knows—there may be a second someday." He broke off these personal reflections to regard Elliott thoughtfully. "What are we going to do about Schöller?"

"I think he'll be feeling pretty safe up there," Elliott said. "We shouldn't have much trouble surprising him."

"We?" Dulles asked. "You know our problem with the Swiss. They've been pretty damn helpful all along, especially Wirth. Don't want to embarrass them. If Schöller asked for political asylum, that'd put 'em in a spot. . . . "

"I could handle it myself," Elliott said quietly.

"Could you? Could you?"

"I think so . . . now."

"Those Russian charges, of course, are ridiculous," Dulles said.

"It's the sort of thing that could be true about him."

"Could be? It's no more than wild rumor. Our War Crimes people have got nothing on him. Nothing substantial."

"He took good care to stay behind the scenes and not put his name to anything."

"He's clean where the Jews are concerned. Had nothing to do with them. Nor with prisoners of war.

Any crimes he may have committed were against his own sort. . . . "

"I have one or two lines on him, sir, that I think alter that viewpoint, which is one I also at one time entertained, briefly."

"You did, huh? It also occurred to you?"

"It just passed through my mind, but then I began to see . . . "

"What? That he's a rough fellow. I agree. I agree. That his hands are not the cleanest? I'm ready to concede that to you. On the other hand, Howard, I've been thinking . . . "

"You sound as though you are defending him, sir."

"No. I'm not defending him. But I'm a lawyer, and I'm trained to see the defense case even when I'm conducting the prosecution."

"I'm not sure I follow what you are getting at, Mr. Dulles."

"Howard, let me tell you a true story. Back in 1929 Secretary of State Stimson closed down America's cryptanalytic effort with what became famous words. *'Gentlemen do not read other people's mail,'* he said. Well, I can tell you, Howard, that when Stimson became Roosevelt's Secretary of War, he was obliged to change his viewpoint pretty smart. When the fate of nations, the lives of soldiers, and a way of life that we cherish, are at stake, we cannot afford the self-indulgence of being gentlemen. Or moralists. We have to do what's practical. And what will serve the larger end-purpose. With humanity, I hope and trust, always with humanity. But without namby-pamby sentimentality. The fact is, Howard, I'm pretty damn sure that Gestapo Müller has gone over to the Soviets. Now we've got to consider what that means for us. It means that through him the Soviets have got access to the biggest network of paid informants and undercover agents ever built up. Many of them are in our automatic-arrest category and can therefore be blackmailed to work for the other side. Given that situation, Schöller could be damn useful to us. There are his files. And there's what he knows in his head. The very fact that we have got him means the Russkies couldn't be too confident about using the Gestapo apparat. I'm thinking out loud, Howard. I'm letting you in on my line of thought that I've been pursuing ever since you told me your news this morning."

"We're talking about a man who was one of the linchpins of the whole Nazi system."

"That's arguable. In any case, it's beside the point. Whatever he was, we can turn him around. We can make him over. He can be rendered politically acceptable. I'll vouch for that. As you say, he's worked behind the scenes. Not too much known about him. He can continue like that. He doesn't have to come out."

"What are you proposing, sir?"

"Well, the way I see it, Howard, is this. Supposing you go to Schöller, whom you've so astutely tracked down, and I regard that as a great feather in your cap, oh surely, a great feather in your cap, and supposing you said to him, 'The deal is on.' Tell him what happened on the Fricktreppe was an aberration on Quantregg's part. He was not acting on my instructions. If Schöller is still suspicious, tell him I'm willing to consider making good part of the financial loss he suffered on the steps. I suspect he is a man who likes money and he's lost most of it. That'll draw him. Supposing you did that, how would that strike you, Howard?"

◆ 41 ◆

Schöller had climbed up into the roof space of the annex.

Through the small grimy skylight he could survey

the whole area. High and remote and wintry-looking with snow clouds lying against its peaks, the pass on this particular morning was bleak in the extreme. The escarpment on both sides gave a feeling of somber confining walls. They rose deeply scarred, cold, and sheer to hem in the few houses and stores and mountain inns.

From where he was, he had a clear full view of the pass. Cars coming from either direction could be seen approaching a long way away. No vehicle would be able to take the narrow steep winding track up to the Gasthaus Rey. Anyone coming up would have to do the final climb on foot, in full view. There was no other way. All around the inn the sides of the Col were starkly bare, devoid of cover. The woods only began to the rear.

Schöller remained most of the time in the annex. When he did go out—to get some exercise—it was usually at night and he confined his walks to the wooded slopes, where he could wander around for miles without any chance of being seen.

He had no conscience about anything he had ever done. Anyone in his position would have had to do the same. He had never, personally, gotten involved in any of that *Schweinerei* that went on. The killings that he had carried out, on the instructions of Heydrich and others, had always been clean. Like Baron Kettler in '38. A quick backward jerk of the head over the high ladder-back of the chair, and the neck broke like a matchstick. The man was working for British Intelligence. Had to be removed. The others were the same. He had never killed anyone unless there was a good reason, and had never got any satisfaction out of killing itself, like some did. Just from doing a job of work which had to be done, and doing it well. He had professional pride. He was a good policeman. He knew police work.

It was foolish to pretend you could do police work, under any regime, dealing with criminals and murderers and ambitious ruthless men, and keep your hands lily white. The intellectuals didn't know all that had

322

to be done so they could sit back and listen to Mozart. What did they know?

But he knew, he knew what had to be done. You couldn't always say these things openly—because people paid lip service to certain pretenses that went down well with the general public—but anyone who knew anything about the realities of power, knew what had to be done.

What troubled him most was that people might tell his son lies about the sort of man his father was. With this in mind, he began to write down an account of his life's activities, but in the end he gave up, feeling that it made too brutal reading for a child, that he would not be able to grasp the necessity of certain acts. Not being one of the intellectuals, he couldn't really explain it properly in words.

What did the innocent American know! A kid— wet behind the ears.

What he regretted most was having let himself be taken in by Dulles. He had believed that he could trust him. Coming out of the bank in Berne he should have taken more precautions, maybe should have gone out some back way, hidden the money and the file index away, in a safe deposit box—got the clerk to post the key to a Poste Restante. Then he'd have been in a position of strength vis-à-vis Dulles. Yes, yes, that was the way he should have done it. . . . Mistake. He always corrected his mistakes.

He certainly wouldn't make this mistake of trusting anyone again. What you could rely on was your own quickness, and skills, and nothing else.

From the top of the annex he kept a regular lookout for any sign of police vehicles coming into the pass, though he was confident he would not be traced here. Nobody would connect the Reich Special Investigator with the broken-down old innkeeper of the Col des Mosses.

But he had made a plan in case he was tracked down. On his walks he had planned an escape route for himself through the wooded slopes, leaving caches of food in different hiding places on the way, as well as extra clothing and a variety of false passports. Just in case.

323

His hoard of Swiss francs he always kept in bags next to his skin.

Elliott left Berne in a black legation Cadillac. Six A.M. He hadn't eaten any breakfast. His stomach felt raw and empty. He drove fast through the long, quiet residential streets, with their clean-swept pavements and washed gutters. Out of the salubrious city and into the sudden countryside, the Cadillac glided on its overluxurious suspension, rocking the driver in soft beige comfort.

It was a straight fast road along the valley of the Aare, and he made good time. The long, low-roofed farmhouses flashed past rapidly until he began to see the mountains, only faintly at first. He thought there was something vaguely sinister about them, the way they stood in such still groups in the dim morning.

Soon he was at Thun, passing the lake, and saw hikers with feathered hats, rucksacks on their backs, and long red or yellow stockings up to their knees.

He was looking out for the signpost to Gwatt and Zweisimmen, and when he spotted it, he took the sharp right-hand turn and began the gentle ascent into the mountains.

At first the road followed a railway line and the Simme, with those Swiss covered bridges crossing the torrent. As he got higher, there were abrupt views through the trees of distant peaks, high snow, and glaciers. Climbing: the feeling of an all-encompassing chill, the air turning jagged. Wind and cloud. Gray, gray.

He felt gripped by a sense of occasion. Days are not all the same, and this was not a day to be blurred and lost among others. This was the day on which something was going to happen.

They expected you to turn your mind around, again and again, till it was a whirligig, forever changing its position in accordance with the needs of the moment.

That was what they expected. Flexibility of response. Mr. Dulles was a clever man, no doubt about it, and ten moves ahead of everybody else—while the others were still fighting the Nazis, he was thinking ahead to the new struggle and adjusting to the particular demands of that. No more simple black and white questions: goodies and baddies. Instead everything was gray, and uncertain.

It was that kind of a day. Clouds and light drizzle. On a day like this you found out what you were going to be.

He realized he must have gone wrong somewhere because he was passing through the ski resort of Gstaad, which was not on the route he had been given. When he consulted his map, he saw that he had made a slight looping detour. Procrastinating. Best now to go on through the Col de Pillon, and then back to the Col des Mosses. Marginally farther than turning back. But he did not like turning back. Best to keep on.

The ground was still rising. The houses became more scattered and simpler as he got higher up. Some were just shacks. He passed through a succession of drab mountain hamlets, with tumbledown structures in weathered gray wood.

At this altitude the mountain peaks had the still whiteness of a dream.

He realized he must be close now to the Col des Mosses. First came an old stone church with a stone tower, then further along a few cafés, some houses, one or two Hôtels du Col. As he came into the pass, the car seemed to have entered a wind tunnel. Outside the buildings, the flags were practically being ripped down from the tall flagpoles.

Elliott stopped the car, opened the glove compartment, took out Quantregg's Colt .45 automatic, and slipped it in his breast pocket. As he got out, he felt pummeled by the rush of cold air. The escarpments overhung the pass like massive question marks.

He looked around. From the pass road the ground rose abruptly. There were a number of houses scattered about the lower slopes before the woods began. Patches of dirty-looking snow here and there and a white hard tinge to the tops of the trees. But the thaw was now in the last phase.

He went into the bakery and asked where the Gasthaus Rey was. The baker's daughter pointed out the place, in an isolated position, some considerable way up the side of the Col.

"How does one get there?" he asked.

"By walking," she said, pointing to the unnoticeable track that curved and twisted upward, disappearing in places, only to continue somewhat arbitrarily from another point further on. Over the years rockfalls and erosion had caused such deterioration there was no possibility of getting any kind of vehicle up there.

Elliott left the car and started to climb. He did not attempt to conceal himself. If Schöller was keeping a watch, he would have seen him by now and recognized him.

As he clambered over the rough unlevel ground, he felt totally exposed—no cover anywhere. A risk he had to take. No other way of getting up there. He was becoming breathless out of proportion to the actual steepness of the climb. He wished he had taken a drink; that would have been a help. Schöller would no doubt offer him one.

He thought about the human waxworks around the farm table, and he thought about Maritza and her father, and he thought about Quantregg, and about Baron Kettler, whose bruised body had been found floating in the Danube. He couldn't help his thoughts. He had not acquired the trick of mindlessness. . . .

He was nearly there. It really was in a most run-down condition, this old pension. Looked uninhabited. Not a sound came from it. Perhaps in his determination to find Schöller he had drawn false conclusions from the available facts. Perhaps he had misled himself into thinking he had found Schöller. . . .

He rapped on the door, strongly, harshly, a night knock. No answer. But he knew that Kremer was there. The baker's daughter had said so. So he rapped again and shouted. He tried the door. Locked. After about five minutes of this banging and shouting, the door was opened by an unshaven bleary-eyed man.

"I'm looking for someone. You know who I mean."

"Nobody here. Go away. Go away."

"I *know* he is here."

Peering into this wreck of a face, Elliott saw only

326

blankness and incomprehension. Perhaps he had been wrong thinking Schöller would have come here.

"You used to know Ernst Schöller. You were detectives together, in Munich before the war. I know it was a long time ago, but you were friends. . . . "

"Yes, I remember Schöller." He shook his head. "What makes you think he is here?"

"Because I don't think he had another friend. Where else could he go? He did you a favor once, and he didn't do many of those."

"Haven't set eyes on Ernst Schöller in twelve years . . . "

"No?"

Now Elliott was sure the innkeeper was lying.

"I'm going to take a look around."

He pushed past and started striding rapidly, determinedly, from room to room. The one with the big green tile stove had obviously not been used for years, judging from the damp clamminess of its walls and floors. He went out. Kitchen. Dining room—with a bed, a worn old leather armchair, from which the stuffing was coming out in different places, a table on which stood one unwashed plate, one beer glass, one knife and fork.

Ignoring the innkeeper's protests at this unjustifiable intrusion, Elliott ran up the stairs to the second floor and started throwing open bedroom doors. These rooms were all very cold and damp and bare. No indication that anyone had slept in any of them recently.

He went to the window and looked out. About twenty yards across a cobbled courtyard was the annex. It surprised him because from the front it was completely concealed.

Elliott leaned out of the window and called, "Schöller! Schöller! I want to talk to you." No answer. In the dim interior of the annex he thought he saw fleeting movements, but couldn't be sure. Up in the attic? Was he up there? If he was, he was keeping well clear of the windows. Probably some back way out. He'd have his escape route ready, wouldn't he? Through the wooded slopes . . .

"Listen, Schöller. I have a proposition for you. Dulles wants to make a deal." Still getting no response, he added, "There's money in it. Mr. Dulles has unvouchered funds he can draw on, in certain circumstances."

From part of the building that he could not pinpoint he heard the question: "Money?"

"Yuh—money. Thought that would interest you, Schöller. Money. Come out. Let's talk. You're not scared of me, are you? There's nobody with me. I'm alone. Go up to your attic, take a good look."

He waited, watching the windows, and his eyes fixed on the attic. He saw some movement there. And then he saw Schöller looking around, surveying the whole length and breadth of the Col.

"You see: nobody," Elliott shouted up to him. He ran across the courtyard and went into the annex and took the rickety stairs, three at a time. He found Schöller in the back of the attic. He smelled and there was several days' growth of beard on his face. There were hollows under his eyes and below his cheekbones. The dusty suit hung loose on him—he had lost a lot of weight, and his eyelids were thick and inflamed. He seemed to flinch away from the light. Suspicion was written all over him.

"Mr. Dulles tricked me once," he said. "Why should I believe him now?"

"I'm here alone, that's the proof. If I wasn't leveling with you, I'd have come with a car full of cops, wouldn't I?"

"I don't know," Schöller said uncertainly.

"Quantregg was a bit batty. No one told him to do what he did . . . "

"What is the arrangement that Dulles proposes?"

"He wants to get together with you. Find those files. Pick your brains on certain matters. He'll pay . . . "

"How much?"

"That's for you to work out."

"Dulles tricked me once," Schöller repeated, and added, "He's tricky . . . "

"You're the tricky son of a bitch," Elliott said.

"I? I played everything straight."

"Not with me, you didn't."

"I did everything as agreed. I safeguarded Sunrise. I saved Wolff's neck . . . Dulles owes me something."

"You tricked me," Elliott said. His voice was still low and contained.

"How did I trick you?"

"The von Niesor girl."

"Maritza?"

"She's dead. So's her father."

"A lot of people are dead. Why blame me?"

"The papers, the exit papers, were no good."

Schöller nodded in agreement. "Yes. It was impossible to get papers at that time."

"You tricked me into believing . . . "

"It was for your own good, and to safeguard Sunrise."

"They killed themselves," Elliott said. "Father and daughter together, with those little pills."

"Yes," Schöller said. "Yes. Many of them did that. I heard."

"But you, you tricky son of a bitch, are still alive. Why you? Tell me: why you?"

"It was the arrangement."

"Oh sure."

"I kept my side of the bargain. Dulles must know I am trustworthy . . . " He was becoming sold on the proposition, Elliott could see. "How would it work?"

"You don't have to come out," Elliott said, "Mr. Dulles'll buy you a villa someplace . . . where would you like to live? He'll make you over. You'll get a tailor-made fairy story to cover all contingencies. And you'll be available for advice . . . to check out certain names. Mr. Dulles figures that if we've got you, the Soviets can't use the Müller apparat, since you can put the finger on a lot of his people. Right?"

"Yes," Schöller agreed.

"That's about it," Elliott said.

"It is not uninteresting," Schöller said. He thought for a while. "I would be very tempted to accept, if I knew I could trust Dulles, but. . . . There are also the files to consider. I know where they are."

My God, Elliott thought, the son of a bitch is bargaining, he's actually laying down conditions, the lousy murdering bastard is going to safeguard his own neck, he's going to protect himself, and win out.

"This is what I propose," Schöller said. "I go now . . . and you do not follow me. Dulles should not try to find me. The same goes for the Swiss. My wife to be released, and taken care of . . . some token advance. From the unvouchered funds you speak of. You follow? Provide all this is kept to and nobody attempts to find me, I will get in touch with Dulles in due course, and I am sure we will be able to come to some arrangement, I am confident of it . . . I think we speak the same language. . . . "

The son of a bitch was imposing *his* terms. *Jeezus!* Something broke in Elliott's whirling mind, the murdering bastard was going to get away with it, a house on a lake, all the home comforts, looked after, protected.

Elliott pulled out the gun.

"You have been given instructions by Dulles?" Schöller asked, all his suspicions returning.

"The agent in the field," Elliott said, "has got to exercise his own judgment on the fine details."

"If Dulles sent you to come to an arrangement with me, isn't that what you should be doing, instead of threatening me with a gun?"

Seeing Elliott falter between opposing imperatives, Schöller seized his chance and slipped quickly past the overwrought young American, being careful not to provoke him to any sudden impulsive action. Such young men had to be carefully handled.

They were outside in the courtyard, and Schöller was walking away.

"It will all be all right if everybody keeps to their side of the arrangement," he said. Things had to be put right, Elliott told himself, raising the gun. Had to be put right. You could not keep turning around and around. Schöller, looking back saw the aimed gun and felt uncertain, could not be sure what the overexcited young American would do—you could assess a person's likely behavior only up to a point. If someone acted irrationally, not in accordance with past character

330

or self-interest . . . you could not be sure what he would do. Schöller had never been less sure of anything. Against all the rules, which said never to bring such situations to a head, he began to run. He was already some yards ahead, and it was not far to the woods.

Elliott was gripping the gun in both hands, to hold it steady, aiming at the running figure. He could not fire yet.

He had to wait until he was once again in possession of his mind. He shouted, "Stop! Stop!" But Schöller did not stop, and he was almost a hundred yards distant before Elliott felt the small area of calm that was like an enclave inside his rage. He had a moment of pure wild satisfaction as he visualized the bullets ripping into Schöller's body. Then he put the gun away and ran after the fleeing man, catching him easily. Schöller was no match for him at running.

Elliott said, "Come on, Mr. Dulles wants you, and I'm taking you to him."

In the car, driving down from the Col, Schöller beside him, the calm in Elliott began to spread. He was feeling better now than he had for some time. Something in him had been resolved, a decision taken, a choice made.

Like Mr. Dulles always said, in this work you had to be ready to deal with the devil himself. Didn't mean you became beholden to him. Not if you were quick enough, and could outsmart the bastard.

• Afterword •

Himmler, wearing a motorcyclist's crash helmet and an eyepatch over one eye, was at the wheel of the small Volkswagen. He was not used to driving himself, and his attention was apt to wander. Just a short while ago, on starting, he had released the clutch too abruptly and the car had gone into a ditch. It had taken his companions, Ohlendorf, Brandt, and Gebhardt, fifteen minutes to push the car back on the road again.

Himmler was wearing the uniform of a corporal in the Feldpolizei, Heinz Hintzinger by name. Gebhardt had turned himself into a general in the Red Cross, and Ohlendorf and Brandt had become civilians.

The journey continued. Himmler was not very good at judging the width of his car and frequently the wheels would jump the curb, almost running over anyone who happened to be close to the edge. At other times, Himmler's driving appeared to be taking the little Volkswagen straight into oncoming trucks, and only the last-minute evasive action of their drivers prevented a head-on collision.

The passengers were all the time in a cold sweat, but the habit of total obedience was strong in them, and none dared to suggest that somebody else should drive.

Himmler was scarcely aware of these various near-collisions, he was almost entirely locked up in his own mind now, and the external world had become of rapidly diminishing importance.

What he couldn't get over was Hitler naming Doenitz as his successor. *Doenitz! I was the natural choice, it was my due. The impertinence of that man, Doenitz.*

"In view of the present situation, I have decided to dispense with your further assistance as Reich Minister of the Interior and member of the Reich Government, as Commander-in-Chief of the Replacement Army, and as Chief of the Police. I now regard all your offices as abolished. I thank you for the services you have given the Reich."

The words of his dismissal kept going through Himmler's brain like some stupid doggerel one cannot forget. How could he, Himmler, be dismissed!

He saw a fist being shaken at him as he nearly ran over a woman, splashing mud all over her. They minded about a little mud, these timid souls!

At the next holdup, caused by streams of refugees blocking the road, Himmler turned abruptly around, and addressing his fearful companions in the back of the car, said, "You will see . . . it will not take long for the Allies to realize they need me as their Minister of Police. Nobody else can deal with the menace from the East. They will find that out. They will find that out."

On May 23, British Military Police examining the hundreds of displaced persons passing through their checkpoints, became interested in a small group, of whom one was a small, miserable-looking, shabbily dressed individual with a black eyepatch over his left eye.

The Military Police escorted the little group to interrogation camp No. 031 near Lüneberg. There Captain Tom Selvester, the Camp Commandant, took a good hard look at the man with the eyepatch, whose papers identified him as Heinrich Hintzinger, formerly of the Feldpolizei. In the face of this scrutiny, the insignificant-looking individual removed his eyepatch, put on his spectacles, and, now clearly identifiable, said in a very quiet voice, "Heinrich Himmler."

At once Military Intelligence was summoned. That evening Colonel Michael Murphy, head of Secret Intelligence on Field Marshal Montgomery's staff, was about to question Himmler. He had already been searched, and one phial of poison had been removed from his clothing. Suspecting something, Murphy called for a doctor to conduct another search. Himmler opened his mouth, as instructed. There was something black between the teeth. As the doctor turned the open mouth toward the light to see what this black thing was, Himmler snapped his jaws shut, breaking the capsule of cyanide. Within seconds he was dead.

In the course of the days and weeks following the end of the war in Europe several other top Nazis were found and arrested, including Ernst Kaltenbrunner, who was tried at Nuremberg and subsequently hanged. Others, including Gestapo Chief Müller, were never found or accounted for.

As a reward for his cooperation with Dulles, General Wolff was not tried at Nuremberg, the Allies stating that there was insufficient evidence against him. After serving for four years as a witness in other war-crimes trials, he was allowed to resume his private life.

In 1964 he was put on trial by a German court and sentenced to fifteen years for being "continuously engaged and deeply entangled in guilt." His closeness to Himmler throughout the years was considered ample evidence of his complicity in the crimes of the SS.

After winding up the OSS operation in Berlin, Dulles returned to the United States. On September 20, 1945, President Truman sent a curt letter to Donovan, the colorful head of OSS. It said simply, "I want to express my thanks for the capable leadership you have brought to the war-time activities of OSS, which will not be needed in time of peace." The shutdown of the service was ordered as of October 1.

Dulles returned to his law practice in New York.

In Washington the service chiefs found themselves competing fiercely with each other for one of their war prisoners, General Gehlen, Hitler's former head of Eastern intelligence. After much in-fighting a deal was worked out and Gehlen now became America's spymaster in Germany. He was given remarkable freedom of action and millions of dollars to rebuild his espionage networks, particularly those sections that extended deep into the Soviet bloc.

In 1947 Truman called in Dulles to advise on the reorganization of America's diffused intelligence agencies. On the basis of his recommendations a new Central Intelligence Agency was created. Dulles stayed with it and in 1953 became its Director. That same year John Foster Dulles had become President Eisenhower's Secretary of State. The Dulles brothers were in pretty close agreement about most things.

In furtherance of the Cold War strategy to which both subscribed, Allen Dulles made extensive use of Gehlen's organization and did not ask questions about the people it employed.

Among these, it is known, were a number of former members of the Nazi secret police.

THE BEST OF BESTSELLERS
FROM WARNER BOOKS!

A STRANGER IN THE MIRROR   **(89-204, $1.95)**
by Sidney Sheldon
This is the story of Toby Temple, superstar and super bastard, adored by his vast TV and movie public, but isolated from real human contact by his own suspicion and distrust. It is also the story of Jill Castle, who came to Hollywood to be a star and discovered she had to buy her way with her body. When these two married, their love was so strong it was—**terrifying!**

SAVING THE QUEEN by William F. Buckley, Jr. **(89-164, $1.95)**
Saving The Queen is the story of a dashing CIA agent, assigned to London after World War II to find out who is leaking American secrets about H-bomb development to the British. "A mixture of wit, charm and audaciousness."

—**The New York Times**

THE BONDMASTER by Richard Tresillian   **(89-384, $1.95)**
Never has there been a story of slavery on such a vast scale with such power and sensual electricity! The Bondmaster relives history at its most shocking as it tells a searing saga of tenderness and torment.

AUDREY ROSE by Frank DeFelitta   **(82-472, $2.25)**
The novel on reincarnation. Now a Major Motion Picture! "Is it ever compulsive reading! The author . . . . can unobtrusively gather up a fistful of our nerve ends, and squeeze. If **The Exorcist** was your cup of hemlock you'll be mad about **Audrey Rose**."—Cosmopolitan